FASHIONED BY FLAMES

THE PROTECTOR GUILD BOOK 6

GRAY HOLBORN

ISBN: 9781963893052

Cover by: DamoroDesign

Edits by: CopybyKath

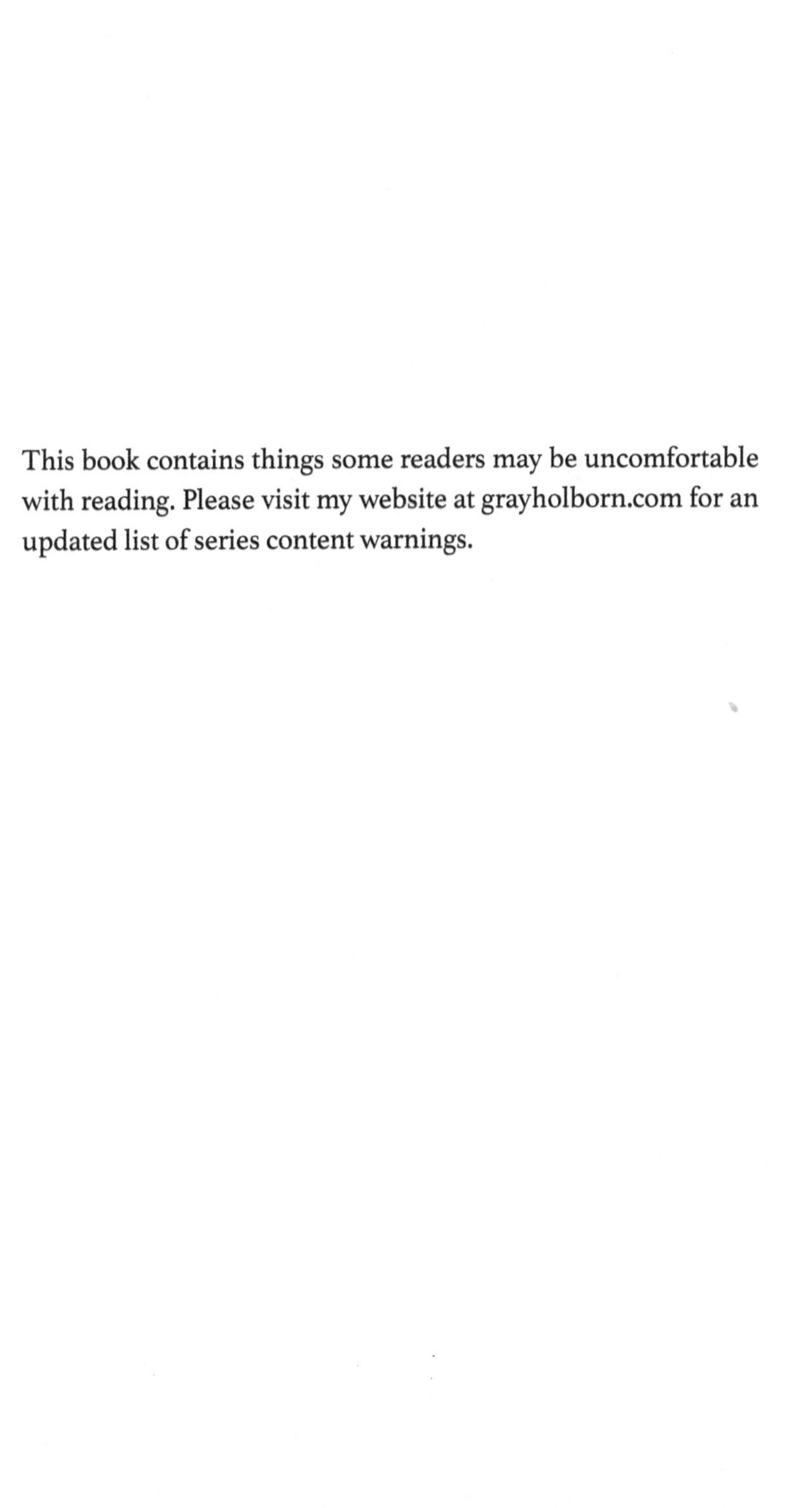

This book contains things some readers may be uncomfortable with reading. Please visit my website at grayholborn.com for an updated list of series content warnings.

1

WADE

"I believe these belong to you, more or less."

The fracture in the all-consuming silence sent my heart racing.

It was a strange feeling—being so alone with no thoughts but your own, that you started to suspect nothing else even existed anymore, maybe it never had. That was until something outside of yourself pulled you back, grounding you into the reality you were hovering aimlessly above, just out of reach.

Instantly, my brain tried placing the deep, unfamiliar voice, but I couldn't. No one had visited me here other than the cloaked man and Max.

My muscles tensed as I lifted my body off my sorry excuse for a bed and stood up, my hands instinctively ready to fight whichever new piece of shit hell had to throw at me. I'd been on even higher alert than normal since Max landed here. Hope had a strange way of blending with fear—like now that I had something to lose, I wanted desperately to grab onto it and keep it safe.

When I saw them there, crowded in my cell, I fell back

down onto the bed—excitement and panic and fear all fighting for center stage low in my gut.

They looked like shit, but they were alive—they were here.

"Eli? Declan?" The words came out in a whisper, like my body was subconsciously afraid that saying their names too loudly would give me too much hope. The sort of hope I wouldn't be able to come back from if it wasn't really them.

Them...and some guy I'd never seen before. He had a no-fucks-given kind of vibe, and the sort of expression usually reserved for watching paint dry on a wall.

Ignoring him, I got back up as soon as the shock faded and rendered my body usable again. It took less than a moment to close the distance and wrap my arms around Declan as she collapsed onto me. She was cut up pretty badly and covered in blood, though I couldn't tell how much of it was hers. When I pulled back slightly, to get a better look at her, to solidify the reality that she was, in fact, here, I saw that her eyes were wide and strained with an unfamiliar sort of fear and discomfort.

She choked back a gag and my stomach tightened for her. I'd only been shifted through space twice since being pulled into hell, but both times it felt fucking awful—like my body was ripping apart and sewing itself back together all at once. Even the memory of the feeling made me taste bile.

But I'd survived it, which meant that she would too. She just needed a moment of fresh air...which she sure as hell wasn't going to get in my little cell.

I pulled her back to me and breathed her in, burying my face in her neck, simultaneously happy to see her and afraid of what, exactly, it meant. They'd found me. Like, *actually* found me. But now they were stuck in the same dungeon as I was, with no way out.

My friends were powerful, the strongest of our kind, but they were no match for the things hell had in store.

I pushed the brief wave of relief away as shame took its

place. They shouldn't be here, should never have come looking for me. Even though my dreams with Max were the one thing getting me through this whole experience, part of me wished I'd never had them; that I'd never lured her and everyone I cared about into the sort of situation that horror films were made from.

As soon as Max had teleported out of my grasp after her visit, I'd half convinced myself that I'd imagined her visit. That she hadn't really dragged herself and my team to hell. That she was some desperation-conjured hallucination my brain concocted to make my agonizingly slow death somewhat palatable.

Now that Eli and Declan were here though, I felt the final wisps of that possibility disappear in the wind. Or, well, the stale air, maybe.

Eli looked far worse than Dec did; all of his weight was still leaning against the strange man, his eyes glassy and empty like he wasn't completely conscious or aware of what was going on around him.

My stomach dipped as I took a step closer to them, unsure of whether or not I should reach for him or let him be. His expression looked so vacant, so far from the mischievous intelligence I was used to seeing on his face. Without it, he was almost unrecognizable to me, like a phantom image of the Eli that I knew.

"What the fuck happened to you guys?" I asked, though I was terrified of the answer. "Where are the others? Where's Max?" Had she gotten caught? Had the cloaked man punished her for leaving her cell and visiting me? I reached one arm towards Eli, but he groaned as the man set him down on the floor, with neither roughness nor care.

Without a word or a second glance, the man dissolved into nothingness before my eyes—there one moment, gone the next.

Was everyone in hell capable of teleporting? The Guild was truly out of its depth if that was the case. How did I spend so many years studying, so many years mastering all of the information about demons that I could get my hands on, and still be so completely unprepared for this world? What chance did we have of surviving this place?

I stared briefly at the stone spot the man had been standing on. No matter how many times I watched people teleport in front of me, my brain still couldn't make sense of it. Couldn't figure out how a person could be standing in front of me one second, and then simply disappear the next. I knew magic was real, obviously. I hunted vampires and werewolves, for crying out loud. But this was some next-level fuckery.

Leading Declan quickly to my makeshift bed of rags, I forced her to sit down and catch her breath, and then I crouched down by Eli. His pulse was faint as I pressed my fingers to his neck, barely a soft flutter for me to pick up, even with my heightened senses.

"What the fuck happened to him?" My hand trailed clinically over his body, uselessly trying to fix...whatever this was.

If any of my friends died during this ridiculously ill-conceived rescue mission, I'd never be able to live with myself. I'd have preferred for the cloaked man to kill me in those woods where he'd found me than be responsible for losing another member of my team.

"Magical blade thing," Declan responded, her own breathing labored as her wide eyes stared unblinking at me. Her voice was raspy and anxious, the way she sounded when she was woken unexpectedly in the middle of the night—on edge, ready for a fight, ready to protect.

I stared at Eli's abdomen, his black shirt wet with blood. My jaw tightened as I remembered the peculiar feeling of my body being torn to shreds from what was likely that very blade not too long ago. I was no longer an easy creature to kill, but that blade had nearly done it.

"Wade—you're ali—"

Her sentence was cut short by the reappearance of the man from before, only now he arrived with two new passengers—the platinum vampire that Max had freed from Guild labs, when this nightmare first started, and a raven-furred werewolf. Atlas's wolf had a tawny-brown coloring, so I knew instantly that this wasn't him.

I scanned the room, like he might appear next at a moment's notice, if I just wished for it hard enough. Then again, did I really want him here, locked in this dungeon with me?

Only if the alternative was that he was in deeper trouble—or worse.

"There," the man said, swiping his hands together as he looked around at my cell, which had grown significantly more compact by the addition of so many bodies. He scrunched his nose, like merely being in our presence was disgusting to him. "That ought to keep you all occupied for a bit."

"Wai—" but my request died on my lips as the man's ethereal blue eyes shifted to mine. He shot me a shit-eating grin and a wink, before he disappeared once more.

I knew how much energy and concentration it took for Max to teleport just once. But he'd done it four times in the last minute or two. And with four bodies in tow. How the hell did any of us stand a chance against any of these guys? We were fucked.

Arms wrapped around my neck with enough force that I almost thought I was being attacked. But when I tensed under the pressure and shifted my head to the side, I was met with a face full of Declan's tangled dark hair and a familiar waft of strawberries—though it was buried under about a week's worth of grime and blood.

The familiar scent that had perfumed half of our cabin engulfed me, and I let her collapse against me, shifting slightly so that I could return the violent hug with equal force. She started shaking against me as her shock wore off, and I felt the unfamiliar droplets of tears against my skin. Dec rarely cried. Not in front of people anyway. And most certainly not in front of the enemy.

For her to be breaking down in front of a vampire and werewolf had to mean that she'd been through some shit. I clenched my jaw as I thought about what that might mean for Atlas.

My eyes darted to the intruding pair, hovering over Eli, and I tightened my arms around Dec. Was this some sort of test? Throwing a pair of demons in my cage to see who would survive the scuffle? It was the sort of game theory I'd expect from hell anyway, but at the moment neither of them seemed particularly ready to pounce.

"Talk to me, Dec. I need to know what's going on. Is Eli okay? Atlas? Have you seen Max?"

"You're alive," she repeated, her voice watery like she was holding back a sob and another rough wave of tears. "I mean, I believed her of course, that you were imprisoned here, that you were still alive in some capacity, if altered a bit. I wouldn't have hopped through a portal into hell just for shits and giggles. But I think somehow I didn't quite let myself believe it, didn't fully let myself hope. But she was right. We found you."

I didn't want to alert her to the fact that in the process of 'finding' me, she'd gone and gotten herself in the exact same position she was trying to rescue me from.

Instead, I pressed against her, trying to curb the anxiety rolling through my body, as she processed what she needed to process. "It's good to see you too."

And it really was. As much as I didn't want her here, didn't want any of them here—not even Max—I couldn't deny that the hole in my chest that had been eating me alive, draining away the last vestiges of hope and humanity I had left, felt smaller somehow. Just from their appearance.

"You look different," she whispered, words choked and tight. "More...just more, somehow." I started to pull away from her a bit, to give her space, knowing that she was seeing whatever transformations the incubus had made. But she pulled me back to her with surprising force considering her condition and shook her head. "Not in a bad way, still you."

My body loosened, fell deeper into the hug. She knew what I was—I knew that Max had told her, that they'd all figured it out. But she wasn't afraid of me. Didn't despise me for housing an incubus beneath my skin.

"This is quite heartwarming and all," a deep, bored voice echoed around us. "Truly a sight to behold. But we need to focus on the fact that the little protector has been left alone with Lucifer, of all people, and we're packed like sardines in a tiny stone room that smells like week-old piss and shit."

I pulled away, shoving Declan behind me slightly as I studied the vamp. He didn't look much better off than Eli, his hand pressed against his stomach as he leaned in a half-seated position against the wall. His strange eyes were mismatched and focused on me with an emotion I couldn't read, though he seemed to be disguising the brunt of his pain quite well.

My team had almost gotten themselves killed trying to capture him after his escape. And now, here he was, trapped in my own supernatural cage. It was like the universe was laughing at us all.

His words caught up with my brain a moment too late, anger making way for shock. "Lucifer?"

The vamp grinned, his sharp canines flashing briefly as his gaze met mine, the challenge clear—I wasn't the only demon in this room. "The one and only. Apparently some of the ancients are alive and officially back on this plane. Two of them anyway. No clue how, no clue why. But there you have it—you've met them both. Our girl's gone and gotten herself in the middle of one giant, apocalypse-sized clusterfuck."

Our girl?

My teeth clenched and I felt soft fingers prying at the tight fist balling my fingers. Declan was trying to untangle them, to get me to relax.

"You knew that the Devil was real?" she asked, brows bent in accusation, but I didn't miss the brief look of betrayal in her eyes.

She... trusted him. At least enough to be shocked by his deception.

All I knew about this creep was that he'd manipulated Max into letting him out of his glass box, only to almost get her—and my entire team—killed. Hell, myself included. He was the catalyst that eventually led to me getting my neck snapped in the first place. And then he'd somehow manipulated them all into letting him escape a second time.

Now, they were all trapped in hell thanks to him—in more danger than they'd ever been before. And Dec *trusted* him?

What the hell was I missing about this guy? Did he have hypnotic powers or something?

"Don't pout princess, it does nothing for your face. Trust me, I may have joked about it, sure, but if I actually thought there was a flying hippo's shot in hell that the ancients were still alive, you'd know it. I wouldn't have joined this ridiculous venture into hell—I'd have grabbed the girl and gotten the fuck out of dodge before shit hit the fan. Especially that particular ancient. Up until today, he's mostly been lore. It's long been assumed that most of the ancients were killed or left the realm during the creation of hell." He let out a long, exaggerated sigh. "This particular change-up will certainly make whatever fight is brewing infinitely more interesting."

"The Devil," I said again, chuckling as my eyes darted between them, expecting the hell-version of a hidden camera host to make themselves present any moment now. "You're pulling my dick."

The vampire tilted his head, considering. "Not currently, but if that would get you to focus, and give us whatever information you have on the guy, I'm not opposed to it. Far less messy than peeling off each fingernail until you squeal."

With more agility than I was used to, I closed the distance between us, my forearm pressing against the fanghole's throat until he was pinned against the wall. I wasn't as strong as a vampire, sure, especially not after who-knew-how-long in solitude, but the incubus beneath my skin wasn't without a heavy dose of power either.

He cocked a brow, that arrogant smirk of his looking more and more like a permanent fixture, rather than a passing taunt. "I guess she has a type, then, doesn't she? I wonder, is this the same position you put her in when you're fucking and feeding off of her? Draining her dry of her life force?"

It felt like he'd run a vat of acid straight through my chest, and the truth of his words made me almost wish that he had. I knew now that Max had enough power, that she wasn't affected by my demon half in a dangerous way anymore—but that hadn't always been the case. I'd hurt her. If he was right—and he *was* there when it happened, after all—maybe I'd even almost killed her. The suggestion of that alone sent a white-hot rage bubbling through my veins, eclipsing any calm and cool I'd been trying to project onto the immediate situation.

And, because I was me, that bubbling rage had to go somewhere, otherwise it would eat me alive.

"Shut your fucking mouth before I thread your lips together with your fangs," I bit out.

His eyes narrowed and he simply grinned, like he could see the self-loathing inside of me and found it amusing to watch and poke at.

I shoved the hand that wasn't holding him against the wall

against his stomach wound, pressing into it. I wanted nothing more than for him to feel the anger that I felt, the pain. I couldn't contain the liquid anger pooling inside me anymore, not after everything we'd all been through.

A deep, raspy groan pulled from his lips, but it quickly turned from the sound of agony to something disturbingly almost sexual.

"I have to say," he laughed, the sound deep and hollow, "I didn't quite see what she saw in you at first." He shrugged, though the movement was stilted under the pressure of my forearm. "I get it now. Hell has awakened something in you, hasn't it?" He shook his head, eyes glistening with mirth. "Don't worry. Max seems to be curious about blood play too, and the boundary between sex and violence has always been slippery at best for sex demons. Your power is nascent though, barely a gentle lick along my neck, so be careful not to rely too heavily on a thrall you can't yet control. It will get you killed." I felt his smirk rather than heard it. "Again. And next time, you might not come back."

My stomach hollowed, and my grip on him loosened instantly. I still didn't understand the incubus or how my new powers worked. I couldn't turn them on or off at whim—and unlike Atlas with his wolf, it wasn't like I could use some obvious transformation to mark the distinction between us. I hadn't spoken to anyone since waking up as something unfamiliar, other than Max and the cloaked man—the former knew little about my powers and the latter seemed to revel in keeping information just out of reach, like a carrot on a stick. I certainly hadn't been trying to use it on this prick.

"Yeah? How about we do an experiment and see if I have enough strength to permanently detach your skull from your spine?"

"Now, now, kitty," he said, voice a gravelly purr that made my stomach recoil. It was clear that he didn't fear me at all, that he found me nothing more than a nuisance or, even worse, a thing to pity. "Let's not pretend like you're a baddy. After all, we're all only in this mess because of you. We've been braving the world of hell, trying to protect Max at all costs, while you've been kept in a safe little cage like a guinea pig. None of us would be here if you hadn't gotten yourself captured by the Devil like a damn damsel in distress. Er," he paused, expression oddly thoughtful, "whatever the male equivalent of a damsel is. A dame? No, that's not right. Dam? Ah, fuck it, it's great alliteration either way. The point is, a little appreciation would be nice. Your friends came an awfully long way to find you. This is hardly a grateful welcoming party you've got going on here."

"You'd know all about being stuck in a cage, wouldn't you?" I felt my skin heat as I tried to contain the anger and guilt building inside of me and bury the emotions before I exploded, before I did something that I couldn't control. Deep down, I knew that he was right. That all of my friends—Max included —were in danger because they were trying to save me. Hearing it from a vampire? That just made the sting so much worse. "If you hadn't botched your first escape plan and tricked Max into letting you out of the lab, none of this would've happened."

I knew it was a shitty thing to say, but I said it anyway. I'd never felt as useless as I had during these last few months. I'd done nothing but waste away in a dingy cell. Part of me wished that I'd never even reached Max through my dreams—the darker parts once again going so far as to wish that I'd never survived the cloaked man's attack at all. If I hadn't, they wouldn't be here. They'd be sad, processing through their grief, but they'd be alive and tucked away safe and sound at Guild Headquarters.

Declan's brows furrowed as her eyes landed on me and I desperately tried to push back the thick thoughts that were starting to emerge. The darkness inside of me had grown strong over my time here, the amount of force it took to keep it at bay was becoming more and more of a struggle. Everyday I felt a little bit less like the version of myself I used to be, the version of myself I recognized. I wasn't sure how much longer I could last—how much more I could fight the darkness from consuming me completely.

The vamp opened his mouth to respond, but Declan cut him off before he uttered a word.

"Jesus, we don't have time for this. Darius—back off the kid. He's not used to your shit and hasn't learned how to tune you out yet. And he's been through a metric shit ton of trauma since we've last seen him." She stood up, but the motion was too quick for her current state and she sat back down on the scraps of fabric I'd used as bedding. She scrunched her nose up, and I felt my cheeks warm in embarrassment. This place hadn't been cleaned since I'd arrived. Months ago. I hadn't even had a change of clothes or a shower. I was used to the stench now, but clearly that was an acquired state. "Wade, look, as annoying as Darius is sometimes, he is not the enemy. He's saved our asses more than once. We owe him. And even if we didn't, we don't have time for this pissing contest of depravity. Let him go. And then tell us what you know about the man who brought you here. As much as it kills me to say, the fanghole is right—this situation is infinitely messier than we thought it would be. We need to work together if there's any chance of getting ourselves —and Max—out of here alive."

We?

"You can't seriously trust this asshole?" I couldn't hold back the disgust in my tone. Dec was the last person on the planet I'd ever expect to look at a vampire with even an iota of respect. What the hell had been happening while I was locked up in this shithole? I glanced down at the wolf that was sitting calmly, still as a statue and as far from us as it could get, watching with yellow eyes that were filled with a layer of intelligence that made the hair at the back of my neck stand up. "And what the hell is up with the wolf? Where's my brother?"

Declan let out a long sigh, the sort that parents often reserved for a particularly long day with a toddler.

The realization that I was causing that sort of tired frustration loosened some of the animosity storming through me, but heightened the guilt. Still, it was enough to bring my heart rate down. I nodded, a silent apology.

She stood up again, but much more slowly this time, and walked over to me. She nudged my elbow until I did as she said and let the vampire go. I hadn't even realized I was still pinning him.

"That's the only bit of good news we've gotten since dropping into this place." She nodded to the wolf, her lips relaxed in a small grin, despite the tension weighing us all down. "Show him."

The wolf had been so still since arriving here, that it was almost shocking to see it come to life now. It stretched, limbs long and lithe, like a cat waking from a nap in the sun. It shook its head, the fur around its neck waving through the air like a lion's mane. Yellow eyes latched onto mine as the creature started to shift.

I'd seen Atlas shift before, but it never stopped being a weird experience filled with a strange sort of macabre fascination. Watching the transition was like watching literal magic unfold before your eyes—the closest we ever got to seeing the physical reality of the supernatural before things like teleportation and hell came into the picture.

The wolf's body contorted and popped, legs growing longer and more sturdy, arms bending at the elbow, fur receding back into a face that was flattening into softer, more delicate features. The yellow eyes were suddenly shot through with streaks of blue, until the wolf started looking more like a girl than a wolf

—and then suddenly like the spitting image of a very specific girl.

One I knew.

"H-how?" I took a step towards her, hardly registering the fact that she was standing in front of me naked. Her eyes were on the ground, her shoulders hunched slightly. "Sarah? Is it—is it really you?"

She nodded, as her eyes met mine, her lips tugging in a soft, tentative grin that used to make my knees wobble. Without another word, she closed the distance between us, hugging me so hard that I could feel each pad of her fingers as she pulled me to her. I'd always been attracted to Sarah, even more so after we were bonded, as if the supernatural forces at play were lighting my way to her with a twinkling path. But holding her now, even with her bare boobs pressed against my chest, suddenly felt no different than if I'd been hugging any other friend. Like Eli or Declan.

Only one person made my stomach dip in that way now, made me feel that excited kind of anxiety that always made my body explode into a swarm of butterflies. That feeling was reserved entirely for Max. It was locked in, impenetrable, whether I liked it or not. From the moment I felt it, I'd never been so sure of anything in my life. And they weren't even butterflies. Something with bigger wings, like my body was alive with a bunch of fluttering eagles the second she was near me.

But Sarah, here, in the flesh, filled me with a soft warmth, and I could feel a heavy weight dropping so dramatically from my shoulders that I almost tipped over from the shock of it.

"You're alive?" I breathed her in, trying to rectify the reality of the situation with what I understood. "But they took you— you were dead."

She'd died because I didn't get to her in time, because I didn't save her. That haunted look in her eyes the night she was killed showed up in every nightmare I'd had since—my name on her lips as she called to me and my brother to help her. But we didn't. I didn't.

My throat started to clog with emotion as I felt her in my arms, felt her hair tickle my face.

"I was changed, not killed—though I was about a hair's breadth from death's door. Almost didn't make the transformation. That's what they tell me anyway. I've been in this realm, unable to reach any of you, since then." She pulled back slightly, blinking away the sheen of moisture that lined her eyes. "Until you knuckleheads got the bright idea to go traipsing into the lion's den of all places. How the fuck did this happen? How did you get here?"

Declan looked over her shoulder as she bent down to tend to Eli. He still wasn't particularly responsive. "Forgot to mention that Wade's an incubus now too. So basically your entire bond family is cursed. We need to rename Six something cool, like the Demon-ators or something."

"That's not cool, it's dorky," I said, but I couldn't completely swallow the grin tugging at my lips.

"What?" Sarah looked at me, assessing, like she'd be able to pick out Dec's lie if she just stared hard enough.

"It's true," I said, but I didn't want to get into it, not right now. I was still raw and we were in the presence of a vampire that made me want to throw my head against the wall. "Where is Atlas?" I asked again, ignoring Sarah's wide-eyed expression as much as I could. I still hadn't fully processed the fact that she was a wolf, I'm sure it would take a while for her to piece together my changes as well.

"He's fine," the vamp said, nostril curled slightly in disgust. "Or maybe not. I imagine they won't let him live if he doesn't pull himself back from the edge. That kind of liability is a danger in this realm. I'm surprised the girl's pack even bothered caging him in the first place."

My eyes narrowed as I tried to process whatever the hell that meant. "Liability? What edge?"

"He's feral," Sarah added, wrapping one of the pieces of fabric from my bed around her body in a makeshift toga of sorts. Her cheeks reddened as my eyes latched on to hers.

We'd never had that kind of relationship, though she knew that I'd always wanted to. I'd always hoped that, with the bond, she'd stop seeing me like a friend, that she'd be inspired to pursue something more. But she was always too hung up on Atlas. And now, I completely understood the futility of it. I didn't think I could so much as look at another girl now that Max was in the picture—sex demon or not, everyone else was ruined for me. It was like some vital part of me was fused to her now—immoveable.

"Feral?" I asked, trying to connect the dots of their partial stories into something that made a semblance of sense to me.

She shrugged, eyes hooded like she was sinking into her thoughts. "It happens sometimes with turned wolves. He never melded properly with his, never fully embraced the transition. The wolf embodies everything he hates most about himself. He resisted it too much; they never truly became one."

"And how does he fix it?" My heartbeat started to thud against my ribs as I saw the answer written across her face before I even asked it.

"Generally, they don't." The vamp answered, voice lilting with intrigue, like this was the first interesting thing to happen since he'd been dropped into this room—like he hadn't just issued my brother a death sentence. "In all fairness, I did try to warn him this would happen. Several times, if I recall correctly. Grumpy, you were there, weren't you? You heard."

My hands curled into fists. Suddenly I wanted nothing more than to carve that snarky grin off his face and dance on his dead body.

Dec shot him a look. "Shut up, you ass. This is why everyone we meet wants to instantly gut you."

"Max doesn't." His statement was matter of fact, like it was an ironclad argument and the only one that mattered.

I glanced around the room, trying to find something I could stab him with, but part of the whole being imprisoned thing meant that weapons weren't exactly—

"You have a blade." I stared at the familiar dagger sheathed against Dec's thigh. "They let you keep a blade?"

Unconsciously, her fingers tightened around it, like pointing out that it was there made her suddenly think that it wasn't. "Yeah, I guess they forgot to confiscate it. Might come in handy for getting us out of this dump."

The vampire laughed, the sound low and harsh. "That blade is useless against them. They let you keep it as a symbol of how little harm we can bring them. It's nothing more than a taunt."

I reached for Declan, unsheathed her dagger, and pressed the point against the fanghole's chest. "I'm pretty sure it will still get the job done with you, won't it?"

His brow arched as he stared me down, unflinching. "Sure, let's see what happens to your friend if you do, shall we?" He tilted his head towards Eli. "I can withstand the damage far better than he can."

My confusion must've been written plain as day across my face, because Sarah let out a low sigh. "He's bonded to Eli. You can't touch him."

While I didn't press the blade in any further, I didn't remove it, either, as I craned my neck towards Declan, waiting for her to point out the obvious. But she stayed silent, lips pressed into a firm line. "Protectors don't bond with vampires."

"Not a mate bond," Declan clarified as she ran a hand roughly over her face. She looked so worn, like she'd been carrying the weight of the world on her shoulders and it was slowly drowning her. "It's complicated, but with this particular blood bond, any injuries Darius incurs have a chance of mirroring themselves in Eli. If one dies, the other will likely follow. It goes both ways."

"This how you convinced them to keep you alive, then?" I asked, but I took a step back all the same, dropping the blade to my side. My eyes darted from the wound I'd noticed on the vamp, to where Eli was still leaning against the wall—expression more present than it was before, though he still hadn't said a word. And then my gaze dropped to his abdomen, where blood coated his shirt.

"Actually," Dec said, gently pulling her blade from my fingers and resheathing it at her side, "Darius saved Eli's life. Hell, he's saved my life a couple of times now, too. As obnoxious as he is, we kind of owe him." She walked over to Sarah and slumped down next to her, forearms leaning against her knees. "If it helps, he starts to grow on you."

"Aw," the fanghole said, drawing the word out long and high as he held his hands to chest. "You're going to make me weep."

"Kind of," she added, but there was no venom in her tone—only an edge of teasing that reminded me of her rapport with Eli.

My stomach tightened as I took a few steps away from the ass. I needed some distance from him, if I wasn't allowed to kill him, but my options were limited in a room that was hardly large enough for me, let alone five. "Why's Eli seem so much worse off then?"

"While he's stronger than most protectors," Darius tilted his head to the side while he studied Eli, eyes narrowed and focused as if something about my friend surprised or confused him, "he's still not as difficult to kill as I am." His eyes darted back to mine as he shrugged. "Plus blood bonds aren't all that predictable. Especially with the magic of this realm as temperamental as it's been—now, more than ever. For all I know, the bond could randomly sever itself tomorrow and then we can all live happily ever after, killing each other without trepidation."

"One can dream," Dec said on an exhale as she leaned her head back against the wall. She was doing that thing she always did—trying to disguise how exhausted and drained she really was. Even in a prison in the depths of hell, the girl hated looking vulnerable.

"You're kidding yourself if you think I enjoy being tied to this jackass. He's constantly almost dying. Honestly, I've never feared for my life more," the vampire looked up, lips moving like he was silently counting something, "and I've been in quite a few seriously dire situations in my time. I'm almost impressed."

"Most of the time, I'm only dying because someone's kicking your ass," Eli said, so quietly I had to strain to hear him. His eyes were focused as he pressed his palms into the ground to stabilize himself. Each breath he took seemed labored, but there was more vibrancy in his expression than there'd been when he'd first arrived.

"How do you feel?" I asked, though I realized the ridiculousness of the question as soon as it left my tongue. "Probably as awful as you look."

"Worse." A small laugh escaped him, but it quickly turned into a low groan. "Good to see you too, Wade." His voice was gravelly and breathy, like he was speaking during the final stretch of a marathon. "I take it you haven't figured out how to get the fuck out of this place, yet?" His eyelids closed tight, like a new wave of pain was rolling through him. "Gotta say, hell's a bit of a bitch. But, on the plus side," he shrugged, the movement making him grimace, "if I die, at least I take out the fanghole too, right?"

I crouched down next to him, pressing my fingers to his neck to check his pulse. He swatted me away, but then gave in.

It was steadier than it had been, but it still wasn't great. "You're going to need to regroup a bit before we try to storm the castle, so to speak." I turned back towards Dec and Sarah. They looked exhausted too, and there was so much blood crusted over their skin that I couldn't tell how much of it was theirs, or how many wounds had healed over. "So..." I said, as the complete clusterfuck of our situation settled around me like a heavy snowfall, "can we circle back to that whole Lucifer thing, or is now a bad time?" I dropped my weight down until my butt hit the floor next to Eli. Their silence clarified more than their words could. "So, it's true then."

I let my head fall against the wall as they all nodded, an odd menagerie of silent bobbleheads, each expression more terrified and shellshocked than the last, like they still couldn't quite believe it themselves.

"And Atlas?" I scrubbed a hand over my face and then cracked each of my knuckles, wanting to do something, but limited in my options.

Dec's eyes met mine. They were filled with the hard determination I'd come to rely on during most of our missions. She had a way of calming us all down, centering us. "Atlas will pull himself out of it. I know he will." She bit her lip as she shook her head softly. "It's what he does."

For a long while, nobody said anything. We just sat, listening to Eli's labored breathing as he slid in and out of consciousness. We had no supplies to tend to him, though I doubted that even if we had, we'd be able to do much other than wait. Magical blade wounds weren't exactly in our training guides. Honestly, I didn't know how he was still breathing in the first place.

Even the vampire had stopped mumbling criticisms of my prison cell and taken to sitting with his face pressed into his palms, like he was sinking into himself.

As much as I hated that they were all here, I couldn't

pretend that I wasn't relieved to have company. Months alone—and hell, with the solitude as deafening and disorienting as it was, I still wasn't even sure how long I was trapped down here—had worn at me in a way that nothing else had before. I could feel the anxiety clawing at my lungs, the fear scraping against my skin. And worse than that was the insufferable, unending boredom that grew so loud, I often found myself dissociating just to survive.

Having them here, it eased some of that, just as Max's visits had done.

Plus, as small as it was, there was at least the illusion of a chance that together, we could find a way out of this shit show. Dec, Eli, and Sarah were three of the smartest people I knew. They'd saved my ass on more than one occasion. And it didn't hurt having the power and strength of a vampire on our side for once—if we really could consider him on our side. Maybe the five of us could find a way out of here somehow, get to Max and Atlas and actually make it home. We had far higher odds putting our minds and strengths together as a team than we did individually.

The Guild had been wrong about a lot, but it had gotten things right with teams—when we worked together, we flourished.

I glanced at the vampire, his body far too still to be human, and tried to process the fact that we were—temporarily, I hoped—tied to another demon. Between me, Sarah, Atlas, Max, and him, we tipped the scales from a team of protectors into a team of the very creatures we were meant to protect the world from.

I snorted at the absurdity of the situation, the quiet sound harsh and surprising enough in the silence to draw everyone's eyes to me.

I opened my mouth and then closed it again. We should be planning, should be figuring out how to find Max and get out of this mess. But how did we plan an escape from a creature that I'd thought was concocted from fairytales and human mythology a mere day ago?

He could teleport, he had blades that made our own weapons look like feathers. And I had a feeling that he probably couldn't be killed with a simple stab to the heart—even if we somehow managed to find a way to strike him there.

A pair of feet materialized before my eyes—bare and caked with dirt. When I glanced up, the biggest breath of air I'd taken in days—weeks—filled my lungs. "Atlas."

His eyes were pure gold, like he was on the edge of a shift, his expression tight and unreadable.

"Figured he might want to join the party, now that he's done with his time out. For now, anyway." The man who'd brought the others here stepped out from behind my brother—his brows lifted in a way that made it difficult to tell whether he was bored of us all or deeply amused. "I don't think he'll kill any of you," he shrugged, glancing at Atlas briefly, "but I'd give him some distance all the same. I gave him a pair of pants. You're welcome for that."

And then, as quickly and silently as he'd arrived, he left.

"Atlas, you're you," Declan said, as she walked over to him.

He recoiled the second her hand touched his bare arm, his face cold and hard as he turned away from her.

I stood up and took a step towards him, but stopped when his eyes met mine. They flashed briefly with recognition, with relief, but there was a wildness there that I wasn't used to seeing. And, deeper down, something dark. Something haunting—or haunted.

Without a word to anyone, he moved as far from us all as he could—which was to say, only a few inches at most—before sitting on the cold floor and burying his face into the pocket created by his arms and knees, sinking into himself just as the vampire had.

2

MAX

Ro would occasionally call me the spawn of Satan as a joke, usually after I'd landed a pretty gnarly hit to his abdomen during a sparring session.

The sudden realization that I quite literally was the product of the Devil did not compute.

At all.

"Come again?"

The man—Lucifer, apparently—exhaled long and slow, like he was tasked with handling the most petulant person in the realm. And well, seeing as he was the Devil, I'd have figured he was used to dealing with far worse. "I am your father."

I bit back the Star Wars joke that tried escaping from my lips, hating that my brain's way of dealing with shock was by throwing humor at it like spaghetti on a wall. Nothing ever stuck. Not in situations like this.

"Like," I said, drawing the word out as I stared at him, "literally, you mean?" My voice sounded like an echo, unfamiliar and hollow. I'd only just started processing the fact that I was part-demon—a succubus to be exact. But... "the antichrist? No. No way."

I wasn't ready for this shit. I wanted to go home, to rewind the last few months—back to the good old days when most of the members of Six hated me, but when we were all alive, and healthy. Normal.

Something that could only be called a soft chuckle escaped from his lips as he shook his head softly. "Not the antichrist." Apparently I'd spoken that out loud. I felt so disconnected from myself that even my thoughts weren't my own. "There are no heavenly prophecies about you. You simply came from my seed."

"Ew. Stop. Right there." Devil or not, I was not going to listen to the man who supposedly created me talk about his... seed. Fucking nasty. Even I had my limits.

"My kind very rarely procreate, you know. It's been thought for centuries that we no longer could. Most would be excited by the idea that they hold that kind of power running through their blood. You shouldn't even exist, not really."

Well, I didn't really care what other people would be feeling in my shoes. All I knew was how I was feeling—and that was completely, irrevocably, decidedly *not* excited.

I was freaking the fuck out.

I wanted to go back to being a regular run-of-the-mill protector, back before I knew that the whole world was a hell of a lot more complicated than I now understood it to be. "Well, I'm going to take a risk and just be completely honest here, but if I was going to have nifty powers, I'd much prefer they didn't come from the literal embodiment of evil. So, yeah, I'm going to have to respectfully decline."

He arched a brow, looking all sorts of villainous as he took a step towards me. "Your conceptions of good and evil are childish and naive at best—ignorant and deadly at worst. I am not what you think me to be. And the world—both here and in your realm—is far more complex than you could imagine. So, can we move beyond this now? There are important things to discuss. We need to get you ready. I need to know you can survive long enough to do what I need you to do."

Yeah, because getting over the whole 'meeting my bio-dad and learning that he's Lucifer' was totally a one-second meltdown, nothing more. Apparently the Devil was just as out of touch with reality as he thought me to be.

Apple and tree and all that.

But I'd seen some wild shit in the last few months, the kinds of things that would make most people detach from reality and live the rest of their days out in the woods, away from the world. Hell, maybe that's why Cyrus did just that for so many years. Part of me really missed that lifestyle, the simplicity of it.

The best coping mechanism I'd come up with? Avoidance. And if I was going to get myself, Darius, and the rest of Six the hell out of hell, I didn't have time to linger on the things that pulled my psyche in twenty different directions. So, 'spawn of Satan' was going to go take a number and stand next to 'succubus' and 'sex with multiple people' in the back of my mind where I didn't have to look at or acknowledge it.

"What is it that you need me to do?" I curled my fingers into my palm. Sinking into the sharp pressure as my nails dug into the flesh, using the pain to ground myself in the moment, to focus. Cyrus always said that focus was most important when it seemed unattainable. Something told me he hadn't quite imagined this particular situation though.

He took a long breath, his shoulders relaxing in relief. "I'm sure even someone as naive as you can tell that the barrier between your world and this one has not only grown thin, but has become increasingly temperamental and unpredictable. There are leaks everywhere. The magic that threads through the supernatural world and the creatures that inhabit it is unstable. It was a slow degradation at first, but now things are unraveling at an unparalleled speed."

I nodded, ignoring the jab. If the dude really was Lucifer,

throwing out some sarcastic comments was probably his version of being nice and welcoming. Charming even.

At least this was something that even members of The Guild would agree on. This year had seen an increasing number of supernatural creatures crossing the barrier into our realm, and doing so in unpredictable, new patterns. Wolves and vampires working together, attacking Guild boundaries and protectors—it was all new, and all terrifying.

But Darius had mentioned that the hell realm had changed too, that the magic had grown more unstable and chaotic since he'd abandoned it, the place left in literal shambles as the inhabitants led a sort of scavenger lifestyle I was used to only in dystopian films. I'd thought it was just because hell wasn't supposed to be all rainbows and kittens, but it had become increasingly clear that this world was changing far more rapidly than even ours.

"Hell has never been a peaceful place," he continued, hands folded together softly at the base of his back as he started to pace, like he was about to lead a sermon. I held back a laugh at the irony of it. "A prison, yes. A space designed to separate and control the creatures deemed too powerful to exist in your world. But it's never been like this. Resources are almost impossible to come by for those without power, or without the protection of those with power, anyway. The magic is strange now–bitter–changing the very atmosphere." He paused, eyes lifting, briefly, to meet mine, "Changing the very creatures that live here, down to their blood. The realm is disintegrating. The magic is tainted. And when it reaches its tipping point, there will be no point of return. Every creature in this realm will be destroyed."

My protector-brain shoved my personal problems aside and kicked itself into high gear. Wasn't this exactly what The Guild dreamed of? A world free of supernatural monsters that preyed on defenseless humans?

But then that would mean that people like Darius, like Wade and Atlas, like me—that we were all disposable, all evil and worthy of death. And I knew that wasn't the case.

While most of the creatures I'd encountered in hell had tried to kill me, something told me that the realm was populated with just as much good as bad—not that those terms really meant anything to me anymore.

How many innocent supernatural creatures would be destroyed in a catastrophe like that? It wasn't a risk I wanted to take, but something told me that if The Guild got wind of this situation, they'd take full advantage of the opportunity to rid the world of hell for good.

"And this world isn't the only one that would be affected," he added, tone surprisingly soft for someone who claimed to be the Devil incarnate.

My eyes lifted to his, and I tried to see myself in his features. We both had dark hair and eyes, though his were a touch deeper, the pupils and irises blending until it was impossible not to recognize this man as a demon. His skin was a light golden-brown like mine, but where I was small and lined with soft muscle, he was all hard angles and edges.

I didn't see myself in his expression, in the coldness of his glare, in the arrogance of his lips.

A ripple of fear coiled in my gut as his eyes met mine again. I tried to trample it down, to pretend that I was talking to someone less terrifying—like this was just Cyrus debriefing me for a mission. But no matter which mind tricks I tried to play on myself, the truth of the situation was impossible to ignore. "What do you mean?"

"I mean that if this isn't handled properly, it's entirely possible that the hell realm will take out the human one in the process—cannibalizing it into nothingness."

"Like a black hole?"

"Perhaps. Or like something far darker and more dangerous

than even you and I could imagine. It's a very delicate balance that's been upset—the two halves feed each other. Without one, how can you expect the other to survive? Protectors," he spat the word out like it tasted foul, "might be willing to risk everything to maintain and strengthen their power, to wipe hell and the creatures that challenge that power off the map once and for all. But in doing so, they run the risk of destroying everything. Including themselves."

"And why me?" I furrowed my brows, trying to think back to everything I knew about Lucifer. None of that lore was fed to me through protectors or any of our people's mythology—everything came from human-created media. Everything I knew about him was biblical in nature or stretched out in strange, fantastical ways in books and movies. That's what I thought, anyway. Now, I wasn't entirely confident about anything. "You're one of the original archangels, right? Why can't you solve this mess? I'm just a girl." My stomach felt hollow and like a rock all at once, the thought that everything and everyone I ever knew was in danger...how was someone supposed to process that shit? The far corner of my mind where I kept all the 'do not touch' stuff could only hold so much undealt-with angst before it became impossible to ignore.

And right now, that corner of my brain was bursting at the seams.

His nostrils flared slightly as he scratched his cheek, the soft sound of his fingernails scraping against his beard the loudest sound in this cell.

"Archangel. I hate that term," he muttered, shaking his head softly like he was trying to focus himself. "The superstitions you've been fed are nothing more than that. Hell isn't biblical. It's a prison. One created by protectors and angels alike, many, many years ago. The blood of our original line and progeny was used to create this barrier. And, for the most part, it's remained quite strong through the centuries. But then you were born—the first direct descendent from one of the ancients since hell's creation. Your mother was more than I thought she was. From the moment you took your first breath, the barrier between this world and yours began to change. Your blood, your power—I think it's the best way to fix it. The best chance to stabilize the magic that's become so unpredictable and dangerous to us all."

I stood up, suddenly deeply uncomfortable in my own body, but then sat back down again as my head went all dizzy and cloudy. I felt like a ticking time bomb, like one wrong move and my body might be responsible for taking out the entire world. Talk about pressure. "You *think*? Think is a pretty weak word to use when existence as we know it is at stake. I need you to give me something that's got a little bit more confidence and meat backing it if you expect me to buy what you're selling here."

He grinned, but there was no humor there, only an acute awareness of how well and truly fucked we were. The sight of his white teeth, the tight clenching of his jaw, made me feel like throwing up. If Lucifer was scared—or, at the very least, nervous—then things had to be next-level bad.

"These times are unprecedented for a reason—fate and magic are fragile, unpredictable. I've made deductions with what I know, but my powers are very limited at the moment. I need your assistance to help reveal the missing puzzle links." He shook his head slightly, meeting my gaze in an unflinching stare again. Each time his eyes met mine, I felt ice flow through my veins. "Trust me, I'm not exactly keen on staking my survival on some barely-adult girl who has about as much control over her powers as a new giraffe does over its legs."

"Pieces," I muttered, the word little more than an unconscious breath.

He bent his brows together, nose scrunching up slightly in

an expression that looked misplaced on someone of his stature and mythology. "Pardon?"

I cleared my throat. "Puzzle pieces, not puzzle links. You mixed metaphors."

"This is what you focus on?" He let out a long sigh, then turned his head to the ceiling, left hand covering his face. "This is the girl who's supposed to save us all? Why are the fates so damn cruel? We're set up to fucking fail before we've even really begun. Maybe death is what we deserve."

Well, at least he was as melodramatic as I expected the Devil to be.

"My friends," I interrupted, my skin going warm with embarrassment. I didn't process shock well, I thought we'd confirmed that already. "What will happen to them? Are they safe? Can I see them?"

He shrugged, glancing down at me like I was the most ridiculous creature he'd ever laid his eyes on. "That's dependent entirely on you." I opened my mouth to ask him to clarify, when he pressed on with a look that wasn't quite an eye roll, but something that gave off the same vibe through stillness. "Do you ever stop with the questions? If you work with me, if you develop your powers quickly and efficiently—if you help me infiltrate The Guild, they'll survive. Or at the very least, I won't be the one to kill them. I have very little control over what messes other creatures get themselves into. And judging from the way they showed up, I have a feeling they are very capable of getting quite messy."

"And if I don't? If I can't?"

"They'll die. But so will most of us if we don't figure out how to stabilize the barrier, so it's not like their fate will be particularly unique or notable." He shrugged, as if he'd done little more than tell me the time or comment on the weather.

"I need to see them." I stood, straightened my posture, ready to go.

His lips pulled into a tight grin, eyes flashing with venom. "You don't dictate the situation here, girl. Make no mistake that your needs and wants are of almost no consequence to me. What I need is for you to get some rest—you're of no use to me like this. After you've slept, we will begin your training."

"But—"

"You'll not leave this room by yourself. You are not to wander the corridors without Samael present to escort you."

I clenched my jaw, suddenly feeling like a scolded child—only in this case, I was being scolded by the Devil of all people. "And Ralph? Is he with my friends too?"

He narrowed his eyes. "Which one is Ralph? The wolf?"

"My hellhound."

He arched his brow like he was amused. "I imagine the hound is with Sam. Get some rest."

And then, without another word, he disappeared.

My first thought was to shift to my friends, to disregard his rules and find them to make sure they were okay. But as much as I hated to admit it, he was right. I was fucking exhausted. It was as if the single suggestion of getting rest had infiltrated my body with a heavy, immovable weight. I felt drugged, dazed, like something was pulling me under a strong current. And I'd be no use to them if I ended up teleporting around the dungeon in a never-ending game of Marco Polo.

So I promised myself that I'd close my eyes—just for a minute or two.

~

SOMETHING HEAVY FLEW INTO ME, tightening around my chest until it felt like I couldn't breathe.

Panic started to rise in my body and I focused all of my attention on conjuring fire, until I picked up on a familiar scent of vanilla and spices.

"Izzy?"

Her name came out as little more than a grunt, but rather than release me, she simply squeezed me harder.

I didn't fight it, I just sank against her, wrapping my arms around her with just as much force.

"You're okay?" Her voice was wobbly, like she was fighting back tears. "I've been so worried. We haven't heard from you in ages and things—things are bad, Max. So fucking bad."

I pulled away a bit, so that I could get a better look at her.

Her cheeks were streaked with tears, like she'd been crying long before I showed up. Izzy was always a ray of sarcastic sunshine. She lit up every room she walked in. But something was off. Her skin looked duller than usual, her gray eyes that were typically so full of life looked harder, more guarded. I scanned the room, concerned that she'd been taken some-where, that she was hurt.

But I only saw the same purple and black bedroom in which I'd spent many nights staying up until dawn watching movies. She was home, tucked up safe in her cabin at Guild Headquarters. Rather than sending a wave of relief through me like it should have, it only heightened my concern.

I couldn't remember her ever looking this upset and fraz-zled before. She usually took everything in her stride. Last time I dream-walked to her and announced that Wade was an incubus, she did nothing but ogle him and roll with the punches.

"Izzy—what's wrong? What happened?"

Her lips pressed together tightly as her chin wobbled, like she was doing everything she could to keep a fresh batch of tears from cascading down her face. "It's bad, Max. It's really bad."

"What is?" I gripped her elbow and led her back to her bed, forcing her to sit down and collect herself. I'd never seen her like this. Her body shook against me and I forced her to take a few big breaths with me. "Are you okay? Are you hurt?"

She shook her head, and my shoulders relaxed slightly.

"It's my fault," she said, her words stammering slightly. "He went after you. He's been a fucking wreck since you went to him in his dreams, and he's been working nonstop trying to bring you back, to reach you. He was convinced that you were in trouble and determined to get to you before it was too late. So he snuck out a few times, hunting down any hint of demon presence to try and get a clue as to where you were—a clue about how to reach you. And I helped. I should've talked him out of it, should've told Seamus or Cyrus. I should have done something."

The blood in my veins went cold. "Ro?"

I sat down next to her, the weight of her shoulder against mine the only thing keeping me steady. It felt like it had been a lifetime since I'd seen my brother, but it had probably only been a few days since I dream-walked to him. Before I'd been ripped from that dream, I made him promise not to do anything reckless.

He'd agreed, hadn't he?

No. I'd been pulled from that dream to Eli—the last thing Ro had seen of me was me writhing in pain and then disappearing from his sight.

Of course he wouldn't have been able to just sit tight and do nothing. If the situation had been reversed, I sure as hell wouldn't have been able to.

"Izzy," I said, my voice cold, fingers trembling uselessly in my lap. "Izzy, I need you to tell me that he's alive. Tell me he's okay. That it was just a scare."

She closed her eyes, and I watched, transfixed, as a few tears escaped between her lashes.

"He's alive," she said, after a moment that felt like a lifetime.

She took a deep, grounding breath, and I watched as a steady resolve and determination eclipsed her expression. "But it's bad, Max. Really bad. We'd been tracking the group—the one that took Wade a few months ago. Looking out for any intel that we could get on movements with groups of wolves and vampires. Attacks," she shook her head, and her stormy eyes met mine. "Things have gotten really bad since you've left. Like worse than it's ever been before. Something's been triggered, and there have been nonstop raids and attacks across the world. Seamus, everyone is freak—"

"Izzy." I tried to calm the panic that was rising so quickly it was making me see spots. Dream-walking across realms was more difficult—reaching Izzy and Ro here was far more draining than reaching any of the members of Six had been. I wasn't sure how much time we had. "I need to know what happened to Ro—is he okay?"

She stood up and started pacing. "Right, sorry, I'm rambling. We got a lead about a small group—it was only a small lead, we weren't expecting to actually run into demons. He made me stay and distract Cyrus, do some intel back here, but then he went with Arnell and Jer." She stopped pacing and dropped her forehead into her hands.

Jer and Arnell were members of Ten and some of the first friends I'd made since joining The Guild. And my brother, he was already halfway in love with Arnell. The thought that they'd all been working to bring me back made my chest hollow out with guilt.

Every muscle in her body was coiled and tight. The hem of her shirt was nothing but ragged, stray threads, like she'd been pulling at it all night. "Max, there was an ambush. They're all alive, they made it back. But he was bitten. And-and it's bad."

My stomach felt hard and my head light—like my body was disconnecting from itself, no longer fitting together properly. I tried to shove the storm building in my gut away, to turn off the fear clawing at my insides like a feral creature locked in a cage.

"Bitten by what?" I tried to keep my voice as calm and collected as I could, knowing that Izzy was trying to do her own emotional gymnastics to ease me into this.

It could all be okay. Maybe she was overreacting—still locked in the heat of adrenaline that came with the job of welcoming teams back from dangerous missions. Werewolves occasionally killed protectors, and very rarely changed them, but a lot of the time, those bites were survivable. As long as it wasn't a—

"Vampire."

I nodded as the room grew blurry and I fought like hell to maintain my grip on the dream. "And the others?"

My voice sounded foreign, like it belonged to another body on the other side of the room. There was no emotion to it, even though I felt like I was being ripped in half by a million different things competing for attention—fear, rage, anger, guilt.

"They were beaten up pretty badly, but on the way to recovery. Seamus is looking after them all, it's expected they'll be alright."

"Is Ro speaking? What did Cyrus say?" I felt my heartbeat pounding against my ribcage. Cy had been bitten by a vampire years ago. He still walked with a limp from the battle, but he was alive and still probably the most badass protector I'd ever met. He could help Ro through this; we'd pull together.

Everything would be fine.

"He hasn't woken up. Max," her shoulders slumped as she dropped her gaze. "Arnell got him out, but—Max, it's a neck bite."

My lungs felt way too tight, like no matter how hard I sucked air in, I couldn't take a full breath. Protectors could heal from vampire bites but neck wounds were another story.

I'd survived one when I first joined The Guild, but I was the only protector in memory who'd ever come back from that wound.

And that's because I wasn't a protector. Not just a protector anyway.

A desperate piece of me hoped like hell that Ro was a secret demon too. That Cy had decided years ago to quit The Guild and collect a few demon-protector orphans to stave off loneliness. But in my gut, I knew it wasn't true. I'd always been a bit different, a bit off. Ro had always been a superstar—the ideal vision of what a good protector was supposed to be. He'd never exploded into flames, or teleported across space, or... healed someone.

I stood up too quickly, my head dizzy from the flash of excitement, and stepped towards Izzy. "I can fix this."

Her brows bent down as her fingers laced gently with mine. "Max, I don't think—'

I shook my head. "No, really, Izzy. I've been healing people. I know it sounds batshit, but I've healed Eli and Declan through dream-walks. I don't really have a total grip on it yet, but maybe I can heal Ro."

She opened her mouth and closed it again, fighting to find words. "You can heal people." It wasn't a question, she simply nodded and resumed her pacing back and forth, some of the cool, calm, control she always harnessed seeping back into her posture. "Okay. I'm choosing to not unpack that right now. I know you're part succubus—" she waved her hand at me when I started to interrupt. "Ro confirmed. I'd figured it out on my own, and then pestered him until he validated me, because I'm a needy bitch and don't like being in the dark. But, that's not important. My point is, you're a succubus. What's one more set of nifty powers, especially since, so far, they're both really goddamned useful right now, right? And probably the best chance we have of getting you back here is relying on your inner demon. So, channel that shit, girl and get your ass here now."

This was one of the many reasons I loved Izzy. The girl couldn't be unsupportive if she tried. I ran up and hugged her again, hoping like fuck that this wouldn't be the last time I ever saw her. That I'd find a way back to her and the rest of my family as soon as possible—Devil be damned.

"Chances that you'll be home later today?" she asked, words garbled around a mouthful of my hair. "If the answer's 'no', which I suspect it is, can you please just tell me where you are, what's going on? We've been trying so hard to reach you— Cyrus has barely even been on campus since you left and the guy has bags big enough to hold my personal arsenal permanently camped out under his eyes."

"I should go to Ro," I said as I pulled away from her. Things were too complicated to run through right now. Even an outline of the last few weeks would take me an hour to get through. If I ever made it back home, I'd tell her everything—every last detail about what I'd learned about myself, about hell, all of it. But I didn't have the heart to tell her now, to see her anxiety spiral more than it already had. Especially since telling Ro had resulted in him winding up in a vamp-induced coma. "I don't have very much control over my dream-walks yet, and mostly just get unconsciously pulled to people. It could take me a while."

"Guessing I can't make that jump with you?" she bit her bottom lip, and I could see the fear bubbling over in her eyes— they were wide and focused, like she was afraid that if she blinked, I'd dissolve into nothingness.

I understood, it was the way I felt when I'd visited Wade's dreams in the early days—each time I'd woken up, I was filled with an awful sinking feeling that it hadn't been real, that he was still dead and my grief was playing cruel tricks on me.

I shook my head. "Movie night when I'm home, though.

Promise. And a shopping spree. I've been in the same outfit for what feels like a year and I'm pretty sure that I smell worse than the gym does after a full day of people training in it."

Her chin dimpled slightly, and I could see her swallow back her emotions. Unable to say anything else, she simply nodded, sniffling quietly as she stood taller. Protectors were so goddamn good at swallowing their emotions, at turning fear into something productive. It was both impressive and sad—we never were given the space to simply sink into our feelings.

I closed my eyes and focused all of my energy on Ro. I'd visited him once before, and I tried to conjure that same feeling —that desperate need to see him—while ignoring as much of my own fear as I could. That would only make the process more difficult.

It required more than simply drawing up an image of him in my mind's eye—it was a complicated process to bring him to life. My thoughts swam with the way his face would pull into a cocky grin right before landing a particularly good hit during our sparring sessions; the way he'd roll his eyes at me, smiling all the same, when I'd ask him to rewatch an episode of Buffy with me for the thousandth time; the way our eyes would meet, communicating a world of silent laughter, when Cy would start up on one of his well-trodden lectures about willpower and focus.

While I didn't necessarily feel the same pull to Ro that I often felt with Wade, it was easier to reach him in a lot of ways —we had a lifetime of connection. Well, ten years of one anyway.

Ro and Cy were my compass home. They always would be, no matter what else had changed over the last few days.

It didn't take long before I felt something shift around me. When I teleported, I was acutely aware of my body, how it was dissolving and restructuring itself. It was a terrifying, almost painful awareness. This was the opposite. The world shifted around me, changing and falling in and out of focus. Even with my eyes closed, I could feel the atmosphere around me shift—the smells, the temperature, the texture of the floor beneath my feet.

My head swam with the strangeness of it all, my stomach lurching slightly as I reoriented myself to the new surroundings.

Familiar white walls greeted me as I opened my eyes, the light bright and unforgiving as I scanned a room I'd spent a fair share of my time in, during my brief months at The Guild. The usual gentle whirs and abrasive beeps sounded around me as my eyes landed on a prone figure on the hospital bed.

Ro.

His dark blond hair was caked against his damp forehead, his face tense even in sleep, like he was still battling the demons who put him there. Blood-soaked bandages covered his neck and upper shoulders, the hospital bedding and gown pulled up around him.

"Ro," I whispered, almost afraid to wake him.

He didn't stir.

Gently, I laid my hand against his, pressing slightly.

No one else was in the room, but that made sense to me. I'd never encountered anyone other than the dreamer in these dream-walks. But usually, when I visited, the dreamer was always awake. Even when Eli and Declan were injured terribly, they'd still been conscious when I'd visited them, almost like they'd been waiting for me.

My stomach tightened as panic started to take hold, squeezing until it hurt to breathe. I said his name again, louder this time.

Nothing.

I shook his uninjured shoulder gently, tapped his leg, screamed for him to wake up until my voice grew rough with wear.

Nothing. Just the annoying sounds of a hospital room and me—completely alone with my brother's body as he fought off the venom creeping through his system.

I wanted to destroy the vampire that had done this to him—wanted to rip the demon to shreds until its blood coated the floor. Wanted to cause the same kind of pain and fear that it had caused my brother, that it was causing me now, as bile rose up my throat. Was this the demon lingering beneath my skin? The fury that boiled hot and angry felt both familiar and not, and I was caught between harnessing it to turn it against the world and cooing it back down into a box where it couldn't touch anyone—myself included.

But as I studied Ro, I realized that a creature like Darius had done this to him. That Darius had probably killed more protectors and humans than I could count in just the same way. That we all seemed to have a strange darkness battling inside of us—Atlas, Declan, Eli, Wade. Even Ro. We all had blood on our hands. None of us were untouched by it, not anymore. Maybe we never were.

I leaned against the chair at the side of his bed, guessing that Cyrus had been occupying it in the physical realm. Confronted with him like this reminded me of the early days of dream-walking to Wade.

He'd been asleep then too, and I'd been nothing more than a disembodied observer, watching and waiting with a budding anxiety. Unable to interact. Unable to break through.

What had changed?

When I'd spoken to Villette, the succubus Darius introduced to me, she'd mentioned that very few lust demons could traverse the realms. Their—*our*—power was connected to the hell realm. Was it possible that I just wasn't strong enough to reach Ro from this distance?

I pressed my palm to his pulse, letting the slow, fluttering beat ground me to the situation, to calm my panic in the way that only Ro ever knew how to do. He was my anchor back to a simpler time, a quiet innocence that propelled us through our strange lives.

The gentle lull was unsteady and strange, and I could tell that something was off.

Every muscle seemed tense, like his body was in the middle of an epic fight for his life, even in sleep.

Slowly, I leaned my ear down to his chest. I did nothing but lay there, listening to his heartbeat, searching within myself for the strange threads I'd found when healing the others.

Khali had mentioned that healing would be easier if I was bonded to the person I was healing. But there were so many different kinds of bonds in our world—the mate bonds that The Guild forced, the blood bond between Darius and Eli.

Ro and I had something stronger though, something pure, something that no magic could touch or complicate. He was my family. Home. If anyone was a part of me, it was him.

I focused all of my energy, every molecule of myself on calling to Ro—searching for him with my mind, lingering on every detail of what it felt like growing up with him. He was strength and friendship embodied. Even when he was being a stubborn asshole, it was always with a strange love and warmth that only Ro could conjure.

When I'd spilled my heart out to him in that dream, he'd held me close, been my lifeline of support. He'd taken on vampires and werewolves trying to find me. I had to find him now.

We stayed like that for what felt like hours, though I knew it couldn't really have been that long. I could feel myself growing tired, like simply lying here was draining the little energy that I had left.

But then, as if out of nowhere, I felt it—the flutter of a tether, an ethereal thread so incandescent and subtle that I'd almost missed it.

It was different, fainter than the threads I'd felt with the others—and I could barely focus my attention around it.

Still, it was there.

I placed my hands against his neck, figuring those wounds were the most dire, and relied on that tingly heat that started to grow under my skin. At first, it had frightened me—feeling my body change and zap with a strange energy. Now, I welcomed it, felt the warmth as if it were a comforting hug.

The sounds of the hospital suite were like a fragile echo now, until the steady beat of my own pulse, each breath that I exhaled, were the only things that I could hear. My head started to grow dizzy, my eyelids too heavy to lift back open.

I felt Ro's muscles tense slightly, underneath my palm, and doubled my focus, trying with a quiet desperation to push all of my energy, everything I had into helping him—into getting him to wake up.

But he didn't.

My body grew sore and my head felt like it was weighed down with a pile of bricks. I laid it down on the corner of the bed, resting it just for a second.

Only that second grew into another, and another after that, until suddenly a sharpness pulled at my chest and I lifted my head with a jolt.

The cold white room was replaced by the heavy gray walls of my cell.

"No. No, no, no, no." I scanned the room, like Ro might reappear if I just kept looking hard enough.

My arms shook at my sides as I stood up, the sudden movement enough to make my vision swim. I dug my fingers into the wall for purchase, and leaned against it, letting the stone wall chill the sweat coating my forehead.

I'd gone too far, but it still wasn't enough. I knew that it would take a while for me to restore my energy, knew that Khali had warned me that overexerting myself during the healing process could turn bad quickly, but I didn't care.

Nothing mattered but getting to Ro.

I'd felt something while healing, even if it wasn't with the power or force I'd experienced when healing the members of Six. I just had to hope that it would be enough for now, that it would be enough to pull Ro through until I could reach him again.

I laid back down on my rock-hard bed and squeezed my eyelids tight, begging for sleep to take me under again. But it was like my body knew I would try to heal him again once I did fall back asleep. Instead of granting my desperate desire, my body protested, until I was somehow too exhausted to sleep.

"Fine," I grumbled, after a useless thirty minutes of tossing and turning. If I couldn't help him on my own, I would find someone to help me do it.

Hell, I'd even settle for Lucifer at this point. He was terrifying in his own way, but I'd face him a million times over if it meant that I could get to Ro again. And time was of the essence.

"Lucifer," I screamed, my voice sharp and echoey as it bounced around the room. I screamed for him until my voice went hoarse, using every name for the Devil I'd ever heard. Unsurprisingly, he didn't do anyone's bidding. So I was left with nothing but a sore throat and an exponentially heightening anxiety about what was happening to my brother back at Headquarters.

I couldn't wait. Couldn't sit here and do nothing when I knew that he was fighting for his life.

At the risk of pissing the Devil off even more than I already had, I had no choice but to disobey his orders. I needed Wade. Dream-walking had been much easier when I was with him, whether because of the energy he provided or simply the quiet companionship, I wasn't sure. Maybe he'd developed some tips and tricks during his time here. Between the two of us, he was the veteran seduction demon.

I closed my eyes and teleported.

Well, it wasn't as easy as all that. I was drained and exhausted and afraid, so it took me probably close to an hour of trying to move my body from one space to another for anything to actually materialize from the desire.

Still, eventually, I made it happen. And when it *did* happen, I collapsed on my ass on the opposite side of my wall, making it not nearly as far as I'd been aiming for.

Honestly, I was lucky that I'd made it through at all, without leaving behind a limb. I needed to learn the details and risks of this whole jumping through space thing, because up to this point, I'd mostly gotten by with nothing but a bit of luck and stubbornness.

The hall was dark and empty and I was too tired to try calling on the fire to light my path. I had a feeling I was going to need the little energy I had left momentarily.

With one hand on the wall to my right to ensure that I didn't face-plant onto the floor, I ran as quickly as I could, my breathing ragged and hurried as I tried to shove the images of Ro's wounds from my mind.

After a few minutes, I stopped, panting as my palms rested against my knees. I was so fucking winded. So much had happened in the last few hours—from finding out my entire life was a lie, to trying to fight off a pack of werewolves and vampires, to dream-walking to another realm. As strong as I was growing, my body couldn't handle the absolute clusterfuck I was putting it through for much longer. I needed food, like a proper steak—or a whole cow—and about a week's worth of supernatural-free sleep.

"Lucifer," I yelled again, though it came out as raspy croaks, my throat raw and dry. "Cloaky, get your ass back here."

Was it a bad idea to taunt the Devil? Probably. But I was

desperate and if I didn't find him or Wade soon, I was afraid it would be too late for Ro.

I could survive many things. Losing him was not one of them.

With a slow, deep breath, I straightened back up, and took off at a wobbly run, trying to ignore the way my vision swam, or how difficult it was getting to make the muscles in my legs follow my instructions.

"You would think with as all-powerful as he's supposed to be, he would hear if someone was—ugh—" I choked on a giant puff of hair just as I slammed into a large, warm rock wall and, once again, landed with a heavy thud on my ass.

A low, rumbly growl vibrated around me, and there was just enough light to make out what looked like a very giant paw about half an inch away from my feet.

"Er," I cleared my throat and braced my palms against the floor in case I needed to quickly propel myself up, "what are the chances you're a friendly?"

If I was supposed to help the lord of the underworld rescue hell, than I sure as fuck hoped that the creatures I encountered down here would at the very least not instantly make a meal out of me. Right?

The growling grew louder and I knew from the depth of the sound that I was most definitely dealing with a hellhound, but also that I was not dealing with *my* hellhound.

Slowly, so as not to instigate the animal into attacking, I lifted my hand a few inches in front of my face. A familiar tingling sensation crept along my skin as I focused all of my fear and rage and anxiety on lighting myself on fire—which seemed about as counterintuitive and reckless as yelling insults at an absent devil.

Instead of the bright, swirling fire that I was used to seeing when I conjured fire, I was staring at a laughably small sputter of flames no larger than what a gas station lighter could produce.

Still, I'd take what I could get at this point. Carefully, I moved my hand towards the creature until a swath of fur black as night was all that I could see—fur so dark that it took me a moment to realize it was in fact fur and not more empty corridor.

Peering down at me was a pair of indigo eyes, narrowed and focused with an intimidating precision. But they were familiar eyes.

I let out a relaxed sigh, my body melting with relief as the barely-there flame disintegrated into nothing.

"It's you," I said, my lips lifting in a small smile that I wasn't sure he'd be able to see in the dark. Dogs could sense friendliness, couldn't they? Here's hoping. I'd met this hellhound once before while wandering this labyrinth of hallways, and I was beginning to suspect that he acted as a sort of neutral guard hound down here. He most certainly was not one of the hellhounds who'd been fighting my team outside anyway.

More importantly, since he hadn't killed me then, I had a feeling that he wouldn't now, no matter how intimidating his growl and stare were. He'd been the closest thing to a friendly face I'd met since traipsing into hell, not counting my friends anyway.

With things as dire as they were, right now, that small sliver of not-murderous intention counted for a lot.

"Can you help me? Can you guide me to...anyone?" I knew Ralph could understand me, no matter how much that proclamation made people roll their eyes, and all I could do was hope that this hound could too. "Do you know where Ralph is? Or my friends? Or even Cloak—"

Soft jaws clamped gently around my forearm and pulled me up with impressive force. The feel of his sharp teeth against my skin made my stomach dip as a scream lodged at the back of my lungs—but eventually my brain processed that while the pressure holding me was strong, it wasn't rough. He hadn't broken skin.

With a toss of his head, the hound used my forward momentum to lob my body towards his back.

For a moment, I thought he was stuck in the decision between ripping my throat out or doing as I asked, and just as I thought he might actually land on the former, a familiar tightness gripped my chest as chills tingled down my spine.

The destabilizing tug of being pulled through space rolled through my body. I tried to resist, to pull away, but every last ounce of strength I had was depleted.

The dark hallway slipped into a darkness so heavy that it became impossible to hold onto consciousness.

So, I let the darkness take me under.

3

MAX

A bone-deep warmth spread through my body, somehow both gentle and urgent as it enveloped me. Part of me wanted to resist it—to let go and fall into a deep, dark abyss, to sleep for a few hours or days or weeks. To rest and forget about all of the things nagging at the back of my mind. But then a brief, flitting image of Ro alone in a white room flooded my thoughts. The sight of him there, like that, sent a fresh wave of fear rolling through me and I pulled onto the warmth with every atom in my body, letting it infuse me with strength.

With each passing second, my focus grew more clear, less hazy.

"She's coming to," a deep, smooth voice said, startling me in the darkness.

"I'm aware, seeing as I'm the one facilitating it." This voice was more familiar, and my body tensed instinctively, even though I couldn't quite place it.

"Do you just wake up every day and choose to be an asshole? Doesn't it get exhausting over the years?"

"You would certainly know."

I peeled one eyelid open, and then the other. There was a brief rush of shock as light flooded my vision, but my surroundings started to settle after a minute.

"Ah good," the familiar voice said, "there you are."

I lifted my head slightly, trying to find the speaker, but it felt like my body was both floating and weighted down.

"Easy," the other voice said, and I felt a gentle pressure against my shoulders, lifting me until I was leaning back on something soft but firm.

Dark blue eyes and shaggy black hair came into focus.

"You," I said, my voice hoarse and softer than I'd intended.

He arched a brow, a shit-eating grin peeling the corner of his lips up. "Me. You can call me Sam."

Sam. The man who'd almost gotten me and my friends killed a few hours ago out of sheer boredom. Fucking prick. But he was also apparently the man who'd sent Ralph to me. I wasn't sure what to make of him just yet, but I damn well didn't trust him as an ally.

My heart started racing as I scanned the room, looking for the giant hellhound that I'd met in the hallway. But he wasn't here.

Instead, my gaze fell on Lucifer, his focus leveled on me like he half-expected me to make a run for it and never look back. Honestly, he wasn't completely wrong. The thought had crossed my mind.

"What were you doing in the halls when I explicitly told you to get rest?" There was no anger in his voice, no emotion at all—just a cool, collected ambivalence. Somehow that was more terrifying than meeting his rage would have been.

I was no longer in the winding dark halls. Instead, I was in some sort of office or den, fashioned with a large black armchair and mahogany table. I was seated on a couch, the material soft to the touch, but not the sort of design meant for long movie nights and relaxing hangs with friends. In that sense, it suited hell just fine.

The room had a cold, minimal sort of decor, like the goal was to discourage anyone from lingering too long here. Still, compared to the flat slab I'd been sleeping on in my cell, the couch was a luxury. The thought that either of the men in front of me had bothered setting me anywhere but the floor seemed strangely absurd and out of character for them both. One had used me as a glorified cage fighter, and the other had kept me in a dungeon.

There was a large window, and the sight of a soft blue sky and the dim filtering of light that washed over the room was enough to ease some of the tension in my body. I wanted to walk to the window, to feel the soft light on my face and look out over the view. After days of being cooped up in that small, stale cell, I could feel myself itching to explore, to stretch.

But how had I gotten here? As soon as the question occurred to me, the remnants of my dream came rushing back to the forefront of my mind, like a funnel ripped wide open.

"Ro." I cleared my throat and stood up straighter. My body felt more like my own now. The strange warmth was dissipating with each passing moment. I felt stronger, less drained than I had even before teleporting outside of the complex. "I need to go."

"You don't really get the point of the whole being imprisoned thing, do you?" Sam leaned back against the wall, his eyes darting between me and Lucifer like he was watching a tennis match—but with the mild amusement of someone who only marginally appreciated the sport. "She's not the smartest girl I've encountered, so I guess she really is yours."

Lucifer ignored him, his entire body still. It was the kind of stillness that came from a predator mid-hunt, like he was waiting to pounce. I just wasn't sure whether it was at me or Sam. "You'll go back to your cell and we'll work on a training regimen in the morning once I've figured out what to do with the pack of misfits who seem to have come as a sort of unimpressive package deal."

My friends. I needed to find them. But before I did that, I needed to help Ro.

"You don't understand—it's my brother. He's been attacked by a vampire and I dream-walked to him. I tried to heal him... and I think I did somewhat. But not completely. I can't let him die."

A flash of surprise swept over Sam's face, gone just as quickly as it had come. "You can dream-walk between realms? And heal in the process. That's...almost interesting."

"You have no brother," Lucifer said, though there was almost a slight edge of insecurity to the statement, like he was questioning the truth but didn't want to state it.

A chill ran down my spine at the realization that I was related to this man. For so long Ro and Cy were my only family. They always would be. But a small, annoying part of me was curious to learn more about the man standing in front of me—and, perhaps even more so, about my mother.

"Please, you don't understand. He's family. He's my person. I need to get back to him." I wasn't sure why I thought appealing to his empathy would help my situation—it wasn't like the Devil would be able to understand love or affection.

"No." Lucifer shrugged. The movement was subtle, but it made me want to punch him all the same. "What do I care if some random boy dies? Thousands die each day. One more is just a blip. Irrelevant. You'll get over the loss. Perhaps it will even make you stronger."

Rage boiled low in my gut, but I tried not to let it show too much. I couldn't win a battle with the two creatures before me —not with any of the fighting techniques I'd spent a lifetime learning. Reason, manipulation—these were the only tools that I had at my disposal here. "Then help me heal him. I can go back to sleep. Teach me how to heal him through my dreams—completely this time. I don't know how much time he has."

"You won't be able to do that," Sam said, interrupting the clear 'no' his friend was about to utter. "Even if your demonic powers are more developed than I'd originally been told, that's not something that is possible across realms. Especially if you're not bonded to him." He let out a sigh, his dark eyes flashing to mine. The intensity I saw there almost made me flinch. "And you'll probably end up putting yourself into a coma or worse trying again. It's too much of a risk for us to take, when things are as...precarious as they currently are. Honestly, I'm surprised you made it as far as you did after waking up—or that you even woke up at all. You got lucky."

My fingernails dug small crescents into my palm as I saw the same resolve mirrored in them both. "Then let me go back to him, heal him in person."

Lucifer let out a soft chuckle that made the hair on the back of my neck stand up. "It took a very long time to find you, girl. And longer, still, to lure you here. Have I not made it clear that, despite the fact that we would prefer almost anyone else, we are stuck with you? Our realm as we know it is, quite literally, at stake here, and I will not risk everything on the whims of some teenage girl and her cumbersome emotional attachments. I won't let you out of my sight, not until I've gotten what I need from you. Half of hell is avidly hunting for you now. And if The Guild finds out what you are capable of, they will happily destroy you with little discussion or debate. You will stay here and you will train—until you've learned how to master your powers and obey orders. Then, once you've proven your use, we will talk about our options for next steps."

My teeth locked together so furiously that I was shocked none of them cracked. Our eyes met and I refused to drop my gaze, to back down. Rather than infuriate him, as I thought an attempted show of dominance might, the corners of his eyes creased in amusement.

I could feel them both toying with me, and while I didn't want the world to end or whatever, I also wasn't exactly certain that someone claiming to be Lucifer was a trustworthy person whose word I should take at face value.

I needed to talk to Six, to Cyrus and Ro. Which meant I needed time and to get home as quickly as possible.

"Way I see it," I started, keeping my voice as even as possible, despite the fact that I could feel my fingers trembling against my legs. "There are two options. You can either lock me back up in that cage and play the game your way."

"I like that option," Sam said.

"In which case," I continued, shooting him a glare that only led to an infuriating smirk, "I'm going to fall back asleep and help my brother. Even if it means that I die or drain myself in the process. And once that happens, I won't be able to help you."

Lucifer let out a low sound that was somewhere between a chuckle and a grunt, but I didn't miss the way his hand clenched into a fist at his side. "You wouldn't."

"Family might not mean anything to you, but it's everything to me," I snapped.

"What's your other option, then?" Sam took a step towards me, and I could see that something about this dilemma finally caught his attention. "You said there are two. What happens if we play this game your way?"

"You let me go home—make sure he's okay."

"Not a chance—" Lucifer started.

"And I'll do as you say after he's okay. After I'm sure that he's no longer on the brink of death. I'll work with you, I'll develop my powers. I'll repair whatever damage is done to the magical system to the best of my ability, so long as I'm not harming my people in the process."

I still wasn't sure that I believed him, or that helping the Devil was in the best interest of most people, let alone the family I'd be leaving behind at The Guild. But at least agreeing to go with things would buy us more time.

"You will need her back at The Guild eventually," Sam cut in. His chin rested on his hand as he stared at me. "And she'll have protection if you give her back that odd menagerie of a team she seems to have collected and that you now have locked up like sardines. Might actually be a good idea to put them to use. Give us eyes and ears where we need them."

The silence stretched for a long moment, the expression on Lucifer's face as impassive as it always seemed to be.

I tried to calm the raging thump of my heartbeat, but it was the only sound I could hear.

"And if your brother is already dead, what then?" he asked, tone absent of all empathy and compassion.

Maybe I didn't want to know more about my mother—I couldn't imagine that she was exactly a person of discerning taste if this was who she'd chosen to procreate with.

I pushed the rush of panic that filled my lungs down at the thought of Ro not making it, but a heavy heat coated my skin. When I looked down, I saw the flare of fire, the colors swirling together furiously.

"She definitely will need to work on impulse control," Sam said as he took a step forward, examining the small plume. "Her power is strong, but she's woefully behind in understanding how to use it. It's almost embarrassing really. I thought your progeny would be more...impressive."

"If Ro is gone," I said, ignoring him, "I still need to be there, to see him. But give me my team, let us work together on this. And I swear that I'll," I waved my arms awkwardly, taking a deep breath until the flames slowly disappeared, "get this under control."

Lucifer's eyes narrowed as he turned toward the window. I

got the feeling that whenever he looked at me, he was counting down the time until it was acceptable to look away—like staring for too long made him uncomfortable. "You'll need to get that under control. If anyone at The Guild sees what you can do, you'll be, as they say, completely screwed."

I nodded, unable to say anything at the risk that my voice would betray the pain that reality caused me. Ro would be there for me no matter what. He'd made that abundantly clear. And I was pretty certain that I could count on Izzy and Cyrus to be in my corner as well. But I'd been around protectors long enough to know that if I stepped one foot out of line—showed that I was...different in any way—I'd end up locked in the lab or decapitated faster than it would take me to say "hellhound." Even Six was terrified of me, of what I could do. I hadn't forgotten how they'd lied to me—the way they communicated with each other when they thought I wasn't paying attention. If they didn't trust me, I didn't stand a chance of expanding my fan base of protectors very far.

"You'll come back here in two weeks," Lucifer continued, and I tried like hell to disguise the rush of excitement that had my hands twitching. Was he agreeing to let me go? "Your being here helps stabilize things on this side of the realm, even if your absence destabilizes things in your realm, as I suspect is the case. It will be a game of immaculate balance as we develop your powers and find the tools that we need."

I nodded, trying to ignore the part about how my coming to hell had potentially made things worse back home. Another thing to deal with later, when I had the ability, time, and emotional stability to do so.

Sam shot Lucifer a look of surprise. I had a feeling that the Devil rarely made compromises.

Not for the first time, I wondered about the nature of their relationship. They weren't killing each other, and they appeared to be on the same side. But there was also a tangible animosity between them that I couldn't miss even if I tried. They gave a new definition to the word frenemy, of that much I was certain. More lethality too.

"Deal," I said, trying to rush things along before he changed his mind. "I'll do whatever you ask if I can save my brother. You have my word."

Lucifer turned to me, the look in his eyes chilly enough to send a dark shiver deep through to my bones. He grinned, harsh and unkind, and something about it instinctively made me squirm, like my body could guess what was coming before my brain could. "I'll need far more than your word, girl."

When I said nothing, he nodded, taking my silence as answer enough, and pulled out a sharp blade. It didn't have the ethereal glow that the dagger he'd stabbed Wade with had. Instead, it looked plain and well made, the sort of weapon I'd expect Cyrus to cherish. But the lack of preternatural doom and gloom didn't calm any of my unease.

"Luce," Sam said, his voice a low, warning growl, "you can't—'

"Enough." Lucifer didn't yell, didn't shoot his friend a deadly glare, but the cool calm of the word was somehow worse, sounding harsh and threatening to me, even though I wasn't the one it was directed at.

Sam clenched his jaw, dark eyes glistening with something I couldn't begin to decipher as they shot between me and the man who held Ro's fate in his hands.

Satisfied that he'd get no further interruptions, Lucifer raised the weapon.

It took everything I had not to flinch in response, not to do something to defend myself. Instead, I kept my gaze on his, trying to relax some of the tension I felt building in my face and shoulders. I wouldn't fight him, not on this. Not if it was my only way to get to my brother in time.

I exhaled the breath I'd been holding as he brought the tip

of the blade to his own palm, carving a long line down the center. I don't know why I didn't expect the Devil to bleed, but it seemed strange seeing his dark blood pool in his hand, looking no different than the same that ran through my blood, that ran through humanity's blood—all of it the same.

Silently, he turned the blade so that the handle faced me. I waited for a beat, confused, until I gripped the blade in my hand, unsure what he wanted me to do with it.

Was stabbing him in the heart on the table? Because I'd gladly take that option if it was.

"You've learned nothing in your supposed school, have you? Nothing but lies about your own people," he muttered on an exhale, his impatience with me running even thinner than usual. He nodded at me, eyebrows raised and eyes wide, as if trying to hurry me along. "Your turn. This is a blood oath. It will ensure that you follow through on your side of the bargain—I make no deals without guaranteeing that they are met."

I knew there was the whole 'never make a deal with the Devil' thing, but sometimes, a girl had to do what a girl had to do.

With a quick, deep breath, I nodded, pressing the sharp metal into my skin and trying not to get too grossed out by the fact that my blood was intermingling with Lucifer's. Even if we really did share DNA.

All at once, I remembered a similar scene, from a week or two ago. Darius was trying to convince Villette to teach me how to stop Wade's advances—little did we know then that I'd be the demon in need of stopping. They'd cut their palms, just like this, shaking on a future favor. I didn't understand it then, but he hesitated before clasping her hand with his—as if he had to take a moment to steel himself. Blood oaths, apparently, were not things to be made lightly.

"How exactly," I started, trying to frame the question as

kindly as I could, at risk of scaring him off from letting me go home, "does a blood oath bond me to you?"

"If you do not uphold your bargain," he said, raising an eyebrow before lifting his palm towards me to shake, "either an aspect of your will becomes mine—"

"Or..." I urged, anticipation making my voice croak. He had a habit of drawing information out slow and languid, like half of his joy—if the Devil was even capable of joy—came from making me sweat.

"Or you die." It was Sam who responded, his tone sharp and gaze lasered in on me. I could feel his judgment licking at my neck even when I turned away from him, no longer able to meet the heated anger in his eyes. "Blood oaths with the Devil are little more than a death sentence. No one with more than two brain cells would shake that man's hand right now."

They would if they had Ro in their lives—and if the alternative was losing him.

"You must shake with intent," Lucifer said, like he could read the decision on my face as I made it.

Without another thought or glance, I grasped his hand in mine, the cut on my palm stinging slightly from the pressure and what felt like a strange, unaccounted-for tingling warmth. When I focused on the juncture of my skin against his, I could feel something almost familiar, but entirely strange—like some invisible force was forging me to the man. Though less intense and sharp, it felt almost like the strange tethers I'd traced in my mind as I healed my friends.

"Careless girl." Sam shook his head and though I could feel his disappointment practically drowning me, he hadn't done anything to forcibly stop me from creating the oath—and for that I was deeply grateful. "I'll monitor your hound while you're away. You're going to be an easy target as it is—so it's probably best if he stays out of sight unless absolutely necessary. The last thing we need is him calling attention to you while you infiltrate The Guild. In the meantime, I'll step his training up as well. He's proven far more useful than I've given him credit for—it's time he reaches the next level of his potential." For a long moment, he paused, staring at me with a strange intensity, like he'd completely forgotten that Lucifer was standing there with us.

"Thank you," I whispered, shattering the ominous calm of the room. "Ralph is very important to me, it will help to know that he's safe and looked after." I wasn't sure why I said it. This man had done nothing but taunt and torment me since my first meeting with him, but for some reason I found myself believing that he wouldn't let my hellhound come to any harm.

There was a flicker of something in his eyes that stirred recognition. It felt like a strange sort of déjà vu, the kind you'd experience in a dream, where the words I was looking for were right on my tongue, but I couldn't get the muscles of my mouth to form them. It felt suddenly like I'd met him before, even though I knew that couldn't be the case. He didn't have the sort of face I'd be likely to forget.

He opened his mouth to speak, but before any sound left the man's lips, Lucifer took a step forward and wrapped his hand around my wrist as that familiar feeling of unbecoming came over me.

My vision shrouded in darkness and when I came back to myself, head dizzy and swimming from the strangeness of the travel, I was in another room.

Gone was the subtle light coming in from the window.

I was back in a dark, gray cell. The air was stagnant and thick with tension.

It wasn't my cell, though it was one that I was intimately familiar with.

"Wade," I said, as soon as my lips could form words.

My eyes found his instantly, and the simple sight of him in front of me sent a rush of calm through my body. He had a way of instantly making me feel like I wasn't alone, like he was there to help carry some of the weight on my shoulders. We were in this new, strange life together.

Only his wasn't the only gaze on me. I scanned the room and saw them all—the members of Six and Darius—staring at me and Lucifer with a range of expressions and emotions in their eyes. There was a girl too, one I'd never seen before, though something about her felt familiar to me. I couldn't place what it was.

She appeared to be naked, wearing nothing but some of the fabric I recognized from Wade's makeshift bed. I shoved the uncomfortable dip of jealousy in my belly down as far as it would go—which was honestly not very.

"Hi," I said, awkwardly stepping away from Lucifer's iron grip, but finding the room too small and crowded to create any real distance between us.

Even with all the anxiety coursing through me...even with all of my concern about the fact that Ro needed me and that I was standing in hell next to Lucifer himself—my father, no less —I *still* couldn't keep my thoughts from wandering to the fact that I'd had sexual encounters with almost everyone in this room since the last time we were all together.

The new, naked girl and Lucifer were the only exceptions. Talk about an awkward as fuck entrance. I found myself struggling to meet anyone's gaze for longer than a moment. Conversations needed to be had, but this was not the time for them.

"You're here."

"Where's he been keeping you?"

"Has he hurt you?"

Declan, Wade, and Darius all stood, and took a step towards me. The mixture of fear and relief warring across their features was identical with all three.

"I'm okay." My voice came out as a soft rasp that echoed

around the room, my cheeks reddening under all of their appraisals.

Atlas was tucked far back, sitting against the wall with his arms leaning against his knees, like he was trying to make his body as compact as possible. His dark eyes, shot with gold, met mine, but other than the light pulse of his jaw muscles and the slight flare of his nostrils, he made no other move. If he was surprised or startled by the fact that I'd just teleported into this little chamber with the Devil, he covered it superbly.

"Ah yeah, him," Darius said, scratching the back of his neck. "He's gotten rid of the wolfy exterior since you've last seen him at least." He shrugged, like he thought Atlas was a lost cause. "Hasn't spoken a word though, so not sure he's really all, you know," he tapped at his forehead, "there, if you know what I mean?"

I nodded, unsure how to respond or what to say to any of them. I wasn't sure what everyone here knew, but the last time I'd seen Atlas, he wasn't a wolf. He'd had me pressed up against a wall with every inch of my body on fire for him, every touch of his skin against mine sending electricity down my spine like my bones were nothing but live wires.

Darius's eyes narrowed as he studied me, his head tilted slightly in that way of his—like he could see so much more than anyone else could. Like every thought I had was printed onto a scroll—one he needed only to unravel to read.

I cleared my throat and looked down at Eli. His forehead was coated in a sheen of sweat, his fingers pressed against the wound at his stomach. Without a thought, I moved towards him, my hands outstretched, but a hard shove into my chest stopped me instantly.

"No," Lucifer said, his arm outstretched in front of me. "You've only just regained your energy. And you've made it abundantly clear that you have no control when it comes to energy exchange."

"Don't touch her." Declan took a step forward, squaring off with Lucifer. Her lips quivered slightly, but she pulled back the fear into a smooth, confident canvas.

Every muscle in my body tensed, the silence as we waited for his response like a thick, choking fog.

From the corner of my eyes, I saw Lucifer arch his brow, but he didn't instantly strike at anyone, or kill Declan where she stood. He seemed almost...amused.

"And how exactly would you try to stop me if I did?" His voice was smooth, but like the hard, flat slide of a blade, rather than the velvety tenor I usually associate with smoothness.

Declan's jaw clenched, her green eyes darting briefly to me before she straightened her posture and turned back to the Devil. The implication was clear—she had no intention of backing down.

"Ridiculous children, the lot of you," Lucifer muttered under his breath before dropping his arm from where it hovered, blocking me.

In a flash so quick it was like watching lightning, he knelt down by Eli.

"No," I screamed, but Declan pulled me back to her chest as I lunged for them both. "Don't hurt him."

Lucifer's hand pressed against Eli's abdomen, pulling a loud, agonizing groan from him. When he turned back to look at me, his eyes were shot through with pure black.

At first, I thought he might be draining him—that seemed like the sort of power someone like him would have. But after a long, tense moment, some of the color started to come back into Eli's face, and while Lucifer didn't exactly look weakened, I could see from the tension around his mouth that whatever he was doing was wearing on him, taking a toll, even if only a small one.

"You're healing him," I said, not because I'd meant to, but

because I was stunned by the realization and the observation had fallen from my lips unbidden.

The air seemed to pulse around us, the energy thick and oppressive.

"You'll need protection," Lucifer said, his neutral expression faltering slightly under the strain. "A half-dead protector is only marginally more useless than a healthy one, but in this case every precaution must be taken, if you're insisting on toying with your life—and, by design, mine."

"You're really going to let us leave?" I was still pressed against Declan's chest, my back melding against the curves of her like a glove.

As if she realized it just as I did, she stepped away, dropping her arms from me. I realized the warmth and comfort of her presence only when the absence stole both away, like a sharp breeze in a dark hall.

"I need ears inside The Guild as is—we don't yet have all the information that we need for fixing this problem. Sam, my people, and I will work on things on our end. Perhaps it is best for you to continue hiding in plain sight."

I glanced around the room, almost every expression filled with a mixture of shock and confusion—every expression but Darius's. Generally, he was good at disguising his emotions, but the disbelief in the furrow of his brows was clear as day.

"You're letting us leave, just like that?" His eyes met Lucifer's, unblinking. "Why? Why just let us go after you've spent so much time getting her here?"

Lucifer's nostrils flared slightly, and I could tell that while he seemed to almost admire Declan's courage, something about Darius's challenge hit a frayed nerve. "I don't need to explain any of my decisions to any of you." He nodded his head towards me. "If the girl wants to fill you in, she can. All that matters is that you will all see to it that she is protected—from protectors and creatures from hell alike—while she does what she needs to do. She will be brought back to me every couple of weeks, where I will help her harness and learn to use her powers."

"No offense," Eli said. He looked almost back to normal, but my stomach dipped at the trademark smirk on his face. Something told me Lucifer wouldn't find his wit as endearing as most people did. "But what makes you think any of us would let her come back here? Ever?"

"Eli," Declan snapped, "shut up."

"He's right," Darius said, fingers scratching absentmindedly against his jaw. "Someone as powerful as you," he turned back towards Lucifer, "is intelligent enough to know that we wouldn't return of our own volition. What aren't you saying?"

I wasn't sure why, but I didn't want to mention the blood oath just yet. I knew it would be met with reproach from them all and it would just get us bickering about a path that had already been forged.

Lucifer's lips flattened into a straight line, but when his eyes met mine, I knew that he wouldn't bring it up either. I could tell that any small sliver of patience he'd afforded us was running on empty. "Your friends are as insufferable as you are," he bit out as he turned to me. "I'll be glad to have some of my peace restored with you gone." He shook his head softly, like he was weighing something, his sharp features clear and discerning, even in the shadowed room as his gaze met Darius's. "This girl should not exist. But she does. A very graceful, tentative balance must be maintained—something you should be all too familiar with, even if you've ignored and abandoned your duties of maintaining that balance."

Darius's jaw clenched as he met Lucifer's stare with a heavy glare. I wasn't sure what he meant by that, but he continued before I could press him for more information.

"She's of age now, is coming into her powers, and, most importantly, has crossed the shadow barrier into hell—a rupture that will usher in a complex web of butterfly effects that even I won't be able to predict. She will need to return here often to keep things moderately stabilized. And if she doesn't learn to develop and use her powers—quickly—they will most certainly kill her within the next few months. Perhaps you can focus on her looming death, if that will keep your attention. I'd go to her, but I'm tied to this place—by blood and bone. My time in the human realm can only happen in small quantities, an hour or two here and there, nothing more. And I'm in a weakened, almost useless state when I make that journey. Not suitable for rigorous training. She will come to me."

His words echoed around the room, everyone silent as they took them in. I got the strange feeling we were being lectured to by a superior—the familiar guilt that only Cyrus could usually manifest in me lingered low in my belly. We'd come to rescue Wade, but was it possible that in doing so, we'd set a dangerous, disastrous domino effect barreling towards our people— towards the entire world?

My skin felt itchy and tight suddenly. I tried not to focus on the part about my powers killing me, but the very act of doing so only heightened my awareness of that growing warmth beneath my skin, the way my anxiety and fear seemed to trigger them into motion.

"And," Lucifer continued, a smug expression plastered on his face as the heaviness of his information, the gravity of it all, tightened around us like a vise. "Just to make sure that we're all on the same page, that none of you attempt to cross me, I will be keeping one of you here with me. Collateral can be a powerful motivator, I've found."

There it was. The twist of the knife that I'd been waiting for. I was okay bargaining with him myself, making my own sacri-fices—but the realization that one of my friends would be under his thumb made my stomach sink with the weight of an anchor.

I looked at the strange collection of people I'd accumulated in this room. All of them strong and oddly essential to my journey home. I couldn't imagine returning to The Guild without a single one of them—even Darius.

If Ro's life wasn't hanging in the balance, I'd offer myself up just to give them all a chance to return.

"Me."

It was the first thing I'd heard Atlas say, and his voice sounded strange as it bounced around the room—hollow and layered with something that I couldn't quite parse.

"No." Wade stood up, fists clenched at his sides as he squared his shoulders and met my eyes. "It has to be me."

Lucifer sighed, dropping his face into his palm. He had the air of someone who didn't have the patience to deal with the room, like a sleep-deprived parent desperate for a few moments away from a pack of toddlers. The pompousness of the gesture had my teeth grinding.

Atlas and Wade were locked in a silent conversation, a battle of wills. I knew from the brief moments that I'd seen them together, that Wade was used to losing these battles with his brother, that he often felt like the kid brother who was constantly bossed around and chided for his choices. It was strange to witness that shift now. Even with Atlas's current mood—a mood that was darker than the storm clouds before a tornado—he didn't back down.

"I don't have control of the incubus." He turned to Lucifer, and I saw the battle across his features as he brought himself to ask his request. "Will you help me learn to use these powers? Before I—" his gaze shot briefly to me before returning to meet the Devil's stare again, unflinching, "before I hurt her, or anyone else?"

Lucifer narrowed his eyes, lip curling in disgust, but he studied Wade with a new focus. I couldn't read the emotion in his eyes, didn't think I'd ever be able to master that particular skill where he was concerned, but I thought I saw something like respect, like the derision he'd been leaking in droves was stifled somewhat, suddenly.

"Let me get this straight," Darius propped his chin on his fist, a malicious smirk lifting his lips. "We risk everything, all of us teasing death probably more times than we've even realized, to break you out of your prison. A feat that no sane person would even consider, might I add. And you want us to just pack up and leave you here, as if this whole thing was for nothing?" He snorted, though whether in disgust or amusement, I wasn't entirely sure. "You protectors sure are a tiresome lot, aren't you?"

"I'll stay with you too." The girl who'd been slumped on Wade's bed was sitting up now, with clear eyes and a rigid jaw.

A flare of respect filled me, competing with the annoying jealousy that still lingered from seeing her naked and wrapped up in the scraps of his linens—sitting on the very bed we'd had sex on not that long ago.

Wade shook his head, but turned to her with a fondness and familiarity that made my traitorous stomach ache. "You need to help Atlas. You might be the only person who can. I'll stay back alone. I've survived down here for this long, what's a bit longer while we figure out whatever the hell is going on, right?"

"No." Atlas stood up, his face flushing with anger, wiping away the monotonous despair he'd been sinking into.

Wade shook his head, preventing his brother from saying anything more. "Trust me, it's for the best. And not just because of the power. I can dream-walk. I'll be able to communicate with Max, to keep an open line with you all far easier than she can do on her own. I also," he tensed slightly, and drew out a long pause, "I don't know that I can go back to The Guild. Everyone thinks I'm dead. They'll know that I'm not...entirely like I was before, you know? It just makes the most sense. You'll understand and see that truth if you just let yourself. Stubborn righteousness is clouding your focus."

"How can we just leave you here?" My voice cracked as I tried to hold everything back, frustrated that Lucifer was here to witness the small chinks in our armor—each other. I knew what Wade had gone through—the despair and loneliness that made everything feel heavy and impossibly empty. I'd lived it myself, since dropping into my cell, even if only a small slice of what he'd experienced. To have his freedom handed to him on a silver platter and to just... walk away from it? How could he go back to that cell?

As if understanding, as if he could follow my thought spiral with more precision and mindfulness than even I could, he shook his head and reached for my hand. The feel of his cool skin against mine sent a spark up my arm. "It'll be different this time. I know you'll all be home, safe. And, selfishly," he gave me a soft smile, "it will help knowing that you'll be back. Frequently. It will give me time to figure my shit out in the meantime."

His eyes locked on mine, that strange storm of midnight blue eclipsing the icier shade I was used to. I saw in them what he wasn't saying out loud—that he could find out more about Lucifer and what all was going on here. He'd treat it like a mission, and that would give him enough focus and purpose to pull through any suffocating darkness.

I bit my lip, blinked back the tears that were threatening to spill over, and nodded.

"Great," Darius clapped his hands before rubbing them together furiously. "Shall we get started on our travels then? I'm starving."

4

DARIUS

I averted my eyes while the group said their goodbyes to the incubus and tried not to gag at the strange sentimentality of it all.

I'd grown relatively fond of, or, at the very least used to, the rest of Max's group of misfits. They were occasionally entertaining when they weren't trying to be. But I'd only known this particular addition for a few brief moments and, honestly, I wasn't a fan.

Not of the way they all bent over backwards for him, nor of his temper and insecurity. But most importantly, I was particularly annoyed with the easy familiarity he had with Max. The way she seemed to melt into his touch, like she craved it, like it was air.

He pressed a lingering, unashamed kiss to her lips, whispering something in her ear that was too quiet for even me to hear. Easy, welcomed. It made me sick.

She was more open around him than she was around the others, myself included, more liberal with her affections. I wasn't sure if it was just because she'd been having sexy dreams with him for weeks, or if their relationship had been like this before he'd been kidnapped by the pompous angel.

I mean, she had to be attached if she was willing to risk getting herself killed to save him.

I tried not to think about whether or not she'd do the same for me, because I knew the answer was a resounding no. Sure, she'd avoided killing me during The Guild's twisted death matches, but that had more to do with the fact that she wasn't as morally corrupt as the other protectors were. She saw humanity in demons where The Guild saw only monsters.

And the annoying part was that I knew that she felt something for me, that she wanted me almost as much as I wanted her—but she pushed those feelings down, letting them rise to the surface only under the protection of a dream or danger. Her cheeks flushed with color each time she looked at me, and I could see the shame swelling with her lust—she wanted me but she didn't *want* to want me. I complicated things for her, brought out the sides of her that she wanted so desperately to deny.

Would she ever take my hand with the same comfortable ease that she did his? He was a monster too, wasn't he? Sure, he didn't quite have my body count, but I'd met plenty of girls in my day who were rather impressed with that particular set of skills. Murderous bad boys were in, weren't they? That's what some of the bestselling romance novels had led me to believe anyway.

Lucifer let out an audible groan of discomfort watching the strange goodbye transpire inside this small cell. I could tell that he was growing tired of us all, that he found our interpersonal dynamics tiresome and slightly repulsive, that he was uninterested in everyone here but her.

But what did he want with her? And why was her power affecting the barriers between realms so much? Did she have power over portals, was shadow magic woven with her as it was with me? I tried to suppress the wave of giddiness pulling me under. I wanted her to be like me, to belong with me. To not be alone.

I curled my lips, disgusted with myself. Since when was I such a sniveling lovesick prick? I'd always prided myself on being powerful and giving zero fucks about anything or anyone —about putting myself and my ability to thrive first. This girl was ruining everything, and I was letting her.

I glanced at her lips, at the way they turned up at whatever the boy was whispering to her. Lips that were soft and plump— the perfect balance between sweet and spice.

Fuck it, I was a goner, whatever.

The slutty, devil-may-care version of me had had a good run. I was a one-woman man now.

As if he could read my mind, the cheeky incubus smirked, his gaze leaving Max for a brief moment to meet mine. Gloating.

What a dick. Still, part of me was almost impressed—I'd more or less considered him a useless, whimpering thing. But maybe the incubus had more bite than I'd given him credit for. He just hadn't yet grown into his new britches. Perhaps he wouldn't be killed before getting the chance to.

"How do we leave?" I asked, interrupting Max and the boy's final caress goodbye. I could only handle so much. Another moment, and I was apt to rip her from his arms and sink my teeth into her until she made those low, intoxicating moans that had been echoing through my head since our last encounter. I'd been craving the taste of her blood since the moment I'd taken a taste in my dreams—the reality of that experience would be tenfold. I was sure of it. The only thing I wasn't sure of was how much longer I could hold myself back from binding to her permanently. The tethers were already there, I could feel them forming and strengthening between us.

I could leave, resist the pull and sever them finally, or I could give in.

More and more, the latter was looking like the most enticing option. Stories about life bonds and mates had always seemed so gushy and nauseating to me—but now I couldn't deny the fact that I just wanted to sink into her, to claim her and have her as my own for as long as we lived. And, well, let's be honest, the way we were jumping into danger, that wouldn't be for very long.

Instead of answering, Lucifer shot me one of those obnoxious smirks he seemed so fond of—the pretentious dick—and grabbed Max and Declan's wrists before the three of them disappeared from sight.

Atlas let out a low growl, his eyes flashing yellow as he stared at the spot where Max no longer stood. I could see his muscles contracting throughout his body and knew that he was quickly losing control of his shift. Again. I rolled my eyes at the predictability of it all—such a tiresome crew they were. Why exactly did I put up with them anyway? I could end them all in less than five minutes, no more headaches.

But then of course, she wouldn't speak to me again if I did.

Right.

That was why I put up with them.

I wasn't entirely certain how he'd been brought back to himself, at least partially anyway, but I had a feeling that the little protector was behind it. He was as lost in her as I was, he just wasn't processing his emotions with as much success and maturity as me. I bit back my own smirk for a moment, before letting it shine through with unabashed pride. Fuck 'em.

The wolf's eyes narrowed as his gaze met mine, reading my general vibe, if not really understanding my thoughts and how I'd arrived there. He hated me almost as much as he hated himself. Honestly, it was delightful to watch. He was quickly becoming my favorite of her ragtag group.

Before he could do anything truly thoughtless, like try attacking me again, Lucifer popped back in and grabbed him and Eli before disappearing once more.

"What the hell is he doing?" Sarah asked. Her expression was stern, thoughtful, but I didn't miss the way that her fingers trembled with fear. She reached for Wade, their hands latching together as some wordless goodbye passed between them. There was sorrow there—a history that I didn't fully understand.

Maybe I'd get lucky and they'd run off together, leaving one less asshat for me to compete with for Max's affections. A guy could dream.

"Be careful, don't do anything reckless," she whispered, squeezing his hand softly. "I'll do everything in my power to look after Atlas, to help him complete his transition once and for all. You have my word, if it's the last thing I do."

I caught a glimpse of something in her eyes—guilt, maybe —but it was wiped away by a startle as Lucifer popped back in, gripped her shoulder, and dragged her over to me.

"I fucking hate this part," I mumbled, voice distorted as if bouncing in a metal tin, as my body was pulled into nothing and everything at once.

When I resurfaced, I found everyone hunched over, clutching their knees. None of us were used to traveling like that and it was a bitch to get used to.

"I've called in a favor to open a small portal here that will support you all and land you about twenty-five miles outside of your Guild's territory, if it's stabilized well enough. We've got quite a powerhouse here, between the group of us, not to give Luce any more fodder for his already obnoxious sense of self worth, so it should be okay," a deep voice said.

I spun towards it, cringing at the dizzy rush that made my head swim. It was unbecoming for a vampire to swoon or be vulnerable in front of powerful demons.

It was the man from the field—the one who'd had us fighting off a stampede of demons for his amusement before Max and Lucifer appeared.

His eyes narrowed with mirth as he met my glare, like he could hear the tirade of curses I was silently lobbing at him. Fucking prick.

He arched a thick brow as he took a step towards me, his movement somehow both lazy and pompous all at once. "When you return, your vampire should be able to help you find a more stable portal, I imagine. He's certainly more familiar with the shadow than the rest of you."

Every muscle in my body froze as I waited for him to say more, praying like hell that he didn't.

"Have your wits about you," he continued, though he turned to Max—his shoulders relaxing slightly with an earnestness that wasn't there before. "The vampire's not one I'd invest much trust in if I were you."

I felt my heart beat an angry tune against my ribcage as I forced my lungs to inflate with air.

"Says the demon who literally tried to have us all murdered a few hours ago," she muttered under her breath. I tried to ignore the way that small gesture of faith made my stomach sink to my feet.

"Don't go sowing trouble, Samael," Lucifer said, voice a low warning, "we have enough to untangle as it is."

The man simply chuckled, the sound dark and echoing in the open field. He wasn't exactly enamored with Max in the way that the others in our group seemed to be, but I didn't like the way he studied her—like she was a science experiment that he wanted to watch implode. He was clearly amused by her, intrigued even, but where Lucifer seemed sure that she'd be useful to him, his friend seemed less convinced.

Surprisingly, Max met the man's smirk with one of her own, squaring her shoulders slightly as she took a step towards him

—threat clear. She was the only one of our group who didn't seem too distraught from traveling through space. Her brow was a bit clammy, her pulse more elevated than usual, but even that was leveling itself out. With each shift, she'd get more comfortable, gain more control, until one day she'd be as powerful as the two men looming over our group. Maybe even more powerful.

Eyes narrowed, she turned back to Lucifer, meeting him with just as much confidence and animosity as he met her. "I meant what I said before about my brother, and I mean the same for Wade. If anything happens to him, I'm out. You'll have to go to plan B."

His jaw clenched as he waved his palm in the air a few feet ahead of her.

The air rippled in that familiar way it did when a portal was activated. Something was strange about this one, though I couldn't quite put my finger on it.

"This will be open for only a few moments. While you are at Guild Headquarters, I need you to look for something." There was a strange reluctance to his tone as he met her eyes.

"What?" she tensed, and I wasn't sure what had happened between them while we were holed up in Wade's room, but something told me that I wouldn't like the terms of whichever deal she'd struck with him."

I took a step closer to her, until the back of my hand brushed against her fingers. I felt her relax slightly at my touch.

Lucifer shared a brief look with the man before turning back to her. "I don't really know." I could see from his rigid posture that admitting ignorance grated his nerves deeply, and I bit back a grin at seeing the mighty Devil falter, even if just slightly. "Protectors harnessed shadow magic when sewing this realm years ago—they have a powerful store of it somewhere, though I don't know where or even how they obtained it. Or how they've kept it alive and active all these years. All I can say is that you'll probably know it if you see it—you, specifically, will be quite drawn to it and stand the best chance of any of us at locating it once and for all."

"Why will I be drawn to it?" she asked, but I could see the hesitation in the set of her shoulders, like she wasn't entirely sure she wanted to know the answer.

"Like attracts like. Shadow magic runs through your blood, mobilizes several of your gifts. You are an anchor. You come from a strong line of those quite gifted at wielding it," he responded.

"Shadow magic?" Declan asked.

I hadn't heard that term in many years. Part of me wanted to shove Max through the portal and never look back, to leave the incubus boy here and wash my hands of the whole thing.

The River Styx was a few feet away, the strange, iridescent swirls of the water hypnotizing to watch. I took a deep breath, trying to focus on the odd, deadly calm the river inspired.

"Shadow magic is what we call a very specific kind of magic," I said, hoping that if I explained it rather than one of the two goons looming in front of us, I might be able to keep my relationship with the unpredictable forces at bay for a little longer. Max was only just starting to trust me, to want me—the last thing I needed was for her to learn about my past. "It's the magic that's woven through mate bonds—both for your people and the supernatural—it's what creates the portals and barriers between realms, what lust demons pull from when exchanging energy, what healers interact with when mending wounds. Some creatures are created from it, some simply manipulate it, some can't access it at all. It's a complicated element, one that no one truly understands."

"So," said Eli, drawing the word out for a long moment, "it's basically just magic then? That sounds like it covers pretty much everything."

Lucifer shrugged. "Yes and no. Magical beings are not all

the same. We don't necessarily all have identical origins—our magic comes from different sources and ancestral lines, and is used in different ways. Shadow magic is not responsible for vampirism, blood bonds, hellfire, werewolves—most of the things your kind associates with the supernatural. It's a very unstable magic that is almost impossible to control when the balance is off even slightly. It deals with life and death and spaces in between—with energy exchange. Shadow magic is why most incubi and succubi are more powerful in hell than in your realm—this place was designed with it so it can be felt most strongly here, but the creatures who live here are not all anchored by it." He let out a long sigh, dark gaze sharpening as he took a step closer to Max. "The details are unimportant. Heal your so-called brother, discern how they are using shadow magic while you're there, learn what you can of The Guild's involvement. They're as much at fault for the devolving state of things as you are—and, unfortunately, I have no way of knowing the extent of the organization's involvement in this century. Most importantly, don't die—and be back here within two weeks. Not a day later."

With a few more parting words and threats about how he'd make life a living hell for us if we betrayed him or if Max didn't follow through on her promise, he nodded towards where the air rippled.

Not needing to be told twice, I gripped Max's hand in mine, a rush of peace falling through me as she gripped mine back, the feel of her fingers twining with mine more calming than the river had ever been. With a quick glance and nod at Declan, we walked through.

A heavy darkness clouded my vision, my senses, until it was all I could feel. I tried to take a deep breath in, to push against the slow agony creeping up my spine, but my lungs wouldn't work. The magic of the portal licked at my wounds with a salty tongue, as images of all the things I spent my waking hours suppressing flashed through my mind—blood, death, betrayal.

For a moment, I thought I'd be lost to it, the shadow magic finally succeeding in getting what I owed it after all these years. But then a small, warm light pierced through, the anchor at my hand grounding me toward it—directing me with a quiet firmness.

I clung to a soft, lingering vanilla scent, pressing my face into the source, until my body was wrapped around the light, taking it into myself. My lungs started to move again, my vision swimming into focus as the darkness became a gradient of shadows that took shape.

And then my knees buckled, Max's curled against my chest as I blinked away the moisture accumulating in my eyes. Her head was tucked under my chin, her breathing slow and steady. With one deep inhale, I glanced around and exhaled.

We were out. A warm, golden sun beat against my face, chasing away any shadows that remained.

Max let out a soft grunt, startling me out of my daze. My fingers were clawing into her shoulders, gripping her to me like my life depended on it. I let her go, slowly, but kept my hands against her, the warmth of her skin comforting.

"Are you okay?" She seemed completely fine, a bit frazzled, maybe, but otherwise it seemed like the portal hardly affected her at all. I found myself glad for it—that one thing, at least, was easy in her life. The girl had been through a lot in a very short amount of time.

Unable to speak just yet, I nodded, soothed by the realization that she actually cared and only a little bit embarrassed that the portal affected me as much as it did.

My jaw clenched as I felt my muscles spasm, the familiar tentacles of darkness growing stronger, making themselves known as they spread throughout my body, like a second set of veins.

"Fuck I hate those things," a deep voice muttered behind us with a heavy thud.

I turned around to find Eli on his ass, shaking his head slightly as he readjusted to being back in our world.

"You and me both," the she-wolf added, though her arrival was a touch more graceful than his. "I was unconscious last time. That jump is fucking brutal. Any sign of Dec and Atlas yet?"

The grumpy pair materialized just as the question left her lips, both looking disheveled and even more surly than usual.

As many times as I'd seen people pass through portals, it never ceased to be a strange experience. One moment, just a typical landscape, the next a shimmer, until suddenly entire beings came into existence or disappeared from sight. Magic was a bloody mind fuck.

"At least we've all landed in the same spot this time," Max said, a small, tentative grin pushing her mouth into a curve. Surprisingly, instead of moving farther away from me, she seemed to inch closer until I could feel her body heat radiating from where her torso all but touched mine. "I'm Max, by the way. I don't think we've met."

"I've heard a lot about you." Sarah smiled, shooting a coy smile at Eli that made him flush. She reached her arm forward to shake Max's hand. "Formal introductions seem strange when I'm standing here half naked and we've just escaped hell and the Devil himself together, but I'm Sarah. I hear you have an excellent habit of saving my cousin and reckless friends from the brink of death—so I'm very happy to finally meet you and extend my deepest gratitude."

Max's eyes widened as she looked from Sarah to Declan, no doubt belatedly clocking the similarities between the two women. They were alike in so many ways, from their rigid stubbornness, to their 'fuck-right-off' attitudes, but I was beginning to notice small divergences here and there. And Sarah would have changed with the awakening of her wolf, which meant she might as well be an entirely new person from the last time they were all together.

"You're alive?" Max's voice was filled with a sort of reverent awe as her shy grin turned into a smile wide enough to make my stomach do an annoying, obnoxious flippy thing.

As if it were contagious, Declan's expression mirrored hers as the two of them shared some empathetic conversation I wasn't entirely privy to—but that smile faltered slightly when Max's gaze turned to Atlas.

There was no lightness on his features, his moody slump as Eeyore-like as it had been since the moment he'd shown up dressed in his newly acquired human meatsuit.

Something passed between them, and I wondered again about the curious turn of events that had pulled the man from the brink of being lost to his wolf forever.

"Alive and channeling some serious Teen Wolf vibes," Sarah said, voice turning into a snorty chuckle at her joke. "Figure it's best to just come out and say it, rather than have you finding out when I suddenly look like Balto."

The group exchanged some banter that I tuned out, trying to calibrate where exactly we'd landed ourselves. Luckily the portal had dropped us in a pretty discreet patch of woods, with enough thick trees to soothe any concern that we'd been observed.

And while it was nice to have escaped hell once again, I couldn't shake the discomfort at being so close to the lab that had imprisoned me for so many years. I was fucking starving and I'd feel a lot better about being near the lion's den if I had something to restore my strength. Right now, I felt more like prey than predator.

Habit had me confident that no one in the group was likely to take one for the team and offer to let me tap a vein.

"Thank you for trusting me," Max said, her voice piercing

through the babble like no one else's could—it was like my ear was tuned to her radio frequency, patiently waiting for a dopamine hit of a sound byte. "I promise I'll do whatever I can to protect you—I won't tell anyone your secret."

"Yeah, well," Sarah shrugged, a hesitant grin on her face, "I figure that you're okay with Wade and Atlas not being totally human, and you've got a vamp in your cavalry, so probably wouldn't be a tipping point to add one more demon to your address book. Plus, you know," she scrunched her nose and let out an awkward, tentative chuckle, "seeing as you're, the spawn of Satan and all…"

She let the word hang there and the truth of her statement hit me like a semi driving full speed down an icy highway.

Max's features were softer than his, sure, but they both had those dark eyes that had a habit of peeling everyone back layer by layer, like an onion, the high cheekbones, the golden-tan skin. Plus, you know, that whole setting shit on fire and teleporting thing they both had going on.

"She's not—" Declan's voice dropped into nothingness as she stared at Max, a look of horror flashing across her face.

"What?" Eli's eyes darted between Max and Sarah, the grin on his face slowly melting into frustration, like he was waiting for the joke to drop and annoyed it was taking so long.

Max flushed and I could see her breaths growing shallower, panic coloring her features. "H-how did you know?"

Atlas hadn't moved a muscle. He was standing there all shirtless and broody as he stared at Max, just as impassive as he'd been since he'd rematerialized in his brother's dungeon. Honestly, I wasn't even sure the neanderthal could process the concept; his wolf always seemed more intelligent than he was, far as I could tell. He might've been better off giving into it, wearing the wolf's skin permanently. Far more use to us that way anyway. A wolf added strength, a primal sort of intelligence. This man? Nothing but trouble and self-loathing.

Sarah's eyes narrowed as she scanned the rest of us. "I mean, it's obvious isn't it? Lucifer let her go. Like, king of the underworld, the most terrifying man in the history of the world, the one they've made countless books and movies about, the dude known for literally torturing people until the end of their days." She blew out a low whistle. "I know that he isn't *actually* like that, that hell is nothing like the stories humans tell. But still. He let her *go*. Because she asked. And, sure, he was an ass about it and everything, but he's concerned enough for her safety to let us all go with her as protective detail. And the hellhounds? The way she lights up on fire? Did nobody else really—"

I didn't like being made to feel like a toddler. But having it all spelled out for me like that, I could understand Sarah's disbelief. How the fuck had none of us seen it before? He'd literally lured her to hell. Though why he didn't just kidnap her himself, I didn't know.

Silence—all of us were struck absolutely cold. For a long moment, no one spoke. And while I was sure that everyone was staring at Max, I couldn't verify it, because I couldn't take my eyes off of her.

"What the fuck do we do now? We can't exactly bring her back to Headquarters." Eli asked, breaking the moment in an awkward annoying bit of word vomit that surprised exactly no one.

Max's gaze dropped, and I could practically taste the shame and fear emanating from her.

"They'll kill her," he added, like we all needed him to clarify. "You know they will."

"Only if we tell anyone," Declan said, voice firm and strong as she stared at her team member. "And we're not going to, obviously."

Max lifted her head, and stared at the girl, though her eyes were so glassy with unshed tears that I wasn't entirely sure she could make out much more than Declan's general figure. My stomach tightened at the sight and I reached an arm forward, wrapping it around her shoulders and pulling her to me.

Into a hug.

A comforting hug.

What the fuck was happening to me?

"Y-you," Max leaned into my side, whether consciously or not, I wasn't sure, "you would keep that a secret? Why? Especially after—"

The unsaid words lingered in the air—especially after everything she'd overheard them saying. They'd called her a demon, a monster. They'd been going behind her back, spying on her since the moment she'd met them, treated her like the monsters they hunted, and she'd overheard it all.

Declan's brows furrowed as she took a step closer to Max. "Same reason we've kept Atlas's secret a secret. And now Wade's. You're part of the team. And we protect our own." The girl looked genuinely confused as she studied Max, as if the answer to her question was the most obvious thing in the world. But I saw the traces of guilt, in the way she fidgeted with the hem of her shirt, the way her eyes didn't quite meet Max's. She knew that Max knew the truth—knew that she'd at least overheard some things. Knew that she no longer trusted them implicitly, not anymore. "We won't betray you." *Not again* hung silently in the air, lingering and filled with regret—at least on Declan's part anyway. I wondered if Max heard it too. "It's as simple as that," she shrugged, "and as complicated."

Something strangely like respect unfolded in my chest as I studied them all. Atlas was still silent, but the impassive, dark look that had eclipsed his features since he'd returned had wilted some, making way for the shock of Sarah's deduction.

Eli rolled his eyes. "Obviously we're not ratting her out. But, I mean, we can't exactly guarantee that they don't find out that something's a bit," he shrugged his shoulders as he studied

Max, "you know...off. She lights up on fire and teleports. And not always on purpose. We can't exactly explain that away. She's not safe there. Not really. We can't protect her from them."

"She's not really safe anywhere at this point," I said, wanting to be a part of this conversation, this decision-making process, like I was one of them.

But I wasn't.

It was something I'd do well to remember in the future—this gentle truce we all had was tenuous, temporary. It would break and shatter eventually, like most things.

Declan nodded and placed her finger to her lips as she turned back to the she-wolf. "We can't bring you to Headquarters just yet either. They'll lock you in the lab and throw away the key. Maybe we should keep you and Max in a hotel while we look for whatever magic thing Lucifer was talking about?"

Sarah opened her mouth like she was going to argue, but then closed it and only nodded. She was intelligent enough to know that there was no returning to The Guild years after being abducted and presumably killed by wolves without being received by an interrogation committee. She'd embraced her wolf. The version of Sarah the protectors knew years ago would be unquestionably transformed now.

Truthfully, they were beneath her. I didn't know her from before, but my guess was that she'd had quite the—what did they call it? Glow up?

"I'll stay with them," I added, knowing as sure as hell that I wasn't letting the little protector out of my sight any time soon again. I waved my hands at the two stubborn protectors and the wolf, "and you all can work on finding what needs to be found I guess. This plan is barely taking shape, and has too many moving and unpredictable parts for my taste."

"Stop." Max's voice wasn't loud, but it pushed us all into silence regardless. There was a small streak trailing through some of the dirt on her cheek, but any other sign that she'd been close to spilling over was erased. Her eyes were hard, focused, as she studied us all. "I'm going to Headquarters. I need to get to Ro. Immediately. I appreciate you all not turning me over and trying to protect me, but he's dying. Saving him is the entire reason we're back here."

"That, and to get to the bottom of this night magic shit," Eli said.

"Shadow," I corrected.

"Whatever, you know what I meant." Eli shot me a quick glare. I noticed he wasn't able to meet Max's gaze. He was looking everywhere but directly at Max, only casting quick glances when she wasn't looking. "And then we need to get Wade and find a way to bring us *all* home next time. There's got to be some way out of all of this shit. A solution. Something."

The last time I'd seen him and Max in the same place, she'd smelled like sex. Like him. I swallowed my smirk knowing that he was still in the doghouse. Useless twat.

"Yes, of course," she shot back, "none of us would ever just abandon Wade." I didn't bother pointing out that I would happily do just that. I was trying to stay on her good side, after all. "But whether or not I'm going back to Headquarters is out of the question. I'm going. I'm Ro's best chance at surviving, and our best chance at somehow figuring out how The Guild is using shadow magic. Though I have on idea how to even begin tackling that problem at the moment."

Declan nodded, her jaw firmly set. "Alright. You'll go back. Sarah and the vamp will stay on the outskirts while we figure out the best way to keep Sarah safe."

"Yes, exactly—" I started, but then stopped as I processed her words. "If you seriously think I'm—"

"You're a liability," she snapped, her Irish lilt leaking out more than usual in her frustration. A trait I often brought out in her. "We can't go traipsing in with the vampire we set loose and expect you to be well received. And the last thing we need is more attention called on Max. You could get her killed. And you'll *definitely* get yourself killed."

I opened my mouth to push back, to argue, but it fell short. A rarity, to be sure. I *was* a liability. In more ways than any of them knew. And if I ended up back in the lab, I'd be of no use to the girl.

I clenched my jaw, swallowing my annoyance with the situation. I still didn't completely understand why I couldn't just go in there and kill them all. Except for the ones they liked and trusted. Wasn't like the world was a better place with a giant group of blood-thirsty protectors stewing in wait, pretending to rid the world from the very evil they created.

And those sanctimonious fucks thought vampires were the monsters. Clueless.

"Fine," I bit out, the uncomfortable taste of compromise coating my tongue. Unpleasant. "I'll play house with the she-wolf. And I'll even try not to kill her." I glanced at the wolf in question, her glower bringing a small grin to my lips. "For now."

She simply rolled her eyes. "Look, I don't know the details of what you've all gotten yourselves into. But I'll help, obviously. Use me and," she cleared her throat, her eyes shifting as she glanced at her friends, "my new strengths as you want. But I want to know why we are all okay working for Lucifer without talking it out first, and I want to know what the fuck he wants to use this shadow magic for. There are so many variables, and this is some seriously powerful shit we are getting ourselves entrenched in—too powerful for us not to question it first."

Right. Good point. I should've been the one to bring it up. Shadow magic and Lucifer was a deadly combination—more so than maybe any other combination in the world, as far as I knew.

Max took a deep breath, squaring her shoulders as she swiped a hand aimlessly through her hair. Her nose flared slightly, like she was debating how and where to start the story, like she was gauging exactly how much she could trust us with whatever bomb she was about to drop.

I hated how desperately I wanted her trust. I'd never cared much for a thing like that in the past. Her new power over me clearly knew no bounds. Disgusting.

With a final, reluctant shake of her head, she started talking —about the hell realm crumbling, about the realms collapsing, about Lucifer's fears of the universe's survival, blah, blah, blah. All very apocalyptic, all very dramatic. It was hell and the Devil, there was nothing new there.

I didn't much trust the angel, and even if his fears were valid, I didn't particularly care if hell imploded on itself or if the protectors were wiped from the face of the earth. I'd find a way to survive—I always did.

But I did believe him when he said that the girl's powers would kill her if she didn't learn to harness and control them. I knew firsthand what unwieldy magic could do to someone who neglected to own it. That was enough for me. I was on board with whatever she needed.

So as his story spilled from her lips, I focused half of my attention on listening to it, and the other half on studying the others. I needed to be sure they could be trusted, that they wouldn't turn on her—or me—now that they knew the truth of her origins, the kind of power that she had. She was the embodiment of everything The Guild hated, everything it was designed to eradicate.

Surprisingly, I didn't find anger or disgust like I'd come to expect from their kind. The wolf was glowering and difficult to read as always, but I didn't miss the way he inched towards Max, bond mate protectiveness written all over the fear and rage playing out behind his yellow-gold eyes.

The stubborn one had more compassion, more focus as she took in Max's words. She was terrified, rightly so. But something about the softness of her eyes as she studied the girl had me convinced that she wouldn't betray her, not intentionally, not yet. Hell, she wanted the little protector nearly as much as the rest of us did. I wondered if either of them were aware of that or not.

And Eli, well, he was so filled with self-disgust and undealt with angst about his libido, that he could still barely look at Max, chancing glances here and there when she wasn't looking, but each one was filled with a longing that made me almost pleased that I was on the girl's good side. For the most part. At least, if that dream had any foundation in reality, I was pretty sure that I was.

The only wildcard was the new addition—Sarah. Her expression was impassive, and I didn't know her well enough to read the subtle body language as she shifted her attention between Max and her cousin, her expression focused and calculating. She listened closely, nodding along at the appropriate moments, as if Max's story confirmed some of her own experiences and suspicions about hell.

Her footing in the hell realm had been unstable, her allies complicated and powerful. But things weren't any tidier for her here either. She'd been a part of their team, sure, but that was before. Transitioning into a wolf—and doing it in hell—could change a lot about a person. It could rock their very foundation.

All I had to do to confirm that was take one look at the asshat, and the way he was constantly battling his two halves, teetering on the edge of self-imploding. So dramatic. So fucking messy.

As if the murkiness of her loyalties solidified the plan, I was suddenly glad that I'd be sharing housing with the girl—I could keep an eye on her, take her out if and when she became a liability. There were worse things to feed on than fresh wolf.

And if she needed to be taken care of, it would be best if I could do it without any of the others there simpering over her.

Or Max around to convince me not to.

The stakes were too high now—higher than I'd ever thought possible.

I had to admit, when I thought about Lucifer's concerns, they made sense. Hell had changed over the years, but so had the human realm. The magic was unstable—like a frayed live wire just waiting for something to fry.

I didn't know for certain whether that signaled the sort of apocalyptic future Lucifer seemed set on, but I couldn't rule it out either. The important thing was maintaining the upper hand—not letting the angel gain complete control of the situation. He was untrustworthy and too powerful for his own good. A formidable—

"I made a blood oath." The soft cadence of Max's words stopped me short, bringing me back to the group. "To gain our freedom." She paused, biting her lip softly. "Well, my momentary freedom, if I'm being technical about it. I have to be back in two weeks, like he said. And figure out what the next steps are to the whole world ending thing, apparently."

"You did what?" I turned towards her, blocking her from the others' sight as I stared into her eyes, hovering over her like a tower blotting out the sun.

"It's done," she whispered, though she masked her guilt behind defiance as she stared into my eyes, unflinching, unmoving.

She didn't fear me, not in the slightest. I wasn't sure whether that infuriated or pleased me, but the realization had my stomach in knots regardless.

So she'd learned about blood oaths. And decided to forge one with perhaps the most dangerous creature in existence. Lovely.

This little protector sure liked to keep me on my toes, I'd give her that.

"What's that?" Eli asked. "You're not, like, linked to him in the way that I am to the fanghole, are you?"

She shook her head, but I was still blocking her from sight.

"No," I said, my voice flat as I tried to swallow down the rage billowing in my belly. Now was not the time to let the darkness take the seat. This was a delicate matter. I needed temperance, to shroud the drama of this new revelation until it could be dealt with.

"She's just literally sold her soul to the Devil," the she-wolf said, a dry laugh piercing the silence. "A reckless move. You're either very brave or very naive. Maybe both. You must really love your brother. "

"It's done," Max repeated, louder this time, her jaw set. "And my problem to face as it arises. I've promised to return, to help him. I'll figure out the details as they come, but right now, I need to get to Ro. We're wasting time talking in circles about things we can't control."

"*We'll* figure out the details," Declan corrected, her shoulder brushing mine as she closed the distance between us. Her hand moved towards Max, like she was going to rest a hand on her arm, to comfort her, but it fell limply at her side instead.

Again, a wave of something like respect flowed through me. The wolf was amusing, sure, but I think of all of the strange installations in the band of misfits that Max had accumulated, the stubborn protector was my favorite.

"So where will me and the fanghole be staying?" Sarah asked, wrinkling her nose like she was still getting used to the smell of the air on this side of the portal—similar, but strange in a new way. It was an uncanny feeling I remembered all too well.

"There's a hotel in town," Eli scratched the back of his neck. He looked strangely well, considering that he'd been a step from death a few minutes ago. Good. I had no intention of following him into the abyss just yet. Things were just getting interesting. "It's not ideal, having two demons that close to Headquarters. But it's the best option I can think of right now."

"No one will expect them there," Atlas said, his voice gruff.

All of us craned our necks to look at him, startled by his sudden departure from his vow of silence. His eyes didn't meet any of ours, but I could feel the desire pouring from his team, the desperate need for him to come back to himself. For him to be like he was before.

But I knew the truth—that way lay danger. If he was going to survive with his wolf, he needed to let himself be transformed by it, to grow with it into something new, and not continue fighting it like he was.

Declan cleared her throat, like she didn't want to startle Atlas by speaking to him. "Sarah will have to lie especially low. Town still has a lot of humans, but there are enough protectors there that they might recognize her." She exhaled, the stray hairs around her face floating in the fabricated breeze. "Like Eli said, not ideal, but probably our best option to keep you both out of trouble for a couple of days. I can bring you supplies and food in the meantime."

Atlas nodded, his expression tense and uncomfortable-looking, like he was trying to force the wolf inside to take human shape, now that we were back in more dangerous territory for him.

"Will you be alright?" Declan took a step towards him, eyes narrowed, assessing, "going back to Headquarters so soon? Or should you stay with them for another day or two? Eli and I can cover for you, say you stayed behind to tie up some loose ends or something. Whatever you need."

"I'll be fine." He tilted his head side-to-side, like the balance between losing himself and not rested on something as small as a stretch.

Still, he was a stubborn creature. And something told me that when the human part of him was riding shotgun like it was at the moment, he wasn't all that much of a chatterbox. He'd be fine. I hoped. Otherwise, he was another liability I'd have to take out.

I wasn't sure how many of her friends I could get away with killing before the little protector would start to see me as the enemy again.

Max grinned, the curve of her mouth tight, and I could see the nerves starting to flicker across them all. Going back to Headquarters after breaking out a vampire and ignoring direct orders—that would not be an easy thing to gloss over.

She turned and started walking towards a small hill. "Good, let's get going then."

"Max, hang on." Eli took a few quick steps towards her, then grabbed her arm. The second he touched her, he pulled his hand back like he'd been burned, then dropped it down to his side, averting his eyes from her glare as she turned towards him.

"We don't have time," she snapped, her eyes glazing over, though whether with fear for her brother or anger at Eli, I couldn't tell.

"I know. It's just," he scratched the back of his head and shrugged, "you're going the wrong way."

"Oh," she cleared her throat awkwardly and glanced around the surroundings—nothing but an endless supply of trees, grass, and dirt—before turning back to him with a sheepish grin, "er, right. Lead the way, then."

The rest of the walk was silent, everyone lost in the labyrinth of anxieties and problems we didn't quite know how to solve. We were able to sneak both myself and the girl into the hotel room without notice, and Declan grabbed us some essentials while we made ourselves at home.

The place was unremarkable—a couple of rooms with

clean linens, a smallish living room area with a TV and gray-blue couch that had small holes throughout the fabric, a little kitchenette consisting of a dorm-sized refrigerator, sink, and microwave.

Unexceptional. But after our days in hell, it somehow felt more luxurious than I could imagine.

And when Declan walked in with a fresh change of clothes, toiletries, and a raw, bloody steak, I just about kissed her.

Sarah got to work helping her cousin organize things, aimlessly opening drawers and checking closets.

The rest of us simply stood there, caught in a strange limbo. We all knew what the next step was, but everyone seemed stuck, like now that we had a plan and were back, no one wanted to move, to initiate it. None of us would have it easy, and the thought of letting Max walk out of that door and back into the lion's den—especially knowing that those lions would rip her to shreds the second they knew what she was—had my skin crawling.

I cleared my throat, catching her attention, while the others mumbled nonsense to each other, trying to soothe the room's anxiety about separating. "A word, little protector?"

Her eyes met mine, and I didn't think I imagined the way they dipped to my lips before her tongue peeked out to lick her own. She glanced briefly at the others before meeting my stare again, nodding.

Without another word, I walked into the other room. Of the rooms available, it was clearly the nicest, so I would absolutely be claiming it. If I was expected to stay here with a newbie werewolf, this close to Guild Headquarters, I at least wanted to enjoy the strange holiday as much as possible. Plus...I had plans for this bed—hopes, dreams. Eventually.

Her soft footsteps sounded behind me, and the second they crossed the doorframe, I pulled her in by her wrist, my fingers easily closing around it, and shut the door with a quiet snap.

"What are—"

Her words melted away as I pushed her against the wall, and closed my lips over hers. I didn't bother starting the kiss slowly, didn't waste time building it up with the kind of languid teasing I might otherwise employ. Instead, I slipped my tongue between the seam of her lips, and kissed her with the hurried, impatient need that I'd felt since the moment I saw her materialize in that godforsaken field.

At first, she froze, neither encouraging nor pushing me away. For a moment, I was certain I'd imagined it all—that rooftop kiss that had me panting for her like a teenage boy before she was ripped away from me so cruelly, that dream that had me coming harder than any encounter in real life ever had.

But then, I noticed her heart rate pick up, smelled her lust building, even as she tried to fight it, and then, like a faulty dam, she gave in.

Her tongue swept against mine as I deepened the kiss, pulling a low groan from me that she mirrored.

I wrapped one hand through her hair, tugging when I got a handful at the roots, until she was pliant against my body like putty. I pressed my teeth gently into her bottom lip, pulling gently as I sucked on it. She ground against me, and I slid my left hand from where it held her waist, to the outer curve of her ass. With a quick squeeze, she exhaled in surprise, and I slid my fingers lower and between her legs, until they grazed against her core. She was soaked—I could feel it even through the thin fabric of her leggings.

As if realizing it just as I had, she jumped slightly and pulled back, her breaths coming and going in heavy bursts.

"Darius," she muttered, her nose flaring softly as her gaze fell from mine.

I watched the guilt sink into her, recognizing it the moment it started to cloud her eyes, swirling with the lust and need that was somehow both within my grasp and so far outside of it.

I pulled back, trying to ignore the pang of disappointment as I brought my hand back to her hip. Using my grip in her hair to tilt her head sideways, I pressed a chaste kiss to her neck, just above the spot where her pulse flickered like a beacon, calling me in, and then studied her carefully.

I heard a low, deep growl from the next room before a shuffle ensued, and I grinned. The wolf could either smell or hear her—maybe both. Good.

For a long moment, I simply stared at her. Admired her full lips, the deep pink that was brighter from all the blood rushing to them. They were somehow both soft and firm at once—intoxicating. Admired her large eyes that were doing everything they could not to meet my stare, the way they narrowed at the corners in defiance, whether at me or herself, I wasn't sure.

I grinned. "Let's make a deal, shall we? Stay safe, be mindful of the trouble you get yourself into while you're away, and avoid as much of it as possible. In exchange, I promise not to kill anyone." I paused, considering my words. I didn't break promises, it was against the fragile code I'd concocted for myself. We all needed some set of rules to live by. "At least, not until you ask me to. I'll play nice with the werewolves and protectors. I'll even keep out of sight from everyone in town. I'll stay here for as long as you tell me to, guiding you to hell and back as many times as it takes—but I want to make it abundantly clear, little protector."

She swallowed, her eyes meeting mine before dropping back down again. "Clear about what, exactly?"

I grinned, then bent down to press my lips to the shell of her ear. "Clear that I don't care if they all die. That I don't care if the world crumbles and the curtain between worlds collapses," I whispered, my dick hardening even more as she squirmed just so against me, then throbbing altogether as her lips parted, shocked. I wanted those lips wrapped around me. Wanted to do so many things with them that the mere thought of it pulled my own to her neck, licking her pulse, teasing it gently with my teeth.

Her intake of breath nearly ended the whole game right there—the last straw before I pulled her legs around me and entered her as swiftly and punishingly as I had during that most exquisite dream.

But I held back, latching onto the final thread of willpower I somehow still had lodged inside of me. Now wasn't the time. She'd never forgive me if her brother died before she could reach him—not if I was the reason for that delay.

"You've stirred me awake—you've got my attention now. All of it. I'm not afraid of you, of what you are or what you'll ultimately do. On the contrary, I'm intrigued. Excited to watch, to be there at your side as it all goes down, whatever that may look like in the end. So, you see," I continued, shifting my hips so that she could feel how much I wanted her, "I'll do whatever you want me to, little protector, because whether you realize it or not, we are tied together now. And I'll wait as long as I have to, do whatever it takes, to finally reach that moment when I'm sheathed inside of you—no dream-walk clouding your guilt, no shame or adrenaline-filled dances with temptation. I'll wait as long as you need me to for the real thing, for your blood glazed over my tongue, and my name raspy and desperate on your lips —and for you to acknowledge that you want that moment as badly as I do."

Her head tilted up then, almost imperceptibly, like she was unconsciously begging me to kiss her, to follow through on that promise here and now. To unfold that dream in real time, harder and more intense in the flesh.

But I took a step back, creating a wall of space between us before I pushed anything sooner than it ought it to be pushed. I wanted her to be ready, to surrender completely, not to fall into me out of a lust that she couldn't control, that she didn't understand—as powerful and intoxicating as it was.

Her face was flushed, her breathing ragged and inconsistent, her brown eyes wide with too many emotions for me to parse through.

I loved that about her—the way she could feel so many things at once. It was almost like she was living a dozen lifetimes all at once, every sensation and thought available in the world swirling around inside of her, fighting to break through.

As if coming out of a trance, she shook her head and cleared her throat, her gaze looking past me rather than at me as it had been before. "I, er," she cleared her throat again, standing taller now as she pushed away from the wall, "right, I should—um—get going then."

"Would you like a kiss goodbye, little protector? You're lovely to taste, even when I don't bite," I teased.

She shook her head and mumbled something incoherent as she moved towards the door, her hand shaking slightly as she reached for the handle.

With a deep breath, she turned it and left the room, leaving me with nothing but a heated and confused look back before she disappeared from sight.

I let out a soft laugh as I pressed my forehead into the wall she'd been glued against moments before. I closed my eyes and inhaled her scent, forcing myself to believe that she'd be safe and return to me soon.

"Can you at least bring me back something to eat? Preferably something bloodier than a sirloin," I yelled after her, just before I heard the others filter out the front door, closing it behind them without another word in my direction.

I'd take that as a no to dinner, then.

5

———

MAX

The walk back to the main campus was a quiet, stoic one.

Well, for me anyway—all I could focus on was getting to Ro as quickly as possible. I wasn't sure how long it took for vampire venom to completely work its way through a protector's system—no one did, like most magic, it was unpredictable as fuck—but he hadn't looked good during that dream.

Judging by the exhaustion I'd felt draining my energy stores when I tried to heal him, I was very certain I'd done something —slowed the process, fought it back a bit, bought him some desperately-needed time. But I needed to see him, needed to do everything I possibly could to save him.

Declan and Eli were brainstorming stories to tell everyone when we arrived. We needed a plan to explain our absence and the fact that we let a vampire out of the lab in the process of ditching all of our Guild duties. There was no way to deny it— we'd used Atlas's and Eli's blood to get through the locks keeping Darius imprisoned. Blood was just as undeniable in our world as it was in a vampire's, it left an indisputable trace of evidence. Truthfully, I knew there was no possible way that we could talk ourselves out of this one. Not really. Our lives as we knew them at The Guild were forever changed.

I just hoped that I'd be able to see Ro and Cyrus again before paying whatever price we'd have to pay.

They toyed with the idea of saying that Darius used compulsion on us—a thing vampires could sort of use on humans to muddy their inhibitions, but rarely could they use it with any success on protectors. Then there was the suggestion that we claim we'd received a tip about the demon who'd killed Wade and needed Darius's pull within the community to find him. The latter was obviously sort of true, and while I figured it was probably best to stick as close to the truth as possible without revealing any of the many things we needed to keep hidden, it still didn't put us in a good position with Guild leadership.

We'd fucked up.

We were coming back with no intel—none that we could give them anyway—and no real way to justify the long absence we'd taken without explaining why we couldn't exactly call in our location or tips. Phones didn't work in hell, obviously, but the whole point was to keep hell out of the conversation altogether.

"We say nothing," Atlas said, interrupting their bickering. His focus was centered on the scattered buildings ahead of us, ignoring the team members and students who were shooting us wide-eyed looks as we made our way quickly towards the castle that housed the medical center.

My stomach dipped with excitement and dread at the sight of it, and I realized in that moment that as confused as I was about The Guild, this place had started to feel like a sort of home to me before I left it. And I knew, with a sinking feeling, that it'd be difficult to fight my way back to feeling that sort of way here again—like I belonged.

"We don't know what kind of story Ro, Cyrus, and Seamus

have spun in our absence," Atlas continued, "we need to check in with them first. Then I'll handle the rest."

I glanced discreetly at Dec and saw her eyes widen, lips parted in surprise. I imagined a similar expression was likely mirrored on my face. It was the most Atlas had spoken since he'd rehumanized himself.

He cracked his neck from side to side, and picked up his pace, like something about being back at Headquarters was either helping—or forcing—him to come back to himself. The wildness in his eyes was replaced with a steely determination. It was like the old Atlas was coming to life right before my eyes.

Had that wildness always existed in him, even before the wolf fought for control? Had he always had to put on a sort of performance within the walls of The Guild—to be the sort of protector he thought he was supposed to be?

"That makes sense," I said slowly, afraid I'd startle him back into silence again. I was never sure which version of him I was going to get. He made Jekyll and Hyde look downright predictable these days. One second he wanted to maul me, the other he wanted to—well, maul me but in a more enjoyable way. "Cy will be with Ro, so that will kill two birds with one s—"

The word was swallowed by a grunt as I collided with something hard enough to knock my breath from my lungs.

Or, rather, something collided with me.

"You're here. I knew you'd find a way. I was certain of it," the something whispered as it smashed my face furiously against it.

"Izzy?" I mumbled, my voice muffled by the fabric of her shirt.

She let me go from the death grip she had me in, and stepped back a few feet so that I could actually see her.

Dark hair, smooth skin, gray eyes that were glazed over with unshed tears, and a smile that could make a grown man weep. It was her. She was here. I was back.

And I realized in that second that it wasn't Headquarters exactly that had started to feel like home, it was the people I'd met—the people like Izzy, who had quickly woven her way to my heart with all the grace of a bulldozer.

Suddenly the reality that we'd made it out of hell alive sank in—all the other shit disappeared and the thrill of disbelief running through my body had me ready to float away.

"You made it out of hell alive. Fucking wild." She shook her head as she grabbed my left hand in hers, completely ignoring the others. "I knew you would but, damn, that's a story I'm going to need to hear." She glanced briefly at Atlas and narrowed her eyes at whatever she saw there. For a moment, I stiffened, afraid that his wolfiness was suddenly broadcast across his face, impossible to hide again. "In detail. Vivid, vivid detail." She scrunched her nose up in frustration, wiped a stray tear as it slipped past the brim of her lower eyelid, and tightened her fingers around mine. "Raging bitchtits, I want to know absolutely everything." She sucked in a deep breath, steadying herself like she normally would before a particularly vicious sparring match. "But later. Just this once, I can wait. Right now, let's get you to Ro."

Just as quickly as she'd run towards me, she started to run away, dragging me behind with a surprisingly strong force.

It took me about half a second to process the sudden jolt, before my legs started working just as quickly as hers. I ignored everyone we passed, barely taking in the startled expressions and shocked chatter that spilled through my ears in fragments and loud, decontextualized exclamations. I was careful not to speed past her too much, hyper aware of the fact that people watching us would notice if I suddenly took off at Edward Cullen speed in the middle of campus—but I could feel my muscles twitching, the anxiety of reaching my brother as quickly as possible competing with the need to remain under the radar as much as I could.

"Jesus," Eli muttered from behind me, his body close enough that I felt the breath of his word reach the back of my neck. I hated that the feel of it made me shudder—that my body seemed to crave him like it normally craved a medium-rare steak. Which was to say that it craved him something fucking fierce. Every atom of my body was buzzing, desperate for his fingers to graze against my skin. Horny succubus needed to be a little bit more discerning—she might not still be mad at him, but I was. "I forgot how fast you were."

For a moment, my thoughts flashed back to a time when I'd gone running, only to stumble upon him at his secret pond. He'd been so open then, so different than he was when other people were around, watching him. The obnoxious fuckboy with the annoyingly sexy smirk had dissolved before my eyes, becoming something different, though equally as sexy if I was being honest with myself. So much had changed since that encounter.

Everything.

Then again, I realized that my early moments with Six were seen through rose-colored glasses. I saw what I wanted to see, naive and gullible. I'd been so desperate to belong that I'd been unable to see the truth—that I could never belong here, never belong with them.

That lake was the same place where he'd first kissed me, using the distraction of the moment and my obvious attraction to him, to go behind my back. To betray me. As soon as the memory resurfaced, I pushed it back down. There'd be a time to come to terms with everything that had happened between us, but that time was not now. Right now, Ro was the only one I had energy for. I was here for one reason and one reason only —who knew if Lucifer would change his mind at a moment's notice and drag me back to hell before I fixed things here?

I had a feeling that as far as dependability and honor went, the Devil wasn't exactly high on either of those lists.

Izzy shoved open the large doors to the main hall, the chatter from the cafeteria buzzing with excitement. It must've been dinnertime—everyone excited to scarf down some food after a grueling day of training.

We didn't stop. Instead, our footsteps echoed around the halls, the number of people in our path decreasing with every few feet that we took—even the nosey ones lingering scattered, like they knew we were headed for our reckoning. When we turned towards the lower stairs, I took them several at a time, unable and unwilling to stop the momentum propelling us forward. The walls grew brighter, the light more harsh as we made our way to the hospital wing.

The tinny scent of cleaning and medical supplies were the only things I could smell.

Izzy slowed as we rounded a final corner and threw open the last door on the right with a surprising amount of grace, given the force. "He's in here. Hurry. I think whatever you did... you know," she glanced back at me, eyes wide as I filled in the gaps "helped him some. But he's still in a bad way. I don't know how much time..."

Her eyes narrowed as they met mine, her words trailing off at whatever she saw there.

Eli and Declan stopped next to me, neither of them out of breath, their expressions soft and filled with concern—the sight of it made my stomach dip. There was so much empathy —so much genuine concern in their eyes that I found myself believing it—or at least wanting to believe it.

When I turned around, I noticed that Atlas hadn't joined us. I started to ask the others where he'd gone off to, but thought better of it.

Instead, I nodded to Izzy, following her in. There were far more important things than tracking the moody wolf's behaviors and oddities.

The gentle, familiar whir of machines grounded me as I stepped towards the bed. It looked just as it had in my dreams.

The sight of Ro, skin clammy and breathing uneven, had me choking on my breath.

His hair was slick and plastered to his forehead, his skin a few shades paler than it normally was. The bandages on his neck and torso were soaked through with fresh blood, like the wound still hadn't closed.

I dropped Izzy's hand and ran to him, swallowing back a sob when I reached him. It hadn't been long since we'd been separated. Not in the grand scheme of things. A week or two maybe—but it felt like a lifetime.

And all that time, I thought I was the one in the greatest danger, thought Ro would be standing over me, concerned and afraid for my life. Instead, it was him. And he was in this position because he'd been trying to rescue me.

I swallowed back the guilt and wound my fingers through his—his skin was cold to the touch. I closed my eyes, a few tears escaping as I did, and focused all of my attention on his wounds. It took me a few long moments to steady myself, to block out the relief of seeing him alive, in front of me, and the fear of seeing him like *this*. Anxiety pooled in my belly, low and heavy. I took a deep breath, trying to center myself.

Healing was one of the more difficult powers for me to control—it required a kind of focus and connection that the others didn't. Not in the same way, anyway.

I felt a slow, creeping heat tingle beneath my hands, like my body was straining to fix all the broken parts of my brother. Even next to him, in the same realm, it was more difficult to find the energy source tethering him to me than it had been when I'd healed the others. Maybe I was still too drained from the journey and all the shit we'd gone through over the last few days.

"What's she doing?" I heard Izzy's voice whisper behind me, the pitch higher than usual, but growing closer.

"Don't touch her."

I heard some shuffling behind me, but I doubled down on my focus. My fingers dug into Ro's neck, like they were deepening the wounds before they could heal them. The sounds behind me disappeared into indistinguishable babble, the disarming shock of the ceiling lights dimming into something soft and calm until it felt like Ro and I existed on another plane, like we'd floated away into a fragile cocoon.

For a moment, all I could focus on was the building heat. If I concentrated hard enough, I could almost feel the strange magic moving from my veins into Ro's. His skin felt warmer to the touch and though I couldn't quite explain how I knew it to be true, I could tell that I was healing him, could feel his life force growing stronger as the thread binding us absorbed every ounce of power I could expend—and then I gave him even more. Still, it wasn't enough—I could feel the truth of that more than I could explain it, but I was certain of it all the same.

I tightened my hold on him, focused on the feel of his skin against mine, on his energy signatures and mine, folding them into each other until the boundary between us started to blur and fade.

My breathing slowed down to match his, and then, after that, grew more shallow and erratic. I felt his heartbeat even out under my touch, felt my own pulse gallop at a strange cadence. My head swam as I gripped onto him, willing myself to stay upright, to continue the process. I wasn't sure how long it would take to cure him of a vampire bite, not when the venom had been festering throughout his body for as long as it had, not when healing him was so much more difficult than it had been with the others.

Was I losing my power? Had I used too much up, too quickly? I'd brought Eli and Wade back from far worse than a single bite before—hadn't I? My thoughts felt slippery, my memories more fluid.

A cool breeze blew against my cheeks, cooling the heat coating my skin. When my eyes opened, my vision swam, so I clamped my eyelids closed again, desperately fighting the wave of nausea pulling through my stomach. My head lowered, inch by inch, like it was growing heavier and more impossible to hold up with each breath that I took.

A nap. I wanted a nice, long nap. Preferably back at the cabin, by my favorite patch of trees, curled up in the soft warmth of Ralph's fur—the promise of my favorite meal with Ro and Cy on the other end of it.

The images of *before* made me ache. I'd craved something new, something exciting when I'd known nothing but the walls of our cabin. But this wasn't the kind of excitement I'd meant. Maybe we never should have left, never should have entered into this confusing, malevolent world that seemed hellbent on taking everything I cared about piece-by-aching-piece.

"Stop her," a hoarse voice rang out through my ears, hazy and echoey like I was trapped in a tunnel with it.

Pressure squeezed my shoulders, pulling me away from Ro, but I fought against it. This had to work—I needed this to work. This was all that mattered.

"We've been trying. She's resisting. We're afraid if we interfere too much, we'll make things worse, more dangerous for her."

"Max."

"What's wrong with her? What is this?"

My chest felt hollow, like the air I pulled into it evaporated before my body could do anything useful with it—the strange energy tying me to Ro strengthening with a violence that I couldn't quite control or harness anymore. Our lives were twined into one—every laugh, every fight, every bad movie marathon that we'd shared circled around me until I couldn't contain it anymore. The thread holding stretched taught and slippery. Until it snapped.

A low growl sounded deep in my chest, like it was coming from me and outside of me, all at once. The grief of the echo startled me.

And then, everything went black.

I WOKE UP IN AN ORNATE, dark room. The bed was giant and carved out of a deep, dark wood. The mattress was dressed in a luxurious-feeling black and crimson-red silk. There was hardly any light in the room, other than the soft glow coming from a few lit candles. Somehow, it was both alluring and terrifying— a combination that sent a bolt of excitement and dread through me in a delicious coil.

"You're here," a familiar voice whispered.

I pinched my neck, craning to find its owner. "Wade?"

He was standing next to a large window, though I could see almost nothing through the glass. Was it nighttime in hell?

I shook my head, trying to focus, my skin still tingling with a static energy that was both familiar and not. It was sort of like the strange soreness of muscles tearing during a particularly good workout, the pain yielding to the promise of healing into something new.

Ro. I'd gone too far healing him, pushed the powers beyond my control.

My body felt lazy and languid, and I fought the desire to fall back asleep, though the comfort of the bed was making it damn near impossible, even with the excitement of seeing Wade again.

He looked different from the last time I'd seen him—only a few short hours ago. He'd showered and shaved the stubble that had lined his jaw from months in captivity. He looked stronger, less stressed, his eyes shifting between the familiar light blue that was reminiscent of the Wade from *before* and the deep indigo I associated with the incubus. The two were starting to twine together in my construction of him. I'd spent far more time with Wade since his incubus was awakened than I had with him in our world. Was it wrong that I found myself more attached to him now than I had back then?

My eyes dipped to his bare chest, where a peculiar new ink coated his shoulder in sleek lines and intricate curves. Something about it was familiar, though I'd seen him naked enough to know that it was new.

"Where are we?" My voice sounded groggy to my ears, deep and low and like it was coming from someone else—somewhere else.

He took a step towards me, eyes narrowed like a lion latching onto its prey. There was something different about him, more powerful almost. It was the sort of energy I always felt from Atlas when the wolf was rising to the surface, just before he lost control of it. He chuckled, though it was more a sound of frustration than humor. "Lucifer finally decided to let me out of that cesspool. Wash up, get a proper meal. Thought it would be a sign of good faith to you, if he treated me less like a prisoner—a way to honor your agreement or whatever. A way to lure you into helping him, into being more...agreeable."

I glanced around the room, taking in the hardwood floor that quadrupled the square footage of his cell, the large velvet red chair in the corner of the room, the furniture that was simple but expensive-looking in its simplicity. Timeless and expensive. I'd seen so much desolation and destruction in hell, that it seemed strange to imagine it as also opulent and beautiful, if still filled with a sort of mysterious darkness. "Definitely an upgrade, I'll give you that."

Wade took another few steps closer to me, his bare feet soundless as he did. "Food, clothes, a shower that felt like a fucking orgasm. If I didn't hate the man so much for putting us all through this misery, I'd owe him a life debt. As it is, I'm biding my time, working with another succubus to learn how to control my powers until you come back."

The disgust in his voice was palpable, but something about the quiet rage sent a wave of excitement through me.

My eyes dipped to the band of his sweatpants—a light gray shade that did little to disguise the lines of his dick. I felt my heartbeat pick up as I forced my gaze away, trying to calm the sudden need to tackle him coursing through my veins.

It was an electric thing—putting an incubus and a succubus into a dreamscape together. Enticing. Enthralling. Impossible to ignore.

As if that jolted me back to reality, my head spun back to him. "A succubus?"

"Yeah, she's apparently a friend of Lucifer and Sam. Initially, that made me hesitant to accept her help, but turns out that she's not nearly as insufferable as they are. Silver lining, I guess. She's been around once or twice, giving me tips on how to use and reign in the lust, even control the dreamscapes to an extent, which is kind of fun. Good change of pace and a nice way to escape when the claustrophobia starts to fold in on me."

He focused for a long moment, his dark eyes swirling with the now-familiar shade of blackish blue as his hand reached towards me, finger lightly touching the tattered black shirt I was wearing.

Almost as quickly as he'd touched me, he pulled back, a smug grin tugging at his lips.

A deep jolt shot through my stomach and I pushed away the image of Wade practicing his incubus powers on someone who wasn't me. I had no right to feel jealous—after all, I'd had more-than-friendly relations with his closest friends... including his brother. But I couldn't deny that the red-hot bubble boiling in my gut was a deep sort of jealousy that I wasn't used to.

When I met his eyes, I saw an odd mixture of amusement and heat that seemed strange in the moment.

"What's so funny?" I cleared my throat, hating how freaking insecure I was feeling under that gaze, knowing that he'd been with another woman. I wanted to ask how *with* her he'd been exactly—were we talking a kiss, a caress, or something more... just more—but my courage was buried deep, far below my pride.

He said nothing, just continued to stare, though I noticed that his gaze was directed more towards my chest than my eyes.

When I started to call him on it, I glanced down. The tattered black shirt had been replaced by a lacy black corset-style bra—one far more detailed and uncomfortable than anything I owned myself.

"H-how?"

His grin deepened as he took a step closer so that his legs pressed against my knees. "I'm a quick study. I can teach you, if you'd like. I liked being your tutor, as brief as it was. I've thought about continuing those sessions many times over the last couple of months. They turned into some of my fondest daydreams."

I let out a quiet, breathy moan, as images of my body twined with his over a pile of forgotten books fluttered through my mind. I could feel the succubus starting to emerge, even through the exhaustion—or perhaps because of it. My energy stores were drained after healing Ro, and rolling around with Wade seemed like the most pleasant way possible to fill them back up. I was a succubus. He was an incubus. The lure of sinking into those roles for a while was a delicious proposal.

His fingers trailed lightly up my arm, over my shoulders, until they traced down my collar bone, grazing where the black lace met my cleavage.

I could feel my skin pebbling under his touch, like my body was coming alive just from the nearness of him—the strange tingling sensation from the healing magic making way for something deeper, darker, more intoxicating.

I leaned forward, ready to give in, to let myself revel in this moment—just as eager for it as the succubus was. But then his words came back to me, and my thoughts were flooded with the images of him being *tutored* by someone else—a succubus who was probably far more alluring and sensual than I could ever pretend to be. I'd met exactly one succubus in my life and she was the definition of sex on legs. She wasn't the kind of girl I could compete with, and I hated the thought of competing with women in general.

Wade was smart—there was no denying that. There was a reason he was tapped to be the one to catch me up on all things Guild history in the first place. But how had he learned this trick so quickly? Developed a command over his powers so seamlessly when it was such a chaotic struggle for me?

"How has she been here multiple times? We've only been gone for a few hours," I snapped, my tone more terse and clipped than I'd intended. Jealousy was not a good look on me.

He arched a dark brow, eyes narrowed in confusion. "Max, you've been gone for four days or so now—I've been training nonstop the entire time. Trying to get as strong as possible, get a grasp on these powers as much as I can so that I don't accidentally hurt you or do something that neither of us can control." His fingers lifted to my chin, tipping my head so that I met his stare. His eyes were cloudy, the subtle tease in his expression hardening into something more urgent. "What are you talking about? What's wrong? What's happening there?"

I opened my mouth to push him a little more about this supposed succubus' 'teaching methods,' but snapped my lips closed as the strangeness of the situation settled on me.

Days? Four?

The last thing I remembered was healing Ro. It was taking less and less effort to pull my thoughts together during these dream-walks, the immediate moments of being dazed and confused slipping away into a fragile sort of awareness. But I was certain that we'd only been on campus for half an hour at the absolute most. I'd met Izzy for a brief moment, but the rest was a hurried rush to help my brother. I hadn't even spoken to Cyrus yet.

"Maybe I gave too much," I muttered, more to myself than to Wade. It had been intoxicating, feeling the power beneath my skin, sensing how it flowed from me to Ro. It had almost felt like my power wanted to be drained, like it wanted nothing more than to fix him, stitch him back together until he was whole and well—even if that meant it destroyed itself, and me, in the process. It was like my power understood that if the decision came down to choosing my life or Ro's, it needed to be Ro's. Every. Damn. Time.

Maybe the strange power was more a part of me than I'd given it credit for.

Wade knelt down, his face pressing closer to mine, his soft minty lips drawing me in. The muscles in his jaw were clenched and angular as he studied me for a long moment— his breath cycling with mine in a way that made my stomach dip for a completely different reason than jealousy or confusion.

"What do you mean, gave too much?" There was a rigidness to the question, an underlying warning that made me think the demon was driving the front seat at the moment.

Something about the command in his tone sent a thrill of excitement through me. My body seemed to very much enjoy this side of Wade.

"I was healing Ro," I closed my eyes and shook my head, trying to ground myself in the now—go all Cyrus zen and what not. I was always terrible at mindfulness—an issue that I anticipated would make my grip on my new, sparkly powers more difficult to manage. I got lost in lust so easily during these dreams, it was downright embarrassing how shifty my libido was. Why was he always able to stay focused? Maybe I needed a session or two with this succubus too. I'd talk to dear old dad when I returned. "He was bad. Like I could almost feel that he was on the edge of death, and it was more difficult to heal him for some reason than it has been to heal the rest of you. I don't know why. But I needed to pull him back, to keep him here—there—so I did."

He nodded, though I didn't know which part he was responding to. "That's probably why you're here now. I felt this strange pull—suddenly overcome with the need to sleep, even though I was in the middle of a session. I think you were reaching for me, searching for a source to pull from, to bring you back." He let out a sigh, his head dipping so that it rested on my lap. "If I hadn't been working with Serae, I could've come sooner, could've helped."

"Serae." The name felt metallic on my tongue. "What kind of work do you do with her exactly?" I hated how much my stomach clenched as I waited for the answer. I should've been more focused on the lost time thing, more concerned about waking up and getting back to hell before the deadline hit. But for some annoying reason that I was pretty sure had more to do with the succubus than anything else, I couldn't ignore the rage uncurling in my limbs, like it'd had been awakened after a long, deep slumber. And it wanted blood.

He grinned, flashing me a brief glimpse of his perfectly straight, white teeth, cheek dimpling in that somehow both sexy-and-cute way of his that was maddening and a turn on all at once. "Max Bentley, are you, by chance, jealous?"

His amusement only served to fuel my anger and turn it inside against myself. I was being petty. I knew that I was being petty. And now Wade knew it too.

"No," I grumbled, glancing down at my hands as my fingers fiddled with each other, like the movement might somehow help me escape this awful moment. Could I do that whole teleport thing in dreams too? Because now would be the time to learn. Sinking into nothingness, even if for only a few seconds, sounded pretty damn wonderful.

He chuckled, the sound low and annoyingly sexy. "It's okay if you are." The humor fell from his expression as he tipped my chin up again to meet his gaze—eyes narrowed and so dark they were almost black. "The thought of someone other than us touching you in that way, making you squirm the way that I do, makes me want to tear this room apart, brick by brick."

For a moment, my brain snagged on the word 'us,' but then his hand dipped between my legs, and the thought floated away like a kite on a hilltop.

I noticed that I was suddenly dressed in thigh high stockings and a pair of crotchless panties. When his finger slid along the opening of the fabric, an embarrassingly loud moan pulled from my lips. He grinned, his lids at half mast as he watched me.

"While a jealous Max Bentley is an adorable one, let me make something very clear." He slid his finger in a slow, lazy circle around my clit, grinning as I leaned into the pressure. "I want nobody but you. Serae is my aunt. At least that's what she told me, anyway. There's nothing even remotely intimate going on with her. And when she suggested that I practice channeling my powers through others, I told her that I'd touch no one but you." He leaned forward so that his lips were little more than a hair's breadth away from mine. "So here we are." He nipped at my bottom lip. "I'm ready to practice. Are you?"

An aunt. There was more to unpack there, but right now, my body was swimming with a heady intoxication and suddenly all I could think about was letting Wade do whatever the fuck he wanted to me in this moment. Over and over again, if he was game.

Unable to speak, I nodded.

A smirk pulled across his lips as he stood up and stepped away from me, the smile deepening when an embarrassing whine escaped from me.

"Good. First lesson is about power exchange. Lust demons get their energy through the power exchange that occurs with sex, not simply the mechanics of the act. Lean back on the bed." His tone was calm but commanding, and I found myself eager to do as he asked.

When I shuffled myself back awkwardly, leaning my head against the headboard, he grinned.

"Good. Now open your legs."

A wave of insecurity made me hesitate briefly at the thought of exposing myself like that. It seemed intimate in a way that tangling my body with his didn't.

"Do it," he said again, stalking towards the bed.

Chills erupted down my spine at the tenor of his voice and I nodded, doing as he asked. I gasped as a chilly breeze swept between my legs, the sensation extra cooling because of the moisture building there.

Wade grinned, and something about the confidence exuding from him enhanced my attraction even more. It was like I was watching him come into himself before my eyes, like this version of him was the real him—like he no longer needed to hide behind the expectations everyone had, no longer had to fit into the predetermined mold made for him or hide behind his brother's shadow.

Like with Atlas and the mask I saw him slip into the moment we got to Headquarters, Wade seemed to slip in and out of one as well—the demons inside the brothers somehow highlighting the truth of their essence in ways that the protector alone couldn't. It was fascinating, and intoxicating to watch. I wanted to peel back each layer, discover every curve and contour of what made them tick.

"We can use lust and the exchange of energy created by it to transform and manipulate the dreamscape." He arched a brow as another sharp breeze skated over me, the tingling feeling making me squirm, as if to illustrate his point again. "Instead of draining us, using that power helps to fill us up, like flexing a muscle repeatedly, making it stronger."

I nodded. I would definitely consider myself a bookworm, but I was far more into this tutoring session than any other I'd ever had before. My focus latched back onto the strange swirls around his shoulder. "Does this have something to do with why you're tattooed? Wanted to try on a new look in a dream without committing to it first?"

He glanced down at his shoulder, where the strange swirls were gliding around his arm. "This is a temporary rune. They're meant to mimic the ones that were created during mate bonds between lust demons, when they were common that is."

I tilted my head, surprised. "Incubi and Succubi have bonds?"

He nodded, a thoughtful expression on his face. "We do."

I didn't miss the way he said 'we.' It was like he'd come to terms with what he was, what we both were, in the short time since I'd seen him last. I was kind of jealous. I still felt like a bit of a stranger in my own skin, not entirely sure where I fit in this chaotic and unfamiliar new world. I wanted what he seemed to have in this moment—confidence and self-acceptance in spades.

"Like with protectors, mate bonds have become a thing of the past for most demons too. No one really understands why," he paused, brows furrowing slightly, "or maybe they do and just don't trust me enough to tell me. I'm not exactly top order here, you know?"

I nodded, glancing at his tattoo again. The markings were a

dark blueish-black, not unlike the shades I saw in his eyes, and seemed to shine and radiate like a liquid metal. Part of me wanted to reach out and touch them, like they were recognizable to me but not quite right all at once. Unnatural, contrived almost.

"And the tattoo?"

"The runes provide a small boost of power, harnessing the shadow magic with more control than we normally could alone." His fingers stroked one of the lines, and I shivered in response, as if he'd touched me instead. His lips quirked up in a knowing smirk as another cool breeze trailed along my legs— every inch of my skin pebbled and filled with an almost painful sting of anticipation. "Especially when trying to move beyond the hell realm with our dream travels. That's apparently a rare thing that you and I can do—Serae doesn't even understand how we manage it. But it won't last more than a day or two. It'll help me reach you, strengthen our skills, allow us to...practice honing them. For now, while we're apart. They're also helpful with allowing me to identify the subtle nuances of the incubus, to control and recognize the power as I use it. Like a training manual built into my skin."

"Doesn't the power scare you?" I asked, my tone mirroring my own fear. I didn't know what to think about the succubus lurking inside of me, didn't know how to feel about that power, or that which I got from Lucifer, for that matter.

His eyes met mine, and there was a hard vulnerability that made my breath catch, like he could read the thoughts as they filtered through my brain. "Yes. I think I thought of the incubus as separate before. Like a darker power that was taking over me." His eyes narrowed and my lips started to tingle, like a cold piece of ice was being rubbed across them. "Now I understand that it isn't separate from me and it isn't new. This has always been me, the parts of me that I've hidden from the world. And maybe that's a little bit more terrifying to come to terms with."

His fingers twitched slightly at his side, and I could've sworn I felt them grazing along my upper thigh. "But maybe it's a little more exciting too. Nothing is what we thought it was—in this world, or in ours back home." His brow arched and his eyes dipped to my lips. Although he wasn't touching me, I could feel the sensation of his teeth tugging against my bottom lip with just as much clarity and sensation as if they were. "There's a certain freedom here—giving in to it. And since things are seeming pretty dire, now's the time to maybe live a little, you know?"

I nodded, not completely understanding the journey he'd been on in my absence, but wanting to all the same.

"Touch yourself." His tone was calm but authoritative.

It was such a startling transition from the heaviness of what we were talking about, that I didn't know what to say in response.

When I made no move, he tilted his head. "Do you trust me?"

I nodded.

"Good. This can stop in an instant, just say when."

I nodded, nervous but intrigued all at once.

"Then do it. Now. And nothing else until I tell you to."

My fingers trembled slightly at the command in his voice, but I couldn't deny that the power emanating from him had ignited a fire, low and deep in my belly. Slowly, I moved my fingers to my upper right thigh, hyper aware of each sensation piercing through me as I did—of the feel of the fabric grazing against my skin—in a way that I'd never been when alone with myself.

With a deep breath, I stroked from my clit to my opening in a long, languid motion, surprised to find that I was soaked even though Wade hadn't touched me yet.

"Again," he said, voice filled with a low gravel that made my heartbeat quicken.

My gaze latched onto his broad, muscular shoulders, trailed down to the hem of his sweatpants sitting at the base of a deep, v-shaped cut, until I saw the evidence of his own arousal. Something about realizing that he was just as turned on as I was helped some of the insecurity dissolve away, until all that I could feel was the lust.

I met his eyes again, and did as he said, my lips parting on a low moan as I did.

"Good girl."

Something about the gravel in his voice as he said those words made my breath stutter. This was a different Wade than I was used to, and he was pulling things from me that I'd never pulled from myself before, no matter how wild my imagination got in the dark of my room.

"Please," I whimpered, my voice little more than a needy, scratchy whisper. It felt amazing, touching myself while he watched, and I could feel an orgasm building quickly, but I wanted him. And I wanted him now.

"Did I say you could speak?" There were equal parts teasing and reprimand in his voice as he closed the distance between us and kneeled on the bed.

The sheer proximity of him had me almost panting—like the demons inside both of us were already entangled in a knot together, doing all the things I wanted us to be doing right now.

Forcefully, but not painfully, he gripped the wrist of my hand slowly circling my clit and lifted. He studied the glistening liquid without breaking eye contact, and brought my fingers to his lips. The tip of his tongue brushed my forefinger, the small, gentle teasing sensation enough to make me throb.

"On second thought," he said, voice disappearing into a low groan. "I want you to taste yourself."

"You wh—" I swallowed the rest of the word when I saw the warning flash in his eyes. Without another question, I let him guide my hand to my lips and sucked on my finger as he watched—eyes dark and filled with a heat that had me on the edge of coming undone right then and there.

I tasted salty, but not bad and he rewarded me by leaning over and giving me exactly what I wanted—his lips wrapped around mine.

I was greedy then, and swept my tongue along his, reached my hand around the back of his head to pull him closer to me.

I felt a deep groan rumble in his chest and, for a moment, I thought that I'd won—that he was done with this intoxicating game and ready to fuck me until I couldn't tell day from night.

"Please," I begged again, this time my voice was feral and wild and totally unrecognizable to me.

Instead, he pulled back, eyes narrowed with a controlled sort of heat that had my legs clenching around nothing.

I slid my hand back down my body, eager to ease the ache building if he wasn't going to do it for me, but one sharp look from him had my fingers stopping at my hip.

"On your knees."

This was a command I was waiting for—wanting to touch him almost as much as I wanted him to touch me. I knelt, hand reaching for the waist of his sweatpants, when he gripped my wrist and spun me so that I was on all fours, ass perched up towards him.

"I'm pretty sure that I told you to do as I say and nothing more. By my count, you've broken the rules four times." His fingers trailed lightly down my spine, making my back arch under his touch. "This is my game. There are consequences."

I opened my mouth to ask him what exactly he meant by consequences, but remembered the rules instantly, and simply tilted my head so that I could see him standing behind me.

With a wicked grin, his hand caressed my right ass cheek and I knew instantly what he was asking.

I bit my lip, nodding once.

The heat of his hand fell away and came back again with a

sharp slap, the sting sending a sharp jolt of excitement through my body.

He met my eyes again, as if checking in, but I made no comment. His indigo eyes narrowed slightly as he nodded, the knowledge that I'd pleased him enough to make me arch my back even more, ready for consequence number two.

He slapped my ass once, twice, three times more—the sting of the third spank enough to pull a deep moan from me. I could feel my own desire glistening down my thighs and I didn't know if I wanted him to prolong this game with another round of consequences or finally ease the need that felt so on the edge it was almost painful.

"Good girl," He whispered, his lips near my ear as his hand grabbed my ass, cooling the skin.

That alone had me ready to explode.

"As a reward, I want you to touch yourself again." When I started to move back into the original position, he clicked his tongue and tightened his grip on my hip. "I didn't say move. Right here, I want you to touch yourself while I watch you from behind."

I nodded, not sure I had the control to speak even if he'd commanded me to. My fingers trembled with anticipation as they found my soaked folds. I slid one finger in, then two, moaning as my body clenched around me. I'd masturbated before, of course. Many times. But it had never felt like this, had never left my body nearly shaking with waves of pleasure.

I pulled my fingers out and circled my clit, pinching softly as Wade's fingers trailed down my thigh.

"Faster," he said, his other hand moving along my side until it reached my nipple.

I did as he said, the orgasm building and building until I thought I'd collapse onto the bed, exhausted and sated.

"Make yourself come for me, Max," he whispered, his teeth nipping playfully at my earlobe.

As if that was the final spark needed, I came, collapsing slightly until Wade's arms kept me lifted.

I felt his hard dick press against my thighs and my ass and my body shivered with anticipation, nowhere near done with playing this game of his.

He kissed the earlobe he'd just bitten, then down my jawline, drawing soft breathy gasps from me as the aftershocks of my orgasm made way for a new, deeper, lingering need. I leaned back against him, throbbing as the force of my movement pushed his dick through my thighs and along my clit.

"Jesus, you're soaked," he said, the steady control in his voice slipping just slightly as he slid against my core, a grunt pulling from his lips. He wasn't as impervious to this as I thought he was. "Focus on the power, on what you're feeling right now, beyond the lust. Let it wind together and tangle up with the need—harness it."

For a moment, I couldn't even focus on his words, every inch of my body screaming for me to take him inside of me without another thought or word or drawn-out, lingering caress—as sensational as they were. But then something about the tone of his voice woke me up a little bit, brought me out of the hazy lust bubble I was drowning in. A strange electricity seemed to vibrate off of us, between us, just as strong in the spaces we were touching as it was in the ones that we weren't— like the anticipation of touch was more than enough to build the energy and take the need to the next level.

Every sense in my body was heightened, the feel of the air along my skin cooling and ticklish at once, my spine with Wade pressed against it almost as sensitive as my inner thighs during the height of an orgasm. A low moan came from his chest, and I felt the vibration all the way to my core, my eyes going dizzy with the feel of him inside of me, even in that way.

"You're doing it," he whispered, his voice hoarse and breathy, like he was struggling to put shape to the words. "Jesus I don't think I've ever wanted someone as badly as I want you right now. It's almost painful, this connection between us—" he hissed a low breath, his voice scratchy, "so fucking raw. Do you feel it?"

I turned my neck to the side, brushed my lips lightly against him in response, the feather-light touch enough to make us both exhale and squirm against each other, both desperate for more pressure, but equally enticed by the strange discomfort of the tease.

Slowly, I pressed my lips back to his, deepening the kiss as I slid my tongue into his mouth. I moaned as our mouths slid together, my mind flooded with visuals of our bodies doing the same—heated and wet and alive with this strange fire connecting us.

His dick throbbed between my legs again, and I leaned back so that the tip brushed against me, both of us panting as the images of us fucking grew more detailed, more clear.

Wade inhaled sharply, cursing on an exhale. "I can't edge much longer, Max. I'm on the cliff as it is. Fuck."

With a wicked grin that was far more teasing and taunting than I'd normally wear, I nipped at his lower lip, relishing the energy that I could feel pulling into me—like we were both operating this strange tug-of-war with power, only neither of us was growing weaker. We would both win this game, even when we lost.

"Then don't," I whispered against his lips.

Before the word fully disappeared into the air, Wade sheathed himself inside of me—the thrust clean and easy with the moisture pooling between my legs.

"Fuck."

I wasn't sure whether he said it or I did, but my body trembled against him, threatening to collapse to the mattress if he wasn't holding me up.

Both of us stayed still for a long moment, relishing the feel of being connected after the heated, building anticipation.

"How do you want it, Max?" he asked, voice raw and ragged and enough to send a fresh wave of chills along the back of my neck. "Just tell me what you want. I want to make you feel good." He slid a few inches out of me and pushed forward again, drawing a gasp from my lips. "So damn good."

He already had. More than he knew. There would be more time for patience and play, I'd make sure of it. But I wanted him five minutes ago. Now, I needed all of him—no more waiting.

"Hard. Fast," I whimpered as he drew out another slow thrust, "you in control."

He made a sound somewhere between a grunt and a moan, and then the world spun as he grabbed my hip and spun me around so that I was lying back on the bed. He shoved a thick pillow underneath my hips so that my pelvis was lifted slightly.

His lips twisted in a quick smirk as he studied me splayed out in front of him, just as I was at the start of this whole encounter.

I was no longer embarrassed by the ridiculous amount of wetness coating my thighs, no longer wanted to hide myself by closing my legs to his perusal. Instead, I felt empowered by him watching me, turned on even more by the way that he looked at me—hunger and desire competing in his dark eyes.

"Deal." He bent down low, so that his head was just a few inches from me, "but not before I get a taste."

Without another word, he closed the distance and slid his tongue along my core, circling my clit and then entering me with a slow, languid thrust.

I throbbed against him, squirming as my body climbed towards another release, but I held it back. I knew how much deeper the orgasm could go if I let him draw it out, slow and steady. But my patience was only so strong.

My fingers dug through his hair as I whimpered, begging

him for more and to stop all at once—unwilling to give up the feeling but wanting to wait to come with him inside of me all the same.

"You," he nipped at my thigh, "taste," he circled my clit with his tongue again, "exquisite." He sucked, slow and hard. I saw stars. "And, since you've been so good, I'll give you what you asked for."

He widened my legs, lifting one of them behind his shoulder as he entered me again—hard and smooth, just as I'd needed.

He picked up the pace with a punishing force and I pressed my palms against the headboard to help with the resistance.

"I'm," I panted, "so," I moaned as he dug his fingers into my thigh with a bruising force that felt amazing, "fucking," I clawed my nails down his back, "close."

He took my mouth with his, not stopping his thrusts as he bit my bottom lip before sucking and nipping down my neck and chest. When he reached my nipple, he took it into his mouth and bit down hard—the pleasurable sting not unlike the spanking, but new and intoxicating and just what I needed.

My orgasm pulled through me on a scream, my entire body alive and tingling with the force of it. With another two thrusts, he followed me over, his moan of satisfaction matching my own.

For a long moment, neither of us moved, both of us spent and exhausted and sated as we laid there in a pile of tangled limbs and liquid.

A low buzzing filled my ears, my body was fighting to stay awake through each pulse of pleasure still throbbing through me. I was exhausted, but somehow revitalized and energized at the same time—all of my senses heightened and sharpened.

Slowly, Wade crawled up a few inches, before his face fell into my neck against the pillow, with a satisfied grunt. He pressed his lips to my skin, the gesture so gentle in comparison to what we'd just done, but somehow just as thrilling.

I felt him grin into my neck and knew that an even wider grin was mirrored on my own face.

"See," he whispered, voice sleepy and eyelashes fluttering against my skin as he closed his eyes, "sharing our bodies with demons comes with some pretty goddamn good perks, if you ask me."

My smile deepened as my heart rate struggled to regulate itself back to something even close to normal.

For the first time, when I reached for the succubus beneath my skin, I didn't find some unrecognizable force or malicious parasite pushing against the boundaries of my mind and my body.

I just found myself.

6

ATLAS

"We say nothing," I said, barely lending any of them a glance as I traced every familiar building, every face, looking for the thing that didn't fit.

I knew he was here.

I could tell by the way eyes trailed us as we walked, lingering longer on me—like they were all waiting to see my reaction, for the chance to see our reunion themselves.

I wouldn't give them that validation. I wouldn't give *him* that validation.

I felt itchy.

And restless.

I could feel the two halves of me splitting down the seams, both vying for center stage. But even the wolf seemed to understand that he couldn't dominate this scene. Not if he wanted to survive.

He'd seen the labs through my eyes.

And we'd had enough of cages.

It was, perhaps, the only thing we were in complete agreement on.

That, and the ripple of pleasure that went through us every time Max's skin touched ours.

But where the wolf craved that sensation, reveled in it, I resented it. Resisted it with every ounce of willpower I had. The problem was, that power was draining out of me, like holding water in my palms. It was only a matter of time before my hands were dry. Empty.

I felt Declan's eyes pierce me in that way of hers—concern and intuition, mixed together into something uniquely her. She had always been the only person that could help pull me back to myself.

Until Max.

"We don't know what kind of story Ro, Cyrus, and Seamus have spun in our absence," I clarified, my words more clipped than I'd intended. It wasn't their fault that I was on edge. That I wasn't myself. Not that I remembered what 'myself' even felt like anymore. It felt like a strange phantom image, ghostly and impermanent. "We need to check in with them first. Then I'll handle the rest."

How was I going to do that? I had no fucking clue. Add it to the list of things I was quickly losing control of.

I took a deep breath, steadying myself. He was getting closer—I didn't need the wolf's senses to confirm what I already felt in my bones. I walked faster, ignoring the mindless students milling about with their mouths wide like gaping fish. *No time, no time.* I'd deal with them and everyone else. Later. I could fix it all, could soften whatever blows were coming our way, if I had just a few more minutes to puzzle it all out.

"That makes sense," Max said. Her voice was low, but I caught every sound, like my ears were made for nothing but to hear whatever she deigned to whisper in them. "Cy will be with Ro, so that will kill two birds with one s—"

Izzy came storming at Max, bowling into her with purpose. For a moment, I felt the wolf startle, the overprotectiveness of the mate bond already starting to ride on his nerves.Or was it my nerves? My overprotectiveness? My mate bond? It was getting more and more difficult to determine where the wolf ended and I began—had it always been that way?

Naturally-occurring mate bonds were unheard of—I didn't know a single person alive who thought they were possible anymore.

And yet, as unbelievable as it was, there was no denying that there was one slowly tethering me to her now. Not after we did...what we did. Now, every single atom of my body was in tune with her—like I was dissolving and reforming into something completely new. Something terrifying.

What I'd had with Sarah had been fabricated, false—hollow. I could feel that now, taste it even.

The problem was that this ridiculous bond was going to get one—or, more likely, all—of us killed.

My skin felt tight, like I was now sharing my body with two forces I wanted no part of—the wolf, and her.

"I hate all these beady little eyes on me," Eli whispered, his eyes darting this way and that, searching for someone. His father, no doubt. They had a complex relationship, but far more affable than the one I had with my own. They didn't always get along, but he feared disappointing the man. I feared something more nefarious from any encounter I had with the man who'd donated his sperm to me.

"Liar," Declan said, but her posture was rigid. I knew that she was just as aware of the reality of our situation as I was. Coming back after the way we left, it wouldn't be easy.

Max and Izzy started to move towards the Main Hall. Like her own private sentinel, the rest of us followed without question or complaint.

I still didn't know how we were supposed to explain Max's involvement in all of this. It would be one thing if it was just my team—we could chalk it up to a prolonged grieving session after Wade's death. Bad, impulsive decisions weren't uncommon amongst our kind, not with the kind of pressure that we were each saddled with from birth. Going off on a bender—well, it wasn't unheard of, especially with a group as stubborn and emotionally unregulated as mine.

Hell, Cyrus ditched this place for decades after raising hell, and he was welcomed back with open arms. For the most part anyway. There were many lying in wait, hoping for him to fail, greedily watching with anticipation in case he slipped and fell from that shiny pedestal we all put him on. There was no winning—not in this world.

Did he leave for her? The dates almost matched up. I needed to press, needed to find out exactly how much he knew, how much he was keeping from her.

Because I believed her now—believed, wholeheartedly, that she had no idea what she was. I could see it in her eyes, the hollow terror that shone back at us when Sarah put together the pieces that we were all too thick to recognize ourselves— probably because we were too close to the situation. Too close to her.

It didn't help that she was growing on me—even more than the bond warranted. I actually *liked* her. She'd found my brother. Essentially brought the most important person in my life back from the dead. And she'd saved my team more times than I could count.

I saw Declan's hands fist at her sides. I knew she wanted to get out of here, wanted to get our inevitable confrontations over with as soon as possible. Her body was buzzing with so much energy that I was shocked she hadn't ripped Izzy back and dragged the rest of us in a corner to fully map the plan. She hated when things weren't clear—when we had to wing it.

I could feel her and Eli gravitating towards Max with just as much force as I was, whether they felt the draw in the same way I did, I wasn't certain. Wade was right all along—I'm sure he was pleased with himself about that—smug fuck. My chest tightened at the thought of him. He could be smug all he wanted—all that mattered was that he was alive.

Hell, even the vampire seemed more attached to her than I'd realized—she was more than the bored, lustful distraction I'd thought she'd been to him.

Polyandry wasn't unheard of amongst our kind—especially with bonds and childrearing becoming so damn complicated. But five of us? There was no way that we could all be bonded to her. I'd never heard of such a thing.

And natural bonds at that.

I felt his eyes land on me before I saw him. I slowed my steps, shaking my head subtly when Declan's gaze lifted to mine.

Her nostrils flared slightly but she didn't argue. She knew to choose her fights carefully. Instead, she took a deep breath and continued to follow Max as she ran, their pace picking up every second. Max's clean scent lingered in the air behind her as I paused.

I felt my stomach lurch, my fingers twitching like they wanted to reach forward and grab onto her, to bring her back to me, or bring me to her. The tentative bond between us was unstable. It was like a living, breathing thing. And it was hungry. Hungry for what, I wasn't sure. For connection? Permanence? Either way, I couldn't let it happen.

Snapping my teeth together, I forced all of my willpower into letting her go, comforted slightly by the confidence that Dec and Eli would have her back—that they'd protect her in the moments that I couldn't. She needed all the protection she could get—maybe even more so here than in hell.

Even though I knew where he was, I walked the opposite direction. It was the only small act of rebellion I could entertain right now. Plus, I didn't want our meeting observed by the people I'd likely have to train in the next day or two—assuming we were even welcomed back into our positions. Someday, maybe.

The noise of the cafeteria filtered through me and a strange sort of longing hit me in the gut. There were times when sitting in that hall, with more food than we could eat—Wade's nose in a book, pretending to not be staring longingly at Sarah, Eli and Dec bickering over something pointless—had felt like the closest thing to home I knew.

I took a deep breath and turned down an empty hall, taking a staircase on the right that would give us at least a semblance of privacy.

Before my foot hit the third step down, my back was shoved against the wall.

"Where do you think you're going, boy?" his voice came out like a steady, controlled growl, but I knew him well enough to hear the anger lacing each word.

I looked up, meeting a pair of blue eyes that were more familiar to me than my own. The last time I'd seen them, they had carved a hollow hole into my gut at the sight. Wade's eyes. Now, they filled me with a somber peace, knowing that, at the very least, he was alive. If I had nothing else, I had that.

"Father." I gave him a small nod, doing my best to ignore the fact that his forearm pinned me to the wall. The wolf lashed against my skin, enraged and shamed by our position, pinned and at his mercy.

I couldn't show my strength, couldn't let him see the subtle changes in my senses, my reflexes. Tarren Andrews would be the first person to stick a blade through my chest if he knew what I'd become—what I was.

"That's it? Father?" he let out a low huff. "Don't fucking 'father' me right now," the line between his brows was thick and angry, his jaw clenched. For a moment he wavered, until the rage tipped into something softer, something I rarely saw on him. "Atlas, where the hell have you been?"

He took a step back, releasing the pressure pushing me against the cool wall.

For a moment, I let myself take him in, as he studied me. There were bags under his eyes—not an uncommon feature for him, but they were darker than usual, his face paler and more gaunt. The dark blond hair that was usually straight and neat, was shaggier than I'd ever seen it, his jaw lined with stubble that I'd never once seen him wear.

"Atlas," he said again, taking another step back towards me, his arm reaching to my face like he wasn't entirely convinced it was me. "Are you okay? What happened?"

For a moment, I hesitated. It sounded almost like concern. So unlike him.

"Seamus and Cyrus said you were on a need-to-know mission." He shook his head, lip snarling as anger eclipsed whatever mask of kindness he'd been trying to don. "I know it's bullshit. They're covering for you. They're always covering for you, so long as it covers their own asses and makes them look important and valuable. Like they're doing their jobs. There's no discipline here—I should never have agreed to let you come back. Were you and those miscreants of yours off on some alcohol-induced bender again? Things are tense right now, Atlas. You know this. There's stuff at play that you don't understand. We're under a lot of scrutiny. There's no room for mistakes and childish rebellions. I know you're upset about your brother, but —" he shook his head, whatever conclusion he had to that sentence falling into a frustrated grunt instead.

And there it was. His reputation. He was worried I'd sully it. That's all I was to him—someone to make him look good, to continue the family name he cared so much about. Our hollow legacy of fighting until we died, upholding the values of The Guild, never questioning or challenging them, just producing more good soldiers for them to usher into death.

As much as I felt shallow disappointment at the glimmer of

concern I'd misread, I felt an equal sort of gratitude towards Seamus and Cyrus. We'd broken a vampire out of the lab. And still, they'd trusted us enough to protect us—to shield us as much as they could from whatever punishment awaited our return, even if their interference forced them to carry some of it on their own shoulders.

"It was a mission," I lied. I wasn't sure what kind of story they'd woven, but I'd do my best to keep it up, even though the flash of disdain on my father's face showed that he, at the very least, wasn't even close to buying it. I felt the wolf scratch against my skin, ready to lunge at the figure in front of us. He was, perhaps, even less a fan than I was. Another thing we agreed on, then.

He snorted, threading his hand through his hair, lip dipping in disgust as it snagged on a tangle. "Of course it was. And what did it yield, then, son? What information have you brought back for us?"

"Wade's killer," I bit out, repressing the small victory that shot through me as his eyes grew wide. "We found him. Followed the lead we'd been chasing for months. It required some," I paused, glancing to the side for effect, though I knew there was no one else within hearing distance, "non-traditional methods."

His brows lifted with surprise, a sadistic gleam flashing through his eyes. As much of a stickler as he was for the rules, he appreciated blood lust more than most demons even seemed to. I was disgusted with myself for not recognizing the similarities sooner—for not seeing through so many of The Guild's lies. "And?"

Tarren never treated Wade with the kind of... care and attention that he'd treated me. He'd always assumed that because Wade was born of a momentary lust-filled night with a human that he was weaker, that he'd be incapable of honoring the family name and the power that came from it. Wade reminded him of everything he feared—the potential for weakness, vulnerability.

But that didn't mean that he wanted his son dead. It didn't mean he wouldn't want revenge for those who took something from him. Men like my father didn't like having their toys stolen, even when they had no interest in playing with them anymore.

"Dead," I said, the word echoing in the empty stairwell, "now."

He narrowed his eyes. "And the vampire you broke out of the labs?"

Darius was the most difficult thing to explain away. My father could understand revenge, but he could never understand mercy. Not for anyone, but especially not for a vampire.

"Also dead. We got what we needed from him."

"Which was?"

"A location. Seattle—there seems to be more activity than usual over there especially. We used him to track down the pack that killed Wade, promising him freedom in exchange."

"And?"

"There is a sort of freedom in death," I responded, my stomach turning at the small tug of his lips.

"Did you bring back the fucker who murdered my son?" he asked, his hand clasping tightly on my shoulder. "Tell me you have the body."

At first I wasn't sure whether he meant the demon's or Wade's. But then I remembered who this man was. Little would be gained from bringing Wade to rest here. He was after information, another lab rat to send downstairs for his friends to tinker with.

I shook my head. "There were complications, variables we hadn't accounted for in our haste."

His lip curled again, but this time in frustration. I'd given him what he really wanted, a thing to critique. "Sloppy. Very sloppy, Atlas. Wade deserved more than some emotional vengeance mission. We could have had answers. Real answers. That group that killed him—there are more like it, the attacks are increasing every day. They're almost impossible to track, difficult to pull answers from. We could have had a chance if you'd handled the mission with more care. Emotions rule far too much of you."

I swallowed the urge to rip Wade's name from his lips. He didn't care what my brother did or did not deserve. All he wanted was power. And if power could be drawn from his son's death, then he wanted every last drop.

"Why are you here?" I needed to get out of here, needed to speak to my team—to Seamus and Cyrus—before my lies backed us into a corner that we couldn't escape.

"This place—the people here—they've gone soft on you all. No precision, no attention to the bigger picture. It's probably why Wade died in the first place. So much carelessness clouding these halls."

I tasted blood as my teeth bit into the sides of my cheek. Holding my tongue was getting harder now that the wolf knew how to break free from its cage.

"I'm here to get things back on track. I should've come earlier, to be honest. If you insist on living here with that reckless team of yours, I'm going to ensure that this place is worthy of you—of our name and legacy. Alleva and I will be doing all that we can to weed out the fat, so to speak. She sees things from my perspective now, understands the uphill battle we face. You've had your time to pout and dick around. Now it's time for you to step into the role you were born for. Beginning with a proper bonding ceremony," he took a deep breath, nostrils flaring as he stared me down. "I never liked that Sarah girl anyway, she wasn't good enough for you. And Wade, he acted like a simpering pup in her presence. Feelings lead to mistakes. Bonds are strongest when they are forged with the strong—

when emotions are removed from the equation altogether. Now, you have another chance to become the version of yourself you were destined to become."

My mouth went dry. What would he do if he found out what I really was? If he learned that his legacy was irreparably cracked? He'd thought having a human for a son was an embarrassment, a tarnish on his reputation. What would become of him if he learned that he had an incubus and a werewolf carrying on the unflappable Andrews name?

"Tumultuous times are ahead, son—these are the times heroes are made, the times when the cream separates itself from the crop, from the rot. I'm going to make sure that when the time comes, The Guild is prepared, that there'll be something here worth preserving."

I nodded, ignoring the flood of anxiety that made it difficult to take a full breath. I had no love for my father, not really. But he wasn't wrong—The Guild wasn't prepared for what was coming. None of us were.

I was able to parse my way through the rest of his babble with a few well-placed nods of agreement before he had to run off to some meeting with Alleva, no doubt filling her in on what he'd learned here. Information was the currency of power in these walls—and he'd caught me early enough in our return that he was certain to have the upper hand in doling it out to those he deemed worthy.

I felt a sharp wave of nausea run through me. At first, I thought it was just my body's reaction to being in his presence, to hearing him throw Wade's name around as a bargaining chip. But the wave grew stronger, more grounded, and I knew that it was something more. Without thinking, I was off— charging down the stairs four at a time, before turning and twisting through the familiar halls that always filled me with equal parts purpose and frustration. I wasn't sure how I knew exactly where to go, how I decided which door to open, but I did. I let the wolf guide me until I wasn't sure whose instincts I was relying on—his or my own.

The sight that awaited me when I opened the infirmary door ripped the air from my lungs as a blanket of dread filled me.

I couldn't explain the feeling. I knew what we were here to do, knew that I'd find Max healing her brother. But something about the way that she was huddled over him, her hair lifting slightly like there was a steady breeze in the room that no one else could feel, seemed off. Everything about her posture—her presence—was wrong, but I couldn't quite pinpoint what was causing it—I could feel it more than I could see it. I breathed in through the wolf, and noted as he did that something was strange about her scent. No, not her scent—her energy.

The stubborn fuse that connected us, the same one that seemed to only be growing stronger and stronger, felt dimmer —less a steady buzz and more a hollow hum.

Eli, Declan, and Izzy were scuffling around, but I paid them little attention—their anxiety heavy enough to amplify my own. We were far out of our element here. For a moment, I caught myself wishing that strange girl—Khalida—was here, to walk her through this, to guide her to the other end. Safe. Unharmed.

Max's head drifted down as Eli grabbed her shoulders to try and snap her out of it.

She was healing Rowan, but she was giving too much.

The warnings we'd been given flashed through my memory —her powers were strong, unstable, she didn't have control. Lucifer's insistence that she could kill herself if she didn't learn to reign them in before they outgrew and eclipsed her.

"Stop her," I said, closing the distance between us. My breath clogged my throat as I reached her, visions of her replacing Rowan on that precipice between life and death swimming though my mind.

"We've been trying," Declan said, her voice wavering and close to tears, "but she's resisting. We're afraid if we interfere too much, we'll make things worse, more dangerous for her."

We were beyond that. She was going to give her brother every last drop of energy she had if we didn't stop her. I almost wished that Lucifer had come with us, to train her as he'd insisted she needed—or maybe that he hadn't let her leave in the first place.

"Max." I grabbed her head between my hands, hoping the contact might break whatever trance she was in.

Her eyes were closed, fluttering beneath the thin skin of her eyelids. Wherever she was, she wasn't with me in this moment.

Fuck.

We couldn't come all this way, go through all that we had, for it to end like this. Hell, she still thought that I hated her. She didn't understand how much she'd fucking terrified me, from the moment I'd laid eyes on her. She didn't understand that—*this*—this exact moment, was the very thing that I—

My head started to buzz, the sounds around us a garbled mess. I forced myself to take a deep breath, clenched my jaw, like sheer willpower could make her open her eyes—convinced that if she just threw me one of those infuriating looks of hers, all doe-eyed and strangely omniscient in that way only she seemed able to manage—that it'd be okay.

"What's wrong with her? What is this?" I felt Izzy move next to me as she spoke, her hand reaching for Max's shoulder, but pulling away before making contact, like she was afraid to unknowingly hurt her, to interfere in something she didn't understand.

A heavy growl pulled deep and low from my chest, startling the girl back. I didn't care. Didn't care if she'd figured it out then and there. The wolf was raging against my bones—grief, fear, and anxiety mashed together until I couldn't tell which were his feelings and which were mine.

All of them. None of them. Both of ours.

I sat on the edge of the bed and pulled Max to me, her body malleable and unresisting as it leaned into me.

The strange breeze that had enveloped her went out at once and I felt a strange tug, like the thread between us was pulled taught, snagging on something. She collapsed completely, her head lolling on her neck like a broken doll.

No. *No, no, no.*

"What happened?" someone—Izzy again, maybe—asked, the words slurred through tears.

My fingers vibrated as I held her, and I could feel my breaths coming in quick, uneven patterns. The wolf was fighting, like he was pacing back and forth, trying to prevent the inevitable shift from coming on as long as he could. I had tools that he didn't—strengths in this world that he wanted to utilize. But I couldn't think, couldn't move, couldn't come up with a next step, another option.

"Atlas." Declan's hand rested on my shoulder, the grip firm but gentle. "Atlas, look."

It felt like she was speaking to me through a funnel, her voice echoey and hard to process.

"She's breathing, Atlas," and then, quieter so that only I could hear, "reign it in."

I blinked, looking up at Declan. Her emerald eyes were blurry as they stared at me, so I blinked some more, clearing the haze.

She took a deep breath in, and then let it out again in an exaggerated hiss, using her hands to mimic the cyclical movement and encourage me to do the same. When I did, she nodded at Max again. "See. She's breathing. She'll pull through. She always does. She just needs rest. Time."

I wasn't sure if she was trying to convince me or herself, but I felt the vice against my chest loosen, if only a little.

I looked down, and found Max sleeping against me, my

fingers gripping her arms so fiercely that I was certain to bruise her smooth skin.

Her head was tilted back at a strange angle, so I laid her back down, supporting her against my chest. And then, slowly, I saw that Declan was right. She was breathing—I could feel each inhale and exhale go through me where we touched.

Not dead. Not yet.

I hadn't lost another one. I hadn't lost her.

The low buzzing sound that turned everything into an echo started to fade away, the wolf inside of me calming down as I did.

I cleared my throat, meeting Dec's eyes again. There was compassion there, but there was fear too. I watched the way her gaze dipped to Max, the way her steady breathing was too focused and deep to be completely natural. She was calming her panic just as she'd calmed mine.

Always the rock, even when she needed one.

I cleared my throat and glanced to the right, noticing Eli leaning against the wall, his stare hollow and flat as he looked at Max, his back pressed against the white paint like he wanted to be as far from here as he could get.

He was folding into himself. It was strange to see him this way, silent and blank—he always had a quip, always had some sarcastic remark to brush away any insecurities he didn't want anyone to see.

His dark hair stuck up in odd spikes and waves, like he'd been running his fingers through it, pulling it in different directions. His face was pale, waxy almost, and I wondered if he felt as nauseated as I did—like I'd been about to vomit all over the floor the second I realized something was wrong with her.

"Somebody," a quiet, but steady voice said, "tell me what the actual fuck is wrong with my best friend." Izzy took a step forward, her brows in a straight, stern line, any sign that she feared me long dissolved. "Right *fucking* now."

I cleared my throat, tried donning my authoritative mask, ready to explain away what she'd just witnessed before forcing her out the door and back to her room. But no words came.

Declan's mouth softened as she straightened up. "We don't know." She studied Izzy in silence for a long moment, like she was debating something, deliberating. When she came to whatever decision she landed on, she nodded and took a step towards her. "Max is more than what she seems. I think you know that. She has... capabilities that we don't understand fully yet. But I think she'll be okay. Sometimes she extends herself —" she nibbled at her bottom lip, eyes narrowed like she was lost in some distant memory, "too far."

"She'll be okay?" Izzy ignored me now, clearly responding to the actual figure of authority in the room. "You're sure."

A flash of something I couldn't read drifted across Dec's expression before it smoothed back into her cool, collected mask. "Mostly."

The girl's jaw set and she nodded, glancing once more at Max before her eyes snagged on mine and lingered for a moment—an unspoken question as plain as day. With a soft smile, she turned towards the door. "I'll get Cyrus. He'll want to know that she's home."

Home. Was that what this was for her?

Reluctant to let her go, I laid Max down on the bed, ready to call Greta for another room to keep her in while she rested, when a low groan sounded next to her.

Rowan stirred awake, his movements both hurried and slow, like he was shocked awake but still stuck in a dream at the same time.

My stomach tightened, and I swallowed back the frustration that he was the one waking up while Max still remained unconscious. He had no idea what she'd done for him—what she'd sacrificed.

Did he appreciate her? Did he love her with the same stubborn ferocity with which she loved him?

"You'd have done the same for Wade, if you could," Declan whispered in my ear, her voice kind but chastising all the same.

I hated that she was right, that she could read me like a fucking book. That, for once, she couldn't just let me linger in the sanctimonious feelings of being rightfully pissed off.

I nodded once and stood up, moving towards Eli where a couple of chairs sat unoccupied. I fell into one, the weight of everything suddenly too much to carry.

I watched Rowan as he processed his surroundings, as he shook his sister, gently at first and then with a rough desperation, as he tried to wake her up; watched the look of relief and anger on his face as Declan filled him in on what had happened.

His hand gripped hers steadily as he tucked her in and spoke to her in calm soothing tones, his voice cracking like he couldn't hold back the sob that wanted to break through.

I could see it then, in the tremor of his fingers, in the wild expression in his eyes, that he did—that he loved her just as much as she loved him. That he would lay his life down for hers, just as quickly as she would do the same.

The realization did nothing to ease the panic coursing through me, but it made me less inclined to detach his head from his spine right now.

Greta walked in, checked Max's vitals, and then—with a shocked and wary attention—did the same with Ro's. She worked quickly and thoroughly, asking questions about the Bentley siblings which only Declan seemed capable of answering with the necessary vagueness.

She was good under stress, good at channeling her fear into something productive—into something helpful. I could always see the cracks though—the way she shot a worried glance at Max with every reassuring point she used to calm or explain things away; the way she'd chewed one of the nails on her left hand down so much that it had started to bleed; the way her breath stuttered awkwardly every few minutes, like she had to remind herself to breathe.

I sat in silence, brushing Greta away, gently, when she tried to assess me, ignoring Rowan when he tried to pull answers from me, his voice gaining volume and vitriol with each question I left unanswered.

He was happy that she was back, but he was also angry that she'd nearly gotten herself killed saving him.

That was something I could understand. I'd be fucking livid if Wade almost got himself killed trying to save me. Heroes in the story never seemed to understand that, never took that pain into account—the kind of guilt that came with being the survivor, with being the one who outlived your loved ones.

The room felt big and small at the same time, filled with a sort of flustered chaos that disinterested me. Greta wouldn't be able to revive Max, wouldn't know what was wrong with her. All the tests and blubbering about were useless.

I felt Eli leave the room before I saw him—didn't notice the solemness of his presence until it wasn't there anymore.

And then the room stilled, as Izzy returned with Cyrus.

Cyrus walked into the room, his gait uneven as he approached the bed. Without a word, he wrapped his arms around Ro, his eyes widening with surprise, then flattening into something softer as he returned the hug.

Cyrus scanned us all, nodding once to me when I met his eyes, before his gaze fell to Max.

Greta tilted her head, her lips curving into a soft grin that etched more lines into her face. "I'll give you a moment together while I gather some things."

When she nodded towards Izzy to follow her out, I thought she might protest, but she let out a quiet, reluctant huff, nodded, and left the room with a muttered, "I'll go grab some food, but I'm coming right back when I'm finished. And I'm eating fast."

Gretta pressed her fingers to Cyrus's shoulder, squeezing briefly, before heading towards the door—brows narrowing in concern when she passed me.

I wanted to reassure her; deep down I knew I didn't want her to worry about me—but right now, I couldn't muster the energy. I was exhausted. Empty.

"She's back." I wasn't sure who Cyrus was talking to—his focus was completely on the infuriating girl lying lifeless on the thin infirmary bed. He wiped a stray strand of hair from her face, the gentle gesture strange coming from the version of him I'd conjured in my head. "I don't know whether to be pleased or terrified."

I saw both emotions warring in his posture as he studied her. He cared for her, there was no denying that. Every muscle in his body screamed that of the protective father. But he'd kept things from her—from all of us.

"You've been lying to us all."

I looked around, trying to locate the speaker for a moment, until I realized that it was me.

Declan walked towards me, spine straight, the back of her hand lightly grazing my shoulder. She cleared her throat. "He's right. You have. You need to tell us what's going on—what you know. About Max. About everything."

Rowan glanced between us, and back to his adoptive father, his expression unreadable as he sat on the bed next to Max, his hand wrapped around hers like a child holding on desperately to a balloon—afraid it might fly away. "They're right."

Cyrus straightened, as if he'd forgotten there were others in the room, before he turned away from Max and toward us. He lifted a thick brow, his dark, impenetrable eyes meeting mine. "I'm not the only one who's kept secrets."

He knew what I was.

Declan stiffened—she edged closer to me.

Cyrus's face softened slightly as he turned back towards Max. "Don't worry, boy. I don't tell secrets that don't belong to me. Never have, and I won't start now." He pressed the back of his hand to Max's forehead, the profile of his face lined with concern. "Where are you, girl? Unreachable, always so damn unreachable—now, more than ever."

"Cyrus," Declan said, taking a step towards him. "Please, what's going on?"

He took a deep, heavy breath as he took in Max's face, like he was afraid it would be the last time he'd see it. Then, slowly, he turned to us again. "When she wakes up." He nodded, his shoulders sagging, his lips turning into a slight frown. "We'll talk when she wakes up. It's not right to have these conversations without her here to hear them. I owe her the truth more than any of you."

"And in the meantime?" I asked, trying—and failing—to keep the anger from spilling into my words. "What the hell are we supposed to do in the meantime?"

His dark eyes met mine again and I saw Seamus in them—the man who'd been more like a father to me than my own. They were eyes that, despite everything, I trusted. "Devote yourselves to training—to guarding her. Seamus and I," he shook his head, "we covered for you as best we could in your absence, though he'll have questions of his own. Questions I can't answer. Don't tell him more than he needs to know, and tell no one else anything if you can help it."

"You're leaving again?" Rowan asked, the bitterness in his voice ringing through the cold room.

Their eyes met, and something passed across Cyrus's face, too fast for me to understand. The anger pouring from Rowan was clear as day. He may have inherited many things from living with the man, but it was his sister's fire I saw mirrored in his eyes now.

Cyrus nodded, glancing down at Max once more. "Briefly. There is someone I have to find. I won't be gone long. It is imperative that I do so as soon as possible." He walked towards the door, paused, and then turned back to us—close enough that I could smell the whiskey coating his breath. "Seamus trusts you lot. Max is naive, but she seems to trust you too." His nostrils flared slightly. "Don't let that trust ring false. Protect her—with everything that you have. Something tells me she will need it in the months to come."

"We will," Declan said, as I simply nodded.

"Hopefully, when I return, I'll have more answers than questions." With a brief hesitation, like he didn't really want to let Max out of his sight again, he left.

The hours passed slowly as people came, left, and muttered about our return in the halls.

Eli returned for a while, he and Declan taking turns arranging things to help us transition back as seamlessly as possible—taking care of what needed to be done in order to allow us to linger on the periphery of the campus, a part of it but not, as we figured out our next steps.

Like Max's brother, I couldn't seem to get myself to leave Max's side. Neither of us spoke much, though Izzy would pester everyone with questions whenever the silence got to be too much for her.

I couldn't shake the feeling that I was here but also not. So much had changed since the last time I was at Headquarters —I didn't know who I was here anymore, didn't know how to *be*.

There were a few moments when it seemed like Max was stirring, coming back to herself in some fundamental way—her skin glowing with a soft radiance, a small almost-grin tilting her lips.

My stomach tightened when I realized that she was probably with my brother—that he was probably the culprit beyond that smile. That she was healing in the way that only they could.

Something fluttered in my chest and I tried to push the frustrating jealousy away—jealousy that he was the one to help her and not me. That he was with her in *that* way. That they had a connection, an ease together that I could never have.

But beyond that, there was a raging relief. I could feel, somehow, that she was okay, that she would wake soon.

The memory of her skin against mine, my tongue tasting hers as I finally gave in to the *want* that had lingered for so long —the want that had become something stronger, a need.

I felt my skin heat from the memory, my mind uselessly pondering where we went from here—how we handled the connection between us, the bond that I couldn't deny was fastening us together, stronger and more irresistible than I'd imagined.

"There you are."

I jumped, the familiar voice pulling me from my thoughts with the speed and roughness of a freight train.

"I've been looking for you for an hour," Tarren walked into the room, the sound of his shoes crisp and echoing in the room filled only with the steady lull of machines and Max's quiet breathing.

I straightened in my chair, my stomach sinking like I'd been caught doing something against the rules, something vile.

His nose curled as he looked to Max, where Rowan dozed in the chair next to hers, his hand resting a few inches from her fingers.

With a nod, Tarren left the room.

I followed.

"This girl smells like trouble," Tarren said, voice a whisper but filled with disgust all the same. "I don't like that she was with you and your team, that Cyrus thinks he can come back here and shove his problems on your lap and ask you to babysit. I don't like her people. The Bentleys—they—" he shook his head, like he didn't quite know how to say what he wanted to say about Max's family.

I knew that he had a stubborn rivalry with Seamus—that the two were never on the same page. And that the feud extended to Cyrus and, to a lesser extent, impatience with Eli. It wasn't new or surprising. Part of the reason Eli and I grew as close as we did was out of a childish desire to annoy our parents, though Seamus never once made me feel lesser because of my father. But I hadn't anticipated that dislike to transfer to Max.

Tarren's eyes narrowed as he took a step closer to me. He was a few inches taller, but he always seemed like an impossibly large presence when he was in the room. "What is she to you?"

I heard the warning in his voice, felt the wolf's hackles rising as we prepared for a threat.

"Nothing." I scratched my jaw and met his eyes. "Just a student I've been charged with dealing with. My team has been tasked with helping her catch up in her training. She's," I took a deep breath, hoping he'd read the wariness rolling through my body as exhaustion, "unremarkable. A duty. Nothing more."

He studied me for a moment, the silence stretching long enough to make my skin itch.

I met his stare—hoping like hell that he was as awful at reading me as he'd always been.

Finally, he nodded, patting my shoulder as he did. "You've been wasted on this place. You and your team should be doing more than training the infants—you deserve better than picking up Cyrus's scraps and trying to mold them into something useful." He shook his head, lost in thought, and I uncurled the fist that formed at my side. "Greta says exhaustion." He let out a cruel laugh. "Do you know how rare that is among our kind? Exhaustion knocking her into a day-long sleep? Seems like she's made of some pretty weak stuff. That's what happens when you're raised by a traitor who ditched his responsibilities decades ago to wallow in his own self pity."

I felt the wolf stir back to life, felt his anger as it curled with my own. I pressed my fingers into my eyes, hoping like hell the wolf wasn't visible. "Yeah, gotta say, I could use some rest myself."

"Tomorrow," Tarren slapped his hand roughly on my shoulder. It was the closest thing to affection he knew how to bestow. "We'll talk tomorrow. You and your team—get some rest. There's work to be done in this place, and I could use your help seeing it through." He nodded towards Max's room, eyes hard. "Sleeping Beauty doesn't need your time or energy anymore. Let one of the lesser teams have her, yeah?"

I nodded, trying to force my lips into a grateful smile, but I only managed a firm line.

He walked away without another word.

I turned, the wolf desperate to get back to guarding over her, making sure she was safe, but paused when my hand reached the door.

Max was on Tarren's radar.

If my father had even an inkling of a clue as to what—who—she really was, he'd lock her up in the labs, torture every ounce of information he could extract from her lips, and then kill her without a second thought.

I needed to keep him as far away from Max as I could. And the easiest way to do that was to make sure that he thought she was nothing—that she wasn't worth more than the cursory glance he'd give any of the other young, inexperienced recruits here. I'd feed into the thing that he wanted so desperately to believe in—his own ego. He'd happily swallow the narrative that Cy had raised two kids without discipline, without respect for or knowledge of everything that The Guild stood for.

Anything to raise his reputation above the Bentleys—above the brothers who'd always matched him in every way.

I could give him a competition with them that he would win —or think he'd won, anyway.

Which meant that I had to be the one to sell it—to make him think that Max wasn't worth the air I shared with her.

I felt the wolf coil inside of me, neither of us comfortable with this strange reality we'd have to create—but both of us in complete agreement that if this was the best way for us to protect Max, we'd commit to it fully.

We'd do as we promised—we'd protect her.

7

——————

MAX

"Well, girl, you certainly have a habit of flirting with death and finding your way back, don't you?"

I opened my eyes to a wild mane of spiky gray hair and a face lined with a map of wrinkles.

I cleared my throat, blinking back the bright light of the room. "Greta?"

She gave a dramatic bow, cringing slightly as she rubbed her lower back. "The one and only. Have to say, as busy and popular as you are, I'm touched to hear that you remembered me." Her voice was raspy but soft at the same time, so that her teasing felt almost as warm as a comforting hug. "Care to share what exactly brought you into this current state?"

I sat up, avoiding her eyes. I didn't want to lie to her, but I knew I couldn't tell her the truth either. Something about the knowing smirk on her lips told me that she had a better idea about what had happened to me than she was letting on. She always seemed to have that all-knowing Yoda kind of vibe going for her.

I made a mental note to do some research on the elderly

nurse as soon as I had a minute. Like most things at The Guild —she wasn't quite what she seemed.

Still, while she might have been a bit of a wild card, she'd been in my corner since day one—even going so far as to help me break into the labs to find Ralph the night that he was captured.

Greta was good people in my book.

At least until someone or something proved otherwise.

Slowly, I lifted myself up into a seated position, grateful when she took a few steps back to give me some space.

Scanning the room, my heartbeat picked up. The dream with Wade was vivid and fresh in my memory, far more so even than my dreams with him tended to be. Maybe we were getting better at the whole turning into demons thing.

Strangely, I found myself more excited about the idea than repulsed. Baby steps.

I felt my cheeks heat at the memory of us *using* our demon powers so effectively, and when Greta's eyes met mine, the question clear in her expression, I found myself abundantly happy that dreams were a private thing—visible only behind my eyelids. Especially in a place as gossipy as The Guild.

Everything in the room was like I remembered it before falling into that exquisite dream. It was strange how disorienting waking up in a hospital room felt—and lately, I'd had more experience with it than most. My head spun from the simultaneous familiarity and strangeness of my surroundings. The room was still stark white and filled with the abrasive scent of ointments and cleaning supplies. But as filled with 'sameness' as it was, I couldn't quite put my finger on the displacement I felt. It wasn't that the room had changed since I'd last found myself lying in one of these beds.

I had.

So, so much. And my feelings towards The Guild and everything it stood for had me on a constant rollercoaster of dizzying and conflicting emotions.

With a rush of panic, I realized that one concrete, very crucial thing was missing.

"Where's Ro?" I didn't bother hiding the fear trembling in my voice. He'd been so close to the edge, so close to being out of my grasp forever—had he made that transition while I was asleep, frolicking with a boy trapped in hell instead of saving him like I was supposed to be?

Greta's grin widened, but when she caught onto my panic, her eyes softened and she pressed a small, firm hand to my arm. "Strangely, your entire family seems to have an extremely impressive ability when it comes to healing. Remarkable even... and made more strange by the fact that you're not even related by blood so the connection ends there." She let out a short laugh, "like cockroaches, the bunch of you—hard to kill, though I suppose many people will want to try. That'll suit you in this life, that's for damn sure. I'm glad for it, all the same. Even if I'm terrified of cockroaches."

She had a habit of murmuring to herself, so that half the time, I couldn't tell if she was still talking to me or entering into some strange monologue, barely aware that I was there to witness it.

I blinked back the tears clouding my vision as I calmed down enough to actually process her words. Hard to kill. That meant—

"He's alive?"

She hummed quietly, nodding as she pressed a cool finger to my pulse. "It'll be a few days before he's back to his normal fighting glory, I think—hard to say with any certainty, since I'm unfamiliar with the exact conditions of his recovery—but alive and well he is. It's a miracle really." She cocked her thin, over-drawn eyebrow, eyes narrowing as she leaned down to whisper. "A miracle, or we seriously overestimated the degree of his injuries. That's what I've reported anyway. I'm old—some might say senile—eyesight and skills aren't quite what they used to be." She let out a dramatic sigh. "Been thinking it's time for me to retire soon anyway, that's what the superiors have been not-so-gently suggesting—perhaps it's time I actually listen and let them pretend they know what they're talking about for a little while longer, eh?" She chuckled, the breeze of her breath cooling the sticky sweat against my forehead. "Well, retire *again*. Maybe it'll stick this time."

I swallowed back the rush of affection threatening to spill over. "Why would you do that?"

I hardly knew the woman, and though I liked her immensely, it didn't make sense why she'd keep these secrets for me. The few conversations we'd had together, I was always a blubbering mess—either dripping with concern about someone I cared about in here, or else dealing with my own injuries.

The humor slipped away from her face, like shade into shadow. She fiddled with a few of her instruments on a small tray, fussed with the blankets that covered my legs before shooting a discrete look to the door. Then her eyes met mine, sharp and unwavering.

"I think we both know that things are not as we've always been told. You were raised by Cyrus. Am I wrong in assuming that you've noticed this too?" She paused, grunting when I shook my head. "It's something I've assumed to be true for a very long time, but current events and the state of...things right now. It's all abundantly clear. I trust people who are trustworthy, not organizations that hide behind secrets and lies and use fear as a way to control people." She nodded, like she was allowing the statement to settle deeper into her soul until it became a permanent fixture there, an anchor to survive by. Her mouth was set in a straight line. "You're good, Max Bentley. The boys, Declan—" she shook her head softly, a shadow of playful annoyance casting over her features, "that brother of yours that hasn't stopped pestering me since he woke up, and even that insufferable man who raised you both—I've always had a soft spot for him, despite the fact that he's kept me far busier than even I like to be over the years. You're all good, of that I'm certain."

She stepped back, but gripped my hand softly in hers. A strange calmness washed over me and I knew with a frigid certainty that I could trust her. Maybe even more than I could trust Cyrus right now. Greta felt like an open book in a way no one else here had—she was difficult to read, sure, but the invitation to try was always there.

"When I think of the alternative—of the lies I've uncovered in recent weeks—" her head jerked to the side as a wave of stampeding steps echoed down the hall, "I think I'll trust my gut on this one. It's rarely failed me before. It'd be a damn shame if it started to at this stage of my life, don't you think?"

"Lies? Wh—"

She waved my question away before I could ask it, her long fingers gripping the railing of the bed. "So, as I've told Tarren, Alleva, and the others who've asked—I was mistaken about Rowan's condition. We all were. His teammates are young. They make mistakes, inflate things into the worst scenario. There are no bite marks any longer, so it's not like they'll scrutinize me or my work too hard. People like to see past the things that disrupt their heavily-guarded beliefs."

Her eyes bored into mine until all I could see was my own reflection—the wide-eyed grateful expression on my face.

"And as for you," she continued, lips tilting into a smirk, "well, you've just had an excessively difficult bout of exhaustion —rare for protectors, sure, but not unheard of when you're running on empty for so many months, as you've been. This world is new to you, overwhelming. Plus, it helps the story that you've only been out for a day. More believable that way—" she raised her hand to stop me again when I started to speak. "I don't want the details, Ms. Bentley. Information is dangerous in the wrong hands—and it can be used as a powerful weapon. Like I said, my gut trusts you and the people you've chosen to surround yourself with. But I want to know as little as possible, for both of our sakes." She paused, leaning over me with a conspiratorial wink. "And, if I'm being honest, exhaustion doesn't seem completely off the mark. You could do with far more than a day of rest. Whatever it is that forced you away and brought you back again, be mindful that you don't run yourself into the dirt before your time. I've seen far too many fall to that fate in my years here."

A day? Hadn't Wade said it had been several since we'd left him with good ol' daddy dearest?

I opened my mouth to thank her, to say something even remotely as meaningful as what she'd just laid out there—the open trust she showed, despite clearly recognizing that something in me wasn't quite as we'd all thought. But before I could garble together a nonsensical phrase, I caught sight of a pair of blue eyes so familiar that the single glance of them packed a wave of relief so heavy that it nearly knocked the wind out of me.

"Ro?" I swallowed back the tears threatening to spill over, but doing so made it impossible for me to speak—like the emotions battling inside of me were determined to make themselves known somehow, determined to escape. Things could only be shoved in that ever-expanding box in the back of my mind for so long. Sooner or later, the tower of bullshit and fear and love was going to spill into a messy heap.

Greta's grip tightened briefly on my hand before pulling away. "I'll let you two catch up. I've got reports and charts to fill out and something tells me that now that you're awake, I'll have fewer bodies pestering me senselessly for updates I can't really give."

I heard her walk away, but my view was covered by a warm brown sweatshirt as Ro pressed my face into his chest, his fingers gripping into my shoulders with a force that was almost bruising.

His body shook against mine, and once I heard him swear softly into my hair and sniffle, I broke.

The tears that were fighting to push out were freed as we clung together, weeping like a couple of dunderheads in the middle of a hospital room while the world collapsed around us.

None of it mattered—not anymore. He was alive. I'd done what I'd come here to do. I could take anything else, face any other evil—Devil or not—so long as he was alive. So long as he was okay.

"You're okay?" I asked on a cracked sob, needing to hear him say it, to confirm what Greta told me himself.

He nodded into my shoulder, pressing me so firmly to him that the shaky breath I let out had nowhere to escape.

"Fine," he muttered, his voice unrecognizable with emotion.

I'd seen Ro cry once or twice over the years, but never like this—I didn't know what to make of the bumbling mess wrapped around me right now.

Instead of questioning and fighting it, for a moment—just one—I let myself sink into him. The familiar musky scent of him enveloped me, and it was enough to make a fresh wave of tears fall. I hadn't realized how terrified I was—hadn't let myself really acknowledge the fact that I might never get to hug my brother again. I squeezed him tighter.

"I don't know how you did it, but I'm okay." He cleared his throat and I heard the tears make way for something I was more familiar with—a bubbling anger that he often fell back on when he wanted to hide his fear. "If you ever leave like that again, Max," he shook his head against me, hugging me to him with even more force, like he was afraid I'd slip through his fingers, nothing but a puddle of water. "You just can't. I need you to promise."

I took a deep breath, letting my senses fill with the scent of him, of home, before I pulled back slightly. The image of him was blurry, like I was looking out of a rain-coated window into the night, but I wiped away the remaining tears and tried to pull myself together.

I couldn't promise him—couldn't say what he so badly wanted to hear. I'd be leaving soon. I'd wasted an entire day in a damn hospital bed. That left us with a little less than two weeks to regroup and look for the mystery source of shadow magic Lucifer was after before I was due back to him and his dungeon of doom.

Ro didn't look like his usual self. The circles under his eyes were dark and hollow, his skin even paler than it had been during the long winter months locked up in our cabin. His sweatshirt was worn and dirty, like he hadn't bothered to wash his things in ages. Had he even bothered showering since waking up? Eating?

None of that mattered. Those were fixable changes. Things he could make right and normal again.

The important thing was that he was here, the deep crescent moon lines in his neck now almost completely invisible— no longer even recognizable as a bite. Greta was right. No one who hadn't seen the marks there themselves would question his recovery. Vampire bites never healed so completely on a protector. We just had to hope that Greta, Arnell, and Jer were the only ones who'd seen the true damage that had been done. Lies held tighter, the fewer people involved.

He was going to be okay.

His hand swept over his neck, covering the area, like my focus burned him.

"You shouldn't have done that," his mouth pressed into a grim line, his nostrils flaring slightly. "You could have died. I can't believe that Izzy even allowed you in here knowing what you were trying to do. You don't understand your," he glanced towards the door, his voice sinking into a scratchy whisper, "*powers* just yet. And people here—they wouldn't understand. You can't just use them like that, you're going to get yourself locked up like Ralph—or worse. You have to be careful, Max. This is a dangerous game you're meddling with."

"Reverse the situation," I snapped, though there was no venom in my voice as I did the same—if Ro had almost died healing me, I'd be just as pissed off as he was. Love was a strange thing, logic got completely fucking thrown out the window. "I'm not losing you. That's not an option. And besides," I cleared my throat, "I have better control than you think. I'm learning. Things are complicated, but we're getting to the bottom of it." I'd tell him everything. About Lucifer, about hell. Ro wasn't someone I wanted to hide myself from, but I didn't know how to start. There were no practice runs for conversations like this—no preparation that could make it easy or simple. "Wade is helping me. And the others—in their own way." I pressed my fingers into my eyes, trying to keep everything straight—who I was mad at, who I trusted. Sometimes it felt like I didn't even know which way was up anymore—I was literally sent here on a mission by the Devil. What the actual fuck was my life?

I straightened up, scanning the room, and tried like hell to hide the hollow disappointment. None of them were here. I had no idea where I stood with anyone in Six at the moment, not on a personal level anyway. They'd made it clear that they'd do what they could to protect my secret, and they were obviously invested in Wade's safety.

Ro's nostrils flared slightly, but he nodded and leaned back on the hospital bed, tucking me into his side.

For a moment, I let myself be comforted—loved—let the absolute clusterfuck of everything slip away and tried to imagine that this was like before—well, before everything. Like it was just me and Ro, huddled up after a particularly grueling sparring match, watching some bad nineties romcom while Cy muttered under his breath about how unrealistic the plot was and how our time would be better spent studying or watching the history channel.

It hadn't escaped my attention that he wasn't here either.

I was royally pissed at Cy, sure, but at the end of the day, he was still Cy. No matter how much he'd kept from me, I didn't think it was possible for me to completely shake the fact that he was, for better or worse, one of my people. Flat out.

But he wasn't here.

A loud crash sounded to our left. I jumped and a familiar heat spread through my veins.

"Well that's new." Izzy's eyes were wide as she hurried inside and shut the door behind her as soon as she was through the threshold. "Seems you've brought a nifty souvenir back from hell. I hope you brought me something equally flashy."

I stared at her, not quite catching her point until Ro let out an uncharacteristically shrill "Holy shit!"

I followed his gaze down to my right hand...which was encased in a thin layer of flames.

Holy shit was right.

I focused, took a deep breath in, and pulled the flame back, using the breathing technique I'd sort of developed over the last few days. The swirl of heat disappeared quickly, but my heart beat furiously against my ribs. Adrenaline was a difficult thing to control.

I thought I'd been getting a handle on my powers—a little bit anyway. One jump-scare from my best friend had me lighting up now? What the fuck was that?

"Er, yeah," I said, as she walked closer to me, "about that."

With a snort she reached over Ro and grabbed my now fire-free hand in hers, studying it carefully as her lips curved into a small grin. "Well, damn. Pretty cool parlor trick, even if it is terrifying as hell. Pun intended. That didn't look like normal fire either—there were so many colors. It was so, I don't know, ethereal looking. Majestic as fuck."

I scrunched up my face, not sure how to go about explaining this to them. "Pretty sure it's hellfire."

"Come again," she deadpanned.

There was a brief moment of hesitation in which I considered concocting some version of the truth that left out the fact that I was a demon spawn—and in more ways than just being part succubus—but then I saw the openness in Izzy's expression, felt Ro's hand squeeze my shoulder. They'd both had my back through all the weirdness so far. They weren't going to run. Maybe it was time to pool my resources, to loop them in and stop hiding from the truth. Time to let the metaphorical bucket of clusterfucks spill open and be vulnerable enough to let them sift through it all. I refused to be one of those people who let their world implode because they insisted on keeping everything from everyone they cared about. I'd read enough novels to know that hiding the truth always led to unnecessary disaster mode and, well, we were already headed in that direction without my stubbornness making matters worse.

"Okay." I nodded, more to myself than to them. I felt a small grin tug at my lips—some of the weight on my shoulders dissipating a bit just from the decision to not carry it all on my own.

As if she could read it on my face, Izzy clapped her hands together with an excited yelp and shoved Ro's legs over so that she had some room on the already crowded bed.

We were scrunched together, legs bent uncomfortably at awkward angles, but something about it felt so comforting I almost wept all over again.

"Story time. About damn time, Max Bentley. I've been dying." She wiggled slightly, stealing some of my blankets to cover her feet.

And so, I filled them in.

On all of it.

Everything from the sex dreams with Wade to the in person sex with Atlas and Eli—during which Ro graciously left to grab us some waters and snacks—to the strange powers that started to emerge after my nineteenth birthday, only to grow tenfold in hell. I told them about the tainted ones, how strange and unexpected hell was, and that Six had been more or less spying on me and keeping things from me for months—about Darius and the pile of confusion I felt where he was concerned. Everything spilled out of me with ease and openness, like a dam had finally given in.

I was done hiding from it all, done hiding from the people who mattered. If Lucifer was right, then the stakes were high and we were all in for a shit show soon anyway. No use burying our heads in the sand about it all.

I pulled stray threads from the cotton sheets, building up the courage to tell them the final thing, terrified about how they'd react, but bolstered by the fact that they were still both here—that they hadn't run away screaming yet. Even when I literally lit myself on fire.

I told them that we'd stumbled into Lucifer's creepy castle, about the instability of the hell realm, and how we got back to The Guild. And then, after a quick glance at them both, I let it slip: "Turns out, apparently, that satan is my, uh, bio-dad."

I couldn't bring myself to look at either of them, worried that I'd see fear or hatred reflected back at me.

Izzy fidgeted a bit, the bed squeaking and shifting as she climbed over me and moved to my other side, leaning back against the pillow so that I was sandwiched between them both.

For a long moment, we sat like that in silence, my heartbeat racing in my ears, a steady hum building as I waited for—I wasn't sure. Panic, anger, fear, disbelief. *Some* sort of reaction.

"So the Devil is real? No shit." Izzy bit her bottom lip as she stared at the mysterious stain on the ceiling above us. A few of her hairs tickled my cheek as she adjusted a bit.

Ro opened his mouth and closed it several times, brows bent in thought as he fought for something—anything—to say. There was a long, heavy silence, until he turned to me and shrugged. "Well, okay then." There was no animosity in the statement, no condemnation, just blanket acceptance as he nudged me with his shoulder. "Now we know at least. Next step is to figure out how to keep you alive and the world from imploding."

I let out a deep breath, my chest suddenly light and my head dizzy with relief.

"Sounds easy peasy," Izzy said, her nose scrunching as she leaned back. "Gotta say, never a dull moment with you two is there? Thank god." She turned to me again, eyes suddenly wide. "Just please tell me that Ralph is okay. I can deal with the end of the world, but I will flip my shit if anything happened to that precious pup."

I nodded, my face splitting into a giant grin, the wave of relief enough to make me float.

8

ELI

"Are you seriously not going to tell me anything more than that bullshit story you lot came up with?"

My dad paced back and forth, his anger making the usually serene pond feel anything like the quiet escape it usually was for me.

I squinted up at the sun, soaking in the stray bit of warmth. If the water wasn't half-frozen over, I'd jump in now to drown out this fight.

We told him partial truths.

That we'd gone after a tip about Wade's murderers, one given to us by the surly ass vampire in the lab.

That Max ran into us during our escape and threatened to report us if we didn't bring her along. I sure as hell didn't want to be around when she learned that particular detail of the story we'd told.

That we made it back—all of us intact. Mostly.

I dug my palm in my chest, trying to rub away the steady ache that had been building over the last week or so—since Max disappeared from the tainted one's nest. Almost dying by mythical blade? Not nearly as painful as this slow, steady, boiling anxiety and fear.

At least she was awake now. Alive. Safe with her brother and best friend, so long as we kept the truth hidden.

"Eli," he snapped again—any humor that usually traced his features long absent. "Answer me. We both know that story you fed us all is total bullshit. I understand why you told it, but I need to know the truth. We need to know what's really going on." His anger softened a bit, his shoulders slumping. "I can't help you—can't protect you—if you don't give me something to go on."

He looked exhausted. I'd known that our disappearance would take a toll on him and the evidence of it was clear as day. The fine lines in his forehead seemed deeper, his skin paler, his jaw lined with a scraggly beard that was in desperate need of a razor or, at the very least, some oil.

But it was his eyes that gave it away the most. There was a hollowness there that made my chest constrict. A hollowness that I hadn't seen since the days after my mother abandoned us.

A hollowness that *I* caused.

I hadn't been able to meet his gaze since I saw it reflected there.

"I told you everything there is to tell. We appreciate that you covered for us—truly we do. But there's nothing more to say. If that's not enough for you, feel free to punish us further. You'll get no argument from me." My voice sounded monotonous and tinny, like it was coming from someone else. I was tired. So fucking tired. But I hadn't been able to sleep since we returned —not while Max was lingering in some dream limbo while we waited around, terrified she wouldn't wake up.

He shook his head, disappointment evident in every clenched muscle. "Vengeance. You really expect me to believe that Atlas led you on a mission guided by nothing but vengeance? And you all just went along with it, shielded by grief? Give me a break. You've given almost no detail about this supposed ambush you all orchestrated—just vague bits of information about Seattle and large numbers of vampires. You returned with no body—all of you looking like you've had a brush with death. Max is drained from *exhaustion*." He sighed. Frustration and sadness warring in every breath he took. I didn't want to stick around to see which emotion won out. "What the hell happened out there? Why couldn't you so much as call? Do you know how worried I've been?" He started pacing, the movements rigid with his anger, until he turned back to me again. "I've been sick with it. Haven't slept in days. These are dangerous times—you can't just go charging into the night. It's so unlike you all—I would never have thought Atlas and Declan would do something like this."

But he could imagine me doing it; he wasn't surprised by my own recklessness, just theirs and the fact that they didn't reign me in this time.

That stung, though he wasn't necessarily wrong. I was the wildcard of the group. I'd built my entire identity at The Guild around taking thoughtless risks and flirting with the boundaries of the rules. But I thought if anyone could see through that bullshit to the real me, it would be my father.

"I'm sorry." It was all I could give him, but it was true. He had experienced a world of hurt—knowing that I was responsible for some of it now made me feel ill.

"This is what we've come to? Lies? After all we've been through together, after all we've worked for? I've kept Atlas's secret. How—" He turned towards the pond, like he could no longer stand the sight of me. A sharp, heavy guilt sank low in my stomach. He'd mentioned when we returned that he'd known the truth—had always known, maybe even before the rest of us did. He protected Atlas, protected me—the knowledge of which made lying to him now all the worse. "How can you still not trust me?"

The taste of bile laced my tongue and I promised myself that when this conversation was done, I'd give myself the day to drown myself in a bottle of whiskey—responsibilities be damned.

I did trust him, that wasn't the problem. These secrets that I kept, they weren't mine to tell. And the risks were too high. Right now, Max's survival was more important than any temporary pain we might experience in trying to preserve it.

While I knew my dad would do everything—give everything—to keep me safe, I couldn't be sure how he'd react to learning the truth about Max, about Wade, about hell. We were at war with The Guild. An invisible one, for now, but I knew that it would grow louder, that sides would need to be chosen soon enough. I wasn't entirely certain yet which side my father would be on. It was a difficult thing—pushing against the very thing that gave your life meaning for so many decades.

"You've kept things from me too," I snapped, the guilt making way for some of my own resentment. He knew that Max was different all along. It was because he'd asked me to that I'd stolen her DNA, that I'd lost her trust. "What haven't you been telling me about Max? About why Cyrus is really here? About what's going on? You can't sit here and preach honesty to me when you've been having me do your dirty work."

He froze, his eyes hardening as I finally forced myself to meet them. Deep brown, a few shades darker than mine, same stubborn expression that I'd inherited through blood and practice.

"You do not have the same clearance that—"

"Bullshit. You and I both know that you and Cy are up to something way beyond issues of clearance. The guy disappears for most of my life and suddenly he's back—no reason at all?"

"The increase in attacks. You know this is why he's—"

"It's more than that. It's her. Where does she come from? What do you know? You've forced me to spy on her, to keep my tabs. I've done that." And look where it's gotten me. "I deserve to know what you're keeping from her. *She* deserves to know."

His brows narrowed, a familiar wrinkle forming between them. "You care for her."

"Of course I do—she's part of my team." I sat down on a large, flat rock, my elbows resting on my knees as I stared at the still water.

"No," he took a step towards me, "it's deeper than that. I mean romantically. You care for her romantically. In a way that's different from your typical...pursuits."

I bit my tongue, kept my focus on the lake. I didn't want to have this conversation with him. Of course I fucking cared about her. Of course I had romantic feelings for her. That was the whole fucking problem. I didn't want to.

I felt a soft pressure on my shoulder and looked up. He was standing above me, eyes rounded as he bent over to look into my own. There was an openness there that scared me, so I turned away.

"Son, do you—do you love her?"

Love.

The word sounded so strange coming from his lips.

Tainted with pain.

Love had destroyed my father—turned his life into a miserable existence that he fought against every day.

Love left me with the shell of a parent for years, and the absence of another altogether.

I'd watched it happen—experienced enough of that agony myself when my mother left.

I had no interest in ever opening myself up to that kind of shadow of a life again. I cared about Max. Deeply. And I'd be a friend to her, family even—I'd treat her with the same respect and affection I reserved only for the members of my team. But the kind of love my father spoke of—that wasn't something I was capable of, wasn't something I wanted, even if I could.

He let out a long, quiet sigh. "Eli—Eli, look at me." Stubbornly, like a child, I kept my focus on the pond. "Just tread carefully, okay. There's so much about her that I don't know. Cyrus has opened up, some, but the man is about as transparent as a stone sometimes. I don't want to see you hurt."

I heard his own pain threaded through that word.

Hurt.

If I was honest with myself, it was too late for that.

Not giving in, not being with Max, knowing that I was responsible for some of her own anger, her own pain—it was a kind of hurt that made it difficult to catch my breath when I lingered too long on it. That's why things couldn't go further between us.

As much as I loved my father, I did not want to become him, did not want to travel the path he'd been forced on.

"I don't want to talk about my feelings. There isn't time or energy for love or romance. This is a war that we're headed towards—don't you know that I get that? That I understand?"

He'd already lamented for hours when we returned about the increase in attacks, about the state of The Guild since we'd left. Things were coming to a head—quickly.

Far sooner than I could have imagined.

"Eli—"

I stood up. I wanted to escape this conversation, push it back on track. We had a mission—given to us by the Devil of all people, but a mission nonetheless. Until we found what we were after, we needed to blend in—to get back to normal. Some version of it, anyway.

He took a step back, slowly, like he was trying not to scare off a wild animal. "Eli, if I've led you to believe that opening up to someone is something to fear, something to be ashamed of,

I've done you a great disservice. What happened between me and your mother, that's not—"

"Dad," I warned. Ice flowed through my veins, clogging my throat. My jaw clenched, my fingers balling into fists. "We're not talking about that. If you want to talk, then you can talk about what really matters. I want to know what the fuck is going on. What do you know? Why did Cyrus—the most anti-fucking-social person known to existence—decide to take in an orphaned baby and raise her by himself? Why did he leave The Guild in the first place and keep her in hiding? Why did you bring him back? Why now?"

Did he know? Did he know what Max was—where she'd really come from? Was it possible that he'd been protecting her all along, just like he'd done for Atlas? Did he know as much as Cyrus, or was he just as in the dark as everyone else was?

It felt strange—both of us dancing around the topic, testing the boundaries of what the other knew, neither of us sure how much we could reveal. I'd never felt so far from him before, so distorted.

He stared at me, jaw muscles working furiously, like he was fighting with himself about whether or not to speak.

Both of us were at a standoff.

Then, he deflated, shoulders sagging, like the fight simply evaporated out of him. He seemed so tired, so empty all of a sudden. "We knew her mother."

I didn't move—didn't dare so much as breathe.

"Cyrus was particularly close to her," he let out a low, humorless laugh, "not close in the way you're thinking," he shook his head, "the direction your head always goes. He was like her mentor, a few years older. He helped train her. I think he saw a lot of himself in her." He grinned, the ghost of a memory visible in his eyes. "She was stubborn as all get out, but she didn't quite fit in here," he tilted his head to the side, "same as Cyrus. But she was strong as hell. Smart too. Sometimes I thought she would even surpass him in skill one day. I used to joke with him about it, try to get under his skin—you know, brother shit."

I cleared my throat, my mouth dry as sandpaper. I didn't miss the past tense. *Was.* "Who was she? What happened to her? Why the secrecy all this time?"

I felt like a child—filled with a thirsty curiosity, desperate for each drop of information he was willing to spill. It was strange, for a glimpse into my father's past to seem so strange and unfamiliar to me. He rarely spoke about his life before me—before my mother—and he almost never spoke about Cyrus. It was almost like he wanted to honor his brother's desire for secrecy and isolation, like talking about him was a betrayal. But things were different this time. He was ready to talk, the shift in the air almost tangible.

He scratched the uneven curls lining his jaw, deliberating again. But it was more brief this time, like he didn't have the energy left to fight. "She was from a particularly strong line of protectors. There are things The Guild keeps from us, things I've glimpsed throughout my life here, but that have become glaringly clear in more recent years. There are protector lines that exist outside of this organization—different from us in some ways, their strengths coming from different sources, different ancestral pathways."

It wasn't news that some protectors didn't belong to The Guild, but I'd never imagined that it was a large, intentional group. Or that they were different from us in some fundamental, important way.

"One line in particular, had worked against The Guild since its very beginning—fighting the very things it stood for, questioning all of our teachings, our philosophies, our ways of life." He paused at the question forming itself on my tongue. "It's not discussed because it's long been assumed that the line died out. The Guild only teaches the history it wants us to learn, that it wants us to keep alive. A thriving resistance that once worked to destroy The Guild? That those holding the protector name worked against our sacred duty to protect humanity from demons and the hell realm? That was a dark story that many leaders feared would sow discontent, encourage copycats—tarnish our name."

"Max's mother was from this line though, the one assumed to have ended?" I guessed.

He nodded. "Cyrus believed so. But she was also descended from a very powerful Guild family. When her mother brought her to The Guild as a young child, few questions were raised. There are stray protectors—those who've been pushed out of our lifestyle or chosen different paths, some end up in unknowing foster systems or are born half-human with a parent who is unaware of our world. Occasionally, when they are lucky, they find their way back to their people, back to us. It wasn't unheard of. The maternal side of her family had chosen such a path a few generations before her." He paused, shrugging. "The records aren't very clear, it's hard to say, hard to trace beyond a shadow of doubt—most of our resources have gone to studying demons, not our own. Plus, they didn't exactly have computers back then, you know? It's easier for information to disappear when it travels through word of mouth, or when a file is misplaced—or *placed*, rather, but in the wrong hands."

"So she was from a different line—she was welcomed back, her mother's family had connections to The Guild, powerful ones it sounds like. What's the problem?"

The chill in the air seemed to get worse, like it was responding to the sadness that washed over my dad. For a long moment, he seemed to soak it in—standing there, against the backdrop of my favorite place he seemed to belong here, like a painting, stuck in time. There was something different about him since we'd arrived a few hours ago—a profound melancholy that I couldn't fully dig out of him. Suddenly, I felt like an intruder, imposing on this rare moment where the mask he so frequently wore dropped away.

"Not unlike Max, she had a knack for getting into trouble, for questioning people and things that she would have been better off avoiding. It's part of the reason Cy took such a liking to her—she frustrated the hell out of him, but there was a wisdom inside her that he respected." A steady breeze picked up and he held his arms close to his body, looking more frail than he was. "Something happened. I don't know the details. I don't think Cy even knows the details, to be honest. She was good at keeping things to herself, making sure others weren't implicated in her choices. But I know enough to know that she broke a law, stole something, angered some very important people high up in The Guild, and then ran away. She was gone for years. And then, one day, she found Cyrus. There was something different about her. The way he described her—I don't know. Something ethereal, almost, something—more."

He let the sentence hang in the void between us until I couldn't take the silence any longer. "Different how? What happened next?"

Seamus shrugged, his frustrated exhale visible in the cold air as it lingered between us. "I don't know. Cyrus never told me anything else. Just that Max was her daughter and that she died. He's protected her ever since, afraid of The Guild's vengeance if they discovered who she was. But more than that, he feared for her safety beyond punishment and living in the shadow of her mother's consequences. There was something different, something fundamentally changed in her mother—and he knew that there was likely something different about Max too."

The succubus.

Her mother was part succubus. It must have been triggered in her, like Wade and Max's powers had been. I felt bad not voicing this to him, not fulfilling my half of the conversation—

not giving him answers, while he was finally providing them to me. But I couldn't do it, couldn't bring myself to fill in the gaps of the story.

"You've kept Atlas's secret for a reason, Eli," he continued, voice low, though there was no disappointment or anger in it, just a bald statement of the truth. "And I've done the same. If Max is different, in the way that her mother was, she would not be treated well here. Even though Cy and I have a reasonable amount of power and respect amongst our people—we are not the law, not the governing body. We are not as important, as valuable, as we may seem to you. Who's to say what would happen to either of them if the wrong people learned the truth?"

"How can you just turn your head and ignore how fucked up this all is? How can you live with this place, the hypocrisy of it all?" The questions flew from my lips unbidden, laced with venom and accusation. I flushed as soon as they did. He was being forthcoming for once and I was attacking him—laying all of my pent up frustration at his feet. I cleared my throat. "Sorry."

His nostrils flared briefly and he returned to his pacing, for a moment, the only sound was his boots crunching on the frozen blades of grass and twigs.

"I haven't." His voice was cold, hard, and I suddenly felt like a child again. "We've been trying to learn what we can—the true history of The Guild, of our kind—helping when we can, from within the system. There are several of us who don't take everything at face value, who've had reason to question and resist certain tales we've been told. But discretion is paramount —one wrong step and everything we've worked towards crumbles. Why do you think I've protected Atlas? Max? That damn hellhound that followed her here?" His eyes widened, like everything was obvious. "Why do you think Cy disappears as often as he does, why I've brought him here? Something big is coming—something none of us understands. We're doing everything we can to prepare ourselves, to keep the things and people we care about safe, while still working towards protecting humanity when and where we can. It's a delicate balance." He shook his head, his gaze at his feet. "Some might even say it's an impossible one."

A soft breeze blew through the surrounding trees. For a moment, I soaked in the sounds of the clearing, the brisk air and briny smell of the water. I felt so removed from the rest of the world when I came to this spot, now more than ever. It was like a small bubble, protected from the monstrosities and evils of the world—a preserved moment of peace, even if it was only ever just a moment, just an illusion of reality.

"Okay." I stood up, brushed the stray twigs from my pants and stretched my arms. I needed a proper night's rest, but I doubted I would get one tonight. I'd been debating whether or not to visit Max, never exactly sure whether it was better or worse to briefly give in to the constant desire to see her. "I believe you. And I trust you." It was the truth. I trusted his intentions, for the most part, even if I couldn't openly convey mine. "But I need you to trust me too. We'll be leaving again." His eyes hardened, the muscle in his forehead tightening as he fought the urge to interrupt. "Soon, probably. And I'll need you to not ask questions, to not get in our way. Things are complicated, with Max, with Atlas—with all of us. And I need you to understand that just because I can't share everything with you, that doesn't mean I don't respect you, that I'm not also trying to protect you and everything we care about."

For a long moment, he held my gaze, a severity in his expression that reminded me more of his brother than of my father.

He nodded once, then turned towards the pond. "This must be what letting your kid grow up feels like. It's terrifying—literally, nonstop terror and anxiety."

I smiled, my chest tightening at the new boundary that stood between us. I'd always provoked my father, frequently challenged the rules governing us at The Guild, but this felt different somehow, final in a way.

"I can't say I particularly enjoy it," he said.

"Honestly, me neither."

We stood in silence for a while, each of us lost in our own thoughts. It felt almost like it used to, when we'd come out here after a long training session, both of us exhausted and frustrated with each other. Something about this place allowed us to just be, to just exist together. It was the one place where all of my rebellions and his severity slipped into their truest form—a shared pain, reflected and refracted in different ways.

"She's been moved off your team, Alleva and Tarren are gearing towards a bonding ceremony with Reza," he said finally, shaking his head when he saw the repulsion on my face. "Don't worry, they're no longer identifying you as an ideal match for her. While Alleva is still intrigued by the idea, Tarren doesn't want his son permanently tied to our family."

I hated the fact that I felt a flush of relief from that. Not even because of the fact that I wanted as little to do with Reza as possible, but because it meant that I didn't have to disappoint my father again when I absolutely refused that order.

After what happened with Max, I had no interest in bonding to anyone, not ever.

It used to seem like a tolerable idea, bonding to someone platonically—like Declan—but now with things as complicated as they were, the thought of bonding to anyone at all made me feel hollow.

"But if you're to be running into danger with this girl, she should be with your team. The fewer eyes on you all throughout these next months, the better. At least until Cyrus is back with answers and to make decisions where she is concerned."

"So you'll put her back with us?" I hated how damn eager I sounded, like a child being offered a favorite toy. "Kick Reza out?"

He shook his head, lips pressed tight. "I can't go against Alleva and Tarren, not right now, not with that. Atlas is his son, not mine." Both of us knew that he was far more a father to Atlas than Tarren had ever been. "But I can find a way to maneuver things a bit, as best as I can anyway."

I wasn't sure what that meant exactly, but I felt a wave of gratitude at his willingness to help, even when I knew he didn't approve—that I was responsible for that look of fear in his eyes.

We sank back into silence again, but it was a comfortable sort of silence—both of us needing a small break from the realities and complications of life with The Guild—time to be alone but together in a way that always made sense with our relationship. Somehow we were always better in the gaps of conversations than we were at actually laying things out with each other through words. We were better at picking up on each other's vague emotions than we were at comprehending each other's thoughts.

Probably because half the time I couldn't even clarify my thoughts well enough for myself, let alone enough to convey them to someone else.

"There's something else you should know." He was several feet away, walking along the pond's edge, his voice carrying through the wind like a soft whisper. Something about him seemed so hollow then, frail.

I nodded, urging him to continue, suddenly itching to leave this place. The haunted look in his expression was difficult to linger on.

"The ambushes are getting worse around the world, but they seem to be concentrated more heavily in the pacific northwest." He paused, and I had to bite my tongue to stop from telling him to get on with it. This wasn't new information. "It's looking like Tarren will, unfortunately, be a more permanent fixture here. He's going to be bringing in some of his own teams. He and Alleva are pulling resources from satellite head-quarters, so it's likely going to get quite crowded in the coming weeks." He bent down, picked up a small rock, and ran his thumb over the smooth surface.

"And?" I pressed, frustrated with the drawn out point he was making. My chest felt tight suddenly, like I couldn't quite fill my lungs all the way when I tried.

"Your mother." His voice cracked on that word, 'mother', and he took a moment gathering himself before turning back towards the water. He was ashamed of his sorrow, wanted to protect me from seeing it. Somehow that only made it worse. "She will be here by morning."

9

MAX

"I mean are you even breathing?" Izzy asked, eyes wide with shock.

"Mmhm," I grunted automatically, stuffing my face with another too-large bite of pizza, my fork already prepped and ready to go with a giant piece of chicken in the other hand. Then I paused and considered her question. It was actually getting kind of difficult to remember the whole inhale-exhale thing when I was so focused on chewing and swallowing. "You have no idea how good this tastes."

"I thought the pizza was actually pretty mediocre today," she said, brow arched, "but I don't want to yuck your yum."

Mediocre? What was she talking about? It was divine. After living in a dungeon for who knew how long, I felt like I'd died and gone to heaven. Unlimited servings of meat, carbs, and vegetables was definitely my version of paradise anyway. "You try bringing someone back from the brink of death and tell me if you're not fucking famished. Plus, they don't exactly have gourmet options in," I glanced around and ducked my head towards our table on the off chance anyone could hear me, "well, you know where. Best I got was some freshly hunted meat cooked over a fire and that feels like it was ages ago."

My stomach dipped at the memory of hunting with Darius. It was the first time we'd spent a decent amount of time alone together, and my stomach did another annoying little lurch when I remembered how not awful that time was.

Until we got ambushed anyway.

Ro glanced down at me from the side of his eye, some of the frustration disappearing at my clear joy, but not completely. "You can't seriously think I'm just going to let you go back there."

Right. We were still on that. After another bemused once-over from Greta, I was discharged with instructions to take it easy for a day or two. The dining hall had been my first stop—after grabbing a quick shower in the med ward and throwing on some fresh training gear they had stored there. That first hit of hot water had felt almost as good as sex. And that was saying something, seeing as I was now part sex demon.

"Can we talk about this later?" I begged, glancing around the room as I stuffed a piece of broccoli in my mouth.

I kept waiting for someone to come get me and take me away. Alleva and Seamus had to know I was back by now, but neither had been waiting at the med ward door with a pair of handcuffs and a scowl, ready to drag me down to the labs or punish me for ditching this place with Six for a few weeks. I felt like I was waiting for my prison sentence, and that not knowing was awful.

I felt every single eye in the cafeteria on me, whispering, like they were all waiting for the shoe to drop too—everyone vying for a front row seat to watch me get reamed out by the adults.

Of course, there were very specific eyes not present at the moment. I hadn't seen Six or Cy since waking up. Ro mentioned that Cy had left campus just before I'd come to, and

I ignored how badly it had stung that he just peaced-out while I was lying in a hospital bed. But I thought Six would have at least come to grab me and fill me in on what the hell was going on here—what our play would be now that we were back. Something.

"Hell-o," Ro sing-songed, as he grabbed the fork out of my hand and pushed my plate out of reach, "are you even listening to me right now?"

That was one way to get my attention.

I ignored the impulse to punch him in the gut for taking away my food, reminding myself that I was happy to see him after the threat of losing him. I shook my head, playing his words back in my thoughts, trying to remember what part of the conversation had made his eyes go all hard with anger like they were now.

Right.

I'd told him I was going back to hell in a few days. I put myself in his shoes again and nodded. I'd be ready to lock him up in the labs myself if the situation was reversed and he'd told me he was going back on a death mission.

I reached forward and grabbed his hand, resisting the urge to bypass the comforting gesture and go straight for my food again. "I get it. Trust me, I do. But what option do I have? Did you miss the part about the—"I mouthed the word 'realm,' "disintegrating around us? Plus Wade is there. I don't have a choice."

"And don't forget the part about your, you know," Izzy pointed to my hand and mimed an explosion, "on the fritz. You need training."

Ro's jaw set in a hard line, but I saw the dilemma unfolding in his mind as he leaned back in his chair—his own food almost completely untouched. "I just got you back. Do you have any idea how—" he shook his head, like he couldn't find the words, and shoved my plate back towards me. "You should finish your food so we can get the hell out of here. All these people staring at us is making me feel itchy."

"Well," Izzy said, popping a french fry into her mouth, "it won't be like last time."

Ro and I looked at her, both waiting for her to explain. I agreed, of course, but I wasn't sure what exactly she meant.

She shrugged, dipping another fry in ranch dressing. "I mean, we're going with you." Her gray eyes met mine, challenge clear as day. "Was that not obvious?"

My chest tightened at the idea of having more people I cared about in hell risking their lives for me.

"Absolutely not," I said, just as Ro leaned back in his chair, shoulders sagging.

"Izzy's right. If you're going, I'm going too." His eyes softened around the corners as he finally picked up his fork and started carefully assembling the perfect, balanced bite of mashed potatoes, meatloaf, and peas.

Weirdo.

Still, I shook my head, needing to nip this in the bud now. Honest communication was my new approach with them and I didn't want to go on pretending there was any chance in, well, hell, that I'd be bringing them *to* hell with me.

"Ro, I get your frustration, I promise I do. If the situation was different and either of you were going, I'd be just as adamant about joining—"

"Don't you dare say but," Ro interrupted.

"She's definitely going to say but." Izzy let out a resigned sigh.

"But," I continued, "you can't come." I raised my hands when they started to protest, urging them to let me continue. "Look, I'm not like either of you. I have tools for surviving that place. It isn't like here. And obviously you know—*he*—doesn't want me dead or else I wouldn't be here right now."

He didn't want me dead *yet*, anyway. Who knew what

Lucifer was going for in the long run. I still didn't trust him, even if I'd made a blood oath with him.

"Well, if we're with you, he probably won't kill us either," Ro challenged, back to swirling his food around on his plate instead of eating it. Such a waste.

Honestly, I didn't know Lucifer at all, but I knew him well enough to know that wasn't the case. He was keeping Wade there as a tool to get me to do as he wished, not out of the goodness of his heart. Did the devil even have a heart?

"It's too dangerous," I said, stuffing my mouth with one more bite of crust on the off chance that would end the conversation. Even *I* was getting full at this point—a truly rare event.

"I don't care." Ro set his fork down and shoved his tray away.

"Me either." Izzy repeated the gesture and leaned back in her chair, arms crossed over her chest.

I bit back the smirk at how childlike they looked in that moment. I was honestly still so happy to have them both near me that I almost didn't even care that we were arguing.

But the stakes were too high on this, and, as much as I knew it would cut them to say, I said it anyway: "Yes, but you both being there doesn't help. It only makes it more dangerous for me. I'm going to be too worried about looking out for you," Ro opened his mouth to protest, but I pushed on, ignoring the flash of guilt gurgling in my belly. "I know you're going to say not to worry about you, but you should know better than anyone that's not how anxiety works. And if I'm focused on keeping you both safe, or worrying about you getting gobbled up by a tainted one, things can go really *really* bad for me. For all of us. I can't stress enough that hell is not what you think it is. The fewer of us there, the better chance we stand. Just, please," I let out a steady breath, meeting both of their eyes briefly before continuing, "help me, but help me from here. If you keep fighting me on this, I'm not going to keep either of you informed—please don't force me to cut you out right now. I need you both, more than you know."

There was a long, unbearable pause while they both processed. They shared a brief look with each other before they turned back to me, nodded once, and let the matter drop.

I exhaled in relief and collected our trays and scraps into one pile. "Excellent. Let's get out of here, I can practically feel everyone gossiping about me and I'm afraid it's going to make me start hating food by association."

"Impossible." Izzy stood up and stretched and I could see the tension from the conversation start to fall away. She shot me a wink that made my own muscles release a bit. "Nothing can destroy the power of pizza. But okay, let's get out of here."

"Where am I staying anyway?" I asked, following her. In the rush to save Ro, I hadn't focused too much on the pragmatics of simply existing back on campus.

The dining hall wasn't too full, but I still expected Alleva or Seamus or someone to come storming in here at any moment. Part of me felt guilty walking around freely, like I was just waiting for one of them to jump out of a dark corner and punish me for convincing Six to jailbreak a vamp and skip town without so much as a ransom note.

Were they being punished somewhere? Is that why I hadn't seen them yet? Why they hadn't been in the hospital room when I woke up?

My breath caught as the possibility flitted through my thoughts.

I shook my head, frustrated with myself for being so damn self-centered all the time. They were probably fine. They just had shit to do—waiting around in the medical ward while I was knocked out was hardly a productive use of time. Especially considering the fact that, right now, time was such a precious commodity.

"With us, obviously," Izzy said as she opened the doors and

started carving the familiar path towards Ten's cabin. "Like we'd let them give up your room or stick you with anyone else just because you took another team on a joy ride. Don't be absurd."

Ro was quiet, and I knew he was still low-key pouting about our conversation, so I looped my arm through his and squeezed him against me—content to be glued to him even if he was in a silent pit of disappointment.

He liked making concessions and compromises about as much as I did.

His body relaxed slightly against me and I knew that we were okay.

I didn't have my phone charged—apparently the battery didn't react so well when crossing into a different realm—so I wasn't sure of the exact time, but the grounds were bathed with the early darkness that came after the sunset, the air a piercing cold. I was doubly grateful to borrow some of Ro's warmth.

"Maybe we just stay in and watch a movie, plan next steps tonight?" Izzy kicked a stray pebble down the path as we walked. "Sound good?"

I nodded, unable to come up with a better suggestion.

While I was excited to spend the evening with them, I suddenly felt the absence of Six sharply—what exactly *were* the next steps? How the hell did we find a source of magic we didn't even know existed? It wasn't like we could just go ask someone like Alleva. I didn't trust anyone with power here, not anymore—not after everything I'd learned. I had a feeling that wherever Six was, they didn't exactly have their top standing anymore. It would make sneaking around and exploring the labs even more difficult than it had been before.

And while a night in any bed with real sheets and blankets sounded phenomenal after Lucifer's hidey-hole, a strange part of me wanted to be back in the cabin with Six.

Then again, that room belonged to Sarah, not me. I'd occupied it for such a short time that I was barely even a visitor there.

"Oh, there's Declan," Izzy whispered, bumping my shoulder gently with hers.

The mere sound of her name was enough to instantly snap me out of my thought spiral.

I scanned the grounds, my heart thumping with an annoying combination of excitement and nerves.

"I haven't seen her for a few hours. She was constantly checking on you while you were sleeping." Izzy paused, lips pursed in thought. "Good movie. Maybe we watch that tonight."

Just as my breath caught at the knowledge that Declan had been there—that she'd cared enough to check up on me, I spotted her.

Like me, she'd definitely had a moment to shower and clean up from the depths of hell. She looked strong as ever, her skin clear and luminous, her long wavy hair spiraling in loose waves down her back. If I didn't know better, I would never have guessed that she'd just emerged from battle after battle with demons only a day ago.

She was standing across the way, talking to a woman with pale lavender hair, their heads ducked close together as they spoke.

I'd never seen the woman before. She looked a couple of years older than me and was breathtakingly stunning—bright blue eyes that were almost as vibrant as Declan's emerald ones. She had one of those ridiculously contagious smiles that lit up her entire face and made the world seem a little bit brighter.

I didn't miss the way that her hand occasionally touched Declan's arm when she spoke, or the easy smile that she seemed to pull from my friend as she listened.

Declan was rarely relaxed, her grins rare and never easy. Other than when she was with Six, I couldn't remember a time when she seemed to actually be enjoying herself around another person.

There was an openness—a familiarity and excitement—in the way they spoke to each other.

A rock settled in my gut as I realized that she wasn't just enjoying herself—she was flirting.

My jaw clenched, belly tight. A flash of self-loathing went through me as I recognized the feeling.

Jealousy.

I wanted Declan to look at me that way—and because she was really interested, not just because my succubus powers were seducing her in a dream.

Ro cleared his throat and I felt a soft pressure on my arm as he squeezed me tighter. His eyes softened, a flash of recognition that melted into compassion as he met my gaze. "How about we save catching you up on stuff that's been going on here and brainstorming our next step plans for tomorrow morning? I agree with Izzy—I think we could all use an ice cream and Sandra Bullock night after the last few weeks. Especially you."

Any of the anger he'd been wrestling with was nowhere in sight. Suddenly, he was just my brother. Just Ro—the boy who could always recognize what I was feeling before I could. The person who did everything he could to ease whatever frivolous pain I felt.

The world was currently doomed and I was mad about a girl—and he was eager to help me patch up both problems, in whichever order I wanted, judgment free.

I leaned into him and nodded. "You had me at ice cream."

∽

AFTER TWO MORE SHOWERS—BECAUSE damn did they feel glorious—I was tucked into bed, listening to the soft rain against my window. I nearly groaned the minute my head hit the cloud-like pillow. So soft, so luxurious. I was going to need a forklift and the promise of bacon if anyone wanted to move me from this spot in the next twelve hours.

If Lucifer was intending on having me vacation frequently in hell over the next few months, I really hoped he invested in some finer linens. Seriously—prince of darkness and all, he should have some better options for his guests.

The brief image of him having a concierge and welcoming his inmates to a fancy spa brought a smile to my face from the absurdity of it all. How was this my life?

Still, even in the comfort of my room, a soft record lulling me to sleep, I found myself restless.

No one from Six had interacted with me even once since I'd woken up. Not that I expected to be on the top of their priorities or anything, but after everything we'd been through, it seemed strange to fall back into things at The Guild like nothing had happened. Almost like I was living an echo of my former life here—not quite able to dig my feet into this reality quite yet. It felt like half of me was still stuck in hell.

And, if I was being honest with myself, a strange part of me was almost excited to go back. I could feel the heady thrum of my power pulling through my veins with each wave of emotion that came over me. I wasn't sure how much longer I could keep it in check. I needed to learn how to harness and control this shit before I got us all killed.

If Lucifer was my best chance at achieving that control, then so be it. At least he'd been more truthful about who—what—I was than anyone else in my life.

Far more than Cyrus had ever been anyway.

I swallowed back the bitterness. As angry as I was with him,

I still missed him something fierce. It stung that he wasn't even here. That he'd left without a word about where he was going —or why. A habit of his that had only gotten worse in my absence, according to Ro.

A soft tapping echoed through my room and I took a deep breath, settling the rush of panic before hellfire came pouring from my fingers again.

I scanned the dark room until my eyes landed on the window across from my bed.

Declan.

She was perched on the small balcony, barely enough room on it for both of her feet to find purchase. Her hair was plastered against her face in long, thick strings—water trickling down her cheeks like a map of tears.

My breath stuttered. Even drenched she was fucking beautiful.

After a moment, I shook my head, forced myself to focus and slid out from under the covers.

I opened the window. "What are you doing here? Is everything okay? Atlas, Eli?"

She waved a hand, signaling they were fine, before she gracefully climbed into the room and closed the window—the soft thuds of rain dulling when she did.

A light cloud of strawberries engulfed me and I lingered near her for a moment, soaking it in, before I cleared my throat and stepped away. Could I be addicted to the smell of her shampoo? More and more, it was looking possible that I was.

"Ten's cabin has a door, you know? You could have knocked." I tried to brush off my nerves with a joke, but judging from the awkward, croaky tone of my voice, it didn't work.

She tilted her head to the side, legitimate surprise in her expression, like she hadn't thought of that. Then, she kicked off her boots, peeled off her wet jacket, and rang her hair out with the fluffy white towel hanging on my chair.

The idea that my towel would smell like her sent a sharp thrill through my spine that I did my best to ignore.

"I don't really want anyone to know I'm here. Every step we take is being monitored. I don't trust anyone right now—only Six, only us."

Her eyes met mine, hard with determination, and my stomach fluttered at the realization that she included me with her team.

I bit my cheek, nodding. "Okay, that makes sense. Can I—can I get you anything? Water or something?"

It felt strange, playing host to a girl who'd climbed into my bedroom through the window.

In a weird way, I didn't know how to interact with Guild Declan. She seemed so at odds with the girl I'd come to know after the last few weeks—like two completely different versions of herself, split in half. And I still didn't know where I stood with her, not really.

She arched her brow, a small grin lifting the right side of her lips. "I'm okay." Her gaze dropped down briefly, studying me as I sat on my bed. I flushed when I realized that I was wearing nothing but a tank top and a pair of lacy underwear. The last encounter I'd had while alone with her suddenly the only thing that I could think about. "I didn't wake you did I?"

I shook my head. "Couldn't sleep." I gestured to my bed. "You can sit, if you want."

"I'm soaked."

"I don't care."

She considered for a moment, and then climbed onto the bed, leaning back so that her head fell on my pillow.

She let out a low groan. "God, I'm never taking a bed for granted ever again."

I grunted in response, lost for words as I studied the gentle rise and fall of her chest. Her arms were pebbled with goose bumps from the chill outside, and I had to force myself not to rub my hands over them to warm her.

For a long moment she stared at the ceiling in silence. "I couldn't sleep either. It's weird being back here. Almost like I'm here but not really. Does that make sense?"

Her eyes drifted down to mine briefly before going back to the ceiling.

"Exactly," I said, leaning back onto my other pillow, my arm a mere inch or two from where hers rested. Being around her felt like a brewing magnetic charge, like even the soft hairs on my arm were stretching to reach her.

Suddenly my blood felt like it was pumping hard and thick through my veins. I took a deep breath, but that only made my stomach tighten more—the rain water making the smell of her shampoo more prominent than usual.

"Things are bad," she continued, her voice low, accent lilting softly, almost melancholic. I wondered what it would be like to listen to that voice every night as I drifted off to sleep. "Worse than I could've imagined. Even after all that we know now—all that we've learned, been forced to question."

That was enough to shove my annoying crush to the back of my brain where the clusterfuck box lived. For now, anyway. "What do you mean?"

Izzy and Ro had filled me in on some things in the brief intermission between While You Were Sleeping and Practical Magic, but I knew that they were still new to the field team, that they weren't given much detail about what was going on. Still, even they knew that things were bad—attacks happening daily all around the world. The entire Guild network was on high alert—protectors from all over the world coming and going at all times.

"I just spoke with Atlas and Eli—" she closed her eyes, like suddenly the blankness of the ceiling was too much for her, "I think it's beyond just the regular lies we've discovered, beyond the uptick in attacks. There are factions and they're all fighting each other."

"Factions of demons, you mean?" Lucifer and Darius had both hinted at such things.

She shook her head once, paused, then nodded. "Yes but more than that. Factions of protectors. Things are breaking here, cracking. It feels like—like all my life I've only ever seen the tip of the iceberg. I'm only now getting a glimpse at what's below the surface. It's haunting." She let out a low laugh. "I hate that fucking metaphor, but that's the best way that I can describe it, you know? Almost like my entire life has been dedicated to a lie."

Factions of protectors? The idea sent my thoughts swimming. "Have there always been factions—or is that new?"

She turned her head, eyes opening and meeting mine. "I think always. Seamus mentioned something about a resistance to Eli earlier. One that's always been there, but has been growing in numbers and strength through the years. The Guild is not as united as we thought."

"Why did Seamus tell him this? Why now—when we're all in the metaphorical dog house?"

"He covered for us—he and Cyrus. It's why we're all walking around, almost like things are normal—to an extent. It's why our punishments and repercussions are far less than what they should be. I think Alleva and Tarren—" she grunted, "probably everyone, really, knows that it's bullshit. Knows that we weren't given special permissions and clearance to leave like we did, accompanied by a vampire."

"Why would they cover for us like that?"

Declan's brow arched. I tried desperately not to stare at her full lips—only a few inches from mine—as she continued. "Isn't it obvious? Max—what we did—there's no coming back from something like that. Not with The Guild. Seamus is pissed—more than I've ever seen him. And he's monitoring our every move, punishing us where he can, pulling us off some of the bigger missions, reigning us in. But Eli is still his son. And he's smart enough to know that if he didn't cover, didn't say that we acted on orders, that we'd all be kicked out. Or worse."

"Worse?"

She shrugged. "I don't know anymore. I want to say we wouldn't be killed. That we'd be booted or demoted or something a little less...final. But I don't know anymore, don't know what to think. Iceberg, remember? It's all new, all unpredictable."

"They know something," I said suddenly, my anger with Cyrus rising again—anger that he wasn't here, that he'd spent my lifetime hiding things from me. "Cyrus. Seamus. I know they do. Something they're not telling us."

Declan stared at me, considering my words. I watched her face soften, likely because my own anger was starting to burst at the seams. Her arm brushed against mine—the touch so light I wasn't sure if it was intentional or not. There was a strange intimacy that settled over us—side by side, in the cover of darkness—just as it had back in that hotel room. It felt like years ago since she'd spilled some of her past to me, not weeks. "I think you're right. But whatever it is, it's clear they want us involved as little as possible. Probably trying to protect us. They have no idea what we've seen though. What we've been through."

"I'm so sick of this," I muttered, my voice watery as I tried to swallow the frustration building in me, to bury it back, where the box of clusterfucks was fit to burst. "I'm so fucking sick of the lies. I can't trust anyone anymore. Everyone is either hiding shit from me or using me. And now I'm like a damn ticking time bomb, just waiting to go off—only I have no idea who has control of the switch. I just know that it isn't me."

Declan flinched, like I'd slapped her, then she pulled back

until there were a few inches of space between us. It felt like a canyon.

"That's fair," she said, eyes not quite meeting mine. "I can understand why you feel that way."

"Can you?" I asked, my voice louder than I'd intended. "Because you're one of those people, Declan. You all are. You've all kept something from me. Lied to me."

She took a deep breath and nodded, her eyes finally meeting mine again, unreadable but full. "That's fair. We did lie to you. We did keep things from you. And we did push you away."

I started to speak, to argue, but whatever was at the tip of my tongue melted away. I'd expected her to deny it, to continue pretending, to continue lying.

"Why?" I asked, the word cracked and hoarse as my vision clouded over. "Why does everyone do that?" My voice lowered into a whisper, like my throat refused to fully form the question buried deep in my chest. "What did I do wrong?"

It felt like a childish thing to say, a silly thing to ask—but I felt it so deep that the question almost knocked the wind out of me as I asked it.

All my life I'd just wanted to belong somewhere—anywhere. I'd been abandoned as a child, raised by a man I thought cared for me, only to learn that he'd been keeping things from me my entire life. I came to The Guild, expecting to find community, my place in the world—only for that to crumble just out of my reach too.

And then there was Six.

I'd felt such a strong draw to them—a certain sort of rightness whenever they were around. Their presence made my skin buzz, every atom in my body bouncing with a sort of aliveness that I'd never experienced before.

But they'd made it clear from the beginning that I didn't fit with them either. It was a constant push and pull. They'd let me close, only to shove me back again. It was giving me whiplash. And Eli—he'd fucking used me, bent me into a million pieces, made me feel more alive than anyone had before, and then wrung me out and left me to dry. I was a tool to him, to all of them, a mission. Now, I'd turned into a problem —one they were forced to help solve.

Declan reached a hand forward, hesitated for a moment, and then gently cupped my cheek, tilting my head up so that my eyes met hers, even though all I could make out through my tears was the rough outline of her shape, the soft contours and dips.

My breath stuttered at her nearness. Even with the anger coursing through my body, I still felt it come alive under her touch, like an electric current.

"I'm sorry," she said, her voice strained with an emotion I'd never heard pulled from her. "I'm so fucking sorry, Max."

She pulled her hand away, my skin cold from the sudden lack, before she leaned back, focusing on the ceiling again as she turned into herself.

I fought the competing desires to drag her back to me and force her away—my own tumultuous push and pull.

"I regret handling things the way that we did—all of it. We shouldn't have lied to you—not for as long as we did." She sighed, tilted her head further into the pillow, like she wanted to sink into it. "At first, it made sense. Something felt... off about you. We all felt it—all tried to ignore it. At first." She paused, a soft smile pulling at her features. "Except for Wade. He never questioned it, never thought twice about embracing it. And when Seamus and Cyrus ordered us to keep our eyes on you—of course we agreed. Mostly because following orders is our job—it's what we've been trained to do. We've never questioned things, never looked too closely at things we weren't supposed to. But partially, I think, because it was an excuse to be near you, to figure out whatever the hell it was about you that didn't make sense to us, that drew us to you like moths to a flame."

I studied her in the darkness, drinking in every word like a drowning man in the desert, my pulse quickening at the idea that they felt the same strange draw that I did. All of them. Was that just the dormant succubus powers, or was it something else? Something deeper?

She ran her hands over her face, the cool, confident composure I was so used to when I saw her disintegrating in the way that I'd only seen it do a few times since meeting her. It was hard to imagine Declan looking even more beautiful than she normally did, but in these moments—when I could see brief glimpses of the parts of herself that she tried so desperately to hide—she was so fucking beautiful it almost hurt to look at her.

"Look, I can't make excuses for the others, and I don't want to make excuses for myself either. Just, Max," she turned towards me again, her head inching forward slightly, closing some of the distance she'd created between us, "just know that I won't betray you like that. Not now. Not again. You're one of us and I'm sorry that we hurt you." She let out a shaky breath that cooled the skin on my cheek. "I'm sorry that *I* hurt you. I'll do whatever it takes to earn your trust back, to make you understand that you matter to us. To me. Things are different now and I promise that I won't keep anything important from you again, not like that."

There was a vulnerability in her expression that I hadn't seen before, her eyes wide, questioning. I could see that this was difficult for her, this openness, and it made my stomach twist even more to know that she was doing it anyway—for me. Because I needed to hear these things.

Maybe it was because I was naive, maybe I just wanted so badly to repair the damage that had been done, to get closer to her, to fold myself into the buzz I got whenever she was around —but I believed her.

I nodded, my chest too tight with unshed emotion to say anything. The small movement brought me closer to her, until her face was only a hair's breadth from mine. Close enough that I could see the dark flecks of green that mixed with light, even in the darkness of my room. In that moment, I wanted nothing more than to thread my fingers through her hair, press my thigh between hers, and fuse our bodies together until the ache low in my belly turned into something else.

We hadn't spoken about the dream—about what had happened between us. And my thoughts drifted briefly to that girl with lavender hair, who Declan existed so easily next to, when every moment with me seemed like a struggle. I wanted to ask, wanted to know if she thought about the feel of my lips against hers, like I did—constantly—if she wanted to taste mine in real-life the way that I was desperate to taste hers.

Most importantly I wanted to know if it was all a fabrication —nothing but the thrall of a dreamscape and the nascent succubus powers that I didn't yet know how to control.

But I couldn't bring myself to ask the questions on the tip of my tongue, because I was terrified of the answers.

I didn't have the courage that she did tonight, didn't have the strength to crack myself open again and spill onto her.

I watched her eyes move between mine, unable to even breathe with her nearness and the heavy desire settling over me. Something flashed briefly on her face, curiosity maybe, or fear.

Her lips parted slowly, the movement mesmerizing.

I licked my own.

Maybe—maybe we didn't need words.

I leaned towards her until there was nothing but a small seam of air between us, my heart beating so furiously I was certain she could hear it in the heavy silence.

A knock pounded at the door, shattering the moment, and we pulled apart like repellant magnets.

"Max!"

Izzy.

I took a deep breath, sat up, and cleared my throat. "Come in."

My voice was shaky, higher than I remembered it, my lips electric with disappointment over what they almost just had.

I felt Declan shift further away, and stand from the bed.

The door swung open.

"I'm fucking raging—" Izzy paused, her eyes landing on Declan and widening with guilt. "Oh—er—am I interrupting something?"

"No."

"No."

We'd spoken at the same time, the haste enough to make it abundantly clear that she had.

Izzy scrunched her face in apology. "Er, right. Um, it's just that I thought you'd want to know that we were scheduled to go on an intel mission day after tomorrow, but um—" her focus darted to Declan briefly, mouth drawn in apology, "but apparently Eli talked to Seamus and Alleva and got them to bench you. Something about insubordination or something. I think he's trying to pull you from our team altogether now—to demote you or something."

A heavy silence enveloped the room as my stomach flipped —the anger that had slowly started to dissipate back with a vengeance.

Izzy's brows tilted together. "Um, you're on fire again."

"Fuck," I muttered, closing my eyes and focusing on the familiar tingling sensation until I drew it back into me. I turned towards Declan. "Did you know about this?"

She raised her hands, shook her head. "Max, I swear I had no idea." She walked towards the window, before looking back briefly. "I promise I'll find out though."

Izzy watched in silence while she disappeared into the

night again. "She knows we have a door right? Or does she just fancy herself as Catwoman or something?" She shrugged, pursing her lips. "Kinda hot though, not going to lie."

I spun towards her, eyes narrowed and jaw still clenched from the news.

She raised her hands, mimicking Declan from a moment ago. "Don't look at me that way. Save that rage for Eli Bentley."

Oh, I planned on it.

10

MAX

I took a deep, steadying breath as I stood outside the gym. I still felt like a prisoner, waiting to get discovered and dragged back to a cell.

Jumping back into the fray by myself wasn't exactly the goal, but I wasn't really sure what to do, where to start. I needed to find Six and start concocting a plan with them.

I'd slept like the dead, my body unwilling to give up the glory that was a pillow and duvet. Ro had left a note taped to my door that he and Ten had an early meeting about their upcoming mission and that I should relax.

The only problem? Relaxing when I knew that the entire world might end shortly was damn near impossible. Especially when alone. When I was alone, all I was left with was that damn box of misery at the back of my mind and I abso-fucking-lutely did not want to unpack that right now.

I shoved open the heavy doors and the creaky hinges echoed around the empty floorplan. Normally, it wouldn't be enough of a noise to draw anyone's focus, not during training, but everyone was on high alert. I felt dozens of eyes pull in my direction, the dull thuds of landed kicks and hits falling from a heavy thunder to a light drizzle.

Making a grand entrance wasn't exactly my plan, but here we were.

My eyes instantly were drawn to a pair of familiar dark brown ones.

Atlas.

And not just Atlas—Atlas dressed in nothing but a pair of black shorts, his torso corded with lean muscles and covered in a slick sweat.

His eyes widened slightly when he saw me before they instantly turned away. Back to avoiding me then. Great.

I walked towards him anyway, unsure what else I was supposed to do. Eli had me benched from Ten and no one had given me instructions for today, everyone expecting me to stay in bed and waste away, apparently.

None of the students and team members even bothered to pretend they weren't gawking as I traipsed through, a realization that made me hyper aware of every move and sound I made, like I was the star of a show I didn't want to be in.

There was a man standing next to Atlas, his posture rigid and stern, like he was auditioning to be a drill sergeant. His face was angular, nose slightly hooked, a glowering expression that was cruel enough to leave a sting.

Strangely, it was directed at me.

"Er," I cleared my throat, and glanced at Atlas, widening my eyes in hope that he could read through my subtext and confusion without me saying anything. "Hi. I wasn't really sure where to go or what to do this morning."

The man let out a low grunt and Atlas balled his hand briefly into a fist before loosening it and stretching out his fingers.

"How is that my son's problem?" The man took a step towards me in that way that men had of trying to intimidate women by taking up as much space as possible. Towering and menacing with bulk and a glare. Without looking away from me, he said, "what are you all waiting for? Get back to work."

His voice was low, but the severity of it carried throughout the room and I heard the familiar squeaks and thuds of shoes on mats pick up in volume.

"Son?"

So this was the infamous Tarren.

I glanced between the two of them, trying not to be obvious about the comparisons running through my mind, but unable to stop from cataloging them all the same.

Atlas wasn't as bulky as his father, nor as fair, but they both had an invisible way of taking command of a room, the energy unmistakable. The glower I'd clocked was also familiar—which was perhaps why I didn't find Tarren as intimidating as he so clearly intended for me to.

His son had been giving me that angry scowl since the moment I'd met him. The fear it initially inspired wore off after a while. Especially after seeing Atlas in his darker moments. Especially after getting railed by him against a dungeon wall.

"Look," I was not going to let this man intimidate me, especially not after I'd just spent who knew how long locked up in the Devil's prison. Tarren was small-time in comparison, no matter how much of a dick he was. "Cyrus isn't here, I haven't come across Seamus or Alleva since I woke up, and I got benched from my current team. I'm not exactly sure what I'm supposed to do." I turned away from Tarren, ignoring the strangeness of seeing Wade's warm, comforting eyes looking so menacing, and glanced up at Atlas. "I just, I hadn't spoken to you since we arrived and I wasn't sure where things stood."

I cringed as soon as those words left my lips, hearing the double meaning just as acutely as I felt it. I didn't know where a lot of things stood between us, not just my place here.

Atlas had slowly been shifting closer to me during the interaction, but where Tarren did so in a prickish sort of way, it almost felt like Atlas was drifting towards me out of protectiveness. As if only just realizing that we were less than a foot apart, he took a wide step back, clearing his throat and dropping eye contact.

"Again," Tarren said, glancing between the two of us, eyes narrowed, "not sure how that's my son's problem."

Okay then. Best way to knock down a douche canoe? Kill 'em with kindness.

I took a deep breath, swallowed my frustration, and stretched my hand forward. "Hi. I think we got off on the wrong foot. I've heard a lot about you, your reputation is quite," I paused a beat, searching for a word that wasn't a complete lie, "impressive. My name is Max Bentley. I'm kind of new here and to this world. Seamus and Cy had me working with Six—"

He raised a hand stopping me. "I know who you are. And while your reputation also precedes you, I am decidedly underwhelmed by it. The Guild is a protected, honored organization. We take it seriously here. I don't take kindly to young, thoughtless girls, coming in and disrespecting it. I don't care who you're related to, or who put my son—however briefly—in charge of babysitting." He crossed his arms over his chest and I bit my tongue so hard I was surprised it didn't start bleeding through my teeth. "You may not have realized it while you've been causing trouble, but things are serious here. My son has more important things to do than look after a girl with a weak constitution and a slimy desire to attach herself to important people around here."

Maybe some douche canoes were impervious to kindness. Meeting Tarren—well—Atlas and his penchant for grumpiness made a lot more sense.

I glanced at the lesser evil of the two and noticed a small thread of gold line the rim of his eyes. Fuck.

"I uh—" I started, trying to keep Tarren's focus on me while

Atlas got his shit under control, "can assure you I don't have a desire to attach myself to your son or anyone else. I was just looking for an assignment. If you want me out of your hair, please convince Seamus to grant me clearance to join Ten's mission and I'll happily do so."

His nose flared briefly, like he was sucking in more anger to power his vitriol. "I don't do your bidding, girl. If you're without a team or prospects of joining one, perhaps that says more than words can."

A dull weight fell on my shoulder and squeezed.

Eli pulled me towards him until our sides were fused together, his signature snark on full display and directed towards the older man. The two of them locked into a silent battle, loaded with a history I didn't really understand. Not for the first time, I realized how much I didn't know about the people and relationships here. Part of the problem with joining the program late meant that I had to slowly piece together a puzzle, only I had no sample image on the box to go off of. Instead, I had to gobble up tiny hints and details where I could pick them up and hope that, eventually, I'd get a picture that made sense.

Like, for instance, the fact that Eli and Tarren clearly had a history, and not a loving one.

"Ah, glad I found you, Max," Eli said, though his eyes never left Tarren's. "Seems there's been a misunderstanding here. I've spoken to my father," Tarren's scowl deepened at that, "and Max is to be under his watch and mine until Cyrus is back and we're told otherwise."

Even though I knew that statement made me sound like a child, the butterflies in my stomach didn't care. This was the closest I'd physically been to Eli and something about him standing up to Tarren sent a small thrill through my bones.

That thrill almost immediately melted away though when my brain caught up to my hormones and reminded me that the entire reason I was put in a metaphorical time out was because Eli decided to get me pulled from Ten. So yeah, maybe not quite a knight in shining armor.

"Well I'm glad that your father has found a use for you. I know he's been rather—aimless these last few weeks. Perhaps it's time he steps down from the heavier tasks and tends to monitoring you and his niece instead. Maybe then my son will have the clarity of focus needed to get things done."

I heard Eli's teeth grind as his fingers bit into my shoulder. Still, he said nothing, just gave Tarren a tight grin, never once averting his eyes.

"Father, is this animosity really necessary?" Atlas had been so quiet that I'd almost forgotten he was there. I was so used to him being such an imposing presence, that the image of him shrinking when next to his father threw me off in a strange way.

I wanted to dig, to understand the odd dynamics of their relationship.

Tarren's face relaxed into a large, exaggerated grin that made him look more feral than Atlas's wolf. "Animosity? Nonsense. Just making sure that we all understand the lay of the land. The stakes are high and I don't want you distracted, not now." His head tilted as he studied his son. "Now, unless you have a problem with letting Eli deal with this distraction, let's get back to your training, yes?"

Atlas's jaw ticked as his gaze dropped briefly to mine then away, like looking at me was painful to him. "No problem. You're right. I could do without any added distractions right now."

I did my best to school my expression, but the sting from his words hit hard all the same.

Tarren nodded, slapping his hand on Atlas's back. "Good, Reza could do with more one-on-one training with you. Seamus has gone too easy on these recruits, I want her so familiar with your techniques that the two of you move like one. Understood?"

As if the mere mention of her had summoned her to him, Reza walked up to Tarren.

"Apologies for missing the first two hours of training, sir," her piercing, blue eyes landed on mine, her brow subtly arching with smug victory. She'd clearly been eavesdropping and was more than pleased with the fact that Tarren liked me about as much as she did. "I was moving things back to my room in Six's cabin and meeting with my mother. I'm very eager to make up for the missed time now."

Tarren relaxed, his face contorting into what I imagined was what passed for an affectionate grin for him. "Not at all, I'm sure Atlas is just as keen. I'm glad to hear you're prepared to put the work in."

Reza was Headmistress Alleva's daughter and she'd decided that she hated me almost the very second that she met me. Worse was the fact that she'd taken over my very brief time as part of Six's team. The room that Sarah left now belonged to her.

"Reza, good to see you," I said, determined to keep trying the kindness thing even if it failed miserably on Tarren. I chanced a quick look at Atlas out of the corner of my eye, trying to read his take on things but, as was often the case, his expression was impenetrable.

I wasn't sure why I thought having sex with him would change his constant hot and cold persona, but I'd be lying if I didn't admit that it hurt regardless.

Reza turned her head up slightly and gave me a curt nod. Where Atlas was difficult to read, her thoughts were clear as day—her fury with me radiated out of every pore, but she refused to give into it in front of Tarren. She was determined to bond with Atlas, so I wasn't surprised that she wanted to continue making a good impression—a strategy I clearly failed at.

"Enough standing around." Tarren clapped his hands and nodded amicably towards Reza and Atlas before swiftly turning his back on me and Eli, and walking away without another glance. Every few steps, I heard him pause beside a sparring match and bark critiques about sloppy technique while making underhanded comments about Seamus and the state of things here.

"Dude makes the devil seem downright jovial, doesn't he?" Eli's eyes danced with mirth as they met mine, the first acknowledgment he'd given me since charging in for my clunky rescue. "Few things are as fun as watching his face turn fifty shades of red. I'm glad there's another one of us to add to the piss-off-Tarren-Andrews- club."

I bit back my own laugh, still pissed as hell at him for getting me in this mess in the first place.

Instead, I ignored him and turned back towards Atlas, expecting him to say or do—something. But like before, he barely even met my eyes. I could almost feel the ice radiating from him.

"Ready?" Reza didn't even bother concealing her delight— Atlas's disinterest in me doing wonders towards alleviating any of her insecurities or fears that I'd be encroaching on her spot with Six.

He nodded and the two walked away, her shoulder practically rubbing against his side, a skip in her step.

I shoved away the gurgling jealousy that had my muscles tensing uncontrollably at the sight of them together like that. I wasn't sure what I expected when we returned, but I sure as hell didn't expect Atlas to go back to his typical asshat self— pretending like I was nothing but an annoying itch on his back.

Not after everything he'd been through in hell.

Not after everything *we'd* been through together.

Now Reza was moving back in, comforting herself in the familiar normalcy of it all. Having her around would make it exceedingly more difficult to plan how we were going to handle, well, everything.

"Let's go. Better not to draw any more attention to ourselves than we already have." Eli's finger brushed against my elbow, guiding me towards a mat at the back of the room, as far from everyone as he could get us. For that, I was grateful.

He peeled off his t-shirt and I tried not to let my eyes linger on every inch of his skin exposed.

Instead, I focused on the ground as I dropped my bag with a dull thud and made my way to the center of the mat.

"Ready?" he asked.

Ignoring proper etiquette, I lunged towards him, sweeping his feet with my leg and ramming my hands into his chest. It was sloppy, and if Cy was here, he'd have a world of complaints to fling at me for such bad form—both in terms of sportsmanship and efficacy.

But bad form or not, Eli landed flat on his ass, reacting quickly enough to pull me down on top of him.

"Jesus, Max, what was that for?" His breath blew a few stray hairs from my cheek.

I did everything I could not to focus on the way his fingers gripped my hips, the heat generated by his nearness. We were touching almost everywhere.

"You pulled me off Ten," I said, voice a low whisper so as not to draw any unwanted ears our way. "You made me sound like a child—blamed everything on me. What the hell were you thinking? Did you expect me to greet you with a smile and a hug?"

He sighed, his eyes softening briefly before the typical Eli-mask was back in place, the signature smirk noticeably absent. "You heard about that?"

"Of course I heard about that." I shoved myself off of him

and stood, offering him a hand out of habit, which he took to pull himself up. "You made me seem like a petulant child."

He raised a brow, hand pointing to where we'd just been tangled on the mat. "Because this was the epitome of adultlike behavior?"

I lined back up, this time waiting for him to give me the signal that he was ready. When he did, I danced in a half circle around him, bouncing on the balls of my feet—waiting to strike. "Now I'm going to be under even tougher scrutiny than before," I swung with my right fist, but he dodged, "which is going to make finding what I need to find almost impossible."

He attacked next, but I was faster than he was—even more so now that I was part demon—and dodged without a problem, landing a strike of my own in the process.

He grunted. "I needed to do something," he swung again, missed, "say something—to make sure we'd have you under our purview. I thought that was obvious?"

"I'm benched from missions." My voice was little more than a growl. "My brother, Izzy, they're going to be out there now without me."

The steady hum of thuds and gasps around us was a suitable soundtrack to the anger boiling in my gut. With a quick scan of the room, I noticed that Tarren was on the opposite side of the gym, his all too familiar eyes meeting mine briefly. They were filled with contempt.

On the mat beside him, I found Declan. Like Atlas, she was caked in a layer of sweat, so she'd been here long before I arrived. She was sparring with the girl from yesterday, her lavender hair wrapped up in a low bun. There was a playfulness to their movements that was impossible not to see. It kind of reminded me of the way that Declan looked when she sparred with Atlas—like they'd been doing it their whole lives.

Who was this girl? Why had I never seen her before?

The distraction cost me a few precious seconds, and Eli

landed an easy hit to my side. I tried to counter it, but it was too late, my movements reactionary and slow.

I swung again, but he was prepared for the maneuver and grabbed my arm, twisting until my back landed with a soft smack against his chest. His arm tightened around me, his voice little more than a whisper that I felt against my ear more than I heard. "Max. You're smart. Think. We can't let you out on missions without us. We have to keep you safe, protect you. You're literally being hunted—and for all we know, by both demons *and* protectors at this point. I gave everyone here a reason to believe that we need to be around you, that we need to keep an eye on you."

"You and everyone else," I snapped, using my little wiggle room to elbow him in the gut and flip him back to the ground.

Once again, he pulled me down with him. "You're just mad that it was me, that I was the one to do it, that I'm the one my father put in charge of keeping an eye on you. It's a more tangible reason for you to be pissed off at me than the real one."

He rolled over so that he was on top of me, pinning my hands to my chest.

I ignored the gibe, but could feel my body blushing at the reminder against my will. This wasn't the time or the place to have that particular conversation with Eli.

"I'm not even on your team," I said, his nose lingering just a few inches from mine. The weight of his body leaning against mine was making it hard to think, like my body was ready to forgive and forget everything he'd done way sooner than my mind was. "Reza is. She's another complication we're going to have to deal with. We can't speak freely in front of her, obviously, and she's stuck to Atlas right now like a damn fridge magnet—and one of the annoying ones that you have to dig your nails under to get it to release."

"Don't worry about Reza, we'll work around her. Just worry

about staying out of trouble when we're not around to help you get out of it. With Tarren and some of the other more elite Guild members here, things are very, *very* risky. And none of us are in the good standing that we were a few weeks ago. Not even Atlas—not even with his father blaming the whole thing on every other member of Six but him."

My fingers bit into my palms. "Do you expect me to just sit by myself in Ten's cabin watching movies for the next week? While everyone else is out fighting—and potentially dying—without me? Ro shouldn't be out there without me. I can protect him in ways that the rest of his team can't. And I can't—" I shook my head, trying to keep the angry tears at bay, "I can't go through that again, Eli. I need to be there for him."

His eyes widened. "Max, calm down. The fire—you're on fire. Take a breath."

I felt the familiar heat before I saw it, my lungs collapsing at the realization of what was happening, of where we were.

With a panicked expression, he lowered his body down, closing the distance between us, half flattening to me as he leaned to the side, blocking us from sight.

"No, don't." I pulled away, afraid of hurting him, but the flames encapsulating my fingers did little more than caress his chest, as if his body was an extension of mine.

Both of our eyes dropped to the fire, where it collided between us, flickering softly as I took deep, steady breaths, until it disappeared altogether.

"Did you—are you okay?" I ran my hands along his chest, expecting to see burns etched into his smooth skin, but his body was just as perfect and untarnished as it had always been.

He nodded, lips parted. Heat flashed in his eyes and I realized that I was basically just groping him on the floor, our legs entwined. Quickly, I pushed myself away and sat up. It felt like my blood was rushing through my veins, a slow and steady ringing filling my ears.

Was this it? Was this the moment that they were all going to realize who, what, I was? After all that we'd been through, all that we still needed to accomplish, was this the silly, reckless end of it all?

But no eyes appeared to be drawn to us, everyone focused and zoned in on their own matches. I searched the room for the person who I was most afraid of seeing me, but Tarren had his back to me as he watched Atlas instruct Reza. He repositioned her legs, and mimed the action he wanted her to take, letting her land a few hits unblocked.

My stomach clenched as her eyes lingered even longer on him than her hands did. Instead I turned and saw Declan.

She looked at me while the lavender-haired girl drew a quick drink from her water bottle. Declan's head tilted in confusion, like she was asking me what was up. There was no concern on her face though, so I was certain that she hadn't seen the little light show—which meant chances were high no one else had either since there weren't any shrieks of terror and no one was coming at me with a pitchfork.

I nodded, signaling I was okay, and her shoulders sank in relief. With a small lift of her lips, she nodded and turned back towards the girl, both of them getting back to their training.

"Fuck," I muttered, my body still jittery from the almost bust. "I don't know what's going on."

Eli studied me, then stood up and held out his hand.

I let him pull me up, ignoring the way my body hummed when his skin met mine. Why was being around them always such a rush? Like electricity was just flooding my veins. It only seemed to be getting worse these days, more intense.

"I guess he was telling the truth. About this at least."

I didn't need him to elaborate on who *he* was. Lucifer. He'd made it abundantly clear that without his help, my powers would soon outgrow my ability to control them.

"But I didn't hurt you. Why doesn't the fire hurt you?"

He arched a brow, the playful smirk back on his lips. "Did you want to hurt me?"

I shot him a flat look, not missing the suggestiveness of the comment. "Obviously not like that."

His playfulness drifted away while he considered, his expression growing darker. "Your powers never hurt me. They only ever heal."

"Yes, but why?"

He ran a frustrated hand through his hair. "I don't know, Max."

But something about the way he said it, made me think that he had an idea.

"Look, right now, let's focus on getting what we need so that we can get you back there before you accidentally blow up a building, okay?" He paused, considering me again. "Not that I think you'll be exactly safe once we arrive there either. You attract danger like no one I've ever seen before. I'd actually be impressed by that if it didn't stress me the fuck out so much."

The latter part was muttered more to himself than to me.

"And where do we start looking for this mysterious magic source? Because so far I haven't experienced any sort of draw while walking through the halls like he mentioned I might."

Eli shrugged. "We start looking for stolen magic in the place that is most heavily guarded and filled with The Guild's deepest secrets."

I let that rain over me for a moment before understanding crept in. "The labs."

He nodded. "The labs."

He got into position, to start another match, but his focus dropped to my hands, like he was afraid I was going to go all candle-hands again.

"Sorry about, you know," I waved my fingers, "that. I'm going to try and keep my emotions in check."

The expression in his dark eyes softened. "Look, if it helps

—the mission that Ten's going on tomorrow. It's all for clean-up and intel. It's not combat based, they aren't expected to run into any acute danger. Compared to some of the alternative things field groups are being sent out for right now, that's about the best you can hope for."

Something about the concern in his voice and the way that he looked at me sent a jolt through me. It wasn't the usual lust or nerves I felt in his presence, but something deeper. Eli didn't always make the best choices, but I knew him well enough now to know that he had good intentions.

"Strange," a cold voice washed over me from a few feet away, "how much your sparring looks nothing at all like sparring."

Tarren closed the distance between us, looking equal parts upset and gleeful, like he was mad that we weren't training, but pleased that he had the opportunity to catch and yell at us.

"If I didn't know better, I'd say your babysitter needs a babysitter."

I was stunned, again, at how unsettling it was to see Wade's eyes looking at me with such sharp hatred.

"Just a quick break, sir," I said, straightening my spine. It made me taste metal to suck up to this man, but I knew that it was the best chance I had of skating under his radar. "We're getting back to it."

He grunted. "It's no wonder my son finds himself in such precarious positions. I should've done more to ensure he was friends with the right people. Those who abide best by our laws, by our ways."

Eli tensed next to me, the look on his face such a pure, controlled anger that I thought he might be the one to light up on fire.

With a satisfied grin, Tarren continued his lazy perusal of the rest of the gym.

"Tonight," Eli said, jaw clenched almost as tightly as his fists, "I'll pick you up tonight and we'll go down to the labs."

"I can't believe I'm not allowed to go." Izzy threw herself dramatically on the couch while she sipped her milkshake. "I mean, did you not promise to include us, whenever it was possible, just yesterday?" She lifted her head and stared at Ro. "Was I dreaming that or did she agree?"

"She definitely agreed," he said, face splitting with a small grin.

"Yeah, well, I don't get to join you both tomorrow, so consider it fair game." I shoved Izzy's feet down so that I had a spot to sit. "Besides, it would look a bit ridiculous to have us all traipsing down to the labs with Eli. Just the two of us, we have a better chance at getting in and out as fast as possible."

She made a sound that could only be described as a giggle.

"What?" I asked, though I had a feeling I knew where her thoughts were heading.

She shrugged. "It's just that," she took another long pull of her shake. I was suddenly angry that I hadn't grabbed one too. The answer should always be yes when it came to milkshakes. "Maybe there's more than one reason you want to ride solo with Eli tonight is all. Unfinished business, a chance to make use of one of those empty rooms in the lab," she wiggled her brows, "I don't judge."

"Jesus," Ro muttered as he rubbed his forehead like he was trying to unhear what she'd just said. "Sometimes I think you forget that I'm her brother."

"That part is just a fun bonus for me," she answered.

He laughed before standing up. "I'm going to go grab some food. I've had enough girl talk to last me the night, I think."

Izzy frowned as he walked away. "Is there such a thing as

enough girl talk?" She turned to me. "I've never heard of such a thing. Especially not when your best girl friend ditches you for weeks to hang out with a team of moody protectors and demons in hell."

"Eli's an ass," I said, ignoring the jab. I leaned my head back against the couch and stared at the popcorn ceiling. He'd spied on me, stolen a piece of my hair while making out with me, and slept with me knowing full well that he was keeping my powers a secret from me. Half the time I still wasn't sure if he wanted to help me or turn me in. It was a betrayal that still made my chest tighten when I thought about it. "In some ways, he's even worse than Atlas, which is really saying something. I can absolutely confirm we will be doing nothing but hunting around for some magical element like a couple of Lara Croft wannabees."

Her face grew serious, some of the humor dulling in her gray eyes as she studied me. "I'm one hundred percent not making excuses for him, but Eli's got a complicated past."

"I know, but—" She shoved her straw into my mouth when I opened it to argue.

"Look, just listen to me for a second. All I'm saying is that everyone here has a past, from long before you came to The Guild. Our childhoods are difficult and for most protectors, those pasts can be pretty dark and complicated. And, well, you have to realize, Max—you're drawn to a group of people who have been through more than most—they've spent years pushing everyone far, far away. They have walls for their walls. No one gets in, not even close." She grabbed my hand, her lips lifting into a ghost of a smile. "Except for you. But with that comes resistance. Trauma, anger, fear—those things don't just disappear when we want them to. In our world, caring about someone is dangerous—it's painful. More painful, I imagine, than death. Those are hard habits to break, hard wounds to close in a few short weeks."

I took another sip of her milkshake—chocolate banana—

and let her words settle over me. It was a rare thing, Izzy going for serious and heartfelt instead of her usual sass. "So you're saying I should just forgive him? Trust him, no questions asked?"

She tilted her head, gave me that don't-be-daft look of hers. "Of course not. I'm just saying, don't write him off completely. As wishy-washy as he's been, he clearly cares—as much as he's capable of right now. Maybe just try to meet him where he's at. Eli's EQ could absolutely use some improving, don't get me wrong. Like, massive amounts of improving. But while he and the rest of them figure out whether or not to rise to the occasion, I just want you to keep in mind that protectors push people away—it's what we're best at. And since finding out what you are capable of, they haven't run scared. That's got to count for something, right?"

I scrunched up my nose, hating that she was right. My life before moving here was uneventful. The most exciting it ever really got was when one of us accidentally broke something during a sparring match or when I got lost in the woods during a failed tracking exercise. Cy never put us through the kind of trauma young protectors on campus experienced. He'd always done his best to teach us, protect us, and show that he cared as much as was possible for him—even though he had his own quiet baggage to sift through.

The protectors here, their lives were filled with constant loss or the expectation that it would come just around the corner. That had to leave some marks when it came to relationship building.

I studied Izzy. She'd thrown her legs lazily across my lap so that she was fully lying down. What had her life been like before me? We rarely discussed our pasts—I knew that, for me, it was because mine wasn't all that eventful. But why was she so quiet about hers?

"*You* haven't pushed me away," I challenged.

She grabbed her milkshake from me and took a long, slow pull, frowning when it made that gurgling, crackling sound that signaled the bottom of the cup. "I'm a bit of a special case. We can't all be this awesome and evolved, you know. Life would be boring." She paused for a moment, considering. "Plus, I think I saw myself in you a little bit. The same quiet loneliness, the same craving for family, for home."

I reached for her hand and squeezed, her soft grin mirroring my own. Other than Ro, I'd never really had a friend before. If I knew that people like Izzy existed, I'd have begged Cy to let us join The Guild years ago. Even with all the dubious mystery behind the organization. If nothing else good came from my time here, Izzy's friendship was enough.

"Yeah, well, enough of that sap." Izzy sat up and swung her legs until her feet reached the ground.

As if the conversational transition was just for them, the door opened and ushered in two members of Ten—Sharla and Jer.

I hadn't seen too much of either of them since my return. Izzy and Ro had been occupying every spare moment that hadn't been consumed by training.

"Oooh, milkshakes," Sharla squealed as she reached for Izzy's cup, frowning when she felt the featherlight weight. "Damn, I'm too late. What are you guys getting up to tonight? We have some last minute things to go over for tomorrow, but maybe we join in on a movie marathon after?"

Her bright smile landed on me, a flash of insecurity in her blue eyes, like she expected me to say no. Sharla was incredibly sweet. And before I'd left, I'd been fast on my way towards considering her a good friend.

But she'd had an ongoing, casual fling with Eli, and I didn't know how to navigate conversations with her now that me and Eli had also been intimate. I'd been a bit standoffish with her since returning, and that wasn't fair. I needed to own some of that emotional maturity Izzy was just going on about and talk to her about what happened—clear the air.

The thought sent a bolt of dread through my belly.

"I've got some plans tonight, but how about we rain check for when you all get back in one piece from your mission?" I offered. At her warm smile and nod, I stood up, suddenly feeling guilty that I'd made her feel even a little bit uncomfortable with my coldness. "Also, there's some ice cream in the freezer and I'm thinking about making my own milkshake. You in?"

"Always," she said, and turned to make her way towards the kitchen.

"Can I get in on that, too?" Jer asked as I followed her.

I tried to swallow my surprise. He'd been unusually quiet since I'd moved back in and had generally made any excuse possible to leave the room when I entered.

"Of course."

A loud knock sounded and Sharla stopped in her tracks. "We expecting anyone?"

Jer pulled open the door and his shoulders dropped slightly at the sight of Eli standing there, his dark hair curling against his forehead and covered in specks of white from the light snowy rain.

"Hey," he announced as he scanned the room, "looks like the gang's all here."

"You here to see Sharla?" Jer asked, his voice sounding almost hopeful as his eyes briefly met mine.

"We didn't have plans, did we?" she asked, walking towards him in the room, her eyes narrowed with confusion but I could tell from the small quirk of her lips that she wasn't disappointed by the surprise. "I've barely seen you since you returned."

A look that could only be described as sheepish crossed his face. I was so used to the cool, snarky confidence that he usually embodied, that I was almost amused by his clear discomfort.

"Oh, er—" Eli glanced at me, back to Sharla, and back to me again as he ran a hand through his hair, cascading the ground with snow flakes that disappeared as soon as they landed. "I'm actually here to take Max." His eyes bugged as the words hung awkwardly in the air around us all. "Not like, *take* her, take her. Just, you know, um—"

Izzy's giggle sounded behind me.

"Extra training tonight. Part of my punishment for insubordination is extra work with Eli, and part of his punishment is babysitting duty," I supplied, more to ease Sharla's discomfort than Eli's.

Jer cleared his throat, his gaze lifting from the ground to my face. "You, ugh, want any other hands on deck to help? I'll have some time and energy for a round or two after we get some final details ironed out."

My stomach sank at the lingering hope plastered on his face. We'd had a conversation, long before I left, that we weren't going to be anything more than friends. But something told me that in my absence, he'd been banking on the chance that my mind might have changed.

It hadn't. If anything, I'd only grown more resolute in the rightness of that decision. I'd felt attraction, deeply, these last few months, but never when I was with Jer.

Sometimes, I wanted nothing more than for all of my complicated feelings towards Six to disappear completely, to feel nothing when I thought about Sharla and Eli together instead of the hollow jealousy I tried desperately to ignore. Maybe then, I could have a calm, nice, normal relationship with someone like Jer. I could bond with someone like him, join Ten's team and actually fit with them in the way they all seemed to fit together. We'd fight monsters and the binary between good and evil would remain intact, unquestioned.

But, deep down, I knew that I didn't really want that. As much as Six drove me wild, I couldn't ignore the spark I felt whenever they were near, my eyes searching for them in every room before my mind could even catch up to the action. They'd all burrowed under my skin, and I wasn't sure there was any getting them out.

"That's okay," I said, smiling in a way that I hoped would be read as kind and friendly, and not suggestive. "We'll be back a bit later. Why don't you guys have those milkshakes without me?"

Jer nodded, his eyes softening a bit as they met mine.

Sharla's head was cocked to the side, her face thoughtful as she studied Eli—after a long consideration, she turned to me, her face cracked into a large grin that reached all the way to her eyes.

When I turned to Eli, he only looked more flustered, haunted even, and it seemed like he was using all of his focus to avoid looking at me.

Whatever passed between them was beyond me.

"Er," I said, the long, awkward pause enough to make my skin feel tight, "should we be off, then?"

Eli cleared his throat and signaled for me to walk out.

With a final glance around the room, I grabbed a jacket and slid into my shoes. "Yeah, let's do that."

"Have fun," Izzy called after us. "But not too much!"

The night air was so cold that I felt it like steel in my teeth with each breath of air I inhaled. I wrapped my arms around myself out of habit, though I didn't feel quite as cold as I usually did. Winter up in the mountains always took some getting used to, but I loved it. Something about the cold and the quiet, the way the white and silver flecks of snow swirled against the night sky, felt like a damn postcard.

Each of the trees were covered in a light dust. It had been a warmer winter this year, the snow rarely collecting above a few inches. Much easier to traipse through with little light to guide us this way.

For the first quarter mile, we didn't speak. I was hyper aware of how close Eli was, his spicy scent surrounding me in a strange warmth as we walked.

I found it impossible to shake the conversation I'd had with Izzy. My brain was torn between wanting to create much-needed distance from Eli—to not trust him or get close—and wanting to grab my metaphorical shovel and dig into him, figure out why he was the way that he was—find out if there was a way in. Neither option seemed easy.

We'd encountered no one on our walk, a rare thing on a campus this large and busy. I had a feeling most students were either getting late-night training sessions in, or catching up on much-needed sleep. The teams were probably all either preparing for or recovering from their latest mission, bunkering down indoors to avoid the chill in the air.

It wasn't even the snow. Since our return, campus felt different—altered somehow. Like even the forest knew that we were on the verge of something terrible. Was this what Darius meant about hell? That it *felt* different upon his return? The magic in the air static, faint but undeniable once you knew to look for it?

The thought of what happened to hell happening to our realm sent a shiver down my spine. I wasn't naive enough to believe that Lucifer was on our side, but I knew in my gut that he was right about what was happening—about the instability of the magic between realms.

After a while, I couldn't bear the silence, the gravity of the situation suddenly all-encompassing.

"Are the others joining us?" My voice was coarse, puncturing the peaceful soundtrack of our walk like a needle in a balloon.

Eli startled, like he'd almost forgotten that I was next to

him, before shaking his head. "Dec is meeting with a friend in town, seeing if she can pick up some leads about what's going on beyond our location. There's murmuring that the different branches of The Guild aren't seeing eye-to-eye. Not with each other and not with the overarching governing bodies, who've been characteristically silent through all of this.

Was she meeting with the lavender-haired girl? I shook my head, trying to cut that thought off before I got even more distracted than I was.

"And Atlas?"

"He was going to try and keep Reza distracted, out of our business for the night, before stopping to check on Sarah and Darius."

"And how are they?" I hated that my heartbeat picked up at the mention of the vampire. I knew that staying inside, obeying orders from a group of protectors, while in enemy territory went against every bone in his body. In stray moments, I'd briefly let myself linger on the heat of my last encounter with him. There was no denying that he'd burrowed under my skin with just as much efficiency as the members of Six had. It was becoming impossible to ignore.

Eli looked at me out of the side of his eye, and for a moment I was certain that he knew exactly where my thoughts had trailed. "They're fine. Both are restless. Neither are the sort to follow orders without grumbling about it. But I think they've kept to their rooms and managed not to kill each other yet, so I think that's the best thing we can hope for. Your vampire seems to have developed a particular penchant for reading young adult vampire novels."

Your.

The thought of Darius being mine sent a charge through my body. I cleared my throat, trying to focus. "I can't imagine that."

"Apparently Declan brought a few paperbacks to him as a

joke, expecting him to scoff or be annoyed. I think she's developing a fondness for intentionally pissing him off—which, for Declan, is really just a fondness. But he's used to being confined, he knows how to wait, how to enjoy the small bits of entertainment that he can find, I think. They didn't have novels for them in the labs. Comparatively, the shitty hotel room must be a first-class vacation to him."

Them—it was a reminder both of where we were going and of the fact that The Guild kept demons like Darius—like me—locked up in cells, as nothing but fodder for their secret experiments.

"Anyway, unfortunately for Sarah, he's been enjoying the process of breaking each story down for her in excruciating detail. Keeps stomping around the hotel simultaneously laughing at everything they've gotten wrong, while using them as evidence that vampires are the most alluring supernatural species in existence." His lips twitched as the image floated between us.

If I didn't know any better, I'd think that Eli was growing almost fond of Darius as well. Maybe I wasn't the only one who no longer saw him as an enemy.

"I'm sure Sarah loves that," I smiled, amused by the idea of them arguing the pros and cons of being a wolf or a vampire.

Eli's face lit up with a true smile—no irony or cynicism in sight. For a moment, things felt easy between us, as they had before hormones and orders went and complicated things.

I felt myself draw closer to him, like his gentle, genuine mirth was a magnet, pulling me in. I took a step back, before I fucked things up between us more than they already were. "Do we, do we have a plan? For tonight, I mean?" I added, biting my bottom lip.

His focus lingered on my mouth for a beat, before he met my eyes. "Not really. Lucey said you'd be drawn to this magic source, wherever it is, which means you're going to be our best bet of finding it. We'll break into the labs, walk around, see if you find anything—if you feel something, or whatever. I'm under strict orders from Atlas not to touch or do anything beyond scope it out and see what we find. Now that we're back, he's sliding back into his usual bossy self."

"Why not? We don't have a lot of time to deal with this."

I hated that they were all meeting and discussing these things without me. It might be petty, but I felt left out—like once we got back to campus, I was discarded as nothing more than a thing to be watched, protected. This was my mission, and I wasn't going to fail it. Wasn't going to let them fail it with their misguided attempts at controlling the situation. The stakes were too high.

He stared at me like I was a goon. "Because we know nothing about it. Once we find it, we'll assess from there. He only asked that we locate it. That's the primary goal right now. That knife of theirs nearly killed me with one strike. There's no way in hell I'm letting you touch it before we know more."

I knew he was right, knew that it was pointless to argue about this particular issue, but I felt my muscles clench regardless. "You think Lucifer really going to be okay with us simply locating it...and then leaving it here? What planet are you living on?"

I watched the muscle in his jaw tick as he took a step closer, his nostrils flaring slightly. "Max, you need to promise me that you won't go near it if and when we find it."

"Or what?" I challenged, my heartbeat picking up again as he took a step towards me.

"Or I'm not going to take you tonight."

"I can always go by myself. I've done it before."

He took another step closer, his eyes boring into mine. "I'll make sure Atlas grounds you for good, we won't include you in any of our plans."

I snorted. "Atlas isn't my father. Neither are you."

"No," his eyes narrowed, his fingers clenched into a fist that was a mere half inch from mine, "your father is much more dangerous. Don't you understand that? This isn't a game, this isn't a power play." He shook his head. "You're not even mad about this, you know we're right. You're mad about—"

The sentence froze in the chilled air between us.

I watched the cloud of his breath fade against my lips, and I suddenly wanted to scream, to push every trace of him out of me. "Go ahead, Eli, finish that sentence. I'm mad about what?"

He studied me.

I watched his pupils dance between my eyes, searching. "I-Max, look. We should tal—"

"Am I interrupting something?"

I turned my head, searching for the owner of the voice, the movement making me realize how very close my mouth was to Eli's.

A man, my age, maybe a bit older, was standing a few feet from us, just off the path towards the Main Hall.

He was cute—dark wavy hair, thick brows, eyes that I couldn't fully determine the color of from this far off, in the cover of night. Like most protectors, he was tall and lean with muscle and something about his posture told me that he'd be a worthy sparring opponent. His lips were thick and full, the top a bit plumper than the bottom. There was something almost familiar about him, though I couldn't put my finger on what.

I felt Eli stiffen next to me, his arm pressing against mine.

"No." He shifted away from me, not breaking eye contact with the man. "We were just on our way in."

"That so?" The man took a step towards us. He cocked his head, dark eyes focused on me like a laser. "Sounded almost like I'd walked in on an argument. A heated one. You sure you're okay?"

Something in the way he said it, made it clear that his question was directed towards me and not Eli.

I nodded, not trusting my voice. My heart raced against my chest. It wasn't against the rules to be out at night on campus, and yet it seemed like we'd been caught red-handed, breaking into the labs already. We'd been careless tonight, letting irrelevant emotions and grudges color our goal.

Like everyone, he was dressed in black. Although he wasn't wearing a jacket suited for the weather, he seemed unaffected, standing there casually in the snow, almost like the temperature didn't affect him the way it did most. He had that too-cool-for-school vibe about him, only something told me that it wasn't posturing, wasn't an act. There was an air about him that didn't fit with most of the people I'd encountered here, outside of Ten and Six.

"I don't think we've met." I glanced briefly at Eli. Every muscle in his body was tense, an expression on his face I couldn't completely decipher, but one that made the anger during our small spat look like child's play in comparison. "But something tells me that you two have."

"Trust me, you'd remember if we'd met," he said, though I couldn't tell if he was threatening me or flirting. Something about the way he studied me made it feel like he could see through me, like he in fact knew me quite well. "But my name's Levi. I'm Eli's brother."

11

____

ELI

"Brother?" Max took a step back from us both, her face flushed as her eyes darted between us. I could practically see her looking for clues, likenesses.

The thought of her seeing him in me made me sick.

"Half." I barely got the word out, my teeth were locked together so tight. It'd been years since I'd seen him, and my reaction to his presence was just as strong now as it had been then.

"No hello, Eli? Beginning to think you've been avoiding me." Levi's shoes crunched in the snow as he took another step closer. When I flinched slightly, he paused, eyes narrowing briefly in confusion before he shook his head and turned his focus to the treeline on his right. He scratched the stubble on his skin and let out a sigh. "Right. Nothing new there, then. Guess I should be grateful to know some things never change."

Max was uncharacteristically quiet, and if I weren't so damn uncomfortable with the task of untying all the knots in my stomach, I'd crack a joke about finally finding the one thing in the world to render her speechless.

A soft pressure closed around my left hand and I glanced

down to find her squeezing it. The small act alone was enough to reduce some of the tension coiling in my body, and when she let go after a second, I almost reached for her hand again.

Levi clocked the encounter, brow arched with curiosity, but I said nothing, had nothing to give to him. He didn't know me at all, and I had no desire to know him. If anything, I was angry —angry that I hadn't considered it a possibility, running into him when my guard was down, him being on this campus at all.

She was here after all, thoughtless of me not to realize that wherever she went, the prodigal son would follow.

I felt him studying me, trying to dissect me, but my mask was thicker than his—impenetrable. With a deep breath, he turned to Max. "You have a name, beautiful?"

Somehow, him flirting with her was even more annoying than when the vampire did it.

Her posture straightened, like she was manifesting strength and control for both of us. "Max."

"Thought that might be the case," he said, eyeing her with amusement. "I might need someone to show me around these parts soon, maybe I'll enlist your assistance."

I bit my tongue, trying like hell to diffuse my rage before I closed the distance between us and decked him in the face.

Not her. He couldn't have her.

"Maybe," she said, her tone neither shutting him down nor encouraging him.

I hated the fact that my chest lightened at her slight chilliness towards him. Max wasn't mine, I didn't want her to be mine. But I sure as hell wanted nothing less than for her to be his.

His lips twitched up in a small grin, clearly impressed with the fact that she wasn't fawning at his advances—maybe even taking the slight lack of interest as a challenge. Smug fuck.

"See you both around then. Enjoy your evening." He dipped

his head back to stare at the sky, the light snow dancing around him like he was a figurine in one of those glass globes children liked to shake. "It's a lovely one, but sometimes the ambiance can be misleading."

Without another word or glance in our direction, he walked away, just as silently as he'd approached.

I thought that Max would immediately grill me about him, that she'd get pissed that I'd never told her about him to begin with. I prepared myself to evade every probing question her natural curiosity would encourage her to ask.

Instead, she touched my forearm, the touch somehow grounding me, even through the thick layers of fabric separating us. When I turned towards her, oddly touched by how such a small gesture could once again make the world feel like it wasn't upside down, her eyes found mine, searching for—something.

"Are you okay?"

Something about the way she asked me that made it difficult to breathe. She cared—she always cared. About everyone. I'd never met someone who so sincerely cared about the people in her life.

I nodded. Being confronted with Levi was always jarring. It was like being confronted with my mother, abandonment issues, and insecurities all at once. I was smart enough to dissect that much of the turmoil seeing him always stirred up. Weirdly, having Max here in the aftermath made it a little less doom and gloom though. I didn't have the desperate urge to hunt down two or three bottles of booze and bury myself deep into the first girl I came across.

"Do you," she nibbled on her bottom lip, like she was searching for what she wanted to say or the courage to say it. "Do you want to talk about it?"

I wasn't naive enough to think that everything was okay between us, that she'd forgiven me pointblank just because my baggage decided to vomit all over our midnight stroll, but the offer made it clear that I wasn't a lost cause to her—that as angry as she was, she didn't hate me. Not completely.

Something about that almost made things worse—it made it harder to pull away from her.

"I, um," I shook my head, unable to shake the surprising piece of me that very much did want to talk to her about it. The part of me that wanted to talk to her about everything. She was one of the few people in my life I found it easy to open up to. It was hard not to sink into that. I forced myself to look up from her lips and nodded in the direction we were going. "We should get going. Get down there before we run into any other interference tonight."

She took a deep breath and nodded with a small smile. I could tell that she was a little bit disappointed that I didn't open up. I'd be curious about the tool too. Levi had a way of adopting that obnoxiously mysterious bad boy thing girls seemed erroneously drawn to.

She started walking and I followed, letting her set the pace as we made our way on the familiar path to the main building. No one else interrupted us. When we finally made it out of the cold, a few people roamed through the halls, but everyone was so busy with their own shit these days that they did little more than nod in greeting before charging off towards whichever errand they were on.

"The thing is," my mouth seemed to be moving out of no permission from me, "I don't really have much to say. I hardly know him. I've only met him twice before tonight, and have never really wanted much to do with him."

Max was thoughtful for a moment, her fingers pulling at the sleeves of her jacket until they swallowed her hands. "That must be hard."

It wasn't. Ignoring him was the easiest thing in the world. When I pretended like he didn't exist, I could pretend like my mother didn't exist either. I wasn't forced to think about the pain that they'd both caused me and my father—didn't have to linger on the fact that she chose to raise one son and discard the other.

"It's not," I said, but the way her eyes darted to the side told me she knew I wasn't being completely truthful. "I'm just glad that I haven't run into my mother yet. My father mentioned she was coming today. Hopefully, like most of the people filtering through Headquarters lately, they'll be busy with a task and out of my hair or, better yet, gone by morning without me having to live with everyone's eyes on me, waiting for me to react."

Her fingers twined through mine, but she didn't say anything. Somehow that was weirdly better. It wasn't a thing we had time to break down right now.

Her dark eyes were filled with so much compassion that it almost hurt to look at her.

I'd almost forgotten that she was familiar with that story— that I'd told her about my mother, about how difficult it was trying to put my father back together after she'd left. It wasn't just a divorce. Protectors almost never broke their bonds. Especially bonds that transitioned into something heavily romantic. When they did, it tore something from the pair, something irreparable. Both of them would always be filled with a hollowness, a sense of incompletion for the rest of their lives, no matter what.

The thought alone made me shiver—but it was the memory of seeing my father's eyes when it happened that haunted me every time I shut my own.

It was a feeling I swore I would never experience first hand. And that meant that as intoxicating as Max was, I didn't want to fall harder than I already had. We'd be friends. Good ones hopefully. But that was it. Platonic.

By the time we made it through the medical ward that was packed with the nursing staff monitoring the latest team to return from a mission, and down to the lab's entry, I realized that I was still clutching Max's hand.

Instantly, I dropped it. "Um, we're here."

"I can see that," she said, brow arched as she studied me with curiosity. She shoved her hand into the top of her leggings and pulled out a keycard that was pressed between the material and her lower belly. I tried desperately not to focus on the bare sliver of skin I'd seen, or how badly I wanted to stick my own greedy fingers down her pants. "I've still got Greta's old card. I thought it might come in useful tonight."

I pursed my lips, impressed. "Good thinking, Bentley. But I also have access down here, so not necessary for today's excursion."

She scrunched her nose, the gesture annoyingly adorable. "What?"

She swiped the card and grinned when the mechanism clicked, letting us in. "Your last name is Bentley too, it's weird that you called me that."

"Grossed out by the prospect of wearing my last name?" I placed both of my hands on my chest in mock hurt, growing more comfortable with the change in our dynamic. Maybe the key was to be myself—to tease and flirt with her still, as was my way with every girl, but not allow myself to actually act on it. Again. "Such a shame, will make the wedding terribly awkward, don't you think?"

It was a joke, protectors didn't do weddings in the human sense, but my stomach flipped at the thought of it anyway, at the sentimentality of the promise and how little it made me want to puke.

She rolled her eyes and stepped through the doorway and into the airlock.

It was so dark that I couldn't see a thing, but somehow that only made me even more aware of her. All that I could focus on was the smell of her hair, the brief touch of her arm against mine as we walked into each other, her warm breath against my skin. Part of me wanted to give in, just this once. To press her up against the wall under the cover of dark, in a locked hall that no one would disturb us in. I wanted to pull those delicious moans from her lips again, taste her tongue, her neck, her clit. It would be so nice to pretend that it didn't count, that it didn't matter.

Instead, I breathed through my mouth until she opened the second door and we found ourselves at the entryway of a long hall. As we walked, I swiped the card from the lazy grip she had on it.

"Hey," she whisper-yelled as I held it above my head, far outside of her reach. "What the hell are you doing? Give it back."

My eyes widened and I held back a laugh. "Not a chance, Bentley."

She made a sound somewhere between a growl and a sigh at that and all I could focus on was how I wanted her to do it again. "Don't call me that you, prick. Give it back, we don't have time for games."

I shoved the card down the front of my jeans, her eyes darkening as she followed the movement. I could see the debate play out on her face—did she go for it or not. If we were anywhere else but the lab—clear enemy territory, she probably would have.

"You have a bad habit of making trips down here by yourself," I chided, pleased that I'd won. This round anyway. "Consider this insurance that you don't go without me—or one of us—again."

It was fun pushing her buttons, but the thought of her getting found out down here by herself, where it was far too easy for them to make her disappear, made bile rise up the back of my throat. All it would take was one person to see her spontaneously turn into a firework and she'd be on the bad side of one of these cages in less time than it would take to blink.

"Alright," she said, the concession enough to stop whatever retort I'd been saving on my tongue.

"Alright?"

She nodded. "I'm not going to break rules for the sake of it. I understand that this is big time now. Life or death—and not just for me. For everyone I care about. I won't purposefully go looking for danger without considering the consequences. You have my word on that."

"Well, er," it was such a dramatic shift from what I'd grown to expect from her that I didn't really know what to say. Max was the queen of impulsive actions and thrusting herself in the path of danger. If she would try to temper that, well, I didn't know what more I could ask. "Alright then."

I tapped the card—and my dick by association. "I'll hold onto this for safe keeping until the world isn't ending then."

She shook her head. "Sometimes I think you're more cartoon than person."

I winked and watched her fight back a smile, but that smile instantly melted into a look of horror.

"What's—"

"Look." She gestured to the window on her right. We'd entered the doorway of the main holding facility, where the demons captured by field teams were put on display for researchers to study and contain. Generally, they kept the majority of them on the lower levels, this was where the extras were kept, rarely more than a handful or two. That wasn't the case now. "Why are there so many of them, why are they crammed together like that?"

The cell closest to her had two demons huddled together. They looked as human as I did, but far younger. Two girls who didn't look a day over twelve were shaking together, their eyes wide with fear as they stared at us, flinching as Max took a step closer to them. At the very least, they had to be sisters, maybe twins, though they weren't exactly identical. The one on the left looked to be the more dominant of the two, her almost-black eyes glaring at us as we approached.

"We aren't here to hurt you," she said, crouching low until she was next to them. "I'm like you. Well, sort of. Here, look."

She held up her hand and I knew that she was going to conjure fire in a bid to earn their trust, to ease the look of fear in their eyes.

"No," I closed the distance between us, hovering over her, and nodded as discreetly as possible across the room.

Her lips parted with understanding when she saw the camera in the corner. "Oh, right. Sorry, I wasn't thinking."

We were going to need to commandeer the footage regardless, but on the off chance that we failed, it would be far better to get caught sneaking down here than it would be for her to get caught out as a fire-conjurer sympathizing with the other demons.

The girls studied her with curiosity, but the hatred mixed with fear in their expressions was unmistakable—partially because their emotions looked no different than ours.

"Vampires?" Max asked, clearly not fussed by the fact that they didn't trust her.

The more timid girl started to answer, but her sister stopped her instantly, with little more than a tug on her curly hair.

Understanding, Max stood and looked at me, her face as broken as if she'd just watched someone take her puppy away. Then again, maybe not. If someone touched Ralph, I had a feeling she'd go protective mama bear before slipping into the existential sadness on her face now. "They're so young."

I nodded, realizing that I felt the same anger, the same sadness at the condition they were kept in. "Why are they keeping so many up here, together like this? I've never seen more than one demon in a cell before."

We walked along the dark hall and found each of the rooms

occupied—most with two or three, some with only one. The other demons were older than the girls, some of them shifted into wolves, their postures exhibiting variations of aggression, fear, or a sort of nihilistic acceptance of their situation. Several charged the glass walls when we passed by, an attempt to escape or attack us—those were the ones who'd clearly only been here for a day or two, the ones who still had hope of making it out of here.

"Oh my god," Max said, covering her mouth with her fingers.

I followed her gaze and found a cell that I'd overlooked—it had two wolves, one showing its teeth at us, the other sleeping in the back corner.

At least I'd assumed it had only been sleeping. Upon closer inspection, I saw what looked like a pool of blood beneath its head, a deadly pillow. Its neck had been torn out, the heart too from the looks of it.

The cell next to it had a similar, equally horrific scene—this time two humanoid looking demons, one sitting proudly next to a decapitated figure, his posture and expression signaling his deep desire to do to us what he'd done to his cellmate.

"They're killing each other." I'd never heard of this happening here before, couldn't imagine why The Guild would allow it to—wasn't the point to study and test them? To better understand the magic that tied them to hell, to find a way to protect us and humans from their violence? "Why?"

A crash sounded behind us, on the other side of the hall. With a quick glance at each other, we charged towards the commotion and stopped short when we saw two vampires thrashing against the walls, tearing into each other. It wasn't quite as explosive as the fight between Claude and Darius had been, but I knew that if the lights were turned on, we'd see the walls decorated in shades of red.

"Stop," Max yelled, slapping her hand on the window, "what are you doing? Why are you doing this?"

The vampires had no interest in her, nor in stopping their grizzly battle.

"Let's go." I grabbed her hand and pulled her to the next door, the one that would lead us where we wanted to go. "We need to get out of here before we attract attention."

"We can't just leave them there to kill each other." She planted her feet to keep me from dragging her.

"We also can't stop them. I don't think anyone is forcing the fighting. Demons are a lot like protectors—there's infighting and territorial disputes. Violence is how power is distributed in this world. Our best chance of stopping the situation is finding what we need and getting to the bottom of what's going on here."

Judging by what we'd encountered in Seattle, and in hell, there was no escaping the death toll, no matter where we were.

"So we just walk away?"

"What's your suggestion?" I asked, honestly curious because I had no better idea of how to fix this shit show without letting the demons loose on the protectors here.

"I—" she closed her lips, considering. "I don't know."

Her shoulders sagged in defeat and a pang of sympathy went through me. "I know. Everything is a mess. We'll figure out what's going on, but the best we can do right now is find what we're looking for, whatever that is." I reached in my pants, her brow lifting in shock and flattening again when I lifted out Greta's card. "Do you sense anything?"

She took a deep breath, closed her eyes. "It's hard, I don't really know what I'm supposed to feel drawn to, what I'm supposed to feel at all."

"Is there an energy signature, something that you feel linked to in some way?"

She inched her way closer to me before opening her eyes

and clearing her throat. She took a step back, breaking eye contact. "No."

Nodding, I swiped Greta's card.

Red light.

Rejected.

"Guess she doesn't have clearance any farther than this," I said, grabbing my own. "I do, though."

Red light again.

"What the hell," I swiped two more times, nothing. Reaching into my thigh holster, I pulled out my dagger, pressed the pad of my thumb into the tip of the blade, and let the blood pool into the collection plate.

Red again.

"What's wrong?" Max bit her bottom lip as she bounced lightly on her feet. "Is it malfunctioning?"

"No," I said, my jaw clenching, "My access has been revoked."

"What? Why?"

"I don't know."

"But you had access last time, right—you and Atlas both. Plus, Seamus—"

Last time. When we broke into the labs to break a vampire out. I couldn't say I was shocked that they were a little mistrusting, even with my father and uncle covering for us.

"Does this mean Seamus doesn't have access either?"

"I don't know." Blood was sacred to protectors—in some ways, we probably valued it as much as demons did. We didn't drink it like vampires, or use it to create binding, deadly oaths, but it was how we passed on our history, our mark on the world. For supernatural creatures, blood told our story, stored our power.

Seamus's blood was used to unlock doorways, and because I was his son, those paths were often automatically accessible to me. It was my birthright, in a weird, archaic way.

Until now.

I scanned the door, noticing new, blinking equipment had been installed above the lock mechanisms I was familiar with. "Looks like they've installed new tech. Maybe now, thanks to us, they're joining the human digital age—going with fingerprints or eye scans instead of the brutality of bloodletting."

"What does this mean?"

I looked at her, even though it was too dark to make out much more than her outline.

"I know, I know, you don't know." She buried her forehead in her hand. "This just made our entire mission impossible."

"Maybe. I don't think Luce is going to take impossible as a reason to stop looking."

"Of course not."

Lucifer's rage wasn't something I wanted to encounter, but maybe Atlas or Dec would have a better suggestion for how to get down there.

"Maybe whatever they're hiding is somewhere else? Not in the labs at all?" She looked up at me, hopeful.

"You mean, maybe they aren't hiding the ridiculously powerful thing they stole behind the security fortress? Seems highly unlikely." I shook my head, considering our options. There weren't many.

"Well, maybe it's not here at all. It could be at another location? Another Guild spot? Somewhere—just, I don't know, somewhere else? It's worth considering. All the possibilities are worth considering right now, aren't they?"

I took a deep breath, she wasn't wrong. "Maybe I can talk to my father. Maybe he or Cyrus can get us in here, if nothing else, just to rule it out."

I felt her tense at the mention of Cy. He still hadn't returned and I knew that there was a whole world of shit they had to work through. More than that, I knew pieces of that puzzle that she didn't. My stomach sank at the realization that I'd have to be the one to tell her, to inform her that her longest tie to normalcy, to family, was built on a giant ass lie. *Fuck.*

Just when I was almost certain she didn't completely hate me anymore, I was going to deliver the news that would send her into a spiral of despair.

"We should go," I said, grabbing her hand in mine and dragging her back to the first doorway.

She didn't fight me as we quickly moved through the hall of doom, the sounds of fists pounding into metal and flesh echoing around us against a backdrop of diminished screams and grunts.

When we made it to the only empty portion of the medical suite, she stilled.

"What?"

"Wait." She bent her brows in focus. "Someone's coming. I can hear them."

I listened, not quite making anything out yet, but maybe her hearing was stronger now that her powers were coming into their own.

It wasn't like the medical ward was off limits per se, but we had no excuse to be in this portion of it—not with us both already on thin ice with the higher ups as it was.

We were only screwed if it was—

"Fuck," I whispered, hearing the voices now myself. "It's Tarren." I closed my eyes focusing. "And Jer's dad, I think."

"Shit, they're coming closer."

I scanned the hall.

"In here." I dragged her a few feet towards them, exhaling when the door to the nearest room opened without resistance. Not locked. Finally, something in our favor tonight.

Probably because it wasn't a room. It was a closet of cleaning supplies.

We pressed together, chest to chest, our legs scissored

together so that we could both fit. The door latched closed, our arms pressed against it, both of us sardines.

If sardines wanted nothing more in the world than to spend all night seducing the tiny fish pressed into them, anyway.

Her vanilla shampoo clouded my senses, mixing sweetly with something clean and fresh—like the ocean. Her arm bent in at the elbow—I felt her thin fingers press against my chest, like she was trying to create a modicum of space between us. All she accomplished though was a caress that sent chills down my spine.

"I don't understand," the man I was fairly certain was Sal, Jer's father, said as he came into earshot. "The recent ones are strong. They're flipping more quickly, more frequently."

"No one understands, that's your job to change." That was Tarren. Every muscle in my body recognized the entitlement in his voice, the snarl. "Run more tests."

"We've *been* running tests."

"Run more, obviously. See if you can identify patterns among them, harvest the element in larger quantities. If more of our teams come back with their bounties, we have a better chance of sustaining things. Or at least stabilizing them."

Sustaining what? What the hell were they harvesting?

Max's fingers gripped gently into me, her way of asking me the same question.

I shrugged, hoping she could feel it.

I knew very little about the labs—not even my father knew the depths of what went on down here—but this sounded new, like they were pivoting directions.

"More bonds. This world, it's all about balance," Tarren said, speaking in fragments now that made almost no sense.

"We've been out of touch with that balance for years." There was a resolute sadness to his voice, the way that it dipped and faded.

"Maybe more power too—eventually—if we can manage it."

They sounded like they were just on the other side of our door now. I held my breath and felt Max do the same, both of us tense with the possibility that they might realize they weren't alone.

"I'll put orders out, make sure that everyone understands—more captures, less killings. It's always been our way, but that's become less clear over the years, they've grown lazy here, prioritizing safety. Risks are what will bring us rewards, it's always been our way. We're losing sight of it."

"We've already lost four of our own in one mission this week," Sal responded, his voice strained with his insecurity. Even he shrank when in the presence of Tarren. "You can't seriously be suggesting that we encourage them to be more careless. Some of the teams—they're so young, practically children fighting out there now. If we're not careful—"

"There'll be more losses than that if we don't act soon. You're too focused on the sentimentalism of a father right now. This is war. I'm concerned with the continuation of us all, with the survival of the human species, and the preservation of the secrets of our world. Small sacrifices are nothing compared to what can be lost—you should know better than that."

"Yes, yes you're right." But he didn't sound completely sure.

"Have the others made similar findings? Reported a similar increase? Similar strengths?"

I could almost feel Tarren's excitement beating against my eardrums. There was a pause, so I assumed Sal answered with a gesture, but they were getting farther away, harder to hear completely. "It could be our salvation or our undoing. If they're growing more powerful while we..."

His voice trailed off until all that I could hear was the sound of my breathing.

Both of us waited in silence, neither of us willing to chance them coming back. The clips that I was able to glean from their conversations were on repeat in my mind, but there were gaps.

If nothing else, it confirmed our suspicions that the cells were full because they were capturing more demons on the field missions. It made sense. We had a huge reinforcement of field teams here right now, people going out on missions every day, joining forces with other branches and satellites of The Guild. Of course that would lead to more encounters, more captures.

But no one had told me that we'd lost so many protectors this week. Why weren't they saying anything? I knew, from my father, that the death rates had skyrocketed while we were gone, that was to be expected with the number of attacks happening around the globe. But in one location, in one mission—without a word?

What more was being kept from us?

Something told me that what we'd find on the other side of that locked door would be even more chaotic.

My heart beat wildly against my chest, against Max's hand, and she slid that hand to my shoulder and squeezed, trying to comfort me.

All that the movement did though was remind me of the fact that we were practically glued together. The awareness of her body against mine only made my heart beat faster.

Without thinking, I wrapped my arm around her waist, pressing her to me.

She startled at first, and I thought she might resist, but instead she quickly melted into the hug—like my touch was just as much a balm to her as hers was to me.

I found myself leaning down, drawn to her lips. We were so close that all I had to do was move half an inch closer and my nose would brush hers.

She leaned into me, tilting her head back.

I wanted nothing more in the entire world than to take her

lips with mine, to see if they still had the power to knock me to my knees, to make me forget every worry and pain.

And, more than that, I could feel that she wanted me to, sense how drawn she was to me, how the tension between us always seemed to build until sometimes it almost felt like it would drown us if we didn't give into it. It was electric, undeniable.

It wasn't even just sex that I wanted. It was everything about her—the way her mind worked, the way she cared about people, the way she was able to peel me back until I was nothing but an exposed nerve.

I wanted her in every way, all the time, forever.

Hell, simply being around her had a way of making me physically feel different, like I was stronger, more intuitive, less focused on myself, like she was a missing link that forged me into something new, something better.

I knew what this was.

Even though I'd never experienced it, even though I fought it at every step.

This was a bond.

A true one. Not the fabricated shit protectors had been contriving for years.

I had a bond.

The second I let myself acknowledge the word, I felt it as truth—it sank deep into my bones, grabbing hold.

Her warm breath swept along my bottom lip and I nearly groaned—the sensation alone had my dick hardening.

What would it be like to give into it? To explore that bond, that link, to its full potential? To nurture it and let it grow, let it strengthen. To connect myself forever to someone like her?

I wasn't sure.

But I knew firsthand a shadow of what it would be like when that bond ruptured—when she made the choice to reject it, to unweave it.

A true bond would be worse than the kind of pain my father went through—unimaginable for me to comprehend. It would be a pain I'd never recover from, a hollowness I'd never fill.

"I think it's safe," I said, my body screaming at me to stay in the bubble, to stay with her, to ignore the potential for hurt. "We should go."

"Oh," she said, her voice quiet, "right. Okay."

Carefully, reluctantly, I untangled my body from hers and cracked the door open enough for the small trail of light to wake me up from whatever spell I was falling under. "Looks empty, let's get you back home before we run into any more trouble. We can discuss the details tomorrow with the others."

She nodded, expression unreadable.

Our walk home was a silent one. The few people we came across were too busy to spare us more than a passing glance.

I focused on the deep chill in the air—used it to ground myself, a distraction to keep me from acting on the over-whelming desire to grab Max's hand, to feel her fingers slide between mine.

Holding hands. I'd never craved that before, not once before her.

As we neared her cabin, I knew that we were running out of time. I could feel her restlessness next to me, though she seemed to have as little desire to speak as I did—both of us spiraling inward, unraveling our own thoughts about the unex-pected evening.

I needed to tell her the truth, to tell her what I'd learned.

"Eli." Her hand touched the side of my arm, and the skin beneath my coat hummed with satisfaction. "We should talk."

Her eyes were wide and round—filled with the lingering pain I knew I'd caused, but also with something softer, some-thing that made my chest squeeze.

"Cyrus knew your mother," I blurted out.

"I—" Her brows bent in, her lips twitched as she processed the words, before they fell into a small frown. "What?"

I took a deep breath and told her everything that my father told me, trying to remember each word, each turn of phrase with a crystal-clear precision—only leaving out our brief tangent about love and my feelings.

My voice stuttered when her face cracked, the heartbreak clear-as-day, broadcasted in every line and muscle of her body. Her expression darkened, her breathing picked up until I grew concerned she might work herself into a panic. I watched her eyes glass over with tears, her chin dimpling as she fought to keep them at bay.

She didn't want to cry in front of me—didn't want me to see the vulnerability, the pain overtake her.

For a moment, I paused, reached my arm forward to offer some sort of comfort, but continued on without making contact. Things were already confused enough, the boundaries too blurred to mess with any more tonight.

When I finished, a heavy silence blanketed us both—her uneven breathing the only thing I could hear.

My stomach hurt just looking at her, knowing that I was the one, once again, responsible for the pain in her eyes—at least partially.

"All this time," she said, the words more a cracked whisper than anything. Her jaw clenched. "He's known all along. And he's not even here to face me, to let me confront him."

"I'm sorry, Max. I really am." I took a deep breath and a step back, needing more space between us before I tried to wrap her in my arms. "Maybe—maybe, I don't know," I scanned the thick tree line, wondering how it could look so peaceful here when so much shit was imploding in our lives, "maybe he had a good reason. For keeping the secrets he kept. Maybe—"

"Don't." She stared at me, unblinking, her cheeks flushed,

hands balled at her side in tight fists. "Just don't. Don't make excuses for him."

"I—" but I swallowed whatever pleasantry I was going to try and wrap this shit fest in and nodded. I couldn't make this better. Only Cyrus could do that—and who even knew if he was capable, if he really did have a good reason for keeping as many secrets as he had?

She wouldn't meet my eyes, and I knew that she wanted to be alone—or at least not alone with me. Maybe Izzy or Ro or Declan were close enough to her inner circle to witness her pain, to listen to her breakdown and analyze all that she'd learned tonight. I wasn't sure. The only thing clear to me was that I was not in that circle, not anymore.

"I'm sorry." I'd never felt those words more deeply than I did now. "For everything. For how I've behaved, for everything you've gone through, for my part in it all. It was a mistake. I shouldn't have—we shouldn't have—I'm just sorry, okay?"

Her lips quivered, her chin dimpling again as she nodded, still not looking at me.

I exhaled as I ran my hand through my hair, searching for something else to say or do other than leave her here like this. But I knew there was nothing. "Tomorrow, in the morning, after Ten leaves, Declan will swing by. She'll update you on next steps."

The tension in her shoulders eased a bit, and I fought back the jealousy that simply the promise of Declan's company could accomplish that in a way that my presence right now could not.

"Goodnight, Max. Try to get some sleep."

I walked away, passed our cabin where the windows were bathed in a warm light, and headed straight for my pond, hoping that after everything the universe had dumped on me tonight, it would be kind enough to ensure that I'd have no more run-ins with Levi on the way.

I'd earned that one thing, at the very least.

12

MAX

When Declan stopped by, it was to have me pack a bag. Apparently, while Ten was out on their mission for two days, I was to stay with Six on their couch. While it was kind of annoying to play the role of the insolent child who couldn't be left alone to her own devices, it was more so annoying because Atlas was still ignoring me and Reza took every opportunity possible to gloat about that very fact. And because she was always around, either hanging off Atlas's arm or trying to suck up to Declan, we couldn't speak freely about anything important.

For five days, I focused on training, trying desperately to stay under Tarren and Alleva's radar whenever possible. Neither of them missed an opportunity to critique my form or comment on my recklessness whenever they could. It was like they could somehow tell that I was a threat to The Guild, that I didn't really belong here, that I wasn't one of them.

In the evenings, I walked the grounds with Dec, Eli, Izzy, or Ro, trying desperately to *feel* a connection to the mystery magic. I kept it to myself that the only magical draw I felt on campus was to the members of Six. Everything else was a dead end. The thought of disappointing a man as infamous as Lucifer was almost as daunting as the possibility of someone at Headquarters finding out what I really was. Each direction I looked, I was surrounded by enemies, people who could crush me in the palm of their hands if they wanted.

Demon powers were overrated—all they came with was more danger and deceit.

While my search for the magic failed, the others tried to pick up the slack.

Atlas tried to reach the lower levels of the lab on his own, only to come to the same conclusion as Eli—his clearance had been removed. And, what was worse, Seamus wasn't able to do anything about it for either of them. When they confronted him, he'd said that Tarren, Alleva, and some of the members of the lab had tightened security after Darius's escape—it was out of his hands and he was already on thin ice as it was. Even he'd lost access to some of the rooms deep in the lab.

Tarren's response, when Atlas asked him about the demotion, was that he needed to find a way to "earn it," whatever the hell that meant.

Which was to say, we were all more or less screwed and stuck in a metaphorical limbo until something changed. The problem was that when it came to life or death shit, 'something changing' could usher in a new catastrophe.

Until I could figure out a new plan, all that was left was for me to run through everything Eli had told me on repeat.

The second he dropped me off the night of our excursion, I ran upstairs and puked, before spending the night curled up on the foot of Ro's bed while he rubbed my back and swore on his life that Cy had never shared any of that with him. Though I didn't doubt it, something about hearing him say it felt like a balm. My entire childhood wasn't a lie. I had my brother.

He'd been sticking to me like glue whenever he wasn't pushed away for meetings. Each day though, he looked better than he had when I'd first arrived, stronger—more like his old self.

"You're done already?" I asked, a giant grin on my face as he stepped off the mat and scrambled for his bottle of water. My body was dizzy with excitement. It had been ages since Ro and I had sparred—and even though our entire world had imploded, it had been a strange sort of magic to pretend like it was before we entered into this life.

"I'm exhausted." He bent at his waist and drained half his bottle in one gulp. "We haven't so much as taken a break in two hours and my ego can only handle so much. I need food and the opportunity to do something other than fall on my ass for a few minutes."

Two hours? I hadn't realized we'd been going that long—I'd been so caught up in the nostalgia of it all.

For a moment, I worried that it was too much for him—that I'd pushed him too far, too soon after his recovery. He'd been on his deathbed a week ago, and here I was draining every ounce of his energy. "Sorry, I got so caught up, I wasn't thinking."

His breathing was labored and I could tell from the way he favored his left side that he was healing from a particularly bad hit, but even through the exhaustion, he seemed exhilarated, pleased. "You're stronger—way stronger than you were before, faster too. Your skills are getting sharper, I'm impressed. I can't keep up like I used to."

I stared at him, my high from sparring with him melting into surprise as I ran the matches over in my head.

Ro and I had always been pretty evenly matched—our strengths and weaknesses balancing out into frequent stalemates.

But that had changed—and I wouldn't have noticed it if he hadn't said something. Today,I beat him in every single match —and I'd been holding back a lot too. Well, he definitely won one of them, but that was because I was focusing most of my attention three mats over during it—where Declan and the new girl were engaged in a fight that looked far more like an intimate, deadly dance than anything. I still hadn't had the courage to ask Dec about the girl, or what their relationship was.

Even though every time she wasn't at Six's cabin during my brief visits, I couldn't drag my mind from lingering on the probability that they were engaged in far more intimate things than sparring.

"I guess I did get the upper hand during most of our matches, probably just one of those days. Plus, you're still recovering," I said.

I must've been frowning because Ro walked back over to me and bumped me with his hip, knocking me down. "I'm recovered and fully capable. But you're misunderstanding me. It's not a bad thing, Max, not something to be afraid of. Honestly, it makes me feel slightly less terrified about everything that you're up against. You've always been good, always been able to hold your own in a fight—but now, you're a fucking force, focused in a way you've never been before. It's your training with Six, among other things," his eyes bugged out, trying to insinuate what he couldn't say openly here. Coming of age, being part demon—my agility and strength were improving so quickly that I often didn't even notice. Especially since I had to operate at half throttle most of the time, to avoid speculation. "Plus, I could feel you holding back a bit too, so who knows what the hell you're really capable of when you need to draw from your deeper pools."

I grinned, my entire body blushing from the compliment. Ro had been working around the clock to make me feel more comfortable with myself and the changes I was going through since I'd been back. It was like having my own personal cheer squad. "Thanks."

"I'm going to grab a bite and hit the books for awhile, why

don't you find another victim to beat up for the rest of the afternoon?" he winked, before grabbing his bag.

Ro was getting pretty good at utilizing the unorganized library at The Guild and had spent a lot of his free time after Ten's intel mission with me and a stack of books, looking for any trace of my mother that we could find. So far, we'd found next to nothing. Just a name—or, rather, a name of someone who showed up exactly once in our research and then seemed to have disappeared altogether.

Sayty Azar.

Her name was listed alongside Cyrus Bentley. He'd put in a request to have her moved to his field team. But there was nothing else. It was almost as if she was a ghost—here but not, gone without a memory or photograph.

"How about you skip the books tonight and just go hang out with that hot boyfriend of yours."

Said hot boyfriend, Arnell, was shooting not-so-discrete glances at Ro when he thought no one was looking. I knew they hadn't seen each other much since I'd been back. Ro was too busy running around like a mother hen, helping me pick up the scattered pieces of my life. And because I missed him as much as I did, and had been so terrified that I'd lost him forever, I'd let him—but I didn't want that for him long-term.

Plus, I had a feeling things between them had been a bit rocky while I was gone, and guilt occupying space low in my gut told me it was because my brother had been so focused on finding me—he wasn't great at dividing his attention up.

I was home now, though, so he didn't have to worry for now. I wanted Ro to have all the things that made those blue eyes of his light up and, since we'd moved here, Arnell was the number one person responsible for that light.

His playful grin flattened as he glanced across the gym, lingering briefly on Arnell.

"I mean it," I said, hands on my hips in mock seriousness.

"No more time with your head in the books fixing my problems until you've sorted out some of yours."

He scrunched up his nose, his shoulders slinking slightly until he looked so much like a young kid being asked to check for monsters under the bed that my heart melted. "Fine. But I expect an entire cake as a reward when I see you later tonight."

"If you handle your shit properly, I won't be seeing you at all later tonight."

With a soft chuckle and another glance at Arnell, he nodded, took a deep breath, and walked towards him.

"I thought cupid was supposed to be a myth," a deep, playful whisper left a warm breeze against the back of my neck.

I spun around and found Levi standing behind me, close enough that I could touch him if I simply held out my arm. Since the night of our introduction, I hadn't seen or heard about him from anyone. Eli went about his day-to-day activities as if the second half of his mysterious family hadn't come crashing back into his life.

"What are you doing here?" I took a step back.

He was dressed in a pair of black joggers and a dark t-shirt, both tight enough to leave little to the imagination. Up close, in the harsh lighting of the gym, I could see that his eyes were a peculiar gray—cool where Eli's were warm—his skin a few shades paler. It was more in the attitude that I could see the similarities between them—the confident, lazy posture, the signature smirk that I hated and loved in equal parts, depending on how annoyed I was at Eli that day. There was something darker about him though—an iciness that Eli didn't have, not once you dove past the surface.

"You sound disappointed." He tilted his head to the side, studying me. "I find *that* disappointing."

Something about Levi reminded me of when I was young, gathering berries in the woods as a child. When I came home with an oversized mug filled to the brim, I ran to Cyrus to show off the spoils. The moment I lifted one to my lips, excited to taste the literal fruits of my labor, he'd slapped it away. "Poison," he'd said, "you have to look closely, it's hard sometimes, to tell the difference between the good ones and the ones that will kill you."

I suppose in that way, he was also like his brother—both two sides of a coin, all in one, an intimidating balance.

"I only meant that I'm surprised. I haven't seen you since the night we met."

"The night we met," he pursed his lips, like he was tasting the memory, "I like the sound of that. Conjures a bit of a majestic scene, doesn't it?"

What was I supposed to say to something like that? Something about the way he spoke to me made it impossible to tell if he was striking to flirt or flay.

"Figured it was time I joined in on some of the action here, got to know the crowd," he shoved his hands in his pockets and scanned the room, looking markedly underwhelmed with whatever he saw. "Seems we'll be staying for a bit."

"Why? For how long?"

He shrugged. I wasn't sure which question he was answering and which he was ignoring. "I was watching you with that boy."

"My brother," I said, though I didn't know why I was volunteering information.

"You're good. Possibly the best I've seen so young. I can see why Eli's protective of you—he's always had a penchant for strong women."

Protective? When had Eli seemed protective? Had they spoken since the night we met?

"Anyway," he continued, unbothered by my silence, "I'd like to have a go, see how I stack up?"

Something about the tone in his voice made me think he was talking about more than a sparring match.

"What are you doing here, Levi?" The voice and the anger lacing it were as familiar to me as my hand.

Atlas.

I felt his presence, knew that he was standing behind me, without even turning to look.

Levi's nostrils flared slightly, his eyes hardening as they stared above me. "Now, now—no need to ruin all of my fun this early in the day, Atlas. I've only had one cup of coffee."

"Go have your fun elsewhere, she's spoken for," Atlas snapped, his voice dipping into a low growl. I spun my head around, terrified that I'd see yellow eyes peering back at me, but they were dark and warm, bleeding through almost imperceptibly with threads of gold—invisible to anyone who wasn't looking for them. "Eli's on his way to take up her training."

"Yes well, he does enjoy a good fight, doesn't he?" The tension between them was thick and stretched for an impossibly long moment. But then, just when I thought they'd scramble for each other's throats, me nothing but a forgotten observer, the animosity evaporated altogether and Levi's face broke into a playful grin. "As I told the lovely Max, I'm just here for a friendly match or two—need to keep in proper shape with things going all topsy-turvy in the world. Wouldn't want to be seen as weak prey out there, would I?"

Something about the way he said prey made me feel like I was the one being hunted.

Atlas took a step closer to me until his chest was nearly pressed against my side. "As I said, she's spoken for and under a very rigid training regimen. If you'd like to practice, there's a global selection of people here available for you to spar with."

I took a deep breath, already tired of the pissing contest that clearly had nothing to do with me and everything to do with their own baggage. Atlas had basically pretended like I didn't exist since we'd hooked up. Which, fine, I got it, the dude had the emotional intelligence of a gnat sometimes. But to go all caveman out of nowhere, after ignoring me for a week just because the new kid wanted to taunt him? There were bigger problems for us to focus on. Catastrophic ones.

Even as I recognized the moment for what it was, I still couldn't deny the traitorous part of my body that purred at Atlas's nearness.

A venomous smile spread across Levi's face. "Are you offering yourself? It has been a while since we've thrown fists— and the last time was both entertaining and educational. It's always a treat, learning how you tick." His eyes narrowed, and my curiosity deepened. I'd heard nothing about Levi, but he very clearly had a past with Six. "Maybe while your father is out, you'll be able to exercise a bit of freedom, flex your claws like old times."

I felt Atlas stiffen against me. Did he know or was that turn of phrase just a coincidence?

Tarren had stepped out some time during my session with Ro, and I knew that there was truth to Levi's statement. If he'd been here, this little spat would have ended before it began. Tarren didn't suffer interruptions to Atlas's training.

"Atlas," Reza walked up to him, her eyes lasered onto the spot where Atlas and I were touching, her jaw clenched tightly as she tried to control the insecurity so clearly etched in every muscle of her body. "Let's go. We have plans in two hours and I want to make sure we get as much as possible out of the time we have to train. We have a lot to make up for."

Honestly, half the time I couldn't tell if she really liked Atlas or if she liked the idea of him, the promise of pleasing her mother by attaching herself to one of the strongest members of The Guild. Legitimate feelings or not, the thought of her with him still felt like someone was bending and breaking each of my bones, one by one.

"It's fine," I whispered, a small part of me intrigued by the thought of sparring with Levi. Clearly Atlas and Eli hated him, but I wanted to know more—to know them through him. "I can use as much practice as I can get too."

Levi's eyes lifted in what looked like a genuine smile. "Excellent, problem solved."

"Great," Reza said, drawing the word out until it sounded almost like a question as her eyes darted from Atlas to Levi.

Unlike Atlas, her reaction to Levi was decidedly flat. She didn't seem to know Levi at all—no one here really appeared to, outside of Six. He was like a ghost here, an outsider. In some ways, I could relate.

Reza's hand slipped into Atlas's as she tried to pull him away, not physically really, but the suggestion was there all the same.

Atlas took a deep breath, glanced at me briefly from the side of his eye, hesitated like he might not leave, and then let himself be directed back to where he'd been training Reza.

Levi's brows lifted suggestively as he centered himself on the mat.

I lined up opposite him.

"Say when," he said, instead of offering me the custom bow.

"Er, okay—when."

He didn't hesitate, didn't wait for me to make the first move before he pushed forward. His fist hit right, then left, and while I dodged them both, something about his rhythm was unpredictable, exciting.

I ducked last second, missing what would have been a pretty gnarly hit to the shoulder and managed to pivot to the side until I was behind him. I swept him behind the knees, grabbing his arm behind his back as he fell.

Rather than surrender, he laughed—a soft, infectious laugh that generated one of my own—He leaned back and twisted out of my grasp.

We were on the ground and then back up again, both battling for control, for the better position. Something about fighting with him felt different than with the others—almost like it was a game, an innocent, violent game. It was intoxicating.

I got lost in the joy of it. Memories of early days, play-fighting with Ro in the spring, while Cy left us to tend to his garden, came flooding in. We'd ignore our usual rules, break them deliberately without Cy there to chide us. Those were some of my favorite memories, just the two of us and a kind of childish energy that seemed so far away, unreachable—until now.

Before I knew it, Levi had my arms twisted against my back, his breath tickling the shell of my ear as I squirmed, refusing to surrender, but trying not to use my full strength or speed at risk of being caught out.

I felt the large grin plastered across my face, strands of my hair glued against my cheek with sweat.

I stepped on his foot, hard, and he let out a groan that was half agony, half laugh as he created enough space between us for me to break free.

"You're scrappy, I'll give you that," he said, his gray eyes bright and wide with excitement.

"You're not so terrible yourself," I said back, smiling despite my efforts to contain it. I still wasn't sure about him—still didn't trust him enough to let my guard down. But I couldn't deny that I was enjoying myself.

Suddenly, like a blind sliding over a window, the boyish glee on his face fell away—the hard, mysterious mask back in place.

I felt my own grin falter in response.

"What's—" I started, but when I turned my head to the side, I saw Eli stepping onto the mat, his lips set in a thin line, every muscle coiled with tension as he stared his brother down.

Just beyond him, Atlas coached Reza, his attention on her, but something in the lines of his posture made it seem like his focus was on us. His gaze flashed to me briefly, the brown lighter than before, though still not obvious to those not as hyper-aware of the shades of his eyes and their meaning as I was. The wolf was closer to the surface than he had been before, and intuition told me it had very little to do with Reza pushing his buttons.

"Eli, glad you could join us." Levi's tone was airy, but his expression was impenetrable. "I was just keeping her warm for you, figuratively speaking." There was a heavy silence, Eli's face blank as the brothers stared at each other. "Right. I'll catch you later, Max. Thanks for the romp."

The muscle in Eli's jaw ticked at that, but he remained stoic, watching silently while Levi hopped off the mat.

Levi wound his way around the training room, studying the different matches, not unlike the way the boys and Dec used to do when they were running the training sessions. For a moment, I wondered if that was also his role back—well, wherever the hell he was from. His form had been interesting, his fighting style thrilling.

Without so much as a hello, Eli dropped his bags and turned to me. "Ready?"

His body was tense, like he was holding back whatever emotion was trying to drip out unbidden.

"What was that about?" I asked, lining up across from him.

"Nothing."

"Okay." I dragged the word out as I bowed to him. "It's just that it didn't seem like nothing."

He bowed, grunted, and lunged towards me. "Drop it, Max," he said as we met each other blow for blow.

We'd gotten better at sparring over the last few days. Sometimes it felt like Eli could read my body, that he knew when and how I was going to strike even before I did.

The fight wasn't unpredictable, like it had been with Levi—with someone new and skilled. There was a familiarity with Eli, our limbs evading and clashing together like they were part of the same puzzle piece.

But today he was off, his movements clunkier than usual, harder—his body telegraphing his decisions so that I could read his intentions half a second sooner than usual.

His jaw hadn't come unclenched since he'd arrived, and when I landed a solid hit on his side, he acknowledged it with nothing more than a grunt before continuing.

"You're angry with me," I said, blocking his hit.

His silence was enough of a confirmation as he circled me.

When we came together again, I used all of my weight to push him down to the ground, bringing myself down on top of him. I felt like a sponge, soaking up his anger and making it my own. He had no right to be pissed at me, to come in here all alphahole and then not even speak.

"What did I do to piss you off this time?" I asked, taunting him now as we wrestled on the ground—just when I gained the control, he'd take it back. The mood swings with these boys made the PMS version of me look like a damn saint.

"Stay away from him," Eli growled out, his hands pinning my wrists to the ground. "He can't—he can't have you t—"

"So, what," I interrupted, "you're done with me and now you don't want anyone else to have a go?" It was a low blow, I knew it the second I said it.

It was a mistake.

His words the other night had cut deep, almost as deep as learning about Cy's betrayal.

He regretted it all—not just his own mistakes and lies, but moving beyond friendship with me. And now he wanted to come in here and police who I gave my attention to?

He looked stricken—the shock making way for too many things I couldn't fully parse. Disappointment, hurt, anger. "Yeah," he said, jaw tight, the warmth in his eyes gone, "that's exactly it. Is that what you want me to say? I don't want my brother to get my sloppy seconds. There, I said it. Now will you stay the fuck away from him?"

I felt like he'd slapped me. My chest tightened until it was hard to get a full breath in. I couldn't decide whether I wanted to pummel him into the ground or go cry to Izzy about the absolute mindfuck that was Eli Bentley.

"Fuck," he whispered, his breath sweeping against my cheek. My body fluttered at the sensation. I told myself it was unbridled rage, that it had nothing to do with the fact that his body was glued to mine, that no matter how many times he was a raging dickhole, I still couldn't bring myself to hate him all the way. "Please calm down, Max—pull it in. I'm sorry, that was out of line." His eyes widened and he dragged my wrists down, flattening himself on top of me. "I was just trying to piss you off, to keep you away from him."

Confused, I looked down and saw the small lingering flames lick along his lower abdomen where my hands were pinned. "Shit."

I took a deep breath, tried to focus, drew the energy back inside, closed the door tight. It had been a couple of days since my powers had gone all wonky—I was starting to think that I was building up a natural control.

Apparently not.

When my hands were no longer novelty lighters he exhaled, relaxing more of his weight onto me.

For what felt like an eternity, we stayed like that, unmoving. I could feel him staring at me, but I couldn't bring my eyes to meet his. The fire was gone, but the feelings that fueled it weren't.

With my left cheek pressed to the mat, everyone looked like they were walking on a wall, the choreographed kicks and punches rendered ridiculous—but no one was focused on us, no one looked like they'd just seen a girl literally spark in anger.

And then my eyes met a pair of gray ones.

Levi.

He was standing at the door, his face blank, but I could tell that all of his attention was leveled on me.

Had he seen?

I couldn't quite tell—maybe his lips lifted into a grin, or maybe it was a trick of the light.

Then, he simply opened the door and left.

"I'm sorry." Eli lifted himself off of me until he was hovering, giving me space as I stared at the now empty doorway, my heart hammering against my chest. If he'd seen, I was fucked. But there was no way for me to know for sure. "I didn't mean that. You have to know that I didn't mean that."

"Then what exactly did you mean?" I muttered, and I hated the fact that I could hear the sadness in my voice, that it wasn't all righteous anger.

I was hurt.

And once again, Eli was the cause of that hurt.

He hesitated for a moment, then pushed himself up until he was seated on the ground, his hip and leg still pressed against me. I unclenched a little—I didn't want to be completely disconnected. "I prefer to pretend like Levi doesn't exist. It's easier that way," he dropped his eyes down to the mat, and I saw the impenetrable-Eli-mask stumble for a brief moment, like it was too heavy to hold up and his arm was getting tired with the task. "Seeing you with him, the way he was making you laugh—I just, I saw red."

I—well, I was confused. But, I think, for the first time, I realized that Eli was confused too. He was giving me emotional whiplash, but something told me that whatever he was doing to himself was just as bad—maybe worse.

He stood up, and I felt the sudden lack of his body against mine.

For a moment, I considered grabbing onto him, pulling him into a hug.

He looked so sad, standing above me with his head hung low, while his eyes locked on to the mat a few feet away from me.

"Look, obviously you're free to do what you want, to hang out with whoever you want. I have no right, I know that." He ran a hand through his hair, kneading when he got to the base of his skull. "You wouldn't be the first person he's taken from me."

I laid there, stunned, searching for something to say to that —but my tongue wouldn't work, wouldn't help me form a response.

By the time I sat up, still speechless and confused, he was already at the door.

~

A TAPPING SOUNDED at my window. I turned to it with a large grin, expecting to see Declan standing there as she had been before.

But it wasn't Declan. It was the last person I ever expected to see standing outside my window, awkwardly perched on the tiny balcony.

"Atlas?" I ran over, opened it with shaky hands, and waited as he climbed in.

I swallowed a laugh at the ridiculousness of it—strong and broody Atlas, folding his body and limbs awkwardly until he was on the other side of the glass.

"What are you doing here?" It was strange, seeing him in my room, like a picture painted in a style that didn't quite suit it.

I shuffled to the side, tried to discreetly shove a small pile of dirty clothes—yesterday's workout gear—under my bed, silently chiding myself for not keeping the place tidier.

"I needed to speak with you," he said, like it was the most obvious thing in the world.

"Through the window, in my room?" I felt myself flush at the realization that this was the first time I'd been alone with Atlas since he'd first transitioned back, at the intimacy of that moment and the oddness of this one. "You could have used the door downstairs. What is it with you guys and sneaking through windows?"

His brows bent in confusion "Who else has been here?"

There was an edge to his voice, but he relaxed when I said "Declan."

For a moment, he scanned my room.

I tried to see it through his eyes—a few stacks of books, a desk, a bed.

I hadn't really had time to decorate, to put my own flair on the place. The wall color wasn't my choice, the furniture hadn't moved an inch since I'd occupied it. It wasn't like Izzy's or even Ro's room. Most of my time living in this room had been filled with grief as I processed what happened to Wade—what I'd thought had happened to Wade.

That period felt like a strange dream, maybe because, partially, it was.

His eyes latched onto the record player, the box of records that I'd gone through—never listening to more than one each night, wanting to savor the gift for as long as possible.

Declan had given them to me for my nineteenth birthday. They were her cousin's and she trusted me with them, wanted me to have them.

"I should probably give those back." I walked over and stopped the current vinyl from spinning—the slow, dark song felt more intimate, more suggestive, with Atlas standing next to me, than it had when I was alone. "I'm sure Sarah would appreciate having a piece of her old life now that she's back."

Back.

I still hadn't processed what that meant—not for Atlas and not for Wade. They were technically bonded to her.

The thought of which made my breath catch, so I walked towards my desk, picking up random things and setting them back down, trying to calm my nerves.

"She'd probably appreciate that," he said, his long finger sorting through the stack, his lips turning up in a rare smile as he recognized a few. What kind of memories did he have of them? Did they stick out to him because he liked them, or because they triggered something he'd felt or experienced with Sarah?

Atlas so rarely smiled, and I had to hold back the urge to walk to him and trace the ghost of it on his lips with my finger. Instead, I averted my eyes, feeling like an intruder, eavesdropping on the intimate moment.

"Can I—" I tugged at the seam of my shirt, grateful that I was still fully clothed, that I hadn't gotten into my bed things yet, "can I get you anything?"

He startled, brows bending in as he turned to me, like he'd forgotten that he was the one who'd crawled into a bedroom.

"Oh, right. We're going to be going on a mission in two days. You'll be coming. We're going to use it as a guise to get you back to Seattle—to, you know. I figured it was best for you to have as much notice as possible, to spend time with your brother or whatever before you leave again—Dec and Eli are both busy tonight, so I'm here." The last part came out more like an apology.

Without realizing it, I'd taken several steps towards him, so that we were only a few feet apart. "Is Eli okay? I haven't seen him since yesterday."

Not since our fight.

I hadn't exactly gone looking for him either. My thoughts were a complete jumble where he was concerned.

I sat down on the bed, awkwardly held my hand out to signal that he could sit too, if he wanted.

Atlas's posture stiffened slightly, like a cat confronted with a dog, stuck in the posture of deciding whether or not to run. Then he relaxed and sat down, keeping a few inches between us. "He's fine, just needs space. Having his mother and Levi here—it's very," he paused, searching for a word, "it's very difficult for him."

I nodded, trying to imagine what that must be like, knowing a mother who'd abandoned you was just within reach, with her other son. Had that been who he'd meant? The one who Levi had taken from Eli? "Levi—"

Atlas shook his head, cutting me off. "That's not my story to tell."

It was odd, Atlas respecting boundaries like that, but something about it warmed me to him, even though I didn't get the information I wanted.

I nodded again, "right, you're right."

He sat silently, unmoving, until I thought there was something else he might want to say. It was like he was reluctant to leave, now that he was here.

"How have things been?" I asked, blushing at my own awkwardness. The man had literally been inside of me a week ago and here I was, getting nervous butterflies just from making small talk.

He turned to me and his lips twitched in a grin that seemed both amused and sad, an acknowledgement that he felt the oddness between us too. "Things could be worse."

We could be dead, we could be found out for what we really were.

"How has the wolf been behaving?" I asked, wondering if

he'd been struggling with keeping the ropes on his demon as much as I had been.

His brow arched, amused, and something in my stomach dipped. This was the most normal I'd ever seen Atlas, the most easy and conversational we'd ever been together. For once, it seemed like he wanted to be around me, like he was missing my nearness as much as I missed his.

"We're better." Something about the phrasing made me feel lighter. He was starting to see the wolf as a part of himself, not some parasite that was simply using his body for the time being. I could almost see my own journey mirrored in him— both of us struggling, but finding a way to learn and see the parts of ourselves we tried to conceal. "It's oddly both louder and calmer when I'm near you. But I don't think it's a surprise to learn that we're—the wolf, I mean—is a bit fixated on you."

My heartbeat skipped and I searched for something to say —it was the closest he'd ever come to admitting that he liked my company, that he craved it. I wasn't sure what to make of the offering.

"I've been having less success," I said, desperate to keep the conversation going, to see where it led, but all I could focus on was the fact that my left fingers were less than an inch from his.The memory of being lifted and shoved against the wall while we devoured each other rushed to focus and I squeezed my legs together as a flash of heat curled through me. "I keep creating small sparks when I get angry. There've been a few close calls."

I didn't want to mention that there was a possibility that Levi had seen. He hadn't mentioned anything or broached me about it, so I figured we were as clear as we could be. I was afraid that pointing out a possible problem that wasn't there might lead to more animosity between him and Eli.

"Eli's mentioned that." He studied me, expression thoughtful, as if he'd be able to dissect the limits and controls of my strange abilities simply by trying to. "Hopefully Lucifer wasn't lying—hopefully returning to hell and training with him for a few days will help."

Hell. Lucifer. We were going back. Voluntarily.

Suddenly simply sitting in my room made me feel dizzy, out of place, like it was mine but also not. How many times would I have to go back? How many times would we survive the journey? How many times could I break protocol before I wasn't welcomed back here? How long until they started to see me as the enemy?

Was I the enemy?

"I think I should go alone," I said, piercing the tense silence between us, "when I go back."

"No."

"But—"

"It's not an argument you're going to win. You need to learn to pick your battles."

"If one of you gets hurt or worse, I'll never—"

"If *you* get hurt or worse, we'll never—"

"How are we going to explain away our absence again?" I exhaled, felt my chest rising and falling. I'd leaned towards him slightly, like the more words spoken between us, the less room for empty space. "Seamus and Cy can't keep pretending to go off book—that's only going to work so many times before they're disciplined and removed from their posts."

His gaze dropped to my lips briefly and he hesitated before pulling away, opening up some of that distance again. "That's what I came here to discuss. Seamus has given the stamp of approval for you to join us on a mission—under Eli's supervision—in two days. From there, we'll split up, whoever returns to The Guild will tell everyone that we were attacked. It won't solve all of our problems, but it will buy us a bit of time at least."

I nodded, considering. It wasn't exactly an elegant solution—

and we'd have to figure out how to explain our absence once we did return—but it was better than anything I'd come up with.

"I'm sorry," I shook my head, started twisting the locket I wore between my fingers, the cool metal grounding me slightly as the walls started to close in. Things were never going to be the same, they were only going to get worse. "I've gotten you all in the world's biggest mess. We have an impossible mission that I'm making no headway on, I'm constantly an adrenaline rage rush away from outing myself as a demon, and the only person offering any sort of solution or path forward through all of this mess is the fucking Devil."

His brows bent in the middle as he watched my fingers open and close the metal clasp. "Why are you sorry for any of that? None of this is your doing. You aren't responsible for the breakdown between realms."

I let out a frustrated laugh. "Are you kidding? Lucifer himself literally said that the magic is growing more unstable because of me. Wade—he wouldn't even be down there in the first place if it wasn't for me."

His hand flattened against mine, pinning my fingers and the locket to my clavicle. I held my breath.

"You're going to break it if you keep doing that," he said. "It looks fragile."

All I could focus on was the feel of his rough calluses against my collar bone, the bottom of his palm resting at my cleavage.

My heart was racing at his touch—and it only raced faster knowing that he could feel it.

As if he was hypnotized, he leaned forward slightly, his hand letting go of mine, but not pulling away. Instead, his fingers drifted against my skin as he traced my collarbone, the light touch making me visibly shiver.

I wanted him so badly that I couldn't see straight—after

days of him ignoring me, having his full attention now made me dizzy with the power of it, the need to keep it.

It was like something in me was calling to something in him, desperate to connect.

"Atlas." My voice was barely a whisper, but it snapped whatever trance he was in. His dark eyes met mine and there was no denying the desire I saw in them. It wasn't just the wolf, it was him. *He* wanted me, I could see that now, there was no more denying it.

His hand snaked around to the nape of my neck, fingers tangling in my hair—he didn't so much as blink.

Just as I was certain he'd give in, that he'd close the few inches between us and kiss me—not with anger or fear or need, like before, but with something more tender—he pulled away and stood up, all in one motion.

"I should go."

"Atlas," I repeated. I stood and followed him towards the window. I was sick of this cat and mouse game, sick of these brief encounters that just wilted away into nothingness. "We should talk about this."

"There's nothing to talk about, Max." As focused as he'd been on meeting my gaze before, he was equally adamant about avoiding it now. "If you have questions about the mission, Eli and Declan should be around tomorrow afternoon. They can fill you in."

He opened the window, snaked one leg out of it.

"And you?" I reached my hand forward and set it on his forearm, his skin hot under my palm. "Where will you be?"

He stared at the spot where I touched him, his jaw tight, his other hand resting on the top of the windowsill to keep him balanced. "I have somewhere to be."

"Right." I understood the dismissal for what it was—whatever I thought was different about him, more open than usual, was nothing but a mirage, a temporary illusion. "Of course you do."

I dropped my hand from him, but didn't move away.

With one deep breath, he hesitated for a moment, eyes still focused on the spot my hand had just rested, and then he swung his other leg out, hopped off the small balcony, and landed with supernatural grace on the frozen ground below.

I stood there, watched him walk away, expecting him to turn on the path that I knew led to Six's cabin, but instead I watched as he went deep into the woods instead.

The desire lingering low in my belly didn't seem to care that he was uninterested in acting on his—if anything, it just made it hungrier.

Eternally frustrated, I peeled off my clothes until I was in a sports bra and boyshorts, and scooched into my bed.

I tried, for a few minutes, to get lost in a novel. Then, I tried a TV show. A movie. Nothing held my attention, nothing got rid of the ache of desire inside of me.

Finally, I gave in, and tried to take care of the echo of want myself, my fingers working slowly, but expertly over my clit as my imagination carried me to that night in the dungeon. It was the least romantic place in the world, but there was something about the roughness of it all, of Atlas finally letting go—giving in to his darker desires, the pain in my back as the wall and his fingers clawed at me, the feel of him inside.

I closed my eyes, arched into the memory, the feeling of connectedness—the heightened excitement, even the anger, taking me over.

I wanted him here, wanted to peel back the layers that I only ever caught glimpses of when he thought no one was looking, wanted to see what would really happen when he finally understood that he and the wolf were the same, were one.

And then, suddenly, as I got close to the release I so ravenously chased, a familiar feeling of thereness and not spilled over me—the breath stopped in my lungs and every atom in my body buzzed with energy. The darkness behind my eyelids grew infinitely more complete, until I couldn't tell where I was—the softness of my bed no longer grounding me.

Just as quickly, the feeling stopped, leaving me gasping for air, my ass collapsing hard on something rough and significantly more firm than my mattress.

I opened my eyes, the sudden, unexpected shift and bright light enough to make me close them again, giving my body a second to adjust.

The walls of my room were gone, replaced instead by ones that were equally sparse and impersonal. My bare feet dug into a worn, scratchy carpet with an obnoxious pattern.

I'd teleported again, and into a place that looked like it hadn't been updated in twenty years—the only exception being a small kitchenette in the corner that looked relatively new, but cheap.

Something about this space was familiar. I closed my eyes and rubbed my temples, trying to ease some of the brain fog that hopping through space and time seemed to generate. My skin was clammy with sweat, my legs wobbly like Jello. I gripped the arm of a blue, well-used couch as I caught my bearings.

There was a door right in front of me, and I could hear the soft whisper of voices on the other side of it.

"I don't understand how you've managed it so quickly," the first voice said, the words hushed and distorted from the distance and wall separating us.

The moment that voice washed over me though, everything clicked.

Atlas.

I'd been thinking about my connection to him and my body decided to drop me outside of his door.

Only he wasn't in his cabin, he was in the hotel suite we'd rented for Sarah and Darius.

"Trust me, it wasn't exactly an easy or graceful process for me. I wouldn't wish it on my biggest enemy." It was a second voice now—Sarah.

Which meant that Atlas had left me and gone to Sarah's... bedroom.

The thought made my stomach turn and I dug my fingers into the couch to ground myself.

I needed to leave, needed to get out of here before they caught me, but I was fucking exhausted and the temptation to eavesdrop too strong.

"Change over and over," she said, her voice filled with a warm compassion. "That's the fastest path. You need to find a way to look at yourself in the mirror and see both you and the wolf reflected back—the faster that you can accept him as not just a part of yourself, but you—the version of you that you will be until you die anyway—the smoother the transition will be. Don't fight him, breathe him in."

"I don't know how to do that. We agree on so few things, see the world in such different ways."

"It's not we, it's I. You're one. *That's* the problem."

"It's not as simple as semantics," he snapped back.

"It is as simple—that simple and that difficult. You are the wolf and he is you. The parts that feel unfamiliar only feel that way because you won't acknowledge the parts of yourself that scare you. Focus your energy on the similarities, the things you and the wolf agree on—deepen that. Start there."

He let out a frustrated grunt. "That's the one thing I can't do right now. Things are complicated at The Guild, you have no idea how much."

Of course—it made sense that he would go to her for help with controlling the wolf. Who better to offer advice on that?

I couldn't deny the sting though, no matter how much I

could follow the logic of his choice. I'd just asked about the wolf, about how he was handling it. And while he'd opened up more than he ever had to me, it didn't come with the vulnerability and ease that he had now, with her.

They were still bonded.

Maybe time and their transitions hadn't broken that link like we'd all assumed. Did he want her in the way that I thought he wanted me? I knew not all protector bonds were sexual or romantic in nature, that they were about team building, trust, strength. But maybe he wanted Sarah in that way—maybe that was why he resisted the tension between us so much.

There was lust, absolutely, but it was possible that the attraction he felt to her far outstripped that which lingered for me.

"My father is back," Atlas said, and there was a long silence that followed. I imagined her comforting him, her hand on his shoulder, on his cheek. Long ago, Tarren had wanted her for him—had chosen that link. "He's—more intrusive, more controlling than he's been in years. Protectors from all over the world are swarming Headquarters right now. It feels like something big is building. They might not know about the fragility between the realms, that hell is collapsing, but they're clearly preparing for something catastrophic. I have no access to the labs anymore, to what they're doing. They're preparing for... something. Your mother is scheduled to get here tomorrow too, I think."

I heard her sharp inhale. "My mother? Is she okay?"

There was so much pain in her voice, so much longing, that I suddenly felt sick—for eavesdropping on the intimacy of their conversation.

I needed to leave. Needed to get out of here before they came out.

"You seem to spy on private conversations rather frequently, little protector."

13

DARIUS

I ignored the annoying flutter in my stomach when I came out for a stretch and found Max standing there. It had only been a week since I'd last seen her, but it had felt much longer.

In my weaker moments, I toyed with the idea of ditching the she-wolf and stalking The Guild campus in search of her—the possibility of getting recaptured be damned.

The girl might as well have a collar and leash wrapped around me at this point.

Declan offered small updates here and there when she visited—recounting all the times that Max got the upperhand when battling Eli while I feasted on some pig's blood that she was able to inconspicuously score from a local butcher. Not as good as slicing open a vein, but it kept my energy up far better than a steak or six would.

The other one—Atlas—completely ignored me whenever he visited, often stomping off into the she-wolf's room, unable to meet my eyes on the off chance we ran into each other in the common area.

Honestly, I didn't blame him. He knew that I saw the parts

of him that he hated most—it was canon now, for him to avoid that internal confrontation for as long as possible. If I were in that headspace, I wouldn't want to look in a mirror either.

Eli was moodier than usual, barely sparing me more than a grunt or two when he stopped by. He'd only visited once, but he hadn't gotten himself killed or seriously maimed since returning to the human world, so we were on fine terms as far as I was concerned. I wasn't interested or curious enough to poke around in his problems.

But she was here now, I didn't have to go on a murderous rampage to make sure that she was okay.

It was a downright excellent evening.

She jumped when I announced myself, her eyes wide with guilt when she turned to face me.

Busted.

That look on her face—full lips parted in surprise, eyes all Bambi-like. Did she have any idea what that kind of look could do to a guy?

"If you're sneaking around, you can't look so shocked when you get caught. There are currently three demons in this apartment—four if you count yourself—and we all have heightened senses. It would be more surprising if you were able to stomp around here unnoticed."

A rosy tint colored her cheeks as she closed the distance between us, making a shushing noise and pressing her finger into her lip.

It made all my school-boy fantasies stretch and wake up. I wondered if she had a cute plaid skirt. No matter—I could buy her one if she didn't.

She grabbed my hand and pulled me back towards my bedroom.

"Well now, this night just keeps getting better and better, doesn't it?" My skin tingled where she touched me, my whole body humming with pleasure now that she was here. Could she feel that too? Or was she still focusing all of her willpower on pretending this connection between us didn't exist? Time would tell.

She closed the door, soft as a mouse and then scanned my room, clearly looking for something though I had no idea what. Her shoulders lifted when she found it and she ran over to the remote lying on my bed table.

Without a word, she turned the volume up as high as it would go without it being too obnoxious.

I tilted my head, pleased with her problem solving. "Smart. Should prevent them from questioning why voices are coming from my room, so long as we speak relatively quietly."

"Good," she said, her body sagging with relief. "I'm not supposed to be here."

"Yeah—" I nodded towards the door and mimed the look of panic that had been on her face just moments ago, "I gathered that, believe it or not. How did you get here, exactly?"

My spine stiffened at the thought that she'd been traipsing through the forest by herself. Those useless tools were supposed to be watching her like hawks, not leaving her alone to do what she did best—get into dangerous situations.

Useless, the lot of them. I should never have agreed to let her out of my sight.

"I teleported," she scrunched up her face and started massaging her temples, "by accident. My powers have been... misbehaving."

I studied her more thoroughly, the pure excitement and surprise of seeing her replaced by concern. Her skin, usually vibrant and warm, looked paler than usual and was covered in a sheen of sweat. It was easy to notice, once I let myself look, because so much of it was on display. "Explains the outfit choice, I suppose."

Her brows lifted in shock as she looked down. Black sports

bra, black underwear, and a smooth stretch of stomach, legs, and arms.

Delectable.

With a pounce, she reached for my bedsheet and wrapped it around herself, letting it trail on the floor like a wedding train.

"Is that really necessary? We're all adults here. It's not anything I haven't seen before, though I'm not sorry for the repeat appearance."

Her cheeks were flushed with red, bringing some color back to her face. We hadn't talked about her dream much—but I was certain it was at the forefront of her mind right now.

She scanned the room slowly, taking in the stack of books littering my desk and the small shopping bags filled with clothes that Declan had kindly brought me.

The t-shirt that said 'bite me' above some cartoonish fangs was my personal favorite.

Her eyes doubled back on the TV. "Were you really watching *Twilight*?"

The volume was on full blast, I was kind of surprised it took her so long to notice.

"Yes," I said, matter of factly, not feeling an ounce of shame, "I finished the books two days ago and Declan let me know there were also some films. They've been keeping me in good spirits. The vampires almost always kick werewolf ass. I like reciting lines to the she-wolf when I get bored. She hates it."

A small smile lifted the corner of her mouth, before her face flattened back into the panicked expression it was stuck in before.

"So why did you teleport here? Miss me too much? I get that quite often."

"I doubt that." She arched a thin brow, glanced at my bed— the covers all in a violent disarray—considered for a moment, and then sat down.

The sight of her on my bed, in nothing but some undergarments and my sheets had the blood rushing straight to my dick.

"I was just—" she fiddled with her hands in her lap, not meeting my gaze, "you know, sitting on my bed one second, and then," she mimed a small explosion with her fingers, "here the next."

I grinned. Her heartbeat had picked up enough to tell me that she wasn't exactly idle or asleep while alone in her bed—she was embarrassed about something...and slightly aroused.

"Thinking about me, were you?"

She rolled her eyes. "No. But now I need to figure out a way to get back."

"You're exhausted. Shifting like that takes a lot of energy. It's a new skill, and I'm guessing this is the best you've fared after a jump so far." I paused and she nodded. "That's a good sign at least. You're here in one piece and alive. Just rest for a few minutes and I can walk you back later when the grump leaves."

She stiffened at that and I tried not to feel too insulted. "No, you can't leave here. Security in the labs is tight right now, I have no idea how we'd get you out if you were caught again."

Oh.

She wasn't avoiding the prospect of spending time with me, just afraid of the possibility that I might die.

How sweet.

I smiled, feeling like the cat who got the cream. I knew she liked the others, but I was growing more and more confident that I was her favorite. "Then you'll shift back. Once your energy is restored."

"What if someone notices I'm gone?"

"It's quite late. Are you expecting someone to come disturb you in the middle of the night? Someone there who might miss your presence for a few hours?" I held my breath, impatient. It was one thing having her ragtag band of admirers to compete with as it was, I wasn't sure what I'd do if someone new entered the mix.

She shook her head, and my body felt light and airy again.

"Excellent, it's settled then." Tonight, she was mine. I walked to my bed and sat on the other side, fluffing the pillows until they were comfortable enough to lean back on.

"What are you doing?" she eyed me suspiciously, like I was skinning a dog and not making us more comfortable.

"Movie night." I grabbed her shoulders and gently pushed her back until her head leaned into the little nest I'd made. She fought me for half of a second, but then sighed, content, the moment her head met cotton. "Obviously. Unless there's something more fun you'd like to do to pass the time?

She shook her head, but I didn't miss the flash of heat on her face.

"Great, can't have you screaming anyway—we're supposed to be quiet. So, movie it is then. I assume you've seen this before?"

I leaned back against my pillows, excited by the fact that, at the very least, my bed would smell like her when she left.

"Of course."

"I'm sorry I don't have popcorn. I know that's usually a movie night staple. I think the she-wolf has some Ben and Jerry's in the freezer if you want me to go steal you some though?"

She shook her head, but smiled. "No, we should stay here. I don't want to risk them catching us for ice cream, no matter how tempting."

We watched for a few minutes and she relaxed deeper into the bed, the lingering anxiety melting away once she heard the front door open and close. Atlas was gone for the evening, which meant Sarah would be nestled in her room for the rest of the night, studiously avoiding me.

She did that a lot, but it seemed pointless. I had no problem reading my favorite lines from Declan's pile of books out loud while standing on the other side of her door. It had become a sort of ritual for us over the last few days.

If I didn't know any better, I'd say the she-wolf was warming up to me almost as much as her cousin had.

I didn't blame her. I was damn loveable.

It would make my life so much easier if people just took my word for it rather than waiting the ridiculous amount of time it took for them to come to the same conclusion on their own.

I turned on my side, face pressing into the pillows, and stared at Max's hand. It lay there, uncurled, just a few inches from mine. For a moment, I thought about reaching out and twining my fingers through hers. I'd never done this before— not even before my years in the lab—sat and watched a movie with a girl, perfectly content just with her company.

I'd seduced women before—and men—many, many times. But this was different.

It seemed so normal, so mundane, but I felt warm and gooey inside.

And nervous.

I was never nervous.

And yet my blood was rushing through my veins, my stomach busy doing that flutter thing it had grown fond of doing lately.

"How are," I cleared my throat and searched for something to say, eager to keep her here even after the risk of Atlas finding her was gone, "things?"

Things?

Jesus, captivity had melted my ability to interact. I used to be so smooth, able to have women swooning with nothing but a look, let alone my ability to dazzle with witty conversation.

Her focus didn't leave the screen, but her lips twitched at my question. The sight made my heart stutter.

I'd done that. I'd made her smile.

I wanted to do it again—and again and again.

"They're okay," she paused, nose scrunching softly, "kind of confusing to be honest."

"Do you want to tell me about it?" Surprisingly, I really wanted her to. I ate up every crumb of her life she dropped for me.

Every muscle in her body froze as she considered for a moment. The silence bled into several seconds, until I assumed that she was going to brush off the offer and continue watching the wedding on the screen as if I hadn't asked.

But then, she did the strangest thing.

She turned her head against the pillow, curling on her side, until we were eye-to-eye, only a few inches apart, her breath mingling with mine.

After a moment, during which I was pretty sure I stopped breathing at risk of bursting the tenuous bubble, she started to talk. Her voice was little more than a hushed whisper, but it spilled out of her like warm milk and honey, detailing the big and not-so-big events in her life since the last time we were together.

I lapped up every word, like a starving man, grateful for every morsel.

I learned about her brother, her friend Izzy, training with Eli, about Atlas's asshat of a father—her words, not mine, though knowing his son, they seemed fitting—and about the thing eating away at her most—Cyrus lying to her about her mother.

When she got to that part, her eyes glazed over with unshed tears and I found myself fisting the bed sheets at my side, ready to track down her adoptive father and break his bones until he made things right and she no longer looked so sad.

She had such a full life and so many struggles for someone so young, so new to this supernatural world. The fact that she let me steal a small glimpse of her thoughts made me want to wrap her in my arms and keep any more harm from finding her.

But that was the thing—I wouldn't be able to keep her safe. Not truly. Not with the world shattering around us, her at the center of it all.

"It's odd," she said, after a long moment of silence, "the more I learn about The Guild, the more I hate it. This place that I've spent my entire life building up in my head as the pinnacle of honor and morality is a lie. The person I assumed I could always trust, no matter what—turns out I can't trust him at all. And I'm not saying that I believe Lucifer entirely, I'm not naive enough to think that someone capable of so much cruelty would be completely trustworthy—he doesn't have our interests in mind, I know that. But it sucks to know that he's right about some things."

My heart did another annoying, heavy thump at hearing her use the word 'our.' I wasn't sure when it happened, but at some point during our trip to hell, I'd moved beyond being just a phantom figure in her life, one that she was stuck with because of a manipulative deal I'd conned her into making. I wasn't sure what I was to her, but it made me feel light as a feather to know that she considered my interests alongside hers.

"But it's clear that he's right about some things," her eyes met mine, "that *you* were right about a lot too. The Guild isn't purely good—good and evil are false binaries in this world. I understand that now. We're all capable of both. And I've seen you do so much good these last few weeks, even when it was reluctantly done or terrifying to execute. I want you to know that I saw it—that I see you." With a smirk she added, "beyond the fangs." she paused, considering for a moment. "You're like us, you know? You don't fit anywhere. But you fit with us now, even if it doesn't make sense. Even if nothing about any of us makes sense." She let out a small, incredulous laugh. "Maybe because of that, actually."

My throat felt thick as I swallowed, trying to come up with something to say to that. It was rare for me to be speechless, but she'd managed to achieve it.

I turned that idea over and over in my head.

You fit with us now.

It wasn't just that she thought I fit with her—she thought that I fit with them all. Like a strange, annoying family of misfits. But family nonetheless.

Surprisingly, it didn't make me want to hurl—instead, I had to swallow back excitement at the thought of belonging.

Sure, I hated them all except for Max, but it was a fond sort of hatred—an entertaining one, anyway. The female protector was almost a friend now, and we had the same taste in books. I was already bound to the Eli twat. While he had a bad habit of almost killing me, I couldn't pretend that he wasn't at least entertaining in the way he went about it.

The brothers, I was less sure of. I didn't really know the incubus well at all, but he'd been fun enough to tease while bored in Lucifer's dungeon.

And the wolf. Well, the wolf was a prick.

But there was a sort of familiarity with his rough edges. Sometimes, I almost swore that when I looked at him, I saw a version of myself. One I worked on burying a long, long time ago.

Suddenly my chest felt tight and I turned away from her, staring instead at the splotchy ceiling—white, originally, but speckled with large stains that I didn't want to investigate too closely.

I'd had family before—by blood and by choice—neither wanted anything to do with me.

And for good reason too.

Would Max feel the same if she found out the truth?

Her soft fingers crawled along my jawline as she gently forced my gaze back to hers. "What's wrong? Did I—should I not have said that?"

I stared back at her, at the blank look on my face reflected in her dark eyes. Not for the first time, I wished that I could rewind time—make different decisions in my life. If not for myself and the people I hurt, then for her—so that I could be someone even minutely deserving of this woman's deeply misplaced affection.

The look of concern melted into something else as her eyes widened, the muscles in her back stiffening as she started to pull her hand away. "Was I wrong? Do you not feel the same? You don't still want to eat us all do you?" A small line formed between her brows. "Like, given the option between killing one of us and eating an—I don't know, a cow or something, you'd choose the cow, right? Or did I supremely misjudge things?"

I broke out into a loud laugh that cut through the vestigial memories of my past and reached all the way through to my bones. "I still very much want to eat you, little protector."

Her breath caught at that, her eyes lingering on my mouth as she swallowed. I wasn't sure if she was entirely aware of it, but her back arched slightly as her hips tilted towards mine.

When she licked her bottom lip, I felt my dick start to stiffen with the thought of my tongue tracing that same path.

"Don't look at me like that," I said, stifling a groan, "it makes my mind think up scenarios you won't want me to act on—not even when the succubus is in control."

For a moment, her fingers twitched in indecision, but then she reached her hand forward again, her nails softly scratching against my jaw, as her eyes narrowed in challenge. "The succubus doesn't have desires independent of my own. I understand that now," she said, her voice deepening as she pulled herself closer to me until our faces were separated by nothing but a breath, her eyes staring into mine until I was certain she'd be able to see all of the things I suddenly so desperately wanted to keep hidden.

I shivered as her hand trailed down my neck to rest at my chest, as she threaded her leg through both of mine until all that I could focus on was the enticing dampness drenching the thin cloth of her underwear against my thigh.

I was suddenly very grateful for my heightened sense of smell.

I'd never been so thirsty before, but blood was just an afterthought.

"And right now," she whispered against my lips before she briefly pressed hers against them in a featherlight touch, "we both very much want you to act."

She pressed her core against my leg, grinding against me.

When her lips pulled back from mine on a soft moan, my brain caught up to my body. I threaded my fingers through her hair and crashed my lips to hers, swallowing her soft, mewling noises.

She tasted sweeter than I remembered and the feel of so much of her skin against me made my head feel dizzy.

But I wanted more of it—I was slowly growing addicted to every single inch of her. I wanted to mark her, lick her, draw every ounce of pleasure from her that I could.

I slid my fingers under the elastic of her sports bra and lifted it over her head. Her nipples were hard already and her thighs tightened against mine when I pulled one between my lips. She was like putty, her back arching and body molding to me as if I was a puppet master directing her, as if she was designed to fit perfectly against me.

With my tongue, I tasted her clavicle, her shoulder, her throat—drawing a particularly delicious groan when I nipped at a spot a few inches below her jaw. I slid my hand down her stomach, pebbling every inch of flesh that I touched, until I reached the seam of her underwear.

In the same breath, I swept my tongue against hers and I slid two fingers into her slick folds. My pants strained at how soaked and ready she was, at the way her hips rolled as she fucked my hand.

"Jesus fucking Christ," I whispered, inhaling her scent. "I don't think I've ever wanted anyone so badly in my entire life." She arched into me again, gasping as my thumb circled her clit. "Fuck that, I know I haven't."

With shaking hands. She pulled my shirt up and slid her fingers inside the band of my sweatpants. When she took me into her hand and stroked me, I groaned into her mouth like a teenage boy.

"Shh," she whispered, and I could hear the grin in her voice. She enjoyed how badly I wanted her, liked the effect that she had on me. "We have to be quiet."

"What? Why?" I asked, pinching her clit lightly and sucking her neck as she tilted her head back. "I want to make you scream until your voice goes all hoarse and crackly." I let out a frustrated growl. "Fuck this fabric. I want it all gone."

I ripped the underwear from her and her eyes sparked with pleasure at the brief flash of pain as the cotton tore against her skin.

Fuck me sideways. This girl was going to be the ruin of me.

"Sarah's in the other room. Wolf hearing. Remember? I'm not supposed to be here." But then her whisper turned into a deep moan when I pushed my sweatpants out of the way and slid my cock against her folds. "Oh my god. Holy fuck."

"Quiet," I echoed, pleased when she stifled her moans by burying her face into my neck so that they vibrated through me. "What do you want, little protector?" I teased her clit with the head of my dick, using every ounce of control I had not to sheath myself inside of her right now.

Her eyes locked on mine, clear and dark and filled with a lust that would have made my knees weak if I was standing.

"I want you." She slid slowly and deliberately against me, and I nearly came right then and there. "I'm done lying to myself, done pretending that I don't. I want you. And I don't want to wait any longer to have you."

Something inside of me shifted and cracked. With one hand at the base of her back, I pulled her to me until her chest pressed against mine. I didn't break eye contact as I slid inside of her. I wanted to watch every expression, every sensation flitter across her face—wanted her to watch the same in mine. "You already have me. You've had me from the moment you walked by my cell in those labs, I just didn't quite understand the extent of it then."

I slid out of her, but not all the way, savoring every second of my body connecting with hers, rolling my hips into her again —and again and again.

I was used to fucking hard and rough, used to blood and bruises and all the fun that came with pleasure and pain.

But this—this was new.

Tender almost.

She placed her hand at the base of my skull and set the pace, riding me so slowly that every inch of me ached and pulsed for her. Not once did she look away.

I felt like her stare would swallow me whole, and she wouldn't get a single protest from me.

There was a soft, quiet strength in the lines of her face, a confidence that made me almost shy—something I'd never felt during sex before.

An electric tingle shot through my spine—one I always associated with a succubus pulling energy from me. But this was so much stronger, so much more intoxicating. Instead of draining me, it felt like I was being filled up—with something better and new. I let myself drown in the feel of it—warm and cold all at once, like my nerves didn't know which way was up.

Her hand pressed down against my mouth, stifling my

groan and I playfully bit down against the side of her hand. Heat flashed in her eyes, the whites swallowed up by a swirling black. She rode me harder, picking up the pace as her tits bounced softly above me. Her thumb traced the seam of my lips, parting them open. She pressed the pad of her finger against my canine tooth, her tongue sliding enticingly over her own.

She pulled me to her so that we were sitting, our torsos glued together with a sticky layer of sweat as she tightened around my dick inside of her.

"Darius?" I felt my name against the shell of my ear, more than I heard it.

I massaged my thumbs into her lower back, taking the nipple I'd neglected before into my mouth. "Mmm?" I asked, pleased when she gasped.

I bit down softly and she carved her fingers into my shoulder blades as she threw her head back, picking up the pace of each thrust.

"You were right," she gasped, her hand coming up to touch my cheek in a move both gentle and possessive that had my heartbeat galloping at a thunderous pace. "I do want you to bite me." My dick pulsed and she moaned. "In fact, consider this me begging for it."

I felt her clench around me as she uttered the words and I had to think of her motley crew of misfits doing a tap dance to keep myself from coming undone so quickly. I wasn't ready for this to be over, not yet. Not when I'd waited so long like a nice, patient, incredibly thoughtful vampire.

Seriously, I deserved a damn trophy.

"Are you sure?" I asked, dragging my focus from the softly beating pulse at her neck to see her eyes. There was a vulnerability there, but also a raging desire that could almost compete with my own. "That's not a passing thing, Max—allowing someone to feed from you during sex. It means something to vampires. Especially when they're with someone that they l —" I swallowed the word back, "like. It means something to me."

I'd fed from people during sex before, but in my gut I knew that this would be different—that she was different.

She slowed her rhythm, brushed her lips softly against mine. "You're not a passing thing, Darius. I'm sure."

My breath got stuck in my lungs at the sound of my name on her tongue. How did she do that? Make it sound so important, so worthy?

I froze, staring at her throat—mesmerized and fucking terrified.

She pulled closer to me, kissed my jaw, my earlobe, the crook of my neck, until my lips were pressed at the crest of where her neck met her shoulders.

I breathed her in, my own blood coursing through my veins in anticipation of tasting hers.

My fangs descended and, unable to resist the open invitation and temptation for a second a longer, they sank into her skin.

She gasped at first, but didn't scream, instead she sank into the feed, like she craved it as much as I did.

My groan spilled into hers, concerns about the she-wolf overhearing things long forgotten as her blood washed over my tongue—warm and spicy and rich.

I'd never tasted anything like her before. It felt like I was in the fairytale fae land—one taste and I was a captive forever.

She had me hook, line, and sinker.

Her fingernails dug into my back, carving their way down in a delicious sting as I lapped her up, each ounce better than the last.

Blood was a magical thing in the supernatural world, but there were no words for how hers made me feel as I drank it in —powerful and strong, like it was an elixir that I'd been desperately needing my entire life. I wasn't sure how I'd survived so long without it.

I felt her pull power from me as I did the same from her, like an infinite loop of energy and ecstasy.

"Oh my god," she whimpered and I started to withdraw before she clutched my head to her neck. "What are you doing? Keep going. I'm so close, this is—this is—"

Could she feel it too? The connection solidifying between us—like brass turned to gold.

A mate bond.

I'd suspected it before. I'd felt too attached for it to be anything less than that. And that early attachment and intrigue just seemed to grow and grow and grow—until it was almost too much for me to bear.

I wasn't sure how or why or if this was permanent and like the bonds my people used to experience years ago, but right now, there was no denying it.

She was perfect.

She was *mine.*

I gripped her wrists and slid her up and down my shaft, speeding up with her gasps as her blood warmed my lips until they tingled.

I felt her clench around me as the waves of the orgasm took over. She fell against me like jelly as mine met hers with equal fervor.

My vision went blurry until all I could see were dancing lights and dots as we collapsed into the pillows as one.

"Fuck," I whispered, stunned silly but clutching her to my chest like she might disappear at any moment—what happened nothing but a delicious fever dream that I'd concocted in my head.

Only my head had never come close to creating anything as spectacular as that.

"Fuck," she echoed, her breath kissing my skin as her body

lifted and sank into mine with each inhale and exhale. "That—that was—"

I nodded, even though she couldn't see it, just as unable to put what that was into words as she was.

We laid like that, simply breathing against each other, as much of my skin against as much of hers as we could achieve, until we were a tired, spent, tangled set of limbs.

As our breathing calmed and the sweat cooled on our skin, she turned to the TV. A demon baby clawed its way out of the main character's belly and she laughed, her chuckle against my chest pulling a mirrored one from mine.

Part of me feared that she'd push off of me at any instant, her eyes wide with regret and unable to meet mine. That she'd talk herself out of what had happened, apologize and make excuses, like she had before.

But when she finally did lift her head off my chest—and only by a few inches, like she wasn't quite ready to leave our puddle of afterglow—there was no shame or fear in the small curve of her mouth or the flush of her cheeks.

She opened her mouth to say something, but I pressed mine to hers before she could get a word out, needing to taste her lips again, just to convince myself that what had happened was real.

Her sharp inhale had me pulling away instantly.

Fingers pressed to her lips and came away with a small dot of red. Her eyes widened as she stared at the small stain.

It was only a drop, but panic flooded my lungs.

Reckless. Thoughtless.

Five minutes in and I'd already ruined everything.

How had I not wiped my mouth first?

But the initial repulsion I thought I saw mirrored in her expression dissipated into something that looked almost like curiosity as she wiped the stain away.

She pressed her lips to mine again, her tongue licking the seam of my mouth until my own met hers.

The kiss was impossibly slow and languid as we explored each other, tasted each other.

I felt my heart beat a hectic drum against my ribs, the pulse throbbing throughout my body. This was so...new to me. So unlike my typical lays. The tightness of my chest, the fluttering in my stomach terrified and excited me in equal measures.

Too soon, she pulled away, her head swaying slightly like she was dizzy.

"Um," her eyes dropped down, a shy smile on her face. "I should probably go soon."

Go? Fuck no.

I didn't want to ever let this girl out of my sight or out of my bed ever again.

"I think I've definitely got the strength to make it back to my room if I concentrate for a few minutes." That delicious blush colored her tan cheeks again.

"You'll come back?" I hated how desperate I sounded, how terrified of rejection I suddenly felt. "When it's safe for you to, I mean. You won't go as long before visiting again, will you?"

I heard the shift in my breathing as I waited for her to answer—suddenly it was almost difficult to look at her, like each time I did there was a chance for her expression to change into one of anger or guilt or regret.

"We're going to Seattle for a mission," she said, pulling herself off of me and into a seated position as she reached for her bra. "Day after tomorrow. It's a diversion. Seamus set it up for us. From there," she picked up the drenched scraps that were formerly used as underwear and shot me a shy smile. I grinned before handing her my black sweatpants. "From there, we're going to make our way back to hell. Hopefully with more ease than before."

I watched her as she sat next to me, mission-face on, hungry at the sight of her drowning in my clothes. "I'm coming."

Her face scrunched up as she considered for a long moment —my fingernails bit into the palms of my hand as I waited for her to push back. But then she simply nodded. "Yes, you should. But we can't exactly sneak you onto a Guild plane."

Relief flooded me. She wanted me there—wasn't going to fight me on this. It was an issue of pragmatics, nothing more. "We can meet at Claude's bar. But if that doesn't work, I'll find you before you reach the portal. I won't let you go to hell without me. That's a promise."

She didn't look concerned or creeped out. If anything, the sentiment seemed to settle inside of her like warm tea. She was done resisting, done pretending that there wasn't an inexorable connection between us—that we weren't linked and a fundamental part of each other now.

With a touch so faint that I almost didn't feel it, she brushed her lips against mine—the feathery sensation sent a bolt of electricity through my body.

I wanted her again, right now—fuck, I wanted her even more than I had wanted her before, if that was even possible.

When I opened my eyes to tell her so, she was gone.

14

MAX

I ran my fingers over my neck, tracing the area, remembering the way it felt to have Darius's fangs inside of me. Painful, sure—but so much more than that. It was a pleasurable sort of pain. One that made my legs wobbly just thinking about it. So different from the other times I'd been bitten.

Maybe because those vampires had been attacking, not seducing me.

And the marks were gone. Part of me was relieved, but a deeper part was almost disappointed, wanting the lingering proof of what had happened.

Strangely, I didn't regret it at all. Sex with Darius was softer than I'd expected, much more so than it had been in the dream. The real experience was cerebral, intimate in a way that surprised me. It added an intriguing layer to a vampire I already had a difficult time deciphering.

My body craved him the second I'd left his embrace, and I had to actively resist the urge to pop back in the next night for seconds.

"Earth to Maxine." Izzy snapped her fingers in front of my face.

"I hate my full name," I grumbled, more out of habit than anything else.

We were on one of The Guild planes, soaring over the mountains on our way to Seattle. The mission was a complicated one, one that required multiple teams. Eli and Seamus had worked it out so that we were traveling with Ten. Of course, Seamus had no idea that we were going to be ditching the mission for a rendezvous in hell, but Eli assured us that he had come to some sort of an understanding with his father.

Another set of protectors would be arriving to meet us in the morning. There weren't very many to spare these days.

She snorted. "That's why I used it. I've been trying to get your attention for five minutes and you've just been sitting there with a dazed, glassy-eyed expression. What were you thinking about?"

My cheeks heated when I met her eyes.

"Ah, I see." She wiggled her eyebrows. "That explains the drool."

I told her about what had happened when we were packing for the trip, desperate to voice it out loud to someone who wouldn't instantly go hunt Darius down and drive a stake through his heart.

Izzy was pretty much my only option. And while she went momentarily apeshit over the fact that I'd willingly had sex with a vampire—I left out the part about letting him drink from me—she eventually settled into a very Izzy-like demand that I give a play-by-play account of events, insisting that she needed to live vicariously through me until her sex life got a "much-needed reboot or included something more exciting than Bob."

Bob was short for 'battery operated boyfriend'—her vibrator.

"What were you trying to get my attention for?" I wanted a subject change ASAP. Too many people were in earshot and I had a feeling Izzy cared a lot less about discretion than I did. Something about that gleam in her eyes and the way she kept glancing at Eli told me that she wanted to throw it in his face for being such a tool after we'd hooked up.

Her rage was stronger than mine was at the moment.

"No fun," she pouted, reading my mind. "We're going to be there soon. Twenty minutes. Time to put your game face on—you ready for the plan?"

The plan.

It was going to be a complicated one to execute. Participate in the mission, plausibly separate ourselves from the rest of the group, and then disappear.

While it was nice that we at least had a first-class flight to Seattle this time, rather than needing to steal a car and take a cramped road trip, we were heading into a much more hostile situation than was ideal. And while I was happy to have Izzy and Ro along for the first part of the trip where I could keep somewhat of an eye on them, I was not stoked about having to leave them behind in enemy territory that could lead to some serious bloodshed.

The last time we were in Seattle, vampires had swarmed our hotel suite like locusts. It was a miracle we'd survived.

I wasn't sure how many more miracles karma had in store for me—or my friends.

"Don't give me that look." Izzy kicked my shoe with hers. "We'll be careful. We know our roles for the gig. I may not, you know," she wiggled her fingers around, "have your particular skill set, but I'm no slouch. I've been hitting the sparring mats hard while you've been away." It was true, she'd improved a lot over a very brief period, and she had already been excellent to begin with. But that didn't stop me from worrying about her. The best protector in the world was little match for even a weak demon. "And, if luck is on our side, we'll be in bed by midnight with enough intel to please even Tarren—no bandages or bruises in sight. They'll be sending in the big dogs for the real mission as soon as they get back from their current one."

Things were never that easy, never that seamless. Not anymore.

"Yeah," I said, though I couldn't shake the guilt lingering low in my belly. I glanced across the plane, where Ro was huddled up with a book. I hadn't seen him turn a single page in the last hour. He'd finally stopped fighting me about leaving again, but he wasn't happy about it.

The light and easy 'gig' had changed dramatically since we'd initially been assigned to the mission. Two protectors went missing in the city less than twenty-four hours ago and we were going in to help the remaining members of the team with the search.

It wouldn't be a super big surprise given the recent uptick in attacks, except for the fact that the team in question was Three. I hadn't met any of them personally, but they were one of the most impressive teams we had. The fact that two of them had disappeared without a trace had sent a ripple of anxiety pouring through Headquarters. It also didn't help that what the remaining members had discovered in the meantime was a game changer.

As suspected, there was a series of mysterious killings in the city that screamed demon activity. Only instead of going after protectors or humans like they usually did, Three reported that the demons were also killing each other—like some kind of supernatural mafia war was ripping Seattle down the seams.

And they were getting lazy, leaving behind evidence that would have the human world eagerly tuning in to and gobbling up all the conspiracy websites they could find if we didn't get a handle on things quickly.

It led credence to Lucifer's comments about competing

demonic factions—which unfortunately meant that his other theories were looking more plausible by association.

Nothing like a good apocalypse to keep shit interesting.

"Hey," Izzy elbowed me in my side, "stop chewing your lip. We're not expecting any real action here. Just getting bossed around by Three, obtaining as much intel as possible, hopefully locating Three's missing team members—who are ideally just off on an extremely untimely bar crawl—and maybe extracting one or two of the demons responsible for the shitstorm in the city right now." She took a deep breath, winded slightly from her list. "Okay, yeah. That's a lot. But realistically, we'll end up scouting until the others meet up with us. No need to ooze concern out of every pore until it's absolutely necessary."

The comment about extracting demons made my stomach clench every time I thought about it. Tarren wanted them brought back alive, to study in the labs—a fate half the members of Six were in constant danger of experiencing.

I wasn't sure why exactly, but Headquarters was buzzing about the high-up out-of-towners' obsession with procuring and studying demons. Like they'd found something new, or were hoping to soon.

Reza's sardonic laugh pulled me out of the thought spiral. She stood behind us, hovering in the aisle with a water bottle dangling precariously close to Izzy's head. "Yeah, Max, don't worry. Nothing to be scared about—just leave the hard stuff to those of us who aren't afraid to face it head on—those of us who actually belong here and are allowed to function without a babysitter."

I clenched my jaw, fists wrapping around the arm rests at my sides. I'd mostly ignored her taunting, chilly stare since I got back, but in the confines of a small plane, avoidance was a difficult strategy to employ.

"Ignore her." Izzy rolled her eyes. "She's just still got a stick up her ass because you and Six went on a secret mission and left her behind to twiddle her thumbs up her ass."

That saying—if looks could kill—it was designed for Reza in this moment. Pretty sure she was skinning me alive with those sparkly blue eyes of hers. She snorted and tried to play it off, but the set of her jaw made it clear that Izzy wasn't completely off. "Please. Everyone worth their salt knows that you manipulated them into taking you like some attention-starved, selfish asshole."

"You know nothing Jon Snow," Izzy said, her voice low and deep and in a strange Irish accent that sounded slightly like a country twang at the same time. "Now go lap up the meager bits of attention you can pull from Atlas while he has nowhere to escape you."

She had a way of joking around one minute and slicing someone from head to foot the next. It was one of those personality traits that made me exceedingly happy that I was almost always on her good side.

"The only reason you're still here is because of who your father is." Reza continued, like she hadn't heard Izzy at all. I could tell from the tension in her shoulders though that she had. "Which is ridiculous. He isn't even your real fucking father." Her voice grew softer as she leaned over Izzy's seat to get closer to mine. "Blood, history—those things matter to our people and you have neither."

Izzy pinched the bridge of her nose. "Everyone has blood and history—and your antiquated bullshit and privilege are stinking up the plane."

"Your plan backfired though, didn't it?" Reza continued, her thin brow arched. "Atlas can't stand to be in the same room as you. And despite your best efforts, you've failed spectacularly at blowing up my future."

"What are you talking about?" I asked. I didn't have the energy to poke the bear like Izzy did. With everything going on, Reza seemed so inconsequential—her frustrations nothing but

insecurities.

A lopsided grin tugged at her lips. "Haven't you heard? Atlas and I are officially going to have our bonding ceremony next month. It's been cleared with our families and with The Guild. Six might be stuck carting you around and treating you with kid gloves like the child you are, but that's temporary. After the ceremony, we'll make sure that we're given the space and respect that we deserve."

My stomach turned to stone.

"Am I invisible? Did you misunderstand me? Let me make myself more clear. Get fucking bent," Izzy shot back as she swatted the blond curls waving around in her face. "We have serious shit to focus on right now. So go sit back down and cozy up to your boyfriend, or you're going to get yourself decked in the face before the mission even starts." She glanced at her fingernails like she was inspecting her cuticles. "I can't be responsible for my impulses when I'm in the presence of this much pettiness."

Reza said something else, but I didn't really hear her. Instead I couldn't draw my focus from a few feet away, where Atlas was sitting, dark eyes locked on mine. They were completely impenetrable. The muscles in his jaw ticked, but then he turned back to Eli, ignoring me again.

It was true.

He was going to bond to Reza.

I'd known forever that this was always the end goal for them—but I'd thought that over the last few weeks, that had, I don't know, changed somehow?

It felt like the air was being sucked from my lungs, and suddenly I felt like I needed to puke. Something deep down inside of me rebelled at the very thought of Atlas permanently linking himself to Reza.

No. Not just to Reza, to anyone.

I tried to take deep breaths in and out, to focus on the mission and how exactly we were going to ditch everyone for a trip to hell. But for the rest of the trip, I did nothing but stare out the window, vaguely aware of Izzy's thumb rubbing small, comforting circles on the back of my hand.

When we got off the plane, we were met by two protectors I'd never seen before. I assumed that they were Des and Regan, the two members of Three who weren't missing, though they didn't smile or introduce themselves. The closest they came was to give Atlas one of those acknowledging bro nods. Neither of them seemed interested in focusing much on the rest of us, but I understood why—we were pawns, here to be used. And they were probably hyper focused on getting their teammates back as quickly as possible.

Instead of wasting time on pleasantries, they got straight to business, separating everyone out by teams, with plans for one of them to join Six and the other to join Ten. They circled various streets on an old school map where they wanted each of us to search. Ten was mostly focusing on the southern half of the city and Six on the northern—where the original attack had taken place. We were going to try and retrace the steps of the initial mission, even though Des and Regan had been doing so nonstop already, hunting for a hint as to what had happened to their team members, or where they might have gone.

No one wanted to say the thing that lingered on all of our minds—that they were most likely dead. I could see it in the set of Des and Regan's shoulders—the gravity that seemed to sink them into the ground. They channeled their tension into action, into assigning roles and pushing us all to the same goal —find out what happened, and don't get dead in the process. They'd save the meatier work for when the other teams joined us later.

I was paired with Six, despite technically being a member

of Ten. I was like Eli's added appendage since I was still essentially on parole—an announcement that made the slightly less moody-looking member of Three stare at me with amusement —Des, I thought—and the grumpier one curl his lip with disgust.

Thankfully, Des was the one joining us.

Reza was right. I really did seem like a petulant child. It was strange, seeing myself through the eyes of those who only heard whispers about me. Still, their mild disgust was far better than the alternative.

If any of them knew the truth, I'd be knocked out and thrown to the labs before I could utter the word "hellhound." That, or I'd meet a far less drawn-out fate.

I knew that the odds of me seeing Izzy and Ro again on this trip were slim—I was to dip out at the first opportunity— so I hugged them both. We tried to be quick, not wanting to raise suspicions with a drawn out goodbye. We'd already said our farewells back in the cabin. But my chest still tightened at the shattered, terrified look in Ro's eyes before he turned away with Izzy and left for their patrol with the rest of their team.

"Okay," Eli nodded to the map, his shoulders stiff, the usual snarkiness in his demeanor noticeably absent. "Looks like we're pretty close to where shit went down, so let's break up, comb through this neighborhood, and see if any signs or tracks jump out at us."

Dec and I nodded and grabbed our small packs.

"Wait."

A large hand clapped on my shoulder. When I spun around, I was less than a few inches from Atlas.

I hated that even now, when we were on a mission with very high stakes, when I knew that he was promised to someone else, my heart still dipped at the feel of him so close.

"Stick close. Don't do anything reckless. This should be

relatively simple, but," he shrugged, and I read the rest in his silence—things were never simple anymore.

I nodded, swallowing the lingering emotion stuck in my throat as Reza walked up to us, brow arched in challenge.

"How many were there?" Reza asked Des. She pulled her arm across her chest like she was stretching for a sparring match, not getting ready to discreetly hunt for signs of demon activity in a busy neighborhood. "And how many of each species are we talking about?"

Des stared at her, said nothing until a family of four walked past us, eyeing our strange group with interest, then shook his head. "I don't know. Regan and I weren't there. We were at a different location. Heard them report a handful of vamps fighting each other through my earpiece, then everything went radio silent. That's all we know."

We split into two groups—Des, Atlas, and Reza in one, me, Dec, and Eli in the other. We walked in relative silence for two hours, never going more than half a mile from the other half of our team, entering into mindless conversation about the weather—chilly with mist-like rain—and various tourist activities—the Locks, the market, some seafood restaurant Dec knew a surprising bit of info about—whenever we got close to a group of humans.

Everything seemed pretty quiet, no signs of any skirmishes, no mystery trails of blood.

Eli even charmed a few shop owners with that winning smirk of his, asked if they'd noticed anything unusual over the last day or two, if crime was particularly bad in the area—inviting the humans that lived here to lead us to any clues they'd unconsciously sussed out on their own, without realizing that they might be linked to demonic activity.

Nothing.

But even so, something felt off. Like the air was charged with something that I hadn't noticed the last time we were in the city. In a strange way, it felt almost like hell had—quiet, but the sort of quiet that came before a storm—we were stuck in the eye, waiting for the shoe to drop.

When we turned down a strange street, we followed an unpaved path towards some shipping containers that lined the waterfront. The area had an old warehouse sort of vibe. No one was around and it was quiet, peaceful even.

"Is it possible that whatever group of vampires Three stumbled upon," I said kicking a large pebble down the path in front of us, "is just, I don't know, gone? It seems sort of unproductive, combing the city by foot like this, hoping something calls to us or pops out of an alley, doesn't it? If vamps don't want to be found, they're not going to be. Besides, they could've even used the portal to get back to hell by now, who knows."

I whispered the last part to Eli and Dec, keeping an eye on the other three about a quarter mile away from us.

Dec tilted her head, considering. "You're not wrong, though I doubt anyone besides us is voluntarily trying to get back to hell."

"This is all just unprecedented for The Guild." Eli scratched his jaw as he stared at Des. "Even the big guns don't know how to handle this shit anymore. All of our rulebooks have just been thrown out the window the last few weeks—we're all kind of like fish out of water, hoping to catch a break or a spare bit of luck."

"Should we try to dip out now?" Dec asked, craning her neck back towards where we'd come. "Tell them we're going to take a break and then just make our way towards Claude's bar? Seems like we're just wasting time at this p—"

Her sentence trailed as she went flying through the air and landed with an echoey thud into the side of an abandoned truck.

Eli and I spun around, just as I heard the rest of our group's feet pound a path in our direction.

We were met with four pairs of dark stares.

They were all varying sizes, dressed more or less like everyone else I'd seen in the city—neutral-colored clothing, jackets with hoods, boots. All of them had matching, malicious grins, the sort that sent chills down your spine. I'd have thought they were a group of pricks, looking to pick a fight, but the power with which they'd thrown Declan made it clear they weren't human.

Demons, then—but which species?

I grabbed my blade from my thigh holster, sensing Eli and Declan do the same thing. Between the six of us, it wouldn't be impossible to take on four demons, so long as they were vamps or wolves, anyway. We didn't stand a chance against anyone with Lucifer's kind of power.

But then six more appeared from the other side of the alley, corralling us like sheep.

Something about the way they circled us, the pleased, lopsided grin on a few of their faces, told me that they'd been watching us—that they knew we weren't humans.

They'd lured us here.

Watched us patiently until we'd sectioned ourselves off from the busier parts of the neighborhood.

Before the others fully reached us, they attacked.

The one closest to us lunged for Eli, and I saw a pair of gleaming fangs from the corner of my eye. Vampires then. At least some of them.

Without waiting for the two that were angled towards me to approach, I leapt towards them, knife poised and ready to strike.

It would be ideal to conceal my speed and strength from Reza and Des, but something told me that if I held back too much, we'd all end up dead.

My blade sank into the first one's chest, his eyes wide with surprise at how quickly I was able to reach him, at the force behind the blow—and then the surprise emptied into nothingness.

For a brief moment, my stomach bottomed at the realization that I'd killed another vampire.

But that doubt disappeared as his friend reached for my neck, fangs distended. He'd recovered from the shock of my speed much more quickly than the dead one had and I knew that trick wouldn't work on the rest of them again.

Maybe my new rule would just be that I wouldn't kill anyone until they tried to kill me or one of my friends. That was my new clear-cut divide—there was no good and evil, just death and survival. I'd do what I had to do to make sure that me and my friends circled closer to the latter.

The vampire's fangs grazed my neck, scraping a thin layer of my skin off. Gross. And ouch. This guy was definitely going in the dead column.

He met me blow for blow and I heard Atlas and the others clash with their own demons in a storm of grunts and groans.

My fist mashed into the vamp's face, his fang digging into my skin as it collided—the adrenaline was so high that I couldn't tell if it was his bones crunching or mine.

A quick scan showed me that everyone on my team—Des and Reza included—was matched with a vamp, some with two, the dust from the ground coating us all in a strange globe of blood, battle rage, and a cacophony of grunts.

The familiar tingle crept along my skin and I knew that I was close to adding fire into the mix.

It was getting more and more difficult to contain the magic, but it also felt stronger—more thirsty than it had ever been before. A small, unfamiliar part of me wanted to obliterate every one of these vamps who'd attacked us, laying in wait thinking we would be easy pickings.

Reza and Des were distracted enough that I allowed the fire to lick the shell of my hand as I punched the vampire in the chest. His lips parted in a scream of agony as he clutched at his torso, trying to peel back flames that wouldn't respond to his will.

Instead, they responded to mine, devouring him until his bright green eyes dulled into that certain nothingness that was growing more and more familiar.

For a moment, a wicked pride flared through me—pure power coursed through my veins and I enjoyed being in control of it, enjoyed being able to protect myself and others.

Okay. Two down.

From the looks of it, it seemed like Atlas and Dec had taken down another, and Des was holding his own.

Maybe we'd get out of this without me having to rely too heavily on my powers.

But then a vampire behind me grabbed my arm and spun me around, a victorious glint in his eye. "It's you. You're the one we've been looking for."

Des and Reza may not have seen me light the other vamp up, but this asshole had.

I tried to shake him loose as he started to drag me to the outskirts of the battle, afraid of using my powers again in case another one of them noticed.

These asshats had been looking for me, specifically? Why?

"Fuck," Eli roared, his blade stabbing into the vampire at his side as he dodged a blow from another. It wasn't a kill shot, but it had the vamp bending over in a loud, angry groan, distracting him long enough for Eli to maneuver himself out of his grasp.

He seemed faster too, more able to hold his own against the demons. Maybe because of all the practice we'd gotten over the last month.

I followed the look of horror on his face and saw more figures emerging from the shadows between the warehouses.

There had to be at least ten more.

Fuck was right.

So much for an easy intel gig. We were well and truly screwed.

I turned to Atlas, hoping that he'd have some idea as to how to get us all out of this mess without me resorting to laying my secrets out for Des and Reza to devour up and package for Tarren's greedy hands.

Yellow flashed in his eyes as they locked on the spot where the vamp's hand clutched me, and I knew that he was just as close to letting his demon out as I was.

Thankfully, Des and Reza were too busy with their own battles to notice just yet, but something told me we wouldn't be able to conceal Atlas's secret if he popped into a wolf in the middle of a battlefield.

Reza's eyes met mine and narrowed, pure hatred seething from them. She peeled back her arm, blood-coated blade pointing in my direction. She was poised to throw and judging from the venom in her icy eyes, was thirsty for a kill.

My heart skipped when I realized she was aiming for me.

Had she seen me use the fire?

She clenched her jaw and threw the dagger.

Only instead of the blade burying itself in my chest, it sailed past my face and landed in the eyeball of the vamp gripping me.

My shoulders sagged in relief and I nodded in gratitude before ripping the blade from his eye socket and burying it smoothly in his chest.

Hopefully he was the only one who'd seen my sparkler trick.

Then, something strange happened. The new demons— also vampires by the looks of them—started to attack not only us, but the original set we were fighting.

"What," Declan grunted, "the actual fuck," her emerald

gaze latched briefly onto me as she elbowed one of the dick-holes in the chest, "is going on here?"

None of this made sense. It was pure chaos. The ground was sprayed with blood, a mix of ours and theirs. The bodies of demons piled up, creating a difficult terrain to navigate as we leapt over and tripped on lifeless corpses. The smell of death coated my nostrils and I tried to breathe from my mouth, sick with the stench.

Another strong arm gripped my left shoulder and spun me around. I gripped the blade in my right hand, ready to stab up through the sternum when I met a familiar pair of familiar eyes—one gold and one black.

Darius.

Only there was a hostility in his expression that I'd never seen directed towards me, his grip punishing, fingers digging in hard enough to bruise.

His eyes widened slightly, like he only just recognized me and it was then that I realized something about him was different—off.

The mottled gold eye that usually peered at me from his right side was on his left, like a distorted mirror. The typical teasing heat I found when I stared into it was replaced by a hardness—a closed-off distance I couldn't reach or even recognize.

Realization dawned slow and hard.

"Claude?" I asked, my heartbeat pounding against my sternum as I flexed my fingers, unsure whether or not I'd need to use my blade in this particular encounter.

Judging from the daggers shooting from his eyes, odds were high that I would.

"You," he bit out, the word clipped. "What the fuck are you doing back in my city?"

15

MAX

On closer inspection, his hair was shorter than Darius's, his posture more rigid, and he was dressed in a nice white button up, rolled to his elbows, that would have seemed ridiculous on Darius.

The blood splattering the front of his shirt was the only thing that screamed "not here for a business meeting."

"You survived hell and somehow made it out alive, then?" He glanced behind me briefly, before pulling me to the side of one of the gray buildings where we weren't in anyone's line of sight. He shoved me roughly against the wall, my hair snagging against the rough concrete. "Impressive, I'll give you that. Perhaps you're even more intriguing than I'd originally given you credit for. But something tells me you're also to answer for the current fuckery roaring through the city."

"You're behind the attacks in the city? The missing protectors?" I wasn't sure why I was so surprised; Claude was scary as fuck, but I'd sort of chalked him up as a reasonably good dude, all things considered. He hadn't killed us—hell, he'd even saved us at one point—so he wasn't *evil,* evil, despite the way his stare was skinning me like a blade.

He was sort of like Darius—unpredictable, powerful, but you could count on him to do the right thing at least twenty percent of the time. Hopefully right now, the odds were in my favor.

His eyes narrowed. "Which attacks are you referring to? Not sure if you've noticed during your travels, but we're living in a completely new world these days. Factions of demons are splitting my city apart, cracking the very tenuous peace I've worked years to create and maintain."

"I mean," I nodded back towards where we'd come from, "just saying, looks like you brought a pack of vampires to an already tense situation...and they are currently trying to kill me and my friends." I ripped my arm from his grip and shoved him away, raising my blade between us, "speaking of which, I need to get back before they actually succeed. So unless you want a showdown with me, I suggest you get out of my way."

I turned to get back to the fight, but he held out his arm, stopping me.

"Why are you here, Max?" His head tilted as he studied me, like I was a confusing art installation and not a girl who'd just threatened to gut him if he didn't let me go. He seemed relatively calm and collected considering the backdrop of bodies hitting the pavement and battle cries sounding around us.

I clenched my jaw, ready to force him the fuck out of my way, then let out a frustrated grunt and dropped my blade at my side. What the fuck was it with these brothers? I couldn't seem to bring myself to kill either one of them.

"We need to get back into hell. The plan was for Eli, Declan, and I to peel off from the group and come find you." I shrugged. "Things got messy."

"That seems to happen a lot where you're involved." He took a deep breath, considered me for a moment. When I made to step around him again and head back into the fray, he tensed his arm, stopping me. "Wait here."

He turned the corner and went back to the bloodshed.

Obviously, I disobeyed the order and followed.

He caught the attention of a few of the vamps, nodded his head towards Atlas and the others, pausing in some sort of silent standoff until his group acknowledged him.

Then he turned around, rolling his eyes when he nearly ran into me. "I see your listening skills haven't improved. My people won't touch yours—just this once. Consider them safe and this particular skirmish over. They'll help keep the ones I don't recognize busy while you tell me what you're doing here. But you have my word that the people you came with won't be killed. Not in this fight, anyway. I make no promises for what fate they may or may not meet after they leave."

I narrowed my eyes, considering his claim. "You seriously expect me to believe the vamps out there aren't going to go ham on a small, mostly defenseless group of protectors hungry for demon blood? Some of our own were taken yesterday—we're looking for them, they're not going to just bow out and leave like this is some sort of jovial match."

He sighed. "Believe it or not, Max, I have more important things to worry about than a few stray protectors and the strange group of comically unwise lackeys you surround yourself with. I have no idea who took your missing protectors. Honestly, pray that they are dead, there are far worse fates than a swift death."

I took a deep breath, craned my neck around him so that I could see my friends. They were taking out one of the vampires from the group who'd originally cornered us—and I saw Claude's group focus their attention on the others. A few of them even started to disperse, one of them carrying an unconscious guy I recognized from the original group. I shuddered thinking what they'd do to him.

Torture, no doubt.

But I believed him for now that my group was relatively safe —as safe as they could be in these circumstances.

Reza was injured and lying on the ground, but she looked like she'd survive. Atlas and Des were still in the heat of battle, but the former noticed Claude, met my eyes, and nodded.

This was our chance. We wouldn't get a better opportunity and it would look like the vamps had simply taken us like they had the members of Three. It was almost perfect.

Eli and Declan were standing shoulder to shoulder, both caked in sweat and blood, though most of the latter didn't look like it came from them. They both glanced around quickly, their shoulders relaxing when their eyes landed on me.

Dec made her way towards me, but when one of the remaining original vamps dove for Reza, Eli stiffened for a moment, mouthed the word 'fuck,' and turned back for her.

For a moment, Atlas tensed and I thought he might throw the plan out the window to come join us. But then the vamp he was fighting punched him in the gut and pulled him back into the fight.

I grabbed Claude's forearm, dragging him away from the battle as Declan caught up to us—hoping like hell the diversion would stick and Des and Reza would be too distracted to notice us peacing off with the enemy willingly.

"Claude," she said, her breathing labored. "That certainly makes part of our task list easier. Almost makes up for this clusterfuck."

His lip quirked at her sarcasm. "I'll tell you the same as I told the girl, my group won't hurt yours—consider it a momentary truce necessary to satisfy my curiosity about what could possibly have you all demanding to go back to hell, when more of its occupants than ever are scrambling to leave."

Dec turned back to the fight, paused for a moment, and nodded. "Okay, let's go. Eli's got Reza's back so it's just you and me, Max."

"Is my brother with you? Or have you finally made one wise decision and ditched him before he gets you killed?"

"He's not with us, but will probably join soon," I said, figuring it was best to go with honesty. Something told me he didn't handle surprises too well where Darius was concerned.

He tensed, but picked up the pace, guiding us back to the main street with precision. "Very well."

He undid his shirt, one button at a time, and peeled it off.

"Woah, woah, woah," Declan started, eyes wide with shock, "what the fuck are you doing?"

He glanced at her, shook his head with annoyance and used the balled up shirt to wipe the few traces of blood from his face and arms. Then, he stepped towards me and did the same, before moving to Declan. She stiffened, a challenge in her emerald stare, but then nodded, relenting.

"Better for me to look like a shirtless tool than to draw attention with blood and gore," he said. "Some of us are still trying to keep away from human perception."

He stopped in the first open store, bought a shirt with a cartoon image of an octopus wrapped around the space needle, and slid it over his head, ignoring the questioning looks from the other customers.

The shirt was about two sizes too small and looked absurdly comedic. I stifled my laugh when he shot me a don't-fuck-with-me look and continued on his path towards...wherever the fuck we were going.

After twenty minutes, he stopped outside of a rundown gas station.

"Er, this isn't your bar," Declan pointed out, words slow and tentative like she wasn't sure Claude was in his right mind and didn't want to push him.

He turned to her, jaw tight. "Obviously. We're taking the bus."

"You don't have a car?" I asked, genuinely surprised. I

couldn't picture someone like Claude riding the bus with normies. Somehow, of all the things I'd encountered in the last few weeks, that was one of the most surprising. Did he really just go around taking bus rides to vampy showdowns?

"I do, but it's back there. The bus will be more discreet for our purposes."

He nodded and I saw the bus curving around the corner like an accordion. When it stopped in front of us, he stepped on and placed a plastic card against a reader.

"Um," I said, glancing back at Dec, "we don't have cash for a trip."

Claude arched a brow, shrugged, then stared at the slumped-over bus driver who looked like he was counting down the seconds until the end of his shift.

It was rare for a vampire to have the power to wield compulsion, but that was most definitely what Claude did. We got on without a problem and walked the shaky aisle to the empty back section.

I sat down next to Declan, Claude across from us, and tried to process the ridiculousness of the moment.

"So, er," I glanced at Declan, hyper focused on the way the side of her foot touched mine. "You're just going to take us back to your bar—no resistance?"

It seemed a little too good to be true, especially since the last time I'd seen him, Claude wasn't exactly eager to be helpful. In fact, he pretty much threatened us and told us to never darken his doorstep again.

And here we were, doing just that.

He studied me for a long moment, his hands folded together in his lap. He'd look intimidating if he weren't still wearing that shirt.

"When you breached the barrier last time," his head tilted to the side, unblinking, "I felt it. Almost instantly, things started to accelerate here. The portal became difficult to close, the taste in the air suddenly metallic. Then, within a few days, supernatural activity in the city exploded." His eyes narrowed. "Only, they weren't entering the city through my portal. I think another one has been ripped open somewhere—likely more than one. Creatures have been spilling in, groups have resurrected old territory wars—the relative peace and privacy I've grown to value have been completely upended. Humans aren't the most intelligent of creatures, but some of them are starting to feel the changes in the air—they know something is coming, even if they don't know what that something is. Tensions are high. Things are changing. My connection to the portal is faltering."

I stared at him, not really sure what he wanted me to say. His findings lined up with what we'd learned at Headquarters —increased attacks, more demons in our realm.

Lucifer warned us of all of this too.

"I'm not sure what that has to do with us," Declan said, her hand balled in the pocket of her leggings.

He grinned. The grin held a devious sort of promise—the sort you might expect on the face of a serial killer before he sliced your fingers off to create a stew. Unpleasant. Terrifying.

"Let's not play this game," he said. "I want to know what connection you have, what you know about what's going on. If I'm satisfied, I'll open the portal back for you. Simple as that."

Was it though? I couldn't exactly tell Claude that Lucifer was my father, not now that I knew there were demons hunting me for that very reason. Would he try to use me for his own bidding—make me a pawn in a tangential battle from the one I was already fighting?

I trusted Darius—implicitly now. But I couldn't extend the same trust to his twin.

Hell if Darius was here, he'd probably spend the bus ride trying to murder him.

But I did, in the pit of my stomach, believe that Claude

really did crave a sort of peace in this city. Not because he despised violence, but because he relished being in control. Control was a difficult thing to maintain during times like this.

So I'd settle for partial truths.

"Hell is disintegrating," I said simply, leaning into Declan's shoulder as the bus took a particularly sharp turn. "We've made," I paused, considering. I couldn't exactly call Lucifer and Sam friends, "acquaintances there who think they have answers to stop it from happening. We're working with them, bringing in what we know from the inner circles of The Guild, to try and put an end to things, to the chaos. Before they truly get out of hand—irredeemably so."

He turned to the window, watching the bars zip past, drunk humans stumbling on the sidewalk in small groups—a mixture of joy and tension in the air. "I see."

"You don't sound entirely surprised," Declan said, leaning forward, elbows on her knees. "What do you know?"

Claude shrugged, scratched at the light stubble lining his jaw. "I suspected as much. Hell is a very precarious creation. The portals require extreme amounts of balance to keep them in line. The slightest shift in power creates unprecedented ripples. As I said, I felt them when you walked through—felt something fundamental tug and change. It's not hard to believe that with things transforming as much as they've been, we're headed towards a collapse of sorts. The air feels ominous, heavy."

I narrowed my eyes. "What exactly are you?"

I knew he was a vampire, obviously. But he was far stronger than any vampire I'd ever encountered. And there'd always been something a bit off about him and Darius—more ethereal and complicated than most demons I'd encountered. They seemed to have an almost otherworldly knowing about them.

A wicked smile spread across his face, revealing fang. "You want to know what I am? Do you care to see me in action?"

The threat was clear. But after having Darius's fangs puncture my skin, I didn't find it particularly terrifying—enticing, maybe, but it didn't hold the weight that he'd intended. Not for me, not anymore.

"What is your relationship to the portal? How are you able to open it? How can you sense the changes so acutely?" I asked. Others had mentioned the shift in the air and the increase in supernatural activity made it clear that more demons were present in the realm, but the way Claude spoke about it—it was as if he could sense the shift, as if it was a part of him.

"He hasn't told you then?" A gleam of amusement glittered in his eyes. "Can't say that isn't surprising. He hates coming across in a negative light when he's trying to make a good impression."

Darius? What did he have to do with this?

"I am a gatekeeper, a guardian. He used to be one too," Claude said, like he could read the question in my expression. "We are inexorably linked to the hell realm, bound to the shadow magic that contains it."

"Used to be?" I asked. I could tell from the smirk that he wanted me to ask, that he wanted me to know the story. For a moment, I considered stopping him—considered asking Darius and letting him tell me his version of events first.

But I didn't.

"Twins are very rare in the supernatural communities—coveted. They tend to be more powerful than most, but they are also great conduits for shadow magic, functioning as a biological system of balances, mirrored images."

Now that I thought about it, he and Darius were the only twins I'd met—in hell, Headquarters, all of it.

It explained, at least in part, why when they fought with each other it was like watching gods crash together.

"They are ideal conduits for portals—the only creatures who can survive the energy opening a portal consumes, because there are two to fuse it through. It's the easiest way to balance the energy, to keep the realms stable. The magic flows between them, restoring and depleting in an ongoing process until eventually they die, worn down from the constant surge, like a rock in a riverbed. It is a heavy fate, but without a pair of conduits, portals can become incredibly destructive and dangerous. It's why I'm so concerned about where all of these demons are coming from—they aren't entering through my bar, but there are no other guardians here."

"But Darius hasn't been in Seattle for years," I said, casting a quick glance down the bus to make sure that we were out of ear shot. Not that humans would believe us if they overheard. "And he said we needed to see you to get to the portal. That the magic prevented him from even providing instructions for how to get to hell."

Claude's jaw clenched. "Yes, I am aware how absent my brother has been. We came to our post through particularly violent measures. It was the only option, at the time—to claw our way out of hell, to keep our family safe, to save our sister. And the magic that binds speech about the portals does not come from the shadow world or our people. It is a different spell, woven into the origins of the realm—as a guardian, he used to be immune to it. That's clearly changed during his long sabbatical."

Sister?

"You're triplets?" Declan asked, her posture leaning towards Claude, clinging to every word of his story. "How did you earn your post then?"

He shook his head. "We are not. That's a story for another time. The point is that we were permanently tied to the shadow realm, to the curtain between the worlds—our power is heightened by it, but it is also completely dependent on it. When the portals become unstable, so does our power. We act as a shield and an extension of the division between realms, mirrored with a set of twins on the other side, in hell. But that balance, that shield cracked when my brother abandoned his post. His selfishness killed people, left some worse than dead, tainted from the perversion of the magic."

"Why did he leave?" I asked, my mouth dry. Was he speaking of the tainted ones? Those manipulated by a tainted magic? Was Darius responsible for the creation of some of those creatures?

The thought that he might be sent a sharp pain through my belly.

Claude shrugged, like he was trying to project nonchalance, but I could see in the set of his jaw, the stiffness in his back that retelling this story hit a nerve, created a small dent in his indelible armor. "My brother does what he wants, always has, always will. He cares very little for responsibility and very little for being told what to do. He doesn't like to be tied down—and there are few things more controlling than a magic that slowly consumes you. It was slow at first—the magic affected him more than it did me, ate away at him and made his demons more visceral. We are stronger when we're near portals, they exist in us, a dual manifestation of sorts, or a parasite.The more time he spent away from his post, without an anchor, the less predictable that part of his power became. Until, eventually, something inside of him snapped and he was never the same. He starved that half of himself. He became reckless, consumed by an unquenchable thirst, a version of himself permanently distorted by resisting and burying the shadow magic." He shook his head, and I thought I caught a flash of regret in his eyes. "He might seem to have his darker impulses under control now, but it is nothing but a well-practiced mask. You'd do well to remember that."

I tried to swallow, but it felt like a rock had lodged itself in my throat.

"And your sister?" Declan asked, though I could hear in her voice that she suspected the same as me.

She was part of the collateral, dead because of Darius's actions.

Claude's gaze dropped to his hands, the shake of his head almost imperceptible—but confirmation enough.

This was why he hated his twin, why he'd nearly killed him in his home, why he was so disgusted that Darius would tie himself to Eli—a protector—when he'd left his own family, hung them out to dry.

I averted my eyes when I noticed Claude studying me. He was pleased with the uncertainty he'd sewn, not happy about the tale, but happy that I finally saw the bigger picture he'd slowly been feeding me puzzle pieces to. He wanted me to despise his brother as much as he did.

Did I? *Could* I?

How did I fold this version of events into the Darius that I knew? The Darius that had chipped away at my walls until I finally let him in. The Darius who'd more or less had a slumber party with me the other night, who'd listened with openness as all of my anxieties came pouring out of me. They seemed like two different people.

Like two different halves—but maybe both made up the whole.

"Maybe—maybe he didn't know," I said, my voice hoarse and cracked. "Maybe he didn't understand what was happening to him, what was happening to those impacted."

"You seem intent on seeing the best in someone who has only shown the worst." Claude arched his brow, leaned forward. "Even if that were the case, he never came back. She died," he paused, the muscles in his jaw tightening with suppressed emotion. "She died trying to take over for him, trying to make up for his shortcomings. And, still, he never came back. Until he brought you to my door."

We rode the rest of the way in silence.

Declan stared out the window, her body tense, like she felt Darius's betrayal as her own.

Their relationship was almost as complicated as mine with him—it had been strange watching their hatred collapse into something softer, something almost like friendship. Would this ruin it?

"This is our stop."

When I looked up, Claude was studying me, expression blank.

Wordlessly, we followed him off the bus, carved the familiar path to the bar.

I nodded briefly to the red-haired man at the door. He'd been here the last time we'd entered. I swallowed my disgust at the way his smile perked up when Declan walked by, his eyes tracing every curve until they landed on her ass. The grin widened.

When Claude met his eyes, the smile dried up and he straightened. "Hi boss. He's in there."

Claude exhaled.

None of us needed to ask who the 'he' in that statement was.

The bar lighting was low, with an almost hazy red. It felt like walking into the aftermath of a storm, and I knew, before I found Darius sitting at a stool, sipping on orange juice, that something had gone down here.

Claude flashed to him, wrapping his throat between his hands and lifting him off his stool and against the wall.

When Declan and I caught up, I noticed two people passed out on their table, two more on the floor near where Darius had been chatting.

"Now, now, brother," Darius cooed, his eyes narrowing on his twin, "they started it. And before you work yourself into a tizzy, don't worry, no one is dead. Only sleeping."

"Let him go, Claude." The bartender—Marge I think her name was—stepped around the bar and rested her hand on his shoulder. She barely reached his chest, but something about her presence had a heady command to it. "D's not wrong. They attacked him. He could've killed them, but he didn't. That's got to be worth something."

A muscle in Claude's jaw ticked, the energy between the two brothers electric and dangerous.

I could practically taste their animosity on my tongue, it was so thick in the air.

I inched towards Declan, stepping in front of her in case this broke into another one of their war-like battles. While I was fairly confident that being the daughter of Lucifer would help me survive their fallout, I didn't think Dec could.

But Darius didn't fight back. Didn't shove his brother off of him or antagonize him. His eyes darted briefly to me, warming slightly, and he raised his hands, palm out, in surrender.

When Claude followed his gaze to look at me, Darius growled, sounding more animalistic than I'd ever heard him.

His twin narrowed his eyes, studying his mirrored self. He inhaled, long and deep. "Something has changed."

Darius peeled his brother's hand from his throat, one finger at a time. "We need to use the portal. I promise we'll be out of your hair once we get through—off to saving the world. I'm a good guy now." He shrugged. "Sort of."

Like lightning, Claude shifted from standing in front of his brother to standing in front of me. His hand wrapped around my neck and lifted me until my toes were brushing the floor.

His fangs elongated and he inched his face towards me until they lightly teased the pulse point of my neck. It wasn't enough pressure to puncture the skin, and tickled more than anything.

"Claude," Marge said, tone warning as her wide eyes darted between the brothers. "Let's not escalate things."

But Darius was there in the time it took me to blink. He ripped his brother from me, throwing him across the room. Claude's nails scraped against my throat as he was forced to let go.

There was a ferality about Darius that reminded me so much of Atlas—the tension so high I didn't want to so much as breathe.

Claude stood up, studied his brother, but his eyes narrowed more with interest than anger—like he'd been conducting an experiment and was intrigued by the results.

"You're bonded," he said, crossing his arms across his chest. "A legitimate one." His impenetrable mask dropped momentarily, legitimate shock on his face—maybe even grief, if I was reading him correctly. "I caught a hint of it before, but brushed it off. It's unavoidable now. How?"

Marge pressed her hand to her mouth in shock, her ruddy-green eyes latching onto me with a renewed interest. "Impossible. She's not even a vampire."

My chest tightened at the word. Bonded.

There was an undeniable connection between me and Darius, I couldn't argue with that anymore. I thought back to that moment a few nights ago, when it had felt like we were one, when the world seemed to tilt sideways until the only thing that made sense was him. But bonded?

Was that even possible?

And why the hell did the mere thought of it send my belly into an explosion of flutters.

"Give us a few minutes," Claude said, his jaw tight. He nodded to the back hall.

"No Eli? Guess my chances of surviving this trip have gone up about seventy-five percent." Darius glanced at me, his eyes glittering with adrenaline. He scanned me briefly before walking up to me and tilting my head so that he could see my neck, could see that Claude hadn't touched me. When he turned my face back towards him, something in my expression made him flinch.

"I see you've been talking to my brother," he said, words clipped. There was a vulnerability in his eyes that shook me, a sadness that was buried just as deep as the demons he kept locked up.

"Yes," I answered, figuring there was no use lying if I was that easy for him to read.

He took a deep breath, nodded. "Fair enough." He turned to Declan, stepped towards her, then stopped, his shoulders slightly slumped. "You're okay too?" He waited for her answering nod, then turned back towards his brother. "I'll be back in a few minutes then."

When they left, Marge focused on me for a long moment, her expression tight. Then, all at once she broke out into a large smile that deepened the lines around her eyes, and wrapped me in her arms. She was surprisingly strong for someone so small.

Then again, so was I.

I sank into her, my body encased in a sudden all-encompassing warmth. Something in my skull tingled and I wondered, briefly, if this was what it felt like, to be held by a mother.

"Thank you," she whispered as she pressed a hard kiss to the side of my head.

"For what?" I asked.

"You might be the very thing to fix them—to help them see the light again." Then, she pulled back from me, wiped the corners of her gleaming eyes with the towel tucked in her waist, clapped her hands together and walked back behind the bar. "What can I get you girls to drink?"

Claude and Darius weren't gone for too long—no more than twenty minutes, but I was already getting a soft buzz thanks to Marge's heavy pouring. She told us stories about the boys, nothing too revealing, just small quirks—that Claude was secretly obsessed with Jeopardy, that Darius was creeped out by cats. Something about the way she spoke about them eased some of the anxiety and doubt that had been rippling in my gut since listening to Claude's tale.

Judging from the grin Declan kept fighting, Marge's clear affection for the boys was having a similar effect on her.

She made them seem so normal, like through her chatter alone she could disarm their darker tendencies.

By the time the vampires rejoined us, I found myself almost liking Claude as a person—even though he'd just had his fangs threateningly pressed to my neck.

The supernatural world was an odd one, but rather than let myself constantly get whiplash from new information and shifts between good and evil, I was trying to just go with the flow.

Marge had a way of easing anxiety. I wasn't sure what sort of supernatural creature she was, but something about her just made me feel cozy in a way that no one else had.

"Ready to go?" Darius asked, though he didn't quite meet my gaze.

"Yep!" The word came out louder than I'd intended, so I decided not to empty the last few sips of my drink.

Claude's lip twitched in an almost smile as he looked warmly at Marge. "I see you've been keeping them well hydrated in our absence."

She shrugged. "If they're willingly going back to hell, figure the least I can do is take the edge off."

When I stood, I could already feel some of the buzz wearing off. It was difficult to get protectors drunk for long periods of time, and I imagined it was even more so with demons.

Darius led the way towards the back, Declan following him.

When I turned to do the same, Claude's hand gripped my

shoulder, though with less pressure and aggression than he'd used during the fight near the waterfront earlier.

For a moment, he studied me, face impassive as always. He opened his mouth, then closed it, like he was searching for the right words or debating whether or not to say anything at all.

When his hand dropped away, I started to walk towards the hall where Dec and Darius had just disappeared.

"Be careful, Max."

I spun back to him and he averted his gaze, scratching his jaw as he stared briefly at the vamps in his bar who still hadn't woken up.

"Something tells me you're diving head first into a battle you aren't prepared for. Your relationship has changed him. I can see that." He exhaled softly, some of the tension in his body deflating a bit. "Though time will tell if those changes are good." When I started to ask what he meant, he shook his head. "Look, he's been permanently touched by a very volatile magic. The demons he's fighting—even if he tries, he might not always be able to keep the darker parts of himself at bay. Keep that in mind when deciding how much of your trust to give him." He let out a dry chuckle, his eyes sparkling with a sadistic humor in that way Darius's occasionally did. "Then again, we all may very well be dead soon, so maybe this all matters less than I think."

As if a switch had been flipped, the familiarity in his expression dissipated and he turned towards Marge. "Close up for an hour while I see them off and," he gestured to the bodies, "handle this."

When he left, I turned to Marge. "It was nice talking to you."

"You too girl," she smiled until I could see the tips of her slightly crooked teeth. That warmth came over me again and I was suddenly sad that I was leaving. "Watch over him and have your wits about you. There's a peculiar darkness in the air." She shuddered, grabbed her rag and started to wipe down the corner. "I pray it disperses without taking too many in the process."

On that ominous note, I left to follow the others, stopping when I saw them through an open door—the familiar alley in the back.

Claude grabbed a knife from his pocket and started to slice his palm, but before he could press it to the invisible place where I knew the portal stood, Darius stopped him.

Silently, he grabbed the blade and made a mirrored mark on his own hand. When he took a deep breath and met Claude's eyes, he nodded. Together, they held their hands up, smearing their blood until two identical swatches were suspended in air. Then the blood disappeared, absorbed by the portal.

Creepy ass magic, but wondrous all the same.

The portal was open.

"Be careful. Trust no one until they unquestionably earn it," Claude said. He was staring at his brother, but something told me he was speaking to me.

"We go together, linked," I said as I stepped up and threaded one arm through Declan's and the other through Darius's. "No getting separated this time."

Declan's body relaxed against me, but I could feel her heartbeat pounding.

With a final nod to Claude, we stepped into hell.

I clung to Dec and Darius, all of us huddled together in a giant hug as the familiar nothingness came over me. Sight, smell, sound—all of it was gone except for touch. I dug my fingers into Declan's hips, leaned into Darius to keep me from slipping away.

It wasn't unlike how it felt to teleport, and, as we swirled together in the ether, A strange, quiet hum started to sound—low and musical and exquisitely beautiful.

I strained to hear it better, my brain buzzing with the newness. It was odd to hear exactly one sound; everything else was blotted out, no breathing, no background noise, just the faint and gentle notes carrying to me from a distance.

Something about it felt sad and hopeful all at once—I could feel it down to my bones.

Then, just as quickly as it came, it left, and we landed with a soft thud on the ground.

I squinted, adjusting to the new surroundings. It wasn't super light out, but it wasn't pitch dark either. The ground was covered with gnarled and knotted roots, the trees shooting high above us like redwoods.

Declan bent over and vomited, her skin pasty and pale as Darius rubbed her back in a gentle circle and pulled back her hair. My heart squeezed at the sight.

This was the man who'd willingly abandoned his family and killed his sister? I couldn't make sense of it.

There was a shadow in his eyes, a hauntedness. I wondered what traveling through the portal was like for him.

Judging from my companions, I'd had the most seamless trip by far.

"Are you guys okay?" I whispered, scanning the forest to make sure that we didn't have any company. You could never tell in hell—I wasn't sure there was such a thing as a safe domain here.

Declan nodded and allowed Darius to grip her elbow and pull her back up.

I handed her the bottle of water in my pack and she greedily gulped down a few sips.

"Thank you."

Darius was silent, but he was present enough to look around, craning his neck slightly like he was trying to pick up sound.

"So now I guess we just need to find our way back to

Lucifer," I said, spinning in a slow circle, like the path might suddenly light up and show us the way. Dorothy had no idea how good she had it. "We still have a few days before the deadline, so it shouldn't be too big of a problem."

Declan tied her hair up in a two-second ponytail that somehow looked perfect and like a stylist had done it.

I averted my eyes. Sometimes she was so stunning it was hard to look at her.

She smirked and I wondered, briefly, if she could hear my thoughts. "Any idea where we are, fanghole?"

After the bus ride with Claude, I was wondering if she'd revert to ignoring Darius or, worse, suggest that we ditch him. Hearing the playfulness in her tone sent a bolt of relief down my spine.

He arched a brow, coming back to himself. "I'm not a hell-forged compass, but I think I have a vague idea of our general region. If I'm right, shouldn't be more than two or three days for us to get there, if we move quickly. Think you can keep up?"

She rolled her eyes, but I caught the small flush on her cheeks. Of everyone in our group, Declan was the most vulnerable—the most human.

I grabbed her hand and squeezed, trying to reassure her as best I could. "Well then, let's get started. No use standing around if—"

A twig snapped close by.

And then another.

We spun around so that we were all back-to-back in a small triangle.

I unsheathed my blade as figures started to emerge from the shadows.

Two at first—then three, then four—and then, just like that, we were surrounded.

16

DECLAN

Just our luck—get rescued from one fight in Seattle, only to fall directly into another within minutes of dropping into hell.

As the figures neared, I noticed that several had glowing, yellow eyes. Most of them were naked. Like an orchestra with an invisible director, limbs started to bend and shift, sending a haunting echo of cracks around us.

Werewolves.

More of them than I could count.

I leaned my shoulder into Max's, the pressure of her body against mine strangely soothing. Words had dried up on my tongue and it was the only comfort that I could offer her. Even if she used her flames, I wasn't sure she could fry this many, not all at once.

"Any chance these are your friends," Max whispered to Darius.

"Max, you need to teleport," Darius whispered, his body stiff against mine. I could feel the anxiety radiating from him, his body vibrating with adrenaline—it was the same charge boiling low in my gut. "Get out of here while you still can."

"I'll take that as a no then," I said.

"I'm not leaving without you two." Her tone was steely and resolute and I could feel her body tensing next to mine. "It's not even an option, so move on to the next suggestion."

Normally, I was a big fan of stubbornness in a girl. Generally, it made them more exciting, more independent and fun to bicker with. Right now, it made me want to throw up.

"He's right," I said, trying to calm the subtle shake in my hand. Last time I went head-to-head with half this many wolves, I'd wound up an inch away from death—saved only because Sarah arrived in the nick of time. And if this was the same pack as the one we'd run from, the one we'd *stolen* her from, then they would make our deaths slow and sadistic. "No use dying out of pride, get out of here. Maybe you can find help."

She grunted—knew I was full of shit. There would be no time to pull help to us. And who would even bother? Lucifer wanted her alive. Something told me he gave zero shits about the rest of us. We had no other allies here.

She was going to die.

She was going to die because she refused to save herself.

I groaned, scanning the horizon for a weak point in their line up. "Summon your fire then and summon it fast."

I shook my head, took a deep breath in, and squared my shoulders. If this was it, if this was where my road ended, I was going down fighting. And I was going to take out as many of these fuckers as I could—maybe then she'd stand a chance.

I dug the balls of my feet into the uneven terrain, trying to get as steady a grip as I could. Two wolves to my right had an arrogance in their posture, a hunger in their eyes as they darted between us, calculating who they were going for first. Their tongues swept across their snouts like they could already taste our blood on their teeth.

I'd seen that very arrogance get many protectors killed in my day.

It was a weakness. One I could dig into and exploit.

They were mine.

I felt a tingling heat behind me and grinned, knowing it was the starting embers of her flames. She was getting better, faster at summoning it to her. It probably should have terrified me, having that kind of violent power licking at my back, but it only sent a thrill of excitement—straight through my belly and low into my core.

Fighting and sex were two sides of the same coin sometimes.

Right now, I needed to focus on the former or the latter was going to get me dead way faster than was useful to her.

"Now," I yelled, charging towards the furry fucks I'd already silently claimed. Before I got more than three feet away from my friends, a large, solid object materialized in my path. "What the—"

My feet skidded through the dirt as I tried to avoid a collision.

The collision was inevitable though and my face went burrowing into a firm, but surprisingly soft surface.

My hands gripped the thick fur and I pulled myself back, tottering slightly as I regained my footing.

"Ralph?" I stared at the warm amber-brown eyes lowered to meet mine. I grinned, wide and earnest. This hound had a way of finding his way to her when we were in a pinch. We seriously owed him like five-thousand boxes of Milkbones if we made it out of here alive.

Unable to stop myself, I threw my arms around his neck and squeezed. If you would have told me three months ago that I'd be this excited to see a hellhound, I would've sent you to the med ward. But here we were, me and a creature capable of killing most demons with little to no effort.

I felt, more than I saw the werewolves stall in their approach, could feel the anxiety rippling through them. Hellhounds were rare, even in hell. And while Ralph was a runt and as lovable as a golden retriever, he had a menace about him that I wasn't used to seeing.

Large eyes that had always held a deep warmth hardened. His sharp teeth were on full display, strings of saliva lining his jaw like he was just as eager to dig into the wolves as they were to dig into us.

He nudged my shoulder lightly before pounding towards the two assholes I was going for. Within two seconds, he'd ripped one of them in half, sending the other falling back on his ass and trying to scurry away, his movements awkward like he suddenly couldn't remember whether he had human or wolf limbs to work with.

I spun around to check on Max and Darius, but they were blocked by another black mass—this one quite a bit larger than Ralph. And far more menacing.

"Fuck," I whispered, my head tilting back to take the creature in. The fear I remembered from my first encounter with Ralph was now roaring through my body as I tried to determine if this was friend or foe.

Max extinguished her fire and walked up to the large creature. She stared into its stunningly purple-blue eyes and nodded, a silent thank you.

She knew him, it seemed, and didn't look even remotely afraid of the giant teeth bared in its jaw.

A friendly then. I hoped.

"I don't know what power you hold over these creatures," Darius said, a bemused grin on his face, "but I have to say, they're a useful tool to have in your back pocket."

The not-Ralph hellhound growled at Darius, its head ducked low, like it was deciding whether or not to rip him to pieces.

Max rolled her eyes, as if the beast was nothing but an over-protective chihuahua.

She walked past him and up to Ralph. He was busy chomping on a wolf femur—a sight that made bile rise to the back of my throat—but he made a happy whine when she pressed her face to his neck.

"I think they're here to take us to Lucifer," she said, scratching Ralph absentmindedly while she turned to me. "They can teleport, like me. And Ralph feels stronger now, more in control—" her eyes narrowed, "I don't know how I can sense that, but I can. Maybe he draws strength from being near his pack?"

"Well, if that's true, we should hitch a ride sooner rather than later." Darius nodded to the wolves around us. They'd stopped their retreat and were approaching again. They were slowly building up the courage to attack. "Looks like the pack is getting braver by the second."

Might have something to do with the fact that Ralph was thumping his hind leg now while Max itched a spot behind his ear. He didn't exactly induce terror when he was around her.

She nodded and wrapped both of her arms around him. "You guys ride with Ralph's friend. I think he's stronger so it'll be easier to carry two passengers."

Ralph's *friend*.

I stared up at the imposing figure next to me again, swallowed thickly. "Right."

Slowly, I reached a hand forward, trying to quell the slight shake rattling my arm. Hellhounds didn't respond well to fear.

The look of revulsion on Darius's face made me feel simultaneously better and worse. My fear was warranted, then, but it would have been nice to have a confidence boost and be proven wrong all the same.

We nodded to each other, then both gripped onto the hound with two hands. I sent a silent prayer to whichever gods existed, and might be listening, promising to find this hound the largest steak possible if he didn't confuse me with his dinner.

He growled again, the vibrations traveling from my hand through to my feet. Shit.

In the corner of my eye, I saw Max and Ralph disappear, a fond grin on her face before she faded into nothingness.

I swallowed again, tried to steady my racing heart. "Right, um, so is it cool if we hitch a—"

The words fell back down my throat as my body twisted and folded into space.

I was almost glad that my body felt so disordered—it kept the bile in my throat from knowing which way to go as a paralyzing dizziness swept over me like a wave.

We landed a few moments later, the world still spinning as I tried to recalibrate my mind and body with the new setting.

Didn't work.

Instead, I fell to my hands and knees and vomited.

Again.

I wiped my mouth with the back of my hand, trying to ignore the acidic taste on my tongue.

When I looked up, the blue-eyed hound was watching me. I wasn't great at reading hellhound expressions, but if I had to define his current one, it would be the canine equivalent of smug.

Ass.

I was definitely team Ralph.

Max was on her feet, eyes glittering bright with adrenaline. These shifts and portal hops seemed to be affecting her less and less. Something about that eased tension I didn't even know I had.

It meant she was getting stronger.

When I followed her gaze, those relaxed muscles tensed back up.

Lucifer.

He stood, still as a statue, his brow cocked with a smugness that made the blue-eyed hellhound seem downright compassionate in comparison.

His lip curled when he looked at the ground in front of me. "Should have had you drop them outside. I forgot how weak protectors could be sometimes."

Shame burned low in my gut, but I lifted myself off the ground and clenched my jaw to keep from doing something truly unwise, like insult the prince of fucking darkness in his own home.

Instead, I'd stick to doing it in the safe confines of my head.

Fucking prick.

We were in a large room—one filled with dark and ornate furniture, but with a taste for pragmatics that I wouldn't have expected from the devil. Large couches, a solid table, bookshelves lining the wall. There was no art and nothing exactly screamed 'let me maim you for amusement,' which I was counting as a win.

Certainly a step up from the crowded dungeon room I'd seen last time I was here.

"You're late." His words echoed around the room, though his voice was quiet.

Darius paled, his cheeks hollowed with a ghostly gray. "We're not. She still has several days to get to you, to meet your deadline."

Lucifer took a step towards Max, ignoring the vampire altogether. "We agreed on two weeks, did we not?"

Why did Darius look like he'd just been told a tainted one was going to devour him piece by piece while he sat there and watched?

"It's been less than that," Max said, her shoulders stiff. Her fingers twitched slightly, like she wanted to reach for her blade. Fat lot of good it would do her even if she did.

Was it even possible to kill him?

Lucifer frowned slightly, brows lifting. "Interesting. Here, you've been gone for a full month. The boy couldn't even reach you through dream-walking these last few weeks. I nearly sent a team after you to bring you back."

A month? What the hell was going on?

"That's—" a line formed between Max's eyes as she tried to process his words, " that's not possible." The confusion bled into fear as she took a step forward. "Wade. You haven't—"

Fuck.

Lucifer let her terror linger in the air for several long moments.

I felt the blood drain from my face and clutched my stomach, thankful that I had nothing left in my system to throw up.

After all that we went through—if Wade was gone because of some fuck up in the magical space-time continuum—was this physics or magic?—whatever—I was going to scream.

He exhaled, and shook his head. "No. I have not killed him," he turned away, walked to a large desk in the back of the room, picked up a large, bronze pitcher, and filled a glass with water. "Yet." His gaze darted from Max, to me, to Darius. Then he shrugged and handed Max the glass. "You'll have to share, I wasn't counting on guests. Not that I would have prepared if I was."

"Where's Wade?" Max asked, her voice tight as she handed me the cup and gestured for me to drink.

I took a small sip and could feel it drip through my body after burning the back of my throat. My stomach turned. I needed to learn to handle teleportation better, and fast.

But queasiness aside, pride swelled in my belly at the sight of her going head-to-head, without fear, with the scariest man I'd ever met. That just as swiftly turned into fear of my own though. He could kill her, if he really wanted to. He could kill us all.

Sometimes, fear was warranted; sometimes, it was a precaution.

"In his room, I imagine." Lucifer shrugged. "Perhaps in a session with Serae. He's been gaining strength, channeling his anxiety into productivity. I'm a reasonable man, I can appreciate the value in keeping someone like him around. At least for now." He shook his head, glanced at the blue-eyed hound and nodded. As if understanding the dismissal, the hound left, throwing one last glance at Max before he disappeared out the doorway. "Curious though. The realms must be changing far faster than I expected. Time is no longer stable, it's malleable, warping—a problem that will likely increase each time you make the jump. That kind of instability…it can be difficult to maintain. We're running out of time."

"So," Max relaxed a little, sinking into Ralph as he sat at her side, "we're good then? With the timing thing?"

A horrifying smile spread across Lucifer's face. "An oath is an oath, my girl. And you have broken your side of the promise, whether you intended to or not."

I understood why Darius looked like he'd seen a ghost now. The same sort of hollowness sank into me. The blood oath, the thing he'd been concerned about since the moment Max mentioned it.

I took a step towards Lucifer, trying to maintain a semblance of strength even though I knew that ultimately I was useless against him. "What does that mean exactly? You can't seriously hold this against her."

He turned, walked towards me, stopped when his boots were a few inches from mine, and studied me carefully. "You're an interesting girl. Brave or reckless, I'm not entirely sure yet. But interesting nonetheless. I can see why she's drawn to you."

"So, the prodigal daughter returns." A man—was his name Sam? I couldn't remember—walked into the room, his tone unreasonably jovial considering the tension encasing us all. He turned to Max and shook his head, making an echoey 'tsk tsk' noise as he came closer. "Did he tell you you're late?" With a shrug, he sank into the couch, propped his feet on the table, and folded his arms behind his head. "I did try to warn you—making a deal with the Devil is never a good idea. Even your fairy tales tell you that much. Stubborn girl though—a lot like your mother that way."

Max startled at the mention of her mother, craning her neck around to see the strange ancient lounging like we were discussing nothing more than a trending hashtag.

He was an odd one, and I couldn't get a read on him.

"Get your feet off the table," Lucifer snapped, his fingers balled into a tight a fist.

"So what's going to happen," I asked, inching my way closer to Max, "if she's broken an oath?"

Lucifer shrugged, walked back to his desk and leaned against it, legs crossed at his feet like we were in a casual business meeting and not discussing my friend's fate. "Whatever I want." He turned his focus towards Max. "Right now, suffice to say, that when I want you here, you'll be here. It's rather convenient, really. I no longer have to worry about you traipsing around through the recesses of hell. Your will is mine. I can draw you to me as I see fit."

Ominous. Seriously fucking ominous. Even if I didn't fully understand what he meant.

That was the thing with him though, he only fed us the information that he wanted to, like watching us scramble for crumbs was amusing to him.

Men were the fucking worst.

He clapped his hands together, the sharp sound echoing through the room. "Now, enough of this. We have much to make up for. Your powers—have they been progressing?"

Something about the gleam in his eye had me wondering if

he'd known this would happen—if the oath and aftermath of our journey unfolded just as he'd expected them to.

Max glanced at me from the corner of her eye. "Um, they've definitely been showing up more frequently, though I don't know if I'd call that progress."

He narrowed his eyes. "Without you summoning them, you mean?"

She nodded, her hands folded sheepishly in front of her.

"She's unstable, who didn't see that coming?" Sam had moved his feet from the table to the arm of the couch, a move Lucifer definitely clocked with a tick of his jaw, but said nothing about. "That's what happens when you have a power block, no guidance, and a handful of bonds only partially solidified."

"Bonds?" I blurted out, my voice louder than I'd intended. I knew that Atlas was definitely bonded to her, but a handful? "As in plural?"

Sam swung his legs down to the ground until he was sitting up, the lazy boredom in his features replaced by a twinkling amusement as he looked at me like he was seeing me for the first time. "Wow. Clueless. The whole lot of you. No wonder she's so unpredictable. You're all unbalanced, every last one of you."

"Summon the hellfire," Lucifer said.

I did my best to swallow my amusement at how absurdly devilish that sounded—like he was auditioning for a spot in a poorly-funded B-movie.

Max planted her feet, stood taller, and closed her eyes, focusing.

After no more than ten seconds, Lucifer crossed through the room. "That long? Seriously? Unacceptable. It should be like breathing—easy, effortless."

He waited, his face a few inches from hers, for another

minute, his body growing more tense with every second that flashed.

Max was shaking, whether with frustration or fear, I wasn't sure. But then, slowly, flames started to lick her fingers. They looked like heat waves at first, but they quickly grew into mesmerizing shades of orange and purple.

Lucifer grunted, unimpressed. "Call them back."

This process took less time, her expression defiant as she met his gaze.

"Again," he barked.

When it took more than a moment, he pressed a blade to her neck. "Let's see if a little motivation will help."

"Stop," I yelled, when I saw her pulse beating erratically in her throat, a bead of sweat trailing past it. "We just jumped through the portal, she's exhausted. And this is pointless dick swinging anyway, you're not going to kill her. You need her. You're just being a prick. Give her some time to adjust."

"It's okay, Dec," Max whispered, her stare darting from me to the asshole in front of her.

"Haven't you been paying attention?" he snapped. "We don't have time."

Max's fingertips sparked.

He dropped the blade to his side and turned to me, his eyes narrowed, considering. "Motivation is the fastest way to learn. But perhaps a change of atmosphere, with a very specific kind of motivation will help."

He grabbed Max's hand and dragged her to me before threading his arm through mine.

"Put the vampire," he tilted his head from side-to-side, unsure, "somewhere, I guess. I'm going to test a theory."

And then, everything went black and upside down for the third time in an hour.

When we landed, before I could fall to the ground again,

Lucifer dragged me to a dark, stone wall, wrapping my wrist in a heavy chain, the loud clank ringing ominously in my ears.

The room was huge, but reminiscent of Wade's dungeon—everything was cold and empty, the area lit only by a few sconces dancing with the same fire Max conjured.

Aside from the manacles pinning me to the wall, and a few more sets scattered around, the room was empty.

"What are you doing?" I tugged my arm uselessly, suddenly feeling claustrophobic. Suddenly hell and the Devil were starting to feel like the start of a Saw movie. Maybe my early assumptions about hell weren't entirely baseless.

"Keeping you contained until I need you," he answered, a wicked gleam in his eyes that made him look almost comically evil. "I don't like my props getting in the way until I want to employ them."

"Let her go." Max ran up to me, her hand cool against my clammy forehead as she examined the locking mechanism.

Lucifer shrugged. "You could shift her away, you know. You don't need me to free her. If you focused on strengthening your skills, she could be out of there in ten seconds flat."

Her hand slid down my arm, a comforting trail. She turned to him, shoulders squared. "So we're short on time and that's your plan? To not only get me to teleport on command—something I'm rarely able to do—but pull her with me? Isn't that dangerous? Couldn't I hurt her if I fuck it up?"

His face split into a crooked smile. "You could kill her. Very painfully at that."

The back of Max's neck flushed, and she dropped her hand away like she was afraid even that would hurt me.

"But you're right," he continued, pressing the tip of his finger against the blade in his hands. "We'll work up to that. I'm not completely without compassion, whatever you might think."

"What—"

Before she could finish, he swiped the blade towards her face, his movement so quick I almost couldn't catch it.

"Shit," Max muttered as she dodged. "What the hell?"

When she grabbed her own blade, he made a soft *tsk*ing sound. "Use your true weapons—fight blade with fire."

Her brows bent, considering, but before she could act on his suggestion, he teleported in front of her, knocking her dagger away with a lazy swipe.

Anger flashed in her dark eyes, but it was laced with what looked like excitement. She raised her hands in front of her, protecting her face, and maneuvered her weight to the balls of her feet.

Sparring was home to her. And the devil was giving her full permission to attack him.

She charged forward, aiming her fist for his face, but he teleported again so that he stood behind her. In one smooth, swift motion, he slid the blade into her back.

"No," I screamed, pulling against the metal at my wrist until the fragile skin there started to tear and bleed. "What the fuck are you doing?"

"I said," he pulled the blade out, frowning as she bent with pain and gripped her back, "to use your true weapons. The weapons that can never be taken from you."

She pulled her hand away and it was smeared dark with blood, her jaw clenching as she turned to him.

He simply shrugged. "It's not a shadow blade, you'll survive."

With seething rage in her eyes, she dove for him, catching him slightly by surprise, just long enough for her to wrap her arms around his middle and drag him down.

But he teleported them both, dropping her to the ground as she recuperated from the shift.

"This is growing tiresome." He shook his head, pressed the

blade to her neck. "Don't waste my time girl, it's a precious thing."

She met his eyes and it was hard to judge who's expression held more vitriol. When she closed her eyes and inhaled sharply, I thought she might be surrendering, but after a long, breathless moment, her hands sparked with fire. Without hesitating, she wrapped her fingers around his wrist.

"Better," he said, lips twitching in a frown, "but still too long to conjure and, ultimately, useless against me, and those of my stature. Shift."

Her skin was clammy and I could see her pulse ticking in her throat as she focused all of her attention on doing as he asked.

Thirty seconds went by and nothing, then thirty more. Finally, she teleported out of his grip and landed a few feet from me, her chest heaving erratically like she couldn't catch a full breath.

"I could have killed you ten times over in the time that took you," he shook his head, a disapproving frown on his features. "Let's try something a bit more motivating, since you seem unconcerned with your own life."

He grabbed her arm and dragged her to the other end of the room, tightening a manacle around her leg.

Her brows bent in confusion.

"You were right." He turned back towards me, walking at a leisurely pace until the distance between us was closed. "I won't kill her. She knows that I won't kill her. Therefore, her life is not very good motivation." His eyes were vacant, cold and calculating when he stopped, a few inches from me—so close that I could smell the subtle spice of his scent. "You, however, are, as they say, free game. And, unlike the vampire, reasonably fragile to help raise the stakes to where she clearly needs them to be."

Without breaking eye contact, he slipped the blade into my abdomen.

I grunted, refusing to scream as warmth spread through my body. At first, it felt little different from being punched in the gut, but when he pulled the blade out, the pain felt both sharp and deep.

"No!"

I heard Max scream, heard the angry metallic echo of her chains, but all I could see was the almost bored look on Lucifer's face. He didn't care one way or another if I lived or survived. Gutting me until I spilled out on his floor was no different to him than if I was a pig sent for slaughter.

He touched the blade to my clavicle, smearing my own blood down my chest, until all I could smell was the metallic brine of my blood. He stopped the painful outline when the point of the dagger was centered between two bones in my lower rib cage. Not close enough to hit my heart, but it would hurt like hell and take hours to heal from.

"Please," Max screamed, her voice muffled through tears and the sound of her trying to break from her restraints. "Please stop. I'll focus, I promise I'll do better, I'll try harder."

Her words were punctured by breathy hiccups, the panic rising in her voice.

Something about the panic screamed to me, made me want to flay the man before me alive for making her feel that. But it also gave me a strange surge of strength.

"You're a monster," I said, doing all that I could to keep the bitter pain from my voice. I wouldn't show weakness, not to him. "Nothing but a power-hungry, manipulative monster."

"For each second that it takes for you to conjure fire," he said, ignoring my curses with little more than a sardonic grin, "or free yourself from your cuff, this blade sinks in another half inch." He craned his neck to Max. "Don't look at me like that, her fate is in your hands, not mine."

"No, this is ridiculous," Max cried, her voice growing hoarse from exertion.

He slid the tip of the blade in, splitting the juncture between my ribs like butter.

I grunted, teeth clenched on my tongue to stifle the pain. I captured his stare with mine, hoping he could read every curse I was lobbing at him in my head.

"Two," he said, as he applied more pressure to the blade, pushing it in further, as he'd promised.

I tried to suck in a breath, but it was sharp and shallow. He'd punctured my lung.

My body wouldn't start to stitch itself back up until he removed the dagger.

A tingling warmth swept over us, brushing my hair back from the sheer force of it, the light so bright that my vision was nothing but a cloud of dancing black dots.

Max's fire. It engulfed us both, like a gentle torch, harming neither of us, even with its power.

Lucifer's eyes widened slightly as he watched the flames lick against my skin, like he was surprised to find me unharmed. But he only let his guard down for a moment, before the shock disappeared and the corners of mouth lifted in the shadow of a smile. "Better."

"So you'll stop?" she asked, her voice winded but coated in a naive hope.

Instead, he sank the blade in further, the swiftness of the maneuver pulling a low groan from my lips before I could bite it back, "No. You've simply proven that I was right. I told you that you just needed the proper motivation, and I've clearly found it. Besides, I told you to teleport out of your chains, not toss fire at my back. You want to save your girlfriend from pain?" He shoved the blade in another half inch, and I fisted my hands at my side until my palms were tattooed with the lines of eight crescent moons. "Then do it."

Max screamed. But whereas her screams had been filled

with fear until now, this held nothing but deep, buried rage—a rage powerful enough that it sent chills down my spine.

I heard the chains across the room clank and then still, the echo going through my bones. In the next moment, Lucifer's hand was pulled from the blade as he went flying backwards.

He landed on the ground, though somehow still looked graceful in the process. Max stood above him, her body heaving with each breath, her eyes black as night and filled with a coldness that turned my mouth dry.

If she'd been looking at me with that expression, I'd have withered up like a prune.

In one motion, she unsheathed her blade and slammed it into his chest, just left of the sternum—in the same exact spot he'd shish kabobed me.

The triumphant smirk on his face dried up immediately as he met her stare, shock widening his hard features.

Ice-cold fear coursed through my veins as I waited for his retaliation.

He wouldn't kill her, I was fairly certain of that. But some things were worse than death—and if she pushed him too far, there was no telling what would happen next.

Rather than lash out at her, he simply pulled the blade out, slow and methodical. He studied it for a moment, the silver coated with a thin layer of blood. Then he simply nodded, his lips puckered like he was impressed. In a fluid motion, as if the wound didn't pain him at all, he stood up, wiped the blood along the side of his pants, and handed the blade back to her. "Good."

She stood there, watching as he walked towards me. Without a word, he removed the blade still buried in my chest without warning—the swiftness of the maneuver had me bent over and gasping to fill my lungs with something other than my own blood.

He stepped back a few feet then turned back to Max. "Now heal her."

Her lips parted as her gaze darted from him to me, where it softened slightly. Without waiting for another beat, she rushed to my side. Her fingers gently combed over my boob as she reached for the wound, and I noticed her cheeks redden slightly.

"Sorry," she murmured, as she pressed the palm of her hands firmly against my ribs.

I swallowed the groan of pain, amused by the fact that someone could be badass enough to stab the Devil in one moment, and gentle and shy in the very next. Such a strange, strange girl.

Her eyes narrowed in focus as she placed her other hand on my neck to stabilize herself.

At first, nothing happened, and I could feel Lucifer hovering on the sidelines, antsy with impatience. This was another skill she wasn't mastering quickly enough for him.

But then a gentle breeze lifted her hair, cooled the sweat against my forehead, and a deep, tingling warmth spread through my body—almost as if the sun were heating me from the inside out. The pain faded into nothing more than a tickle, and then into something that sent a surge of heat through my stomach, a familiar pressure building low in my belly.

Her eyes met mine, but they were black as night, unseeing as they bored into me.

Even still, I felt irrevocably connected to her in that moment, like my body was hers—until the very thought of us not being entangled created an overwhelming tightness in my chest that had nothing to do with a dagger.

I remembered the last time she'd used this power, though—how she'd nearly killed herself from sinking too deeply into the intoxicating magic, the addicting pull of sinking her energy into mine. This was her most dangerous skill—the one that would lead to her death if she didn't get a better hold on the release. She gave too much.

"Max," I said, my voice cracked and hoarse from the intensity and feel of her energy mingling with mine, making it stronger. "You have to stop. I'm all stitched up now, completely fine. Don't overdo it."

But my pleas seemed to fade right through her, unheard.

Lucifer inched towards us, like a dark shadow, brows bent with the hint of concern—the whisper of his fear heightened mine.

"Max," I yelled, my voice strong and loud now that I'd shaken off the initial allure of her nearness. "Please." I turned to Lucifer, trying to dim my panic. "Stop her."

He shook his head, but there was no wickedness in his expression. "That's not how this power works. She needs to learn to let go of it." He turned to me, head tilting with interest. "As her bond to you stabilizes, it will become easier for her to do, she will become stronger."

Bond. To me?

My mouth dried at the insinuation, just as a liquid heat burned in my gut. Was it even possible?

It made sense for Atlas to bond to her—we didn't understand wolf mate bonds well at all, but it was undeniable that they existed and that he was drawn to her by forces he tried desperately to ignore. But there hadn't been a true bond between protectors in many lifetimes. And I'd never heard of one being forged between two women.

"I—" whatever I was about to say fell away as Max leaned into me, like she was losing the energy to keep herself standing on her own.

My eyes darted between hers, looking for a window into her, to wake her up from the trance. Without thinking, I crashed my lips into hers, remembering how, in the dream, it had felt like being doused in a bucket of water, like waking up from a lifetime of sleep.

At first, her lips didn't respond, and I threaded my free hand through her hair, drawing her to me. But then, slowly, I felt her return the pressure—not quite a returned kiss, but like she was coming back to herself, pulling herself out of the black hole she was drowning in.

When I pulled away, her dark eyes started to clear, slowly at first and then all at once, until the familiar warm brown eclipsed the darkness entirely.

"You're okay," I whispered, my lips less than an inch from hers. I ignored the fact that Lucifer was standing next to us. My heart beat erratically against my chest, whether from fear or heat, I wasn't sure. "You are okay, right?"

She nodded, expression blank as she took a step back. With a heaving breath, she turned to Lucifer and punched him in the nose, the resounding crack quivering all the way in my bones.

Blood crept down his chin, lining his teeth like a creek as he smiled—the sight of which sent the hair on the back of my neck standing up.

"Ready for round two?" He sheathed the original blade and pulled out another, this one coated in an iridescent sort of glow.

Shadow magic.

Max's eyes widened as they darted to mine. "No. She won't survive that. That's too far. She's not—"

But before she could finish her sentence, he pressed the blade into my gut, then folded me into his embrace. "Then you better locate her. Quickly. Use your connection to do so, before it's lost altogether."

A tidal wave of pain wracked my body that made it impossible to breathe, to think.

Max disappeared from sight, my body folding in on itself as Lucifer teleported us away.

I wanted to die. There was no coming back from this sort of

misery as the shift pushed and pulled me apart, creating seams and cracks where there were none before.

And then it dulled, turning into a quiet numbness that was tolerable—pleasant, even, in comparison.

Even the pain I carried with me always melted away until I couldn't recognize it anymore.

I could live here, lingering in this nothingness until the world deemed it enough. There was nothing to see, nothing to feel, nothing to hear.

Just nothing.

"It won't be long. She won't fail you. She can't." A cold voice echoed around and around, disturbing the peaceful emptiness, but I didn't bother trying to decipher it, didn't even try to make the sounds into shapes with meaning.

Instead, I floated.

Until, eventually, a powerful snag pulled me, like my body was suspended by a cord reaching its limit but refusing to snap, refusing to let me break free and fall into the pool of darkness below.

But I wanted down there. And so I fought.

Tugging myself away, chafing my fingers on the invisible cord until each thread broke in two.

The final one wouldn't budge. No matter how long I tried, I couldn't get it to release me. It was so determined to pull me back up, to drag me back into the misery of before.

I sliced my palm against it, the pain of it shocking things into focus.

Warmth spread through my body, filling me down to my toes and fingers, until I could draw breath again. I gasped at the sensation, felt my eyes roll in the back of my head as the ecstasy filled me. There was good on the surface too, and so much more of it than the heavy hurt that weighed me down.

I clung to it, my heart racing as the threads wove themselves back together, binding until the cord tying me to the surface was even thicker than before.

"Declan."

A soft pressure against my chest that made it ache, but not with pain.

"Please, please, please wake up. You have to wake up."

The voice was filled with so much sorrow, so much grief, so much wanting.

And so I did as it asked.

When I opened my eyes, the world came spinning back into focus. A pair of dark eyes across from mine.

"Max?" I leaned back so that I could see her better.

"Well done." Lucifer's voice, but I couldn't see him from my position. "Rest for an hour or two. I have somewhere to be. We'll start back up again when I'm back."

She was shivering, body heaving with heavy breaths, cheeks lined with streaks of tears.

The world snapped back into focus and I pressed my palm to my abdomen, expecting to find a dagger, but finding only Max's hand. Her skin still tingled with an energy that called to me, like a melodic voice guiding me through a heavy mist.

"You're okay? You're alive?" she asked, like she couldn't quite believe it, even though I was gripping her hand against me. "I thought—I thought—" she wiped her cheeks with her free hand and took a few steps back.

I groaned when her hand left mine. I wanted her against me, not giving me space.

"I'm okay. I think you healed—whatever that knife did." I didn't want to think about that place, didn't want to revisit how close I'd come to giving into the allure, to slipping into the dark lake of nothingness. I scanned her more closely, remembering the last time she'd tried healing, how difficult it was for her to stop. "You're okay? I didn't take too much from you?"

She shook her head, her eyes now their familiar shade of

brown. "You stopped me. I don't know how, but it was like the power was yours, not mine. You shut it down when I tried to sink into it."

I nodded, though I didn't understand what she meant—didn't understand the intricacies of the shadow magic.

Slowly, I studied the room. Finding myself on a bed, a lamp lighting the plain decor in a soft glow. "Where are we?"

She shook her head, her brows bent like she was noticing the room for the first time. "I'm not sure. One of his guest rooms, I suppose," she spat the word 'his' like the word was filled with venom. "I found you. I'm still not sure how, but I did."

The bond.

Was it possible? That we were linked together, that her magic sought mine out, like attracting like? I still wasn't sure, but the thought that I could be permanently tied to someone like her—it was hard not to get drunk on the possibility of it.

"You're exhausted." I reached for her hand and pulled her back towards me. "Sit. Get your energy back up and we'll figure out what to do next."

The moment I touched her though, heat rushed through my body, settling low in my belly. A heat that I saw mirrored in her dilated eyes.

My focus dipped to her lips. They were full and parted slightly, expectant.

Suddenly all I could think about was sucking on them until she squirmed.

The breath caught in my throat when her tongue unconsciously swept along the bottom one before her teeth gently indented it.

Jesus, did she know what she was doing when she did that?

I squeezed my thighs together, trying desperately to ignore the heat pooling there.

But something about her nearness after healing me, about

having her energy mingling together with mine, heightened the attraction I tried so damn hard to resist.

I wanted her to want me in the way that she wanted the guys. Wanted her to look at me with that hungry look I saw when she watched them, the look I'd talked myself out of thinking I'd seen a few times when she watched me—stolen glances that reflected my own hunger back to me.

I thought I could sit by, be her friend and nothing more. I'd been doing really well ignoring my desire throughout the impending apocalypse. I thought I had anyway. But now, all I could think about was pulling the same delicious noises from her that she'd made in that dream.

A breathy, needy moan escaped from me as the memory flashed through me.

Max's eyes widened at the noise, her focus lasered on my mouth.

And then, as if magnets drew us together—too strong for either of us to resist—our lips met in a desperate, deep clash.

My tongue slid between the seam of her mouth easily, and my body throbbed when it met hers.

I pulled her to me as she licked and nibbled on my lip—I could feel my pulse racing against every point in my body. An electric surge went piercing through me, amplifying every sensation until I felt like just one more touch would have me coming just from a kiss.

"Max," I whispered against her mouth, my voice desperate and needy but it felt too good for me to care, "Fuck, I want you."

As if the declaration woke her up, she broke the kiss and pulled away.

I leaned forward, like my body was chasing the ghost of her.

"I'm sorry," I blurted, panic racing through my body, "I didn't mean to push you. Or upset you."

Fuck. I ruined things. How did I fuck this up so royally?

She shook her head, a frustrating laugh escaping as she

dropped her face into her palms. "You? God no. I'm so sorry. And for before, for the dream." She let out a loud, frustrated groan.

The sound cut through me.

My stomach dipped. I knew that tone in her voice.

Deep regret.

Self-hatred.

I felt myself flush, felt the blood drain from my face.

"It's the succubus powers," she continued, her eyes digging ditches into the floor rather than meet mine. My mouth felt dry as I tried to calm myself down, to re-bury the feelings I had for her. Friends, I could be her friend. I just had to convince my needy pussy that she was getting nothing but my hand tonight. She wouldn't be satisfied—I wouldn't be satisfied—but we'd get over it. Eventually. More important things were happening in our world anyway. My libido wasn't even close to getting top billing. "Any attraction I'm feeling gets really difficult to ignore and it makes other people think they feel it too. I'm so, so sorry. I swear that I will get better at—"

"Wait, what?" I blurted out. I took a breath, stumbling over her words again as they shoved my personal pity party back into the recesses of my brain. "You think that I'm only attracted to you because you're part succubus?"

Color rose to her cheeks. She chewed on her bottom lip again and damn if I didn't want to immediately be doing that for her. "Yes, it enhances and—"

Her words trailed as a giddy laugh bubbled up my throat. "Max. The succubus powers have nothing to do with it. I've been into you pretty much since the moment I saw you." I shook my head as I realized the truth of that statement. "Hell, I haven't even so much as thought about touching anyone else since."

And if I was being *really* honest, she'd played the starring role in every little solo session I'd had with myself since meeting her. My vibrator's battery life could barely keep up.

"But," she scrunched up her face, closing one of her eyes like she was fighting back whatever stray thought was in her head. I waited patiently, barely breathing until she lost the battle. "What about the other girl? Aren't you with her?"

Other girl? What the fuck was she talking about. I hadn't had anything that could be considered a semi-stable romantic relationship in years.

"Max, there is no other girl. Who are you even talking about?"

I wasn't sure it was possible that she could turn even redder, but here she was doing it. How did she find a way to make clown cheeks look so fucking fuckable? "The girl with purple hair. I thought—"

I laughed again, this time louder. "Dani? Max she's an old friend. Was my mentor when I was in The Academy—her role was like mine is with you—" I stumbled over that, not wanting her to think I felt for her the way that I felt about Dani, "only in terms of position at The Guild I mean. I never wanted to lick every inch of her like I do you."

Generally, I would've hated myself right now. I hadn't meant for that last part to slip out, but when it brought out a tentative grin on her face, the regret slipped away. I'd tell her every single thing I fantasized about doing to her if it would make her eyelids go heavy like that.

But just when I thought she'd give in, that she'd sew up the distance between us again, her body tensed. "I don't want to hurt you though—I don't know how to not feed yet. It's different with—"

"The others," I finished. The jealousy that poured through me had nothing to do with the fact that they were attached to her too and everything to do with the fact that they were more indestructible than I was. But Lucifer's words came back to me.

So I took a deep breath, stood up, and walked towards her. "Max, I don't think you can hurt me, not in that way. I feel stronger when I'm with you. Even just now—I could feel your power lingering, but it wasn't draining. It felt energizing. I don't know how it's happening or why, but I think that there is a connection between you and me and that it's more than just attraction and friendship. I think," I paused, tried to suppress the insecurity and fear that she'd laugh in my face, "I think that we're bonded. Or bonding anyway. In the process. In progress—"

I was babbling. I never babbled. Dear god, send Lucifer back here to kill me before I dug myself my own grave.

When I finally mustered the courage to meet her eyes, I found no mockery, no revulsion. Instead, they were wide and bright. Was that—relief? Hope?

"If I hurt you, if I pull too much from you—will you tell me?"

I nodded, unable to bring myself to speak. Was this— was she?

She took a step towards me, her eyes lasered on my lips with a hunger that sent heat pooling in my core. "I'm willing to test this, to go slow and see if you're right—to make sure that I don't hurt you—if you promise you'll stop me if I do?"

I crushed my mouth to hers in answer, swallowing her moan as I pressed her up against the wall.

My hands swept over her body, the gentle curves of her breast, her hip, until I found the edge of her shirt and pulled it over her head. I didn't want slow and testing.

My body was feverish—so many months of this painful, heady want finally getting released. I wanted all of her. I was too terrified that this might be the only chance that we got.

Her lips left mine and trailed across my jaw, down my neck, nipping and biting until I was putty against her. When her hand slipped past the elastic of my pants to pull them down, I kicked off my shoes—my movements erratic and rushed and sloppy.

But her hands were shaking too, and when I slipped my own hand down the front of her pants, I found her underwear drenched.

I brought my finger out and sucked on the tip, tasting her, and she moaned so deep that I felt it vibrate through me.

In rushed movements, like we were timed, we finished undressing.

I slid my leg between hers and nearly came undone already when her thigh rubbed against my clit. I was soaked—and the feel of both of our lust, liquid and slick on each other's legs just turned me on more, if that was even possible.

Her lips captured mine as she guided us back towards the bed. We fell on top of it as one.

She pulled back from me, kneeling over my hips. Dark eyes, swirled with lust. I could see strange swirls in her eyes, like microglitter in a magic crystal ball—could feel her power lick against me, so that even her nearness felt like a stroke to my clit.

With a wicked smirk, she dipped her head down, palming my breast as she nipped and sucked at my stiff nipple.

I moaned and felt her grin against me.

Two could play that game.

I gripped her hips and guided her up until her hands were planted on the headboard above us and her glistening core was in front of me.

With a wicked smirk of my own, I traced her with my tongue—from her clit to her opening in one long, languid movement.

She tasted divine—sweet and earthy all at once.

I licked her clit in slow circles, with consistent pressure. I heard the headboard creak as she gripped tighter, hovering above me.

She was on the edge; I could feel her clit engorge as I sucked and slowly picked up my pace.

"Oh my god." Her voice was deep and primal as she started to gyrate against me. "Fuck that's amazing."

As I added more pressure with my lips, sucking her clit between them, I dipped two fingers into her pussy, gently rubbing the wall of her vagina in a come here motion that made me come when I did it to myself, stroking the g-spot.

I grinned against her as I felt her tighten around me.

"I'm already—" she moaned, "Oh my god, I'm—" her words punctuated with breaths as she spasmed against me, sinking down on my face as the orgasm drained the power in her legs.

The feel of her coming on me nearly brought my own. My pussy throbbed with mirrored pulses, like her orgasm was running through my body.

She climbed off me and brought her lips hungrily to mine, tasting herself on my tongue.

She trailed her fingers in ghostlike touches down my torso until they slid into my folds—wet and slippery as I ground my hips against her.

"I liked that," she said as she kissed and nipped her way down my neck. "That motion," she stuck two fingers in, repeated the motion on me to punctuate her point, then used her thumb to press down on my clit just as she sucked my nipple into her mouth.

I came instantly, my vision clouded with dots of light.

Holy fucking shit.

When my body stopped being jelly, I realized that her head was between my legs, studying me with a hunger in her expression that made my breath catch.

Shyness flashed in her eyes as they met mine—the contrast with the succubus lingering at the surface endearing as hell. "I've never done this before."

"You don't have to."

Her eyes widened. "I want to. I just wanted you to know that I—might not be great at it."

"That's not possible." I felt my lips spread into a smile. "Just do what you like done to you. And I'll guide you towards what I want if that's not doing it for me."

She nodded, then gently licked me, like she was testing how sensitive I was from the last orgasm.

I buried my hand in her luscious hair as she sucked my clit into her mouth, gentle and forceful all at once.

The tip of her tongue flicked up and down as she moved her fingers inside of me again to match pace.

I expected to guide her—I wasn't afraid of telling a girl what I wanted and how—but pleasure pooled over my body in waves.

She was—holy shit she was edging me. She watched me with a lust-filled focus, making sure that I was alright, that my body wouldn't crumble into pieces at the mercy of a succubus. And that focus helped her read me like sheet music until she could play me with the skill of the greats. She brought me to the tip of the hill and then watched as I floated back down, paying attention to every pulse and motion that I made to bring me climbing back up again, but then never letting me fall.

My head got dizzy from the sensation, my ears nearly ringing with the teasing.

Every inch of my body was peppered with goose bumps, the pale peach fuzz on my arms even standing to attention.

And then, just when I thought it would be too much, that my body would explode if it had to wait another moment, she brought me over the cliff, lapping me up as I came.

For a long moment, I was silent, trying to regain myself as she buried her face into my neck.

"Not," my lungs worked overtime in deep, loud gasps, "bad."

She leaned back against the pillow, glanced at me out of the side of her eyes as a giant, shit-eating grin pulled across her face.

Yeah, she knew she'd done great—knew that she'd turned my bones into jello.

A heady warmth spread through my body, down to my toes. I'd had sex before, obviously. But this was different.

This was life-changing sex that made my body feel like it had exploded into a million different pieces and built itself back up into something stronger than before—something more precious, more solid.

My breath stuttered in my chest as a pure, all-consuming affection came over me. I didn't let myself dissect it, wasn't ready to unpack the feelings slowly winding their way through me with a fierceness that wasn't there before—I couldn't ignore them forever, not like I'd been trying to anyway, but I didn't need to tackle them head on right now either.

I had Max freaking Bentley naked and in bed with me. She wanted me. In the way that I wanted her. I was going to float in this momentary bliss for as long as I possibly could.

When she closed her eyes and snuggled into me, I climbed on top of her, hovering, and shook my head. As I pulled gently on her earlobe with my teeth, whispered softly into her ear, "No way. Time for round two."

17

MAX

One moment I was laying in bed, a tangled mass of sweaty limbs with Declan, body buzzing with pleasure, drifting off to a much-needed sleep, the next moment I was sitting in a lavish chaise lounge chair made of the softest black velour I'd ever felt in my life.

I ran my fingers along the material as my thoughts cleared and I caught my bearings.

"See, boy, what did I tell you? Succubi always have an appreciation for the finer things in life—fabrics and upholstery among them. We can feel them more deeply, sink into the sensation of them against our skin. It's a gift, one we should be careful we don't take for granted. An unfamiliar woman watched me. There was something both dangerous and inviting about the tone, like she combined the force of a growl and a purr all at once. Her eyes darted briefly to Wade as he walked over to me. "I'm glad we are finally able to meet. The boy was beside himself when he couldn't sense you—made our training all but useless these last few weeks. And, unfortunately, I don't have the ability to reach those beyond this realm."

Before I could process everything she'd said, Wade's arms wrapped around me and squeezed.

"You're alive," he whispered against my neck, sending shivers down my spine. My body was already hypersensitive after being with Dec, and these dreams had a way of extending that pleasure beyond the physical realm. I swallowed back the desire to jump his bones. "Please don't ever do that to me again."

I nodded, squeezing him back, but then I pulled away, creating some necessary distance between the two of us. I didn't want to go all lust-consumed with a stranger in the room.

As if sensing my heightened state, he nodded and walked a few steps away, where another elaborate chair sat.

"Time isn't aligning properly between realms," I said, straightening my posture and taking a look at the woman watching us.

I wasn't sure how she hadn't immediately pulled my focus. She was, without a doubt, one of the most beautiful women I'd ever seen: deep brown skin, dark eyes that had a sort of knowing light in them, high cheekbones, a figure of perfect curves and angles, and black, curly hair. "You really are the one then. The one he's been searching for. You really are hers."

My stomach lurched.

Hers.

I licked my lips. "Y-you knew my mother?"

The woman nodded, her head tilted as she studied me. "You look like her." A soft, sad smile ghosted across her face. "And you look like him." She turned to Wade, her eyes dancing with a mischievous glint. "She's lovely. I can see why you're so taken. Our family always has had the most exquisite taste. Glad to know that trait lives on in the next generation."

Wade cleared his throat. "Erm, Max, this is my aunt."

His aunt.

It was as if announcing their relationship was the key to

unlocking the similarities between them. The same high cheekbones, accompanied by matching smiles—dimples to boot—his nose the more masculine version of hers. And something about the way she carried herself; her posture had an echo of Wade in his more confident moments.

"You can call me Serae." She stood up from her seat and walked to me, gripping my hand gently in hers. The moment her skin touched mine, I could feel her power lick against me—not in a seductive way like it was when I was with Wade, but like she was reading my energy, getting a taste for it. "You're quite strong for someone with only a trace of succubus blood in her veins. Lucifer's power must have amplified it somehow." She paused, turned back to Wade, not dropping my hand. "Or else my nephew. How interesting."

A shadow crossed her features as she dropped my hand back to my side and studied me.

"Please," I said, taking a deep breath. "How did you know my mother?"

Now that I had a name for her—or I thought I had, anyway—now that there was even the sketch of who she might have been, I was starved for more. It was like nineteen years of desperately wanting to know her had come to a head. One that was impossible to ignore any longer.

I wasn't sure when he'd moved, but Wade was next to me, his arm heavy across my shoulders as he squeezed my bicep.

Surprisingly, I felt more comfort than lust at his touch, as warmth spread through my body.

Serae studied us, her face unreadable. For a moment, I thought she was going to ignore my question. "I knew her. Many years ago. When she found herself here, in this particular pocket of hell."

"Pocket?" Wade asked, focusing on the details while I suppressed the giddiness at the fact that she'd decided to open up.

She nodded. "Hell is not one large, open realm. When it was created, many of the ancients were barred into small pockets. Like mini realms of their own." She flattened an invisible wrinkle in the long silk gown she wore. "It was insurance that they wouldn't band together and destroy this place—that they wouldn't destroy each other or upset the delicate balance of things." She shook her head, a small grin tugging at her lips. "Somehow your mother found her way into Lucifer's sect. It was chaos, of course. But over the years, long after she was gone, the barriers of his particular prison started to crumble, and started to bleed into another. He's been getting stronger ever since, but he's not what he once was."

"She left?" I echoed, trying to find an entry point into all of the new information being given to us, like a rich, decadent buffet. My life had been nothing but a pile of questions and secrets piled high—the thought that I might finally be getting answers, even just a few, was almost overwhelming. I took a deep, steadying breath, met Serae's gaze with my own, tried to project the regal calm that she seemed to exude from every pore. "Where did she go?"

Serae shrugged, a sadness overcoming her gentle expression. She had an odd way of looking compassionate and lethal at once. It kind of reminded me of Wade in some ways—hard and soft edges interwoven and complementary. "No one knows. She was here and then she wasn't. I don't know any more details than that. And no one here speaks about her anymore."

"Because Lucifer doesn't allow it," I guessed.

She didn't confirm, but the hardness in her eyes told me that I was right, or at least very close to the truth.

The thought that he didn't talk about her startled me.

It meant that she had meant something to him. That he cared enough to try and erase her from memory, from his home.

That someone like him was capable of such a strong

emotion seemed incompatible with the version of him that I'd encountered. But it wasn't the first time since discovering his identity that I wondered what their relationship might have been like.

If she was as manipulative and cruel as he was. If she softened him somehow. If it was a consensual relationship, or something more unspeakable.

"You'll do well to be careful in your dealings with him," Serae said suddenly. She tilted her head up slightly, like she was proudly defying him, even though he couldn't reach us here.

Could he?

"What do you mean?" Wade's body grew tense, his brows narrowed as he studied his aunt. He pulled me against him, until we were glued together at the side.

I sank into the warmth that washed over me, let it calm the pounding of my heart.

"Many want the barriers between realms handled in different ways. Lucifer's intentions are not magnanimous. He might have cared for your mother once, but that does not necessarily extend to your well-being now." Her hands gripped the sides of her dress, creating actual wrinkles now.

"He's not just relying on her powers to repair the barriers then?" Wade asked, though he didn't seem surprised.

"His powers are bound up with the hell realm. He does not have access to them. Lucifer is a shadow of his former self, so long as they remain as they are."

"So the realms aren't collapsing?" I asked.

"They are." She tilted her head from side to side, considering. "Or something big is happening anyway, I can't really be sure. No one can. This is new territory for all of us. Hell didn't exist and then it did, the inner workings of it are beyond my pay grade. But if you really can wield power over the great divide, if you truly are the key to unlocking this prison as many seem to think, you need to watch your step."

"Speak plainly, Aunt." Wade's voice was a low growl.

I stiffened, afraid she might turn on him, on us both. I wasn't sure how to take on a fully-fledged succubus in her own dreamscape.

But after a long moment, the air thick with anticipation, she simply grinned. It wasn't warm or welcoming, but laced with a feral quality I associated best with Atlas's wolf. "Some will seek to use her as a tool to trap protectors in this realm, to reverse the conditions we've lived in for many years. Many dangerous creatures have been trapped and stripped of their powers for years and years—forced to live in a world of brutal violence and misery. And of course, while she is part demon, she is also part protector. Vengeance is a powerful motivator. Some will wish to wield her as a bargaining chip—sold to the highest bidder, with little concern for more than the promise of protection. Others might try to breed her, to untangle the bonds currently attaching to and strengthening her energy and forge their own." Her eyes were black and cold as they met mine. "And some will use her to absorb the parts of the shadow barrier that are unstable, leaving behind an unchained, old and powerful magic that few have the balance to restore." She shrugged, leaning back into her seat. "Like I said, unprecedented times, who's to say what happens next. That's as plainly as I can say it."

Well, shit. That sounded ominous as fuck.

And it wasn't even like I was under the impression that things were going to be smooth sailing while working with Lucifer. But damn. Hell's politics and grudges seemed just as complicated and convoluted as The Guild's.

Maybe Claude was right.

My new M.O. was to trust no one but the people who'd

earned it. Everyone else was to be handled with a ten-foot pole. Twenty if I could find one in a pinch.

"So she's basically screwed everywhere she turns?" Wade stood up, his hands clenched at his sides as he started to pace. "What are we supposed to even do with that information? How do we protect her?"

Serae raised a perfectly-arched brow as she watched her nephew. "Have you learned nothing these weeks with me? What do you do? You soak it in. You learn everything that you can. Knowledge is power. If you trace any powerful person in our history, you will discover that their strengths came from what they observed and learned, not just their physical prowess. Incubi and Succubi are particularly well-suited for lingering on the peripherals, manipulating people into giving information they might normally not, deciphering the differences between emotions. Use that. And, in the meantime, you train. Master your powers to the best of your ability. They're your other greatest asset, the best chance you have of surviving."

Wade's jaw muscles ticked as he met her eyes. I watched him consider her words, his shoulders relaxing slightly as he nodded and sat back down.

He trusted her.

I hoped that I could too.

In the meantime, I'd do as she said—get as much information as I could.

"Will you train me?" I cleared my throat, realizing that I was asking a lot. "Like you've trained Wade?"

Her cheeks lifted in a smile, her skin glowing and radiant as she stood up, brushed her hands over her dress to flatten it. "That's why I am here. Lucifer has requested that I get you both in control of your powers as soon as possible." She reached for my hand again, her skin soft and feathery against mine. "You especially. Learning how to manifest your succubus powers will be key in helping you balance your energy. He doesn't take training lightly. You will need to get better control over recharging yourself, so to speak."

"Through sex?" I asked, drawing the question out slowly and trying not to get overly embarrassed about the fact that I was asking the dude-I-was-sleeping-with's aunt about this.

Her brows rose and she shook her head. "No. Well, not completely anyway. We can pull from many forms of intimacy, sex is just the most powerful—the easiest to manifest and often the simplest way to manipulate. People are more pliable, more giving of information when they are consumed by lust. But intimacy, connection, can infuse us in their own ways. It's why our mate bonds, when they formed, were so powerful. It was like having an exponential feedback loop of restorative power and strength."

I turned to Wade and frowned at the black shirt he was wearing. It was a moment before I realized that I'd been unconsciously looking for the tattoo. He'd mentioned bonds between lust demons, how they used to develop and manifest across the skin, a marker of their power.

Serae's head tilted as she studied me, considering. Something flashed in her expression, but it was gone before I could parse it.

"So," she clapped her hands together, a genuinely warm grin lighting up her expression, "I've taught Wade a lot of the basics in our short time together. Now that you're here, you can learn through each other. I'll meet with you as often as I can to help you recognize the boundaries of your power, to isolate and sharpen your strengths, and wield them with more intention and control. Our tools are as political as they are sexual."

A rush of gratitude flooded me and I took a deep, cleansing breath. "Thank you." When she waved her hand like it was no big deal, I took a step towards her, meeting her eyes. "For offering to train me. But also for your honesty and your candor.

I've had very few people in my life be so open—offering truths even when they're difficult to hear. I won't forget that."

Something shifted in her eyes as she nodded. She pressed her hand to me and grabbed Wade's with the others. "Let's get to work, shall we?"

The next few days went by in a blur.

Sam was put in charge of most of my training since Lucifer, it turned out, was wildly busy and seemed to hate being in my presence almost as much as I hated being in his. While Sam was a complete prick who made my blood boil with rage each time we were in the same room, he didn't lean into Lucifer's strategy of torturing Declan to motivate my powers—which subsequently helped keep me from lashing out and attacking him every chance I got.

It was hard work, and made training with Cyrus look like child's play. Every session left me exhausted and drained— mentally, physically, emotionally—and I found myself hating eighties movies for promising quick, chipper montages, when I had to go through the gruesome real deal.

And while my body and brain felt broken and stretched to their limits, I was getting faster at summoning and controlling my hellfire.

Teleporting was a whole other animal and an extreme struggle every time.

In the little downtime I had, rarely more than a few minutes here and there, I visited with Declan and Darius. Their limited options for entertainment meant that they were becoming my favorite begrudging, platonic couple.

Seriously, I'd watch a reality TV show of their bickering with glee.

Neither of us had spoken to Darius about what we'd learned from Claude. The one time Dec even came close to discussing it, he'd turned inside of himself in that way he always did.

We visited with Ralph as much as we could, and the other hellhound had taken to lounging about with us as well, though, to my chagrin, he was less into playing games and getting cuddles than Ralph was. Still, every once in a while, he'd let me scratch the spot behind his ears that he couldn't quite reach. Progress.

So far, hellhounds were the creatures I trusted most in this place, but that was probably because of Ralph. I still hadn't forgotten that the other one was tied to Lucifer and Sam. I had no illusions that he wouldn't betray us to them if it came down to it.

At night, I'd almost always meet Wade and we'd work on getting better at recognizing the strengths and limits of our powers. While I was growing fond of Serae, the sessions without her were my favorite, since those tended to involve Wade, and a bed, and far less clothes.

"You're distracted today," Sam snapped, his blade biting into my neck—not far enough to do any real damage, but enough to draw blood. "If you're not going to focus, why should I waste my time?"

I elbowed him in the abs, doing a fat lot of nothing by way of shoving him off of me. "I've done nothing but train for three," I paused, grunting as he pushed me to the floor, "no, four days. While awake and while asleep. Forgive me if I'm not at full-fucking-capacity."

"Excuses," he lobbed a fireball at me, though it did little more than make my skin tingle. "If you wanted to be coddled, you should never have come back. Hell is not the place for weakness."

I sprang to my feet, shooting a ball of fire at him, but he disappeared before it hit him. When I turned to anticipate his move, I felt his blade press low into my back—farther this time. "I didn't have the luxury of not coming back. Wade's here."

He spun me around, lifted the blade to my neck until all I

could see were his dark indigo eyes piercing me with more precision than his blade could manage. "Also a weakness. Your compassion for your friends might be an admirable quality where you're from, but if you're not careful, it will get you killed one day." He shoved me away, kicking my shin in the process. "If you're going to let that happen, at least wait until he's got what he needs from you. He'll be even more insufferable than he already is if he loses his chance at gaining freedom."

I didn't need to ask who the 'he' was in Sam's statement. Other than Serae, I hadn't encountered anyone else within these walls—not that I had free reign. There was a specific wing of the castle that we could walk freely around, but little more.

So, as far as I could tell, Sam didn't seem to have any friends. He was either with his pack of hellhounds or making me bleed.

"You seem to hate him," I said, dropping my arms to my side. "Why do you stay? Why do you work for him?"

His thick brows narrowed, creasing the skin between them. "I don't work for him. I don't work for anyone." When I grinned in disbelief, he took a step towards me, tension etched in his spine. "We're forced to work together."

"By who?"

His shoulders sank slightly, his lips twisting into a grimace. "I warned you about blood oaths, did I not?"

Interesting. "So you're not friends?"

He shot another ball of fire at me, the flames licking and tingling across my skin just as I managed a teleport. Finally.

"Better, but not good enough," he said, sounding so much like Lucifer I wanted to decapitate him. "If you don't pick it up, I'm going to borrow a page out of your father's handbook and drag one of your friends in here. See if that sparks some motivation." I clenched my jaw, biting back the desire to whip pointless curses at him. "I don't have friends. I told you, relationships are a weakness."

It took me a moment to remember that I'd asked him about Lucifer, the declaration felt so out of nowhere.

And it was so matter of fact the way that he said it—no pity or sadness in his voice, no longing in his expression. Just the familiar numbness in the depths of his eyes that was there more often than it wasn't. Complete boredom. An apathy that made my blood turn cold.

What had happened to this man? There were moments where I thought I saw glimpses of humanity, of compassion—and others where he seemed just as cold and uncaring as Lucifer.

Still, something about that, about the loneliness of his statement, sent a wave of pity rolling through me. I was familiar with the fear of having no one, of not belonging.

I did my best to swallow it back, to ignore it. I didn't want to feel anything for this man. He was an asshole. There was no denying it. He'd made a game of almost getting my friends killed. During our training sessions, his eyes lit up with amusement each time he cut into me. And while Lucifer was clearly invested in saving hell from crumbling into nothingness—whether for his own gain or the less likely consequence of saving the people living here—I earnestly believed Sam didn't give a fuck if we all ended up dead.

Something told me that letting him in would prove his claims true—that compassion could very well be a weakness in some instances.

But those glimpses of kindness confused me more than anything I'd encountered in this realm, regardless of their brevity and transience.

"Why did you send Ralph to me?" It was a question I'd wanted to ask him since the moment I'd mentioned it.

"I told you before," he said, lifting his blade, motioning for me to attack him. He'd been trying to get me to work on weaving my new strengths with my existing sparring techniques. I still didn't have a great grasp of my newfound speed and strength. So much of my training growing up had been designed knowing that I would always be weaker or slower than the creatures I hunted. That was no longer the case. "He's the smallest of the hounds I know. Figured he would be the least conspicuous. And I had no use for him here." He swiped left just as I tried to correct course, drawing a fresh line of blood. "You may be the top out of protectors, but sometimes sparring with you feels like sparring with a baby giraffe. If you don't learn how to flex and control your new muscles, you'll be useless against those who matter."

Those like him. Like Lucifer.

Something told me I didn't want to know how many ancients were out there. I just had to hope that Serae was right, that they were stuck in isolated pockets of the realm—and that hopefully none of the barriers closing them off had begun to disintegrate.

"Yes, but why send a hellhound for me at all? Why did you want to protect me if you're so ambivalent about the collapse of the realms?"

For a moment, his face went blank as he considered the question.

I used that opportunity to attack, confident that I finally had the upper hand, when he snapped out of it and pulled me to his chest, blade cutting into my skin, deeper than before.

My body froze. Each attempt I made to free myself just pushed the blade deeper.

When I gripped his arm, trying to peel it away from me, he spun me around, gripping my hand in his.

His dark eyes were unreadable as he swiped his thumb against the small, pale star imprinted on my wrist.

"It's a birthmark," I said, voice hushed though I wasn't sure why. "That, or a scar. I don't know where it's from."

"Lucifer Morningstar," he said, unblinking. "She loved the irony of it."

"Irony of what?" I didn't dare pull away, didn't dare break the trance that had come over him.

"That someone so grumpy could be associated with such a chipper, hopeful name." A small, wistful grin tugged at the right corner of his mouth. "Used to call him Starry Boy when she was annoyed with him, just to piss him off." The almost-grin inverted into a slight frown. "She must have chosen this symbol as an ode to him when she had your powers bound."

My mouth dried as I tried to wrap my mind around that. "My mother? She had my powers bound?"

He dropped my hand and my arm settled at my side, heavy and strange, like it didn't belong to me anymore.

"Sayty," he cleared his throat, like he wasn't comfortable with her name on his tongue, "and your father came from competing lines of very volatile magic. You are, quite possibly, the only one to have survived such a combination." His eyes met mine briefly, before dropping to the ground. "We wanted her to terminate the pregnancy, knowing her chances of survival were almost zero. But she refused. She ran, knowing that a baby with your blood wouldn't survive here. That you'd be hunted your entire life—the first child born of an ancient in centuries. And born to a line of enemy protectors, no less." He paused, and I was certain that I hadn't taken a breath since he spoke. "A spell weaver bound your magic before she gave birth —she wanted you returned to her people, in hopes that you could be raised never knowing where you came from, what you were capable of. That you could remain hidden. An impossible wish."

"But my powers aren't bound." My voice sounded alien to

me, like I was watching the conversation unfold from behind a glass wall.

He rubbed the back of his neck, shaking his head as he stared at the ground, unable to meet my eyes. The gesture was so human—filled with such a heavy existential exhaustion—that, for a moment, I forgot who he was, what he'd done to me and my friends. Instead, I just felt an all-encompassing pity.

"They were—as much as powers like yours could be bound, anyway. Something that happened in your realm triggered them, warped the spell. Traveling here, going through the portal has expedited that process."

His eyes met mine. The colorful light from the torches made them look more vibrant than usual, the empty numbness I was used to no longer there. Something about them was so achingly familiar. I couldn't put a finger on it.

The more I looked at him, the more I saw that his usual prickishness, the way he walked around here like nothing mattered—it was a salve. He was in pain.

"You loved her." I felt the truth of the words as they left my lips. "That's why you sent Ralph looking for me. You did it for her."

Something unreadable crossed his features before they emptied back into the familiar empty mask he wore.

"I think it's time that you went home," a dark voice echoed behind me.

I spun around, my heart in my throat from the conversation, and saw Lucifer standing there, cloak pulled over his head so that I couldn't see his eyes.

I didn't need to see them—was glad that I couldn't. There was a quiet rage in his stance, in the way he held the shadow blade at his side, the magic pulsing in time with each breath that he took.

"I-I thought you wanted me to train here for as long as I could?" I wasn't sure why I was fighting him. I wanted to get back home more than I wanted anything. But something about the anger in his voice had me concerned.

He pulled the cloak back, revealing dark eyes that were narrowed with even more animosity than I expected. He nodded stiffly to Sam. "Leave us."

Sam chuckled, the sound more menacing than humorous, bowed his head dramatically, and met Lucifer's eyes with a snarky wink. "As you wish."

Then, without so much as a glance in my direction, he disappeared.

I was jealous. Not only because he could call on his powers so deftly, but because I desperately wanted to leave the room, the tension was so thick I could chew on it.

"I need you to return and I need you to put some actual effort into finding the source of The Guild's shadow magic." He started to pace, hands clasped together at his back. This was the first time I'd seen him in days and he was barking orders without preamble. "Things are moving quickly now, we can't wait."

"We have looked." I stiffened when he paused his pacing, dark eyes glaring into me with venom. How was this a man my mother felt safe teasing? How had she survived him? "It's not exactly easy for us at Headquarters. We have very little ability to get beyond their security."

"Excuses," he muttered, and I was caught again by the echo of Sam saying the same thing. They were alike in many ways, perhaps that was why they got under each other's skin so much. "And your particular location is not where your search should end. Follow the chain of command. The realm is made of shadow magic, that kind of magic needs to be fed. It might be unstable, but it isn't starved. Find out how they are harvesting the magic and where they are storing it. That is the key to stabilizing things."

"And how exactly do I stabilize things once we know that?"

"Steps. We take things in steps. I'm working on the details on my end, I need you to fulfill yours."

I ground my molars together, tried to keep my frustration from boiling over. "Aren't you, like, an original dude—back to the origin of the world? Shouldn't you have more information for me about this stuff—powers to keep it from happening altogether?"

For a moment, I thought he was going to kill me dead right there.

But the feral anger in his eyes seeped out into a tired wariness. It was the most human he'd looked since I'd met him. He shook his head like he was trying to dispel the vulnerability through movement. "I'm not what I once was, I have a shadow of the power I used to have."

I remembered what Serae said, about his magic being tied to the realm.

Bound like mine?

"Your understanding of reality is shaded by the mythologies of the human realm, all of them right and wrong at once," he continued. "I've been around for a long time, yes, but that doesn't mean I've been around since the origin of things. There were paranormal beings walking the realms long before me, long before humanity occupied the realm you came from. Ancients are just as curious about the questions and philosophies that occupy your people. We have no answers about meaning or purpose or god. Humanity, protectors—they are not original in their not knowing. The sooner you let these misconceptions go, the sooner you stop trying to understand the world from your narrow point of view, the smoother things will go for you. There is no good and evil, only life and death. And even death is a murky area. You'll do well to remember that."

Neither of us said anything for a while as I folded what he'd said with what I'd heard from Sam and Serae. There were so many sides to consider, so many perspectives to examine—I knew almost nothing about my own history, how could I even begin to unpack the history of our strange, convoluted world? A world in which I learned every day that I knew less and less than I thought I did the day before?

"There is an elder council," Lucifer said, breaking the silence. Something about the way he studied me made me feel more like a peer than a naive subordinate. Or perhaps like a pawn—useful, worthy of some respect, but ultimately disposable. "Start there if you're finding yourself strapped with your location. And there are factions of protectors. From what I understand, after hell's formation, hard divides were created. Perhaps those divides hold some of the answers you'll need."

"When do you want us back here?"

He took a deep breath in, examining his pristine nails, before turning to me. "I don't know. My ability to leave my corner of hell is strengthening as time passes—there are places I need to revisit, answers of my own I need to seek."

"How will I know when to return then?"

The corner of his mouth lifted in an arrogant grin. "The beauty of a broken blood oath means that I can call you to me at a moment's notice. And you will be able to do nothing but heed that call. Part of your will is mine, until that connection is severed. It can be a truly useful magic, when woven with intention and finesse."

It felt like an anchor fell into the pit of my stomach. Pulling me to hell was one thing, but what would it mean, in the long run, to do whatever the Devil asked of me?

I hoped like hell that he was right—that the human mythologies surrounding his identity were false.

Without waiting for me to speak, knowing full well that there was nothing for me to even say to that, he gripped my arm and teleported us away.

After I recalibrated my nothingness into thereness—I didn't

even break a sweat this time, thank you very fucking much—we landed in front of Declan, Wade, and Darius.

We were outside, in the same location we'd teleported from before, all of them standing awkwardly against the hauntingly beautiful backdrop of The Styx. Something about it called to me, and I found myself having to deeply focus on not giving into a very urgent impulse to submerge myself into it.

There was another man there—one I didn't recognize. Judging from the look he was giving Darius that set off raging I-want-to-dismember-him-limb-from-limb-vibes, they either knew each other well from before, or else Darius had made another one of his famously shitty first impressions.

Darius seemed unaffected as always, maybe even a little amused by the animosity dripping from the man. His face split into a disarming grin when his eyes met mine.

Even now, even knowing that I was under Lucifer's control, my stomach still dipped with excitement and something a little friskier than excitement at the sight of that cocky smile.

The knowing glint in his eyes told me he knew exactly where my thoughts were.

"Nash will open the portal for you," Lucifer said, stepping away from me as he nodded towards the man who was giving some serious Grumpy Bear energy. "Be sure to train every day. And, on the plus side, I'll no longer need collateral, so you may take your incubus with you as a sign of good faith. Believe it or not, I'm not needlessly cruel."

I bit my tongue, swallowing the small swell of blood.

18

MAX

"Where the hell would she have gone?" Declan paced the small hotel suite, walking in and out of the two bedrooms, like Sarah would magically appear inside one of them eventually.

Dec had called Atlas fifteen minutes ago, to tell him we were back, that we had Wade, and that Sarah was missing.

Apparently, in true Atlas form, he uttered nothing more than an 'okay' before hanging up.

Now, we were just anxiously waiting for him and Eli to show up, while making sure that Wade and Darius didn't accidentally murder each other before we had backup. Their friendship hadn't really been on the path to improving in hell, but learning that they'd be living together for the foreseeable future hadn't exactly put them in a headspace for bonding either.

"Her mom's here, right? Do you think she went to campus? That she went to see her mom?" I tried to put myself in Sarah's position. If I were her, and hadn't seen Cyrus in months and months—and knew that he assumed I was dead and was going through an impossible grieving process—I wasn't sure I'd be able to resist the temptation to see him.

"Fuck." Declan stopped cold, her face turning a sickly gray shade. "She definitely went to see her mom. Why didn't I think of that?" She ran a hurried hand through her hair as she continued her pacing. "There's no way that Aunt Jay would sell her out, werewolf or not, but if anyone else saw her, she's fucking screwed."

Wade's gaze dropped to the floor and my stomach squeezed for him. Sarah's mom might have been loving enough to overlook her daughter's transformation, but everyone knew that if it came down to it, Tarren would lock Wade away with little more than a second glance. He'd already treated his son like shit when he thought he was half-human.

"And now that none of us have any clearance to the labs, I have no idea how we'd get her out of there if she gets caught," Declan continued.

"Guess they wasted the good breakout on you then," Wade said, meeting Darius's amused stare with a much less friendly one.

Dec's shoulders dropped as her eyes met mine. "Maybe they won't even bother capturing her. Maybe they'll just outright kill her."

The door crashed open and Atlas walked in, his eyes covered with a pair of dark sunglasses.

His jawline was rigid as he scanned the room, his energy electric with tension. For a moment, I thought he was going to wolf out right in front of us.

Instead, he took three giant steps into the room and scooped me into his arms, his face burying into the crook of my neck as he squeezed me to him.

Atlas was hugging me.

In front of an audience.

And, was he...smelling me?

My shock melted into something else as I fell into the embrace, my body humming at the closeness of him.

"You've been gone nearly a month," Eli said, his eyes dark and distant as he followed Atlas into the room. "We knew you weren't dead, Atlas said we would know if you were, but we had no way of having any clue what the fuck was going on. It was fucking maddening—trying to work and train while—" he shook his head, exhaling heavily.

A month?

This whole time scale thing was chaotic and impossible to predict. If anything, I would've assumed that it would have been less than a day here, that they would've just gotten back from their mission in Seattle—our absence little more than a hiccup, crossed wires.

It was going to be a lot more difficult to explain a month of disappearances away.

Atlas detached himself from me and walked to the other side of the room, his movements stiff and awkward, like he was resisting each step, before leaning against the wall. He nodded to Wade, but I was guessing he was fighting with his wolf at the moment, so their reunion wasn't as warm as I thought it would be.

"The portal instabilities are messing with time," Darius said, expression bored like we were discussing the weather and not the wonky mechanics of time. "You haven't been stocking the fridge with any of that pig's blood by chance, have you? Realm hopping always wipes me out and, while it's not my first choice, it's better than the she-wolf's leftover tacos that she's always forgetting in there."

"You're all okay?" Eli asked, ignoring him as he scanned everyone in the room. His voice was rigid and monotone, devoid of the usual snark. "Why'd he let Wade out? What happened?"

I sucked in a deep breath and sat down on the couch next to Darius. "The blood oath. I didn't make it back to him in time."

"Technically you did," Declan interrupted, momentarily pausing her lap of the room, "hell, we were even a few days early. The Devil is just a dick."

"Time got weird on that end of things too," I clarified. "We were away from hell a lot longer than the two week agreement. With the blood oath broken, he can pull me back into hell whenever he wants. I guess he kind of owns my willpower for the foreseeable future. So he let Wade go."

"I'll kill him."

"Are you fucking serious?"

"How do we break it?"

A low growl vibrated the room, but I couldn't tell if it was coming from Atlas or Darius—maybe both.

I raised my hands up trying to calm them all down. "There's nothing to be done about it right now. I don't think he's going to abuse the loophole too much. At least not right now. He was pretty preoccupied while we were down there—I spent most of my time training with Sam and Serae. Besides, in some ways, it'll be more convenient. We won't have to travel to Seattle every few weeks, or travel to his doom and gloom castle once we drop into hell. Plus, we have Wade back, which is totally worth some forced teleportation every few weeks." I shook my head, trying to focus. "But right now, we need to know what's going on with Sarah. How long has she been gone?"

"She was here last night." Eli sat on the arm of the couch, his hand brushing against my bicep. "I've been crashing in the vamp's room most nights lately. It's been nice to get away from Reza. She's on a redecorating kick. Thinks she's moving in permanently so she's using all of her time and energy to kill my vibe."

I tried to ignore the tightness in my chest, used all of my self control on not looking at Atlas, on not dissecting and analyzing every microexpression he tried to conceal.

Besides, while I knew that Eli hated Reza, something in my gut told me he wasn't hiding out off campus because of her.

He'd been doing everything in his power to avoid Levi and his mother since they'd been in and out of Headquarters.

"She was more antsy than usual," Eli continued, his arm around my shoulders now, though it seemed more unconscious than intentional. "Really fucking antsy. I don't think her wolf appreciates being cooped up in here with no end in sight. Six weeks is a long time to stay confined. It's not like we've come up with a plan to integrate her back into her old life—there was nothing for her to even look forward to, not really."

"You think she needed a run?" I asked, my focus unconsciously shifting to Atlas.

He nodded, the muscles in his jaw pumping. When he took the glasses off, his eyes were shot through with yellow, but I could see the brown starting to fight its way back. "It's a full moon. A lot harder to control the wolf if her emotions were already running high, if something triggered her more than usual. I've been trying to contain mine all week. It's been... difficult."

"More like all month," Eli mumbled.

"So maybe she'll come back after stretching her legs?" Wade asked, but I could see in his eyes that he didn't really believe it.

"Protectors aren't the most intelligent creatures, but I doubt even they wouldn't notice a werewolf prowling their territory these days." Darius plopped a hand on my thigh, drawing slow, smooth circles with his thumb.

My stomach tightened at the feel of having both Eli's and his hands on me.

"I mentioned that her mom was back in town again," Eli said, shaking his head. "Maybe I shouldn't have. She's been in and out the last month, like most of The Guild—figured it might help to know she was around, even if she couldn't see her. We watched a shitty movie and killed a fifth of whiskey before I crashed. I didn't see her this morning, but I assumed she was just passed out in her room sleeping off the hangover."

I stood up, reluctantly separating myself from the warmth of the boys and walked towards the door.

"What are you doing?" Atlas was behind me, his breath whispering at my back.

"Going to go look for her obviously. Hopefully no one's seen her yet. If they have, Seamus will know and we'll create a plan to get her out from there."

For a moment, his eyes locked on mine, something almost like regret flashing in their depths. "You can't just go back to campus. You guys have been gone for a month—you disappeared in the middle of a fight with a horde of vampires."

"We'll tell them they kidnapped us," Declan said, her eyes sparkling with clarity. "The Guild knows that demons have been taking our women for months. We'll tell them we broke out."

"You expect them to believe that vamps kept you alive for a month, and that neither of you are worse for wear?" Eli asked, brows narrowed in disbelief like someone just told him that unicorns were real.

Declan's brows burrowed together as she focused, and I could see that pushing into protector mode was helping calm some of the anxiety over her cousin. "We weren't with them for a month. We escaped early on, but we were in the Canadian wilderness. Had no way to reach anyone, no technology—we were just focused on staying alive and getting back here." Her eyes sparkled as they met mine. "When we finally made it to civilization, I called Atlas. He grabbed a plane and picked us up."

Darius puckered his lips, impressed. "It could work. Protectors are notoriously good at believing lies."

"It'll also give us time to look for Sarah." I started pacing, like Declan's adrenaline was feeding into mine. "While you all commandeer a plane. Shouldn't take more than three hours tops from now."

Eli took a deep breath, buried his hands in his pockets, and shook his head. "This is an absurd plan. Like, on the scale from normal to fucking batshit, this takes the cake."

"It could work," Atlas said, inching closer towards me until his hand gently brushed past mine, then immediately pulled away— "but you guys have to go with Eli. Take one of the small helicopters, the ones we were trained to drive for pair missions. If anyone spots you around town before Eli brings the plane back, it's all for nothing. And, that way, when he lands it on Guild property, it won't raise suspicion if you aren't on it."

"I'm the one who has to fly?" Eli's eyes widened, his voice uncharacteristically sharp. "Seriously? I haven't re-read that manual in weeks."

"Eli's afraid of flying," Wade muttered, an amused grin tugging at his lips. He missed his team, missed being a part of all of the planning and scheming—I could see it plain as day on his face. "He taught himself how to fly each aircraft The Guild owns on the off chance a pilot mysteriously dies while he's on one. Knows each manual like the back of his hand."

My chest warmed at the sight of that light in Wade's eyes. He seemed so happy to be back here, teasing his friend like the past few months hadn't happened. Honestly, if he got to come home, back where he belonged, being indebted to Lucifer was nothing in comparison.

"I'll look for her," Atlas said, jaw clenched tight. "I'll be able to track her more easily. It makes the most sense. Eli, you clear shit with your dad."

"Fuck," Eli shook his head, but then nodded when he caught Atlas's eyes.

And so it was settled.

We left Wade and Darius sitting awkwardly on opposite sides of the couch, unable to do more than hope that when we returned, it wasn't to find that they'd killed each other.

Sneaking onto the helicopter unnoticed was surprisingly easy, since Eli was the only person required for lift off. The difficult part was getting him to actually lift off.

"I thought Wade said you can drive every plane?" I asked, trying to stifle my grin.

"He can fly them in theory," Declan said, brow arched. "As in he's passed the necessary tests, knows the mechanics of each of the planes, and has done more simulation driving than anyone I know."

"But he doesn't ever actually drive them?" I added.

He sank into his pilot seat, sweat beading on his forehead as he stared at all the buttons and gadgets like he was about to go head-to-head with Lucifer himself.

I hated how adorable it was.

The guy who could easily summon the nerve to flirt with anything that walked, who could charge headfirst into a battle with demons with a grin on his face—was terrified of being airborne.

I leaned forward and squeezed his hand softly. "You've got this. I know you do."

His eyes met mine, and the vulnerability there made my stomach flip.

It was so damn hard to hate Eli, that I wasn't sure it was worth even pretending that I did. Yeah, he was an absolute asshole sometimes, and he totally ruined my first time having sex by lying to me, but then he'd go and throw a look like that at me and suddenly all I wanted to do was wrap my arms around him and squeeze.

"Besides," I added, trying like hell to ignore the annoying flutter in my chest that exploded whenever his stare met mine, "if we crash, I'll teleport us to safety."

"Or heal whatever injuries that haven't killed us," Declan added, a giant smirk on her face.

"You can teleport with other people now?" he asked, eyes widening.

It had been a joke, but the hope radiating from his face made it impossible for me to form words.

"Yep, training with Luce was pretty damn useful," Declan lied, nudging me with her foot to keep me quiet. "So no problems, let's get moving. We've figuratively been wandering the wilderness for weeks, so no more lollygagging—the starving version of me is absolutely going to demand a trip to a local fast food chain before being forced to thrust myself back into civilization."

"Same," I said, the thought of a burger and fries enough to make me drool. "A month in the wilderness? It's honestly impressive we didn't just eat each other out there."

Eli laughed, his shit-eating grin washing away some of the lingering anxiety in his expression.

I felt myself blush at the awkward phrasing.

When I turned to Declan, she simply winked. "Who knows, maybe we did. I can only be expected to have so much self-control."

Four hours later, we landed back at Headquarters with full bellies and a fresh pair of clothes that Eli had the foresight to bring for us.

We'd had some fun mussing up our hair and rubbing dirt into our skin to help with the ruse. And while Eli was stiff as a board the entire flight there and back, the trip had been pretty seamless.

Before we started to descend, Eli peeled back his white-knuckled grip from the lever and reached for me.

"There's something you should know," he said, his jaw tight with tension. I wasn't sure whether it was because we were hovering in the sky in a metal death contraption or because of whatever was on his mind.

I nodded, encouraging him to continue when he didn't.

His eyes darted briefly to Declan before they landed back on the expanse of sky before us. "Atlas and Reza are scheduled to have their bonding ritual tomorrow."

Bile rose to the back of my throat. When we'd left, Reza had mentioned it would be coming up. The time warp just sped things up far faster than I'd expected. I still hadn't had time to process it. Not when I thought there was a small possibility that —I shook my head, tried shoving down the confusing cluster-fuck of feelings I had for Atlas. Instead, they landed like a heavy rock in the pit of my stomach, permanent and impossible to ignore.

"This is ridiculous. He's already started bonding to Max." Declan shook her head as she leaned forward, huddling closer to Eli. "At least the wolf has anyway, so I don't know how sepa-rated they still are. But either way, it's obvious. Is he just going to fracture that bond and create another?"

Eli tensed, the skin along the column of his neck flushed a pale white-gray.

"What are you talking about?" My spine tingled as I glanced between them. Declan and Darius both seemed convinced that they were my bond mates—and I'd be lying to myself if I didn't feel a peculiar, supernatural connection to all of Six. But something about hearing them acknowledge that connection too made it all more real—made it suddenly terrifying.

And the thought of losing one of those invisible tethers that I clung to—the thought of Atlas being attached to Reza of all people, made me want to turn her inside out.

A low, dark part of myself, hidden back in the recesses of

my mental clusterfuck box whispered the truth I wasn't ready to voice into reality—*mine.*

"There's more," Eli whispered, checking each of the levers and lights like the plane would suddenly combust if he wasn't constantly monitoring. "Your aunt has been a mess since you disappeared—made my dad promise that if we found you, if you made it home, that he'd send in a rushed petition for you and I to" he shook his head, like he couldn't believe what he was about to say, "you know, get bonded as well. As soon as possible."

Declan sank back into her seat, her emerald eyes vacant as she processed his words.

I wasn't sure who looked more disgusted with the announcement—Eli or her.

"Anything else we missed?" I asked, trying and failing to bury the stomach pit with sarcasm.

Eli inhaled, deep and long, then nodded. His grip tightened, if possible, even more than it already was. "They are disintegrating Six—effective tomorrow, after the ceremony. You and I will be folded into another group, same with Atlas and Reza."

None of us spoke. The loud sound of the engine was suddenly the only thing I could focus on—it was somehow impossibly loud and distant all at once, like echoes of the reverberations were pulling through me in waves.

"But Seamus—" Declan's voice pierced through the hypnotizing drone.

Eli shook his head, interrupting her. "Out of his hands. We've had too many close calls and fucks ups lately—Tarren and Alleva pushed the transfers through with almost no resistance."

The last twenty minutes of the flight were spent in a heavy silence—partially because Eli was hyperfocused on nailing the landing, and partially because there was nothing more for us to say or do, other than sink into the new reality we were being forced into.

When we landed, before the engine fully quieted, Atlas was at the door, waiting for us to step out.

"Did you find her?" I asked, as soon as he was within earshot.

I needed good news. I wasn't sure I could handle any more disappointments.

Seamus, Tarren, and a few others were scattered around a bit further back, waiting for us to disembark.

He shook his head, the look on his face enough to make my heart stop.

"What's wrong?" My voice didn't sound like my own.

He glanced briefly towards his father, then back to us. "It's Ten."

Ten.

My brother.

Izzy.

I stopped breathing.

"They were on a mission not too far from here and got separated. Mavis was bit—werewolf," he said, quickly, anticipating the question before I even thought to ask it, "Arnell, Izzy, and Sharla brought him back about an hour ago. They're all okay."

"Ro?" I suddenly felt like I was going to throw up.

"He and Jer got separated from the group during the attack. The others couldn't find them, and they couldn't wait much longer with Mavis in bad shape. They—they aren't back yet, Max." Atlas's hand squeezed my shoulder softly, but I barely felt it. A sharp buzzing noise filled my ears as I processed his words. "They haven't answered their phones. We don't know where they are."

I felt Eli come up behind me, his arm wrapping around my waist.

At first, I thought he was just offering comfort, but then I realized he was helping to hold me up. Suddenly my legs didn't feel like they were working.

"Let's get them inside," Seamus yelled, signaling some of the protectors standing around. "They've been through a lot."

My feet started to move, one step in front of the other, but I couldn't process where they were going or process any of the questions or orders Tarren was barking at us. The world was a blur and all I could focus on was the fact that Ro was missing.

That he wasn't here.

And then my eyes met a familiar dark, impenetrable gaze.

Tanned face with soft frown lines etched in, dark billowing hair peppered with gray.

Cyrus.

He was back.

19

MAX

Cy was back but Ro was missing.

It was such a cruel twist of fate that I almost wanted to congratulate whoever wove it.

And not just regular missing, but the kind of missing that happens when a mission goes bad, the kind of missing I was in the middle of fabricating, like the universe was punishing me.

After the medical staff satisfied themselves that Dec and I were okay—nothing more than a few scratches still left to be healed, Tarren interrogated us.

We'd rehearsed stories on the plane, while Eli mumbled nonsensical lines from the flight manuals under his breath, so the questions weren't too unexpected.

But the man still stared at me from Wade's eyes with intense disgust and distrust, muttering the entire time about entitlement and how "this is what happens when people aren't properly trained."

Still, there was nothing more for them to do other than let us go with instructions to stay hydrated, fed, and to get some rest.

I had no intention of resting though, no intention of finding my way back to Ten's cabin knowing that Ro wouldn't be there.

I'd already begged to go looking for him, had already demanded to know what The Guild was doing to make sure he was found and brought back safe.

But we were on lockdown—both Declan and I benched completely until our statements were reviewed by the council and Headquarter heads.

Seamus had assured me that he was on it, that they were doing everything they could to locate Ro, and that he would tell me the second information changed—but that he ultimately agreed with Tarren. There was nothing I could do. Forcing my way into their investigation would only shift resources away from finding my brother and place them onto corralling me.

I had to wait until Izzy and the others were done being debriefed, though they'd probably be one of the first teams tapped to go find them—they were the only ones who knew what happened out there.

My instincts told me to say fuck it and go after him myself. But too many things had gotten worse because I'd lost my patience, because my rashness had gotten in the way of things.

I couldn't fuck this up. Wouldn't fuck this up.

Until I had more information, I had to bottle up the fear and figure out a plan B.

So, instead of arguing with Tarren and the others, I took that energy and beelined straight for a small cabin that had been unoccupied more often than not these last few months.

My fists pounded on the heavy door, not letting up until it opened with a whiny creak.

"I've been waiting for you to show up." Cy stepped to the side so that I could squeeze in. "Figured it was best to wait out Tarren's questions and the reports, talk to you here. It's better for you if I keep away from him—my presence will only make him despise you more, unfortunately."

I didn't give a shit about Tarren or his history with Cyrus.

Right now, all that mattered was Ro—and channeling all of my anxiety into something productive for once.

"Where the fuck have you been?" I barely even waited for him to close the door behind me before I spun around and stared him down. I knew that Ro missing wasn't Cy's fault, but lashing out at him was the closest thing I had to a relief valve at this point.

Because the reality was, that if Cy had been around, if Cy hadn't spent a lifetime lying to us, neither of us would be in the positions we were in now.

"Max," he shook his head, "I know you're upset, but calm down. Have a seat."

"No. I don't want to have a seat. And I sure as hell won't calm down. What I want is pretty damn clear. I want to know where the fuck you've been," I paused, studying him. He had heavy bags under his eyes like he hadn't slept in weeks, his arms were leaner than I remembered, and something about him just seemed so damn frail that, for a moment, I almost lost my resolve. But then the anger I'd buried over the last few weeks, the rage that had been building slowly with nowhere to go, the fear trembling low in my gut, finally reared. "Why the hell did you keep Sayty Azar from me?"

You would've thought I'd slapped him from the look on his face.

He didn't move. Didn't so much as blink. "Where did you hear that name?"

I shook my head and took a step closer to him. "You don't get to ask the questions right now. I've had to deal with unanswered questions for nineteen fucking years. Only to come here and find out that you've known who my mother was this whole time. This whole fucking time? How—" my voice cracked. I took a deep breath and forced myself to meet his eyes, to confront him with all of my focus. "How could you keep the truth from me all these years?"

"Max," he reached a hand forward, but I took a step back. His shoulders sagged. "It's complicated. So much more complicated than you could possibly imagine."

"Then tell me. Uncomplicate things. Now's your chance—we're not able to do anything but twiddle our thumbs until we're given some idea where Ro could be. Help me out for once—keep my mind off him." I blinked back the film over my eyes, begging my body to stay strong, to not cloud my resolve with emotion.

He sighed, nodded to the wooden table a few feet from us.

I followed, taking in the small cabin. It was open concept, but much smaller than the spaces reserved for teams. Nothing more than a small living room that opened up to a sparse kitchen and dining area.

Cy hadn't adorned the space with any personal touches—in fact, it looked exactly as it had the day he arrived here.

Had he planned on staying? On making a home amongst his people? Or had this always been a temporary stop for him?

I followed him to the table, trying to ignore that his limp seemed worse than normal. It tended to get particularly bad when he was stressed. I took the seat farthest from him.

When he did nothing but stare at his hands, as if they held the answers I was seeking, I couldn't keep quiet any longer. "Did you know that she was part succubus?"

His eyes shot to mine, held my gaze for a breath, and then he nodded. "Sort of. I knew that she was more than just a protector. When she—when she came back. She found me and I could tell that there was something different about her. It was an energy about her, a strength and glow that wasn't there before. One that had nothing to do with the fact that she was pregnant."

"But you didn't turn her in, didn't tell anyone." It wasn't a question—I knew Cyrus had kept her secret or else I wouldn't have grown up with him.

His mouth thinned into a straight line. "She was in trouble. She was scared, absolutely terrified when she came to me. It had been years since I'd seen her, years since she disappeared. And when she showed up at my door, I could tell that she'd experienced an entire lifetime in her absence. There was just a giant, wide gulf between us that hadn't been there before. I couldn't reach her, not like I used to."

Occasionally, Cy had a tendency to sink into his memories, to forget that he was having a conversation, that I was even around him. I gave him a few moments to linger in the silence, before I couldn't take it anymore. "Why did she disappear?"

His shoulders tensed as he stared at his hands, steepled in front of him on the table—fingers bruised and battered from who knew what. "She was being forced to bond to someone she hated. Linking her life to him would, as far as she was concerned, have been a fate worse than death. Right before the ceremony, she realized she couldn't go through with it. She disappeared that night and it was years before anyone saw her again."

"So that's why she left. But why did you leave The Guild all those years ago?" I dipped my forehead into my hands, as so many shifting pieces started to come into focus—I could sense these things were connected but I didn't understand how. "Why did you come back now?"

Cy's eyes widened, surprised by the questions. When he looked at me, it was like he was seeing a ghost—there was a rigid fear in his expression, in the tensing of his posture. He scratched his jaw, the rough grating of his fingernails against his scruffy beard the only sound in the entire cabin. He nodded. Then, slowly, he stood up and walked the two feet to his kitchen. He ruffled through the cabinets until he pulled out a half-empty bottle of whiskey and two small glasses.

"I didn't get on well with those in charge, when I was your age. Like you, I spent most of my time breaking the rules and butting my nose into places it wasn't welcomed. When I was younger, a few years older than you and Ro, a member of my team was bit by a werewolf." He turned back to me as he poured a healthy few fingers of liquor into each glass. Cy was generally a pretty stoic guy, but there was something deeper than that in his eyes right now—a bone-crushing sadness that I'd seen on those nights when he hit the whiskey bottle a little too hard. "When we came back, they told us that she died. But I didn't believe it. The labs weren't always as well-guarded as they are now. I snuck down and found her down there—caged like the other demons that teams had brought back from battle. When Seamus and I went back to break her out a few days later, we were too late."

His voice trailed and I knew with a sinking certainty that she'd been killed.

By The Guild. Like they were going to do Ralph, to Darius —what they would do to Atlas, Wade, Sarah, and me if we ever found ourselves on the wrong side of those thickly guarded walls.

"Anyway," he continued, his tone stronger, more like the Cy I was used to. "I'd had doubts before then of course, heard whispers of protectors resisting the practices and beliefs of The Guild. An underground network of sorts, both outside of the organization and within it. After years and years of digging, I learned the truth. The one they guard more fiercely than anything else." He paused, his shoulder blades shifting and tensing. "Hell was not a natural place for demons—one we were put on this planet to guard. Hell was a place that protectors created—as a way to gain power and an edge over those they couldn't control. Hell drains the people contained within it, feeds on their power to maintain itself. Protectors are more powerful than humans, yes, but we weren't satisfied with that—

weren't satisfied with the fact that a single vampire could take out three or four of us with little difficulty."

He walked back to the table, carrying the two glasses in one hand, the bottle in the other. He set one of them in front of me and I just stared at it. Cy was a heavy drinker, but he almost never offered booze to us.

"Go ahead," he nodded, sitting down again, though he took the chair next to me this time. When I brought the glass to my lips, tasting the sharp liquor, he did the same, relaxing into the familiar comfort it had always brought him. "If protectors couldn't find a way to give themselves that kind of power, they needed to find a way to bind that power, and those who had it. In doing so, they became some of the most powerful creatures in this realm, the ones who held all the cards. Hell isn't a heaven-sanctioned prison, meant to keep humanity safe and trick children into abiding by some arbitrary moral code. It's one that our people created centuries ago out of a bottomless hunger for power, pure greed. When I learned that, I wanted no more part of it. It's difficult to hunt demons when the ones you serve are just as dangerous, just as ruthless."

I took another sip, savoring the sting of the alcohol as it warmed my throat and belly. Lucifer had hinted at something similar, though coming from Cy, it felt so much heavier—so much more real.

When Cy spoke, things always seemed to ring with truth.

"Is there a way to prove this, to show people the truth?" I couldn't imagine it sitting well with anyone that The Guild was lying to us all.

He let out a humorless chuckle and shook his head. "Only those with clearance—very few outside of the council—know the details. And it's not something I could prove to you or anyone else who didn't want to believe it. When your mother showed up on my doorstep, she told me stories. I only half believed them at the time—it was like speaking with a ghost—

but I've replayed them like old documentaries in my mind since then—examining them from every angle. She didn't grow up at The Guild for the first years of her life. She was part of a different line of protectors—one very different from The Guild." He brought the glass to his lips and drained it before pouring himself another, this one significantly deeper. "Their power was different from ours too, their strengths. Your mother, well, she claimed their magic was used to create hell years ago. Unlike all the protectors we know, their power didn't slowly disappear throughout the years in the same way that ours did —because it honored a different kind of balance. That's what she'd call it, though I never knew what she meant. She alway spoke in riddles—especially when she returned from her disappearance. She trusted me more than most, but she still never told me more than she thought I needed to know. Smart that way—good at keeping things close to the chest."

A look crossed his features, and I could tell that he was lost in some distant memory. He shook it off, like he was disappointed in himself for lingering in it. "Anyway, the line she was descended from—when they helped to create the barrier between realms, all those years ago, they realized the mistake they'd made. They realized that it was a magic forged through greed and fear, that the lore The Guild was spinning was one manifested in half-truths and outright lies. Because, you see, protectors are, in fact, demons. Just far less powerful. But just as capable of evil, of harming humanity. Her ancestors separated irreparably from The Guild, and worked to destroy the organization for years, living among humans and protecting those they could. Eventually, it was presumed they died out. Which I believed. Until,"

"My mother," I finished.

He nodded, a sad smile lifting the corner of his mouth. It was an almost invisible twitch, one only someone who knew to look for it would see.

"Why did you come back then? Why have you been helping them?" I didn't mean it to sound like an accusation, but I heard the anger in my voice all the same. My ability at keeping things locked down was shrinking. Dramatically.

"Because of you." When I opened my mouth to ask what he meant, he pressed forward. "Because I couldn't keep you safe anymore. When your mother came to me, with you in her belly, she told me that she'd changed, that she was more than a protector, that her powers had been triggered—she didn't tell me how—but that they could've remained dormant if she'd never left The Guild. She told me she had plans to have your powers bound when you were born, that her ancestors had been confining their power for centuries, many of them choosing to live their lives as humans, the ultimate rejection of everything The Guild stands for. And I thought that she'd done it, that she'd found a way to keep you hidden. But then that day —" when his eyes met mine, I knew that he meant the day before we left our cabin, the day before my entire world turned upside down, "when a damn werewolf and hellhound showed up on our front doorstep, I knew that we couldn't stay. I couldn't protect you there—especially if your powers were dimmed, hidden away. I was in over my head." The chair creaked as he leaned back into it, staring vacantly at the bottom of his glass. "You hadn't manifested any particularly strange skills that would stand out amongst your peers here, and I'd taught you all that I could. I hoped that by bringing you here, letting you train with the best, it could buy us some time while I tried to find a way to keep you safe more permanently.

"There are some who try to fix the broken system from within it, like Seamus. I've never believed in that path personally, but I hoped that if I could rope him in, and the others like him—those working to restore value and integrity to The Guild, that they might have answers I didn't, that they might know more about your mother's history or her people than I did. I don't trust anyone here, but I do trust Seamus—and that was double the support than I had back in that cabin."

When he reached his hand forward to pour another splash of whiskey, I grabbed the bottle, pulling it towards myself.

"Why didn't you tell me any of this?" I took a deep swig, kept it in front of me, my hands gripped around cool glass. "Why make me suffer through a lifetime of not-knowing?"

His face dipped into a frown, the fine lines that had slowly etched into his features deepening. "I always planned to tell you. One day." He inhaled sharply. "But that's the thing isn't it? How do you know when one day comes? At first, I told myself I would wait until you were old enough to understand—ten, eleven maybe. I'd tell you some things then, about your mother, about the dangers of the world you were born into. And then Ro came into the picture. His parents—" Cy paused, clearing his throat. "His parents were friends of mine from before. They left The Guild long ago, had chosen the path of anonymity, of living their lives among humans. When they died, I couldn't leave Ro to grow up in a system that wouldn't understand him. And you—you needed a friend. More than a grumpy old man to keep you company out in the middle of nowhere." He shook his head, his gaze darting briefly to mine then down again.

A rush of anger rolled through me at the fact that I was here to hear Ro's history and he wasn't. Anger, but also fear. Because while I was cozy and safe inside Cy's cabin, Ro was out there— fighting for his life.

"I believe The Guild had them killed. His mother's parents, Rowan's grandparents, were dissidents in their time. They too died mysteriously many decades ago. It is the way, I've come to learn, of those who speak out against our practices, loud enough for others to hear. Another reason I kept things from you both. You are both so stubborn, so headstrong, so fiercely protective of the people you care about—I knew you would have trouble sliding under the radar. And then, when you were teenagers, I thought about telling you again. But I didn't want either of you saddled with carrying the consequences of being your parents' children. I thought you not knowing would protect you both. But you wanted desperately to know where you came from, to find where you belonged in the world. I-I think—"

He trailed off and I poured him an ounce of amber liquid, urging him to continue.

In one gulp, it was gone. "I think by that point, I was secretly holding out hope that we could go on like that forever. You were just two kids. And for the first time in a long time, I felt like," he shook his head, "I don't know, like I belonged somewhere. Like I was meant for something. Like maybe where you belonged in the world, was with me, with Ro. I know we aren't a conventional family, that I'm not—" he cleared his throat, "my own attachments got in the way."

Cy disappeared in a haze of liquid, as I blinked back the tears threatening to fall.

"It became more and more difficult to tell you the truth. To put that burden on you—that protectors weren't what they appeared in The Guild books you devoured as kids, that you had no one but me, that your mother was—" he shoved his glass away, out of reach, and shook his head with a grunt, "I don't know what happened to her. Not the details anyway. I didn't see her much when she returned. She died, I think. I'm sure of it. All I know is that I opened my door one day, months later—a door only she and one or two others even knew to find —and there you were. By yourself, a small, bald-headed baby looking at me with the same stubborn look in your eyes that I'd seen so often in Sayty's. There was a wrinkled letter tucked into a blanket—nothing in the envelope but your mother's handwriting carving the words 'protect her.' And so that's what I did. That's all I've tried to do since the day you showed up on my doorstep." His eyes were glassy, a sight that made my own swim all over again. "But maybe I've failed you. Eventually, I wanted so badly to protect you, to keep you from being hurt, from the disappointments of the world, to give you the version of family that I could, to save you—like you'd saved me—"

His voice trailed off, clogged with emotion he was trying to keep down.

I tried desperately to swallow back the same storm in my throat. I peeled the bottle's label back in flakes, my fingers covered in the rusty orange confetti as I rolled the storm of information through my mind. "Where have you been?"

This was, perhaps, the most I'd ever heard Cy speak in my lifetime, but he still hadn't answered my original question, the reason I sought him out. Since the day we arrived at The Guild, he'd created a distance between us—deliberately leaving campus and telling us nothing about his whereabouts. He disappeared, sometimes for days or weeks at a time, leaving us no way to reach him.

"Like I said, I'd hoped that your succubus powers would remain dormant. After all, your mother lived amongst her peers at The Guild for many years unnoticed. But when you were attacked by that vampire, the second day we'd arrived here no less, I knew that wasn't the case. I also knew that at the rate you were running towards trouble, it would be impossible to conceal your nature for long." His nostrils flared slightly as his gaze darted briefly to mine then back again. "And I'd learned from experience that The Guild did not care whether demons were part protector or not—they dealt with them all the same way. The fact that you weren't even of age yet and were healing at that rate, even with the bind," his hand reached forward, his finger lightly pressing at the star on my wrist—the one I'd frequently see him stealing glances at. I'd always assumed the fear in his eyes when he stared at my scar was because it showed weakness, abnormality. Protectors weren't supposed to mark so easily. But now, I could see that it was fear that I would be found out, fear that my safety would be compromised. "I could tell you were more powerful than your mother initially let on. That meant you were in more danger at The Guild than I'd realized—and that I was the one to bring you here. So, I went looking for her family, for her line of protectors—anyone that might be able to guide me, to protect you."

It hit me then, with absolute clarity. I rolled my lips between my teeth. "You don't know, do you? She never told you?"

His brows bent together. "Know what?"

"I'm more than just a succubus." A small chuckle escaped from my mouth. It was strange, for once, to know more about my history than him. "I'm Lucifer's daughter. When she disappeared all those years ago—it was because she'd found a way into hell."

Cy's entire body stiffened, an expression I couldn't read—one I'd never seen before—on his face.

It felt like he was looking at me with new eyes, I could almost see him folding this version of me into the one he'd created long ago.

The silence stretched between us, neither of us breathing.

"Good," he finally said, nodding to himself. "That means you're more powerful than I anticipated. You'll be better able to protect yourself, in time."

I wasn't sure what I was expecting from him, but it wasn't that.

Fear? Disgust? Sure.

But relief wasn't even in the running.

"You're not upset?" I narrowed my eyes, trying to catch every small movement or gesture he made, like that might signal the truth more than his words, "That Sayty literally saddled you with the Devil's spawn and never even told you? You're not afraid?"

His acceptance was so much swifter than my own had been. Like Ro's—unconditional.

He pursed his lips, considering. "I know nothing of Lucifer or of the hell realm. I'm relieved that you've been there and survived—that suggests that if he knows of you, he wants you alive. That, potentially, he'll be able to protect you better than I could. That's all I've ever wanted for you—safety, the chance to survive and build a life."

Warmth spread through my limbs, competing with the anger still simmering there. I tried to ignore the snarled mess—it was a tangle of knots I'd have to unwind later, when I had more time and energy to tend to them with thought. "You said you went looking for her family; did you find them?"

Loud pops echoed as he crackled each of his knuckles. "It is difficult to find protectors who do not want to be found—particularly when they come from a line that has been thought dead for decades. And even more difficult when you're from a line they despise and distrust. All but impossible when I had no names, no information to go on. Your mother and your grandmother—" he shook his head when he saw the flash of excitement on my face, "she died shortly after bringing Sayty here. They were very private people. No records, no information."

I chewed the inside of my cheek, trying to ignore the flush of disappointment.

"It took a long time, but I finally found one good lead."

My chest constricted, the wrapper confetti now small enough to resemble microglitter.

"Most of your mother's family is dead. But she had a brother, a twin. He disappeared years ago, but if we can find him—or anyone who knew him—it would be a start. Saif was his name."

Saif.

"He never joined back with The Guild? When my mother—when Sayty came?"

Cy shook his head. "I never even knew she had a brother, and I was perhaps her closest confidant here. But twins are incredibly rare among our kind—hell, children are rare as it is these days, but twins are different. They hold a different kind of power, one protectors have never fully understood. In the lab, they've even tried producing them medically, using IVF. It always fails. If we can find him, he might be able to help you harness your mother's powers and tell you more about where you came from, he'd be an invaluable ally."

My thoughts raced back to the bus ride in Seattle—to Claude suggesting something similar, about twins and power stability.

It wasn't much to go on, and I wasn't sure that getting in touch with my uncle was really a top priority here—not when the barrier between realms was potentially shattering around us—but it was another possible anchor that I didn't have before.

"Thank you." I realized it must have taken a lot for him to track down this information. And it meant something that he did all of this because he thought it would help me. But there was still so much to sort out between us. I met Cy's eyes and nodded. "For tracking this information down and for telling me."

"I—" his lips thinned into a straight line as he gathered his thoughts, "I hope that one day you'll forgive me. For keeping the secrets that I did. I hope that one day you'll understand that every decision I've made over the last nineteen years has been with your safety in mind."

The truth in his voice sank low and heavy in my gut. I believed that he really believed that. But I didn't know if I was ready to forgive a lifetime of unnecessary secrets—not from one of the two people in this world that I'd always trusted implicitly.

I opened my mouth, not even sure what was going to come out when Cy's phone started vibrating.

"Yes?" His voice was gruff, devoid of the rare emotion filling it over the last few minutes. "Where are they now?" He nodded, like the person on the other end could see him.

He hung up and set his phone on the table between us, staring at it with disbelief.

"That was Alleva." With a deep breath, he looked up at me. "Ro and Jer, possibly. Two protectors have been spotted on the edge of campus, they're coming in now."

The breath flew from my lungs. "Both alive? Okay?"

Cyrus shook his head. He didn't know yet.

I stood and ran to the door, turning to him as he pulled himself up from the table. He waved his hands at me. "Go, go. I'll catch up."

I nodded, my stomach soaring as I wrenched open the door and flew outside, not looking back as I ran. My feet snapped stray, dry twigs as the breeze blew through my hair—nothing existed but the thought of what I'd find at the end of the sprint. It took every ounce of restraint that I had to slow myself down, to not run with the speed of a demon.

The surroundings were a blur of grays, greens, and balls of warm yellow light as dusk settled in on the campus.

I heard a few people call my name as I passed them, but I wasn't stopping, not until I saw him.

And then, at a clearing ahead, close to the main hall, I saw a large figure emerge from the trees, surrounded by a team ushering them in.

"Ro," I yelled, pushing my body as I tapped just a touch into the speed I was both learning and struggling to suppress.

He was a few hundred feet away when I saw him with vivid

clarity, his figure tall and sturdy on the horizon—amongst a backdrop of protectors in black, like his own private sentinel.

In his arms, was a figure that took me a few seconds longer to register.

Dark, reddish black hair, pale skin caked in dried mud and gore.

Completely still, the neck tilted at a strange angle.

Unmoving.

Jer.

He was dead.

20

ATLAS

"How's she holding up?" Eli asked. He was sitting on the couch like a jackass, his head resting on the floor, back on the seat, feet strewn over the back. "She was close with Jer, wasn't she?"

Close enough that she'd kissed him once. Or been kissed by him anyway. The memory of that sight still made my stomach squeeze.

Declan shrugged, pausing briefly in her path to wear a runway through the old hotel carpet. "She was pretty close with Jer. It's hard to lose a member of your team."

"She's not part of Ten," Wade said. His back was turned to us as he made some pasta on the hot plate.

He'd also ordered from three different takeout menus. After months of living off whatever scraps Lucifer deigned to feed him, our rather limited options outside of the cafeteria probably seemed like a five-star buffet.

I bit back my grin at having him here with us again. I'd forgotten what it felt like to have my team complete.

"No, she's not," Eli agreed.

I did too, but I kept my mouth shut.

"She's staying in with her brother and the rest of Ten tonight," Declan continued, like she hadn't been interrupted by a bunch of testosterone. She was really good at ignoring it after all this time. "She wanted to come help us with Sarah, but I didn't think it made much sense to drag her out. We've searched everywhere."

Dec wasn't wrong. We'd been hunting for her nonstop. I'd gotten a glimpse of her scent on the edge of campus, but it was in such a heavily-trafficked area, that I lost the trail almost as soon as I found it. There was no sign of her in town, on campus, anywhere. It was like she'd just disappeared.

"You haven't checked the labs." The vamp had been uncharacteristically quiet since we showed up. It had been fifteen minutes and he hadn't picked a fight with any of us. Instead, he just leaned against the doorframe of his room.

"Aunt Jay would know," Declan said, but the way she bit her bottom lip made me think she wasn't as certain of that as she sounded. "She would tell us if Sarah had been captured. There's no way she'd just let them keep her there."

I hoped she was right.

"It's possible being close to home made her itchy. Maybe being so close and realizing she could never go back just got to be too much. There's no future for her here," Wade said, and something about the way he said it made me think he was speaking more about his own realizations and fears than hers. "I'm sure living with the obnoxious fanghole—"

"Let the record state that I object to being called obnoxious," Darius drawled, "cunning, dashing—sure. But obnoxious is a stretch."

Wade rolled his eyes, "I'm sure living with the fanghole was...a lot. Maybe she decided to cut her losses and slip out—a good old Irish goodbye. She's been through a lot, maybe she wanted some space to process for a while."

I narrowed my eyes at my brother, hoping he got the

message without me having to spell it out for him. That might be the case for Sarah, but if he even considered leaving, he had another thing coming.

He raised his hands and the scorched wooden spoon in the air, cringing as some starchy water dripped down his arm. "Not saying I would do that, but just saying. Full moon, wolfy energy is high—maybe she needed a break. I just—I get it if that's what she wanted right now. It's hard being cooped up, feeling like your life outside of four walls doesn't exist. Maybe we give her a day or two and then find her when she wants to be found. That's all."

My own wolf stretched against my skin in acknowledgment. If I gave in to his current desires right now, I'd be curled inside the cabin with Max folded against me.

The thought of her in my bed for the first time sent blood rushing to my dick. I adjusted my jeans and sat down next to Eli while Declan resumed her pacing.

"So," Eli drew the word out for a few seconds, his eyes narrowed as they met mine. He looked ridiculous with all the blood rushing to his head. "Are you really going through with it in the morning?"

I schooled my expression into careful neutrality, even as I had to swallow back the bile in my throat. 'It' meant one thing —bonding to Reza.

I nodded as I pressed the cool rim of the beer bottle to my lips. There wasn't a choice.

Since we'd been back, I'd done everything I could to try to convince my father that bonding to Reza was a bad idea—to try and get him to understand that I didn't need to bond to anyone.

Each time I resisted, no matter how subtle, he seemed to only dig his feet in more. Typical.

"You do know you're bonded to Max though, right? Like, I know you're not great at recognizing your feelings, but that's definitely happened. Or has started to happen anyway. Your wolf isn't going to let you just abandon that." Declan shot her all-seeing look at me. It was one she'd hit me with more and more often, since Max showed up—the one that told me to stop lying to myself, to stop being so damn thick.

I averted my gaze.

"We can all agree that bonds are back?" Wade asked, slurping a noodle into his mouth. "And then, once we do, can I please spend the next twenty minutes saying I told you so? Because I called that we were all attached to her from pretty much day one."

"It doesn't matter." I handed Wade a bowl. There were three in the suite, all of them with mismatching patterns, two of them with large chips out of the side.

"You'd break the bond, even if it's already started to solidi-fy?" Eli tipped his own bottle to his lips. He'd spent the better part of the last ten minutes learning to perfect drinking upside down. Toddler. "Even knowing that doing so could literally cut into her, rip a piece of her out."

"Not literally," Wade corrected, but the venomous glare Eli lobbed shut him up. Even though that usually-effective glare was diminished by the fact that it was delivered upside down.

"You've seen my dad." Eli's voice softened, the anger dipping into something else, something even darker. "You would do that to her? It's one thing to let it fade. It's another to sever it altogether. You don't know what going through a cere-mony with someone else can do to her."

The beer bottle shattered in my hand, spilling the few remaining dregs all over my pants.

"Shit." I stood up. Sharp glass cut into my palm, but the wounds were already starting to heal by the time I made it to the sink and ran water over them. For a long moment, I stared at my palms, watching the water turn from dark red, to light, to pink, and then clear again. Eli was right. And so was Wade. I couldn't deny anymore that Max and I were linked. And I had no fucking idea what going through with this would do to her. Or to me, though I cared far less about that. But I knew my father. "It would be better for her to be hurt than killed." Because I knew that if I resisted the bond to Reza, my father would retaliate. He'd look too closely at Max. Digging too deep could very possibly result in her death. "Besides, she'll have her ties to the rest of you. That will probably lessen the wound. It does with the fabricated bonds, anyway."

My chest tightened as jealousy scraped against my ribs. Surprisingly, I wasn't jealous because the others were attached to her, were forming their own bonds. I was jealous because I was rejecting my own.

Eli shook his head, the movement awkward and stilted since it was still pressed into the carpet. But the glare peering through his eyes was enough to get the sentiment across. He thought I was an asshole.

He wasn't wrong.

I spent the rest of the night staring at my ceiling. I didn't want to sleep, because I knew what sleep would bring me— pleasant dreams about Max, only for me to wake up and have to go through a bonding ceremony with Reza.

I'd never wanted to bond with Sarah. Hell, if I was being honest, I never wanted to bond with anyone.

Until I met her.

But the thought of tying myself to Reza, knowing what that would mean for me and Max—for the rest of my team—made it almost impossible to breathe.

I threw my blankets to the ground and took a shower, readying myself for the day. It wasn't even dawn yet, but I was done pretending that sleep would come. My mind was too heavy, my wolf too restless.

The crisp, cool air licked at my skin, and I found myself wishing that I could transform, that I could sink into the wolf for a few hours and run. But I knew that things were too tense now, too many protectors were around campus and the surrounding areas. It wasn't safe. So I settled for a walk on two legs instead of four, until I found myself on a familiar path, staring at a familiar window.

I wanted to see her almost as badly as I wanted to avoid her.

The temptation of her nearness settled the matter and I climbed the tree outside of her window until I was perched on the small not-quite-balcony outside of her bedroom.

My stomach clenched the moment I realized that she wasn't in her bed, that she wasn't asleep. Her bedding was pristine and abandoned, just as it had been when I'd visited the spot while she was gone. Like one day, I'd find myself outside her window and she'd magically appear.

Instead, I spent a month going out of my mind, waiting for her to return to us. Other than the few weeks when I believed Wade was dead, it was the most aimless and terrified I'd ever been.

Where the fuck was she now though?

With a deep breath, I pushed the panic aside, and felt the lingering nearness of her, like her body was calling to mine.

Slowly, carefully, I climbed around the cabin, using the system of ledges, gutters, and trees to balance my weight, until I found myself at a different window.

This room was a disaster—clothes strewn everywhere, plates and cups toppled precariously against a stack of books.

But there was Max. She was curled at the foot of the bed like a cat, while her brother slept—the blue light of the TV casting a haze of shadows over them both.

My body relaxed as I watched her. She looked terrified when she found out about Ten's mission. It killed a small part of me that I didn't comfort her, that I didn't swallow her body in my arms and soothe the ache that she felt.

I knew better than most, the particular ache that came when you thought your brother was dead. It was sharp and unyielding. I'd nearly hugged Rowan myself when he emerged from those woods. Not because we were particularly close—though I found myself watching after him more than usual while Max was away—but because his arrival meant that she'd feel relief from that pain. That she was saved from that despair, at least for another day.

The shock of my own relief haunted me still. I knew now that her happiness meant more to me than anyone else's in the world—even my own.

Was that love?

I shook my head, not letting myself linger on the thought. It didn't matter. Not anymore. I couldn't be with her, not in that way. Not if I wanted to protect her, not if I wanted to keep my father and his colleagues away from her.

My grip slipped slightly, so I climbed back down, my feet landing with a soft crunch on the powdery snow.

As I kicked away the dust, my focus latched back on the window.

Max.

She stood there, studying me, her brows bent in a small frown. She raised a finger, telling me to wait, and disappeared.

Fuck.

I wasn't actually prepared to talk to her.

My heart stammered against my chest until, after a minute or two, she was standing a few feet away from me.

"Is everything okay?" She pulled her cardigan over her shoulders, her hair mussed from sleep.

"I—" I stopped when I saw the puffiness under her eyes, "what's happened?"

Her face scrunched in confusion for a moment, before relaxing. "Oh." She shook her head and rubbed her hand against her temple. "Jer."

How had I forgotten? I felt like an ass. I'd been so happy

that Rowan came back, that he was okay, that I barely even considered the fact that she would be hurt by Jer's death.

"I'm sorry. Are you doing okay?" Before I knew what was happening, I'd wrapped her into my arms, pressed my nose against her neck so that I could be surrounded by the clean juniper scent of her.

She stiffened for a moment, then leaned into me, her arms reaching around my back and pulling me closer to her.

We stood like that, in silence for a few moments—witnessed by no one but the bright moon and the cool, calm night. Something about being close to her settled the whirl-wind storming through my mind, grounded me somehow.

I didn't want to let go, didn't want to leave her—wanted to be closer to her in every way possible.

My head shifted, as hers did the same, like we could communicate through the smallest gestures possible, until my lips found hers—warm, soft, and full.

Kissing her seemed to crack something open inside of me, like I was simultaneously being destroyed and recreated all at once.

Our tongues met, slow and tentative, as we tasted each other. I could still taste the minty flavor of her toothpaste, and hoped that I didn't still taste like booze.

She moaned softly and I pulled her closer, until her body was glued to mine, our lips and tongues moving faster now—urgent.

Her hand slipped up the front of my shirt, the coolness of her skin pressing against the warmth of my stomach. My dick was hard already, throbbing and obvious in my sweatpants.

A crow cawed, the sound echoing and reverberating around us. The sound was enough to bring me back to reality.

I peeled myself away from her, taking a few steps back to ease the temptation to claw her back to me.

Her lips were full and swollen, her skin ethereal in the soft light. Even after a night of crying, she was still the most beautiful thing I'd ever seen.

"I," my chest squeezed as I tried to find the words. "I'm sorry. I shouldn't have—I can't do that anymore."

She was silent for a moment, but I couldn't bring myself to look at her, to see the look on her face.

It was a cruel twist of fate.

I was finally able to admit to myself that she was what I wanted—more than I've ever wanted anything or anyone in my entire life. And I couldn't have her. Not now. Not if I wanted to protect her.

"Right," she said, her tone sad but not angry, "Reza. I'm sorry too."

Her eyes were dark, filled with a swirl of emotion. I wanted to unravel each one, to erase the stuff that brought her pain and amplify the things that made them sparkle with light.

"It's just that it's complicated," I said, wanting so badly to explain myself. To tell her that I wanted her, that I'd never once felt a damn thing about Reza other than annoyance. That I was doing this because of her—for her. That I was trying to protect her from a man who would most likely kill her if he found out who she was—if he found out that she was important to me. But I knew that if I told her these things, she'd resist them. She'd fight for me—for whatever was developing between us, even if it put her in danger. I couldn't let her do that. "This thing, between us."

"I understand." She raised her hand, like she knew what was coming, but didn't want me to voice it.

But I needed to. Needed to end this clearly and completely, so I didn't drown myself in the hope of leaving it open.

"It's over," I said, my stomach in a system of twists and painful knots. "It shouldn't have even started. The bond will erase any fleeting attractions, any lingering affection from my wolf—in that way, I mean."

It wasn't true. That wasn't how bonds worked, but she didn't know that. I honestly didn't think that any bond, no matter how much magic was infused in my connection to Reza could ever quiet the loud roar of my body when Max was in the room.

She nodded, her eyes welling up as her forehead and chin wrinkled, but she swallowed the emotion down, her gaze out towards the line of trees, rather than me. "What's it like?"

I stood still and silent, unable to bring my focus away from the hurt on her face. Hurt that I caused.

She cleared her throat. "The bonds, I mean. What did it feel like when you were bonded to Sarah?"

Like a passing fancy compared to what it felt like bonding to her. It was almost absurd to even think about them in the same way, as coming even close to each other.

"It feels," I studied the facade of the cabin, suddenly wishing like hell that I'd stayed in the confines of my bedroom. I wasn't sure I could go through with the ritual later today, not after seeing her, not after feeling her lips against mine again. I could already feel the wolf resisting, like the tenuous relationship we'd come to—the oneness between us—was unraveling at the seams, just as fractured as the bond with Max would be. "Subtle. My bond with Sarah was nascent, not fully developed."

I let myself glance at her briefly, taking in the strands of dark hair blowing in the breeze, the full lips that were still red from our kiss. She wasn't looking at me, her focus on the disappearing shadow of the moon instead, but I could tell from the stiffness of her posture that she was taking in every word, metabolizing them slowly—lost in thought.

"They take time to solidify," I continued, suddenly uncomfortable with the silence between us. It was like an invisible wall was already building between us. I wasn't sure what she was thinking, what was causing that small divot between her brows, the thin line of her lips, the clench of her right fist. It frustrated me endlessly that I couldn't ask. I so rarely offered her a window into my own mind, it seemed cruel to demand anything of hers. Especially now. But I wanted to peel back the layers, destroy the space building between us until it shattered all the same. "But I did feel stronger, faster, a little more in tune with her and Wade when we were sparring and in battle. Your senses get heightened and you borrow from each other's strengths. It's like a lingering sixth sense. The primary bond—Sarah and Reza in this case—become like a phantom limb, if that makes sense. That's how others have described it anyway. Traditionally, they've also been a way to forge and strengthen community and family. But lately, it seems like The Guild cares more about the power and safety that bonding offers." I ran my hand over my face, suppressing a frustrated groan. I didn't want to think about this. "That's why Alleva and my father are pushing Reza to bond with urgency now. I imagine she's the first of many her age to have them rushed, with things so intense now."

Her eyes were wide now, lips parted in recognition as she nodded. "That makes sense." She turned back to me, the moon reflecting in her dark eyes. "And will you really leave Six? Will the team really be fractured?"

I forced my jaw to relax, lulling the quiet rage that had been boiling in my gut for weeks. The moment my father suggested the idea, I had to spend two days locked in my room, just to keep myself from wolfing out. Everything I'd done over the last decade had revolved around creating my team, and then, protecting it. Losing them felt almost as wrong as losing Max. Like I'd become an outsider to the life I was supposed to live. "My father wants us to join Three."

"What will that mean—for" she took a deep breath, drew her cardigan closer to her with a shiver, though she didn't look cold, "everything?"

I felt the question sink low, burying itself deep in my gut.

The world was crumbling at the seams—the very properties of hell bleeding into our world, potentially destroying them both—Max at the center of it all.

What came next?

I had no fucking idea.

But I knew for sure, no matter who I was forced to bond to, I'd continue doing everything that I could to help her and the rest of Six fight off whatever impending apocalypse was coming for us all.

Even if it meant abandoning The Guild for good.

Or dismantling it piece-by-piece from within the belly of the beast.

21

MAX

"You need more sleep." Ro nudged me, shoving a plate onto the foot of his bed, where I sat with my legs crossed. "Don't think I don't know that you slipped into my room like a creep and slept at my feet." His eyes narrowed, but even with the small gleam of amusement, I could still see the haunted look in their depths. "Or that you snuck out in the middle of the night to talk to a certain werewolf."

"You're the one who needs sleep." I rolled my eyes and gratefully stuffed my mouth with a giant helping of eggs on toast.

Ro'd barely been able to speak yesterday. He was so shaken up after debriefing Tarren, Seamus, and the others upon his return. He and Jer had been separated from the rest—just for a moment, but that was all it took. A werewolf sank its teeth deep into Jer's side and ran, dragging him behind like dangling cans on a newlywed's car. Ro took off after them, no time to find or alert the others and got beaten up pretty badly in the process. By the time he finally found Jer, his body was lifeless. But he still managed to bring him home to his dad when he escaped.

I couldn't imagine what that was like—carrying your lifeless friend for miles, trying to avoid onlookers or draw attention. His phone was gone, he was completely alone. The thought of it made my chest ache all over again—for Jer, but also for my brother.

"I still don't understand why they're starting to kidnap protectors." Ro peeled a piece of crust off my toast and balled it between his fingers, like he just needed something to keep himself busy. "It's like they're using us for something, but I don't know what."

"Or they're looking for someone," I said, reluctantly, quietly. It was a thought I didn't want to voice—because I had a sneaking suspicion that someone was me. Lucifer had warned that different groups of demons were after me, eager to use my connection with him and the barrier for their own ends—I wasn't sure how they knew that I existed, but it was clear now that they did.

Which meant that Jer's death—that Three's missing team members—was on me.

Ro squeezed my shoulder, his expression serious. "None of that."

I swallowed my bite, tempted to take another just as a way out of this conversation. "None of what?"

"Guilt. This isn't on you, Max. None of this is your fault, even if they were trying to find you."

I nodded, not because I agreed with him, but because I was done with this topic. My head still ached from a night of crying. It was kind of wild how quickly my body could heal from injuries, while the emotional pain seemed to only linger, deep and unforgiving.

"His death was fast."

"You don't know that," I said.

Ro sighed, ran a hand over his tired face. "I just wish that we'd gotten those fuckers."

Tarren had already sent a team to the location Ro identified, the large farm where he'd found Jer's body. By the time they got there, the werewolves were gone—the family who lived at the house dead and clustered together in a pile outside one of the barns, like kindling waiting to be burned. The image made me sick.

"I should talk to Cy soon," Ro glanced at me. I'd mentioned my conversation with him, but hadn't given too many details. I figured it was best if the part about Ro's family came from Cy. "You want to come?"

I shook my head. "No, we'll talk when you're back. The three of us maybe. I know that I shouldn't resent him—and in a lot of ways, I understand where he was coming from. I probably would've done the same if I were in his position. But I just need some time to get my head together."

Ro scanned his room, then got up to dig into a small pile in the corner. He pulled out a small blanket, one of the ones we'd brought from home. "Don't worry, I know my room is a mess, but I promise it's clean. Rest here for a few hours, try to get some sleep if you can. I remember—" he wrapped the blanket around me, my body tingling with warmth at the gesture, "I know how exhausting it can be, worrying about someone, not knowing if they're coming back. Rest. Get your mind off the bullshit for a bit, if possible."

My eyes blurred as I nodded, unable to voice the sorry at the tip of my tongue, for fear that I'd start crying all over again. He knew that feeling because I was the one who'd put him through it.

He squeezed my shoulder again, signaling that he heard it all the same, and left.

My head fell back onto the pillow, and I let myself be wrapped in the familiar smell of Ro. My stomach ached, like I was being stabbed, when I thought about Jer. And it was a hurt that deepened even more when I found myself selfishly grateful that it wasn't Ro who'd met that gruesome fate.

Closing my eyes, I forced myself to take a deep breath, to focus on anything else other than that.

But whenever I tried to think about something else, the only thing I saw was the look in Atlas's eyes when he left me standing outside this morning—dark, impenetrable, conflicted, like he was in the midst of some invisible battle.

It took a full minute after Atlas had left before I realized I hadn't taken a breath since he disappeared.

Reza. He was bonding to Reza.

Right now. While I laid here thinking about him, greedily hoping he'd show up at my window again and confess to feeling the intoxicating, overwhelming pull to me that I felt to him.

A sharp pain flared through my chest, making it almost impossible to breathe—like a knife had pierced straight through my lungs.

I sat up, my hands clutching my chest, like they could soothe the invisible ache—but it got worse—sharp and deep.

Swallowing bile, I swung my legs over the bed, using Ro's nightstand to pull me to my feet—but all that resulted in was knocking over a pile of books and a half-full glass of water.

This pain was like nothing like I'd ever felt before—all consuming and spreading, like it couldn't decide where in my body it wanted to land.

I needed to find Izzy or someone.

When I finally made it to my feet, I collapsed to my knees, biting back a whimpering scream.

My eyes slammed closed, the diluted light through the window too much to stand.

A familiar pull locked in my mind, a thread, taught and compromised. And then the pain was eclipsed by a hollow nothingness—only to reform again a few moments later.

When I opened my eyes, I was no longer in Ro's room. I was in the same position—hands and knees—but my fingers gripped into a plush, shaggy red carpet that felt far too lavish to ever suit my brother's tastes.

I scanned the area—a hall, unfamiliar, dimly lit with sconces, and empty. Thank god no one was around to witness me materializing from thin air. I just had to hope that there weren't any cameras out of sight.

The walls were dark and appeared to be made of concrete slabs—an odd choice given the otherwise warm decor. I leaned back, my head resting against a heavy door. It was locked. Like the deeper recesses of the lab, it seemed to require a blood identification.

I knew better than to leave my DNA down here—wherever I was. I had no clearance anymore and I knew that the thin ice I was already precariously standing on at The Guild would fracture and break if I was caught down here.

Turning, I pressed my palm to the door. It seemed to almost pulse against me—steady and lulling. I had a sudden, deep urge to discover what was on the other side. Like whatever I might find would soothe the ache in my body—quieter now, but somehow more pervasive in the dullness, impossible to ignore.

It was like the invisible cord had wrapped itself up behind the door, coiled and insistent—but also warning. I had no idea what I'd find, even if I could open this door.

I scanned the room, looking for...anything. There was a vent, the grating locked, hole too small for me to fit through, and positioned too high for me to climb without any purchase —but something in the gentle vibration down my spine told me that was the route to take.

Closing my eyes, I steadied my breath. Focused on the hollow space I knew existed several feet above the door. Imagined myself just beyond it, where the venting system opened into something that might fit someone my size.

I inhaled, deep and heavy.

When I let out my breath, I was encapsulated in a thick darkness. I felt cool metal against my palms. I'd made it.

I just wasn't exactly sure where *it* was.

The tunnel was too tight for me to do any more than awkwardly shuffle my body along, army-crawl-style—a realization that sent my heartbeat into panic mode.

Small spaces were not my jam, and this was—by far—the tightest space I'd ever been shoved inside.

What if I couldn't teleport back? The power was nascent and unpredictable, and I could tell from the looseness in my muscles, the slick sweat against my neck, that I'd already used more energy than I should have shifting twice so quickly in succession.

The thought of being stuck here with no way out, sent my body into a dizzy frenzy. My vision blurred—though because it was so dark, the blinking fuzzy lights that glazed my eyes were my only tell.

I felt my heart drum a vicious beat against my ribs, my body hyper aware of every pulse point, like I could feel the blood swimming through my veins.

Fuck.

This suddenly felt like the worst idea I'd ever had—worse, even, than diving head first into a portal to hell. At least there, I wasn't alone. I had a clear mission, a goal.

What the fuck was I chasing right now? Some invisible, phantom thread in my body? What the hell was I thinking?

My head swam and, slowly, Cy's voice echoed in my head— his usual gruff lecture about breath work, the importance of finding my center.

I closed my eyes, sank into the memory, imagined myself in the open air surrounding the cabin, the gentle fall of leaves around me as I tried my best not to roll my eyes at his exaggerated exhales.

Clarity.

The dancing white dots of light disintegrated away as I opened my eyes again. I could do this.

Whatever *this* was.

I shimmied forward, into the dark shadows in front of me, following the strange pull that I could only hope was intuition.

After a few twists and turns, a hazy light appeared ahead. I blinked twice, thinking I'd only imagined it.

Excitement bubbled in my belly as I pulled myself towards it, pushing any lingering anxiety and fear of getting out of here alive and undetected away. The vent was slim—no more than two small windows, no larger than letter slots, for me to look through.

There was a fractured room, offered in pieces on either side of the thick metal slit cutting my view in half.

Hushed voices sounded below as I lifted myself up onto my elbows—ignoring the biting discomfort—to see.

Something kept behind this much enforcement had to be important.

A few figures came into my view.

One a man, dressed in a long dark cloak. I only caught a brief glimpse of his features, when he turned to the side, but I was certain I'd never seen him before.

Alleva—her stark blond bob and cutting blue eyes recognizable, even from here.

Tarren—imposing, stiff-postured, but with an excitement I'd never seen in his expression tugging at his eyes. Like he'd won.

Standing between them were Atlas and Reza.

I could recognize them easily, even though they both had a fabric covering over their eyes and thick hoods pulled over their heads.

Atlas looked stiff, deeply uncomfortable, but my body seemed to hum at the sight of him.

He tilted his head slightly, and I wondered, briefly, if he could sense me too.

And while Reza twittered from foot to foot, trying to get comfortable in the candle-lit room, there was a sort of excitement buzzing through her body that no amount of anxiety could quell.

Their bonding ritual.

I was witnessing it.

The realization that I would have to watch this happen made the dull pain flare inside my chest.

This was worse than any claustrophobia, worse even than being stuck in the tunnels alone for hours.

But as much as I wanted to look away, to close my eyes and force myself back into Ten's cabin, I couldn't do it.

Maybe I was more masochistic than I realized.

The man I didn't recognize pulled something from his robes. The way he held it made it impossible for me to see what it was, but when he grabbed Reza's hand and she flinched, I guessed it was a blade of some sort.

When she pulled her hand back towards her body instinctively, I saw the thick pool of blood there, confirming it.

Atlas's hand was sliced as well, though he seemed to be expecting it. He'd been through one of these rituals before, so it made sense.

Both of them were separated by a large podium, covered in a dark shroud. It was awkward and bulging, but something about it sent a shiver down my spine.

I wanted to reach through the impossibly small vent and remove it—to see what was hidden beneath.

"As I said," the man started, his voice dull and monotonous, but not unpleasant, "your vision is clouded to help awaken the bond. This allows you to search for each other through the darkness, to bring life to the invisible tether tying you together. You must learn to nurture that bond, feed it into life, for your connection to strengthen. Through it, eventually, you will grow stronger, unified—a protector's greatest strength is the connection they share with their bond mate."

The knots in my stomach tightened, and I held my breath, terrified that I'd be found out up here.

"Now," he continued, "link hands."

Reza reached her blood-coated palm forward, eager and willing, but even from here, I could see the gentle quiver of her fingers.

Atlas's shoulders stiffened, and for a moment I thought he wouldn't do it. But when Tarren cleared his throat, softly, Atlas relented.

His fingers reached Reza's outstretched hand, and interlocked with hers.

The man pulled back his hood and stepped towards them, a flat look on his expression.

He had wavy blond hair, with light highlights that could be sun or age-touched.

In a slow, low voice, he started to chant something in a language I didn't recognize—the words so hushed and deep that I felt them as vibrations in the air more than I heard them.

A trembling pulse flared through me, so painful I had to bite my tongue to keep from whimpering.

It felt like I was being ripped in half, the fragments separating in jagged, uneven tears.

"Atlas Jeremiah Andrews," the man said, eyes bright like the incantation was alive inside of him, "Reza Marie Pratt, please impale your hands on the stone of our fathers."

Impale? What the fuck kind of cult shit was this?

He pulled the shroud from the large podium. A large, jagged, iridescent stone was embedded inside of a wide, deep stone bowl—the bowl filled with a mesmerizing, glistening liquid-like substance.

A flutter built in my chest, and suddenly, I couldn't bring

myself to look away from their union, no matter how badly I wanted to.

Using their unlinked hands, they sightlessly reached towards the stone, Reza's fingers pulling back slightly as she reached it—like the material surprised her, whether the temperature or the shape, I couldn't tell.

Slowly, they shifted their weight forward, until a slow, thin stream of blood coated the crevices of the stone.

"The circle is initiated," the man whispered.

Tarren nodded, eyes sparkling with pride and something else—a tension that I couldn't quite read.

Alleva didn't seem to be so much as breathing, her attention locked on her daughter.

The man chanted a few more words, then glanced briefly at the juncture of their clasped hands on one end, and where they each bled onto the rock. "Atlas, Reza," he nodded to their parents, "witnesses, repeat after me."

He spoke again, in that unfamiliar language, and the room erupted in soft echoes as the others joined in.

The hair on the back of my neck lifted, my heart beating so fast and hard that I was convinced it would tear itself from the confines of its cage any moment. Something tugged low and deep from within me, though I couldn't distinguish where in my body it originated—it was everywhere and nowhere, an infinite loop.

Fuzzy lights danced in front of my vision, blotting out the figures below.

But through the pain, the only thing I could focus on was the stone below and the shimmering liquid-steam surrounding it—glowing and bright and impossible to pull away from.

Familiar and strange all at once.

I knew with a blazing certainty—a certainty that left me simultaneously nauseous and breathless with the heaviness of it—that I'd found the source of shadow magic that Lucifer was after.

It took every ounce of willpower to tear myself from it, wiggling backwards into my tunnel until I was far enough away from the ritual to be drawn back in.

For several minutes, I closed my eyes, focusing on my bedroom in Ten's cabin. It took longer than it should have, and was more painful than it had ever been.

But, eventually, I landed with a dull thud on my bed—my body and heart heavy with an ache and a darkness that I couldn't fully understand.

22

DECLAN

"You're different." Dani narrowed her eyes, her dark lashes making the blue color pop in a surreal sort of way.

"So are you." I dragged a fork through my breakfast, finding it almost impossible to stomach eating right now.

"Yeah well, trauma. Nothing new," she arched a perfectly-shaped brow, stealing a slice of my toast and ripping off a piece with a shrug, "losing a best friend, a bond, and a team will do that to a girl. I have reasons—clear as day for you to examine and unpack. You have, on many occasions, in fact—much to my annoyance. I want to know what's up with *you*."

Her tone was more sarcastic than sad, the defense mechanism as familiar as my own.

My past wasn't exactly all butterflies and rainbows. Dani knew that. But I knew she wasn't talking about that shit. I had changed in the few months since I'd seen her. A lot.

When Max came bowling into my life, everything I thought I knew was knocked sideways and upside down—revealing new and strange versions of my world that I hadn't considered before. I still didn't understand the final picture, but I was more confident than ever that my compass pointed towards her and my team.

Hell, even if that team included an obnoxious as fuck fanghole.

I needed to visit him later. He'd been cagier since the run-in with his brother.

"Hellooo—" Dani dangled the soggy piece of toast in front of my face before taking an absurdly loud bite. She swallowed, her scrunched face revealing her distaste. "Your life has been an absolute shitshow. And you straight up ditched me here for a month. A *month*. Just straight up left me with these people. What were you thinking?"

I couldn't tell her any of that, for obvious reasons, but I wasn't doing a great job disguising my turmoil from her. And, truthfully, other than Atlas and the rest of my team, she was the one person I'd never felt the need to conceal shit from. This was new territory.

"Atlas is, as we speak, bonding to a girl I can't stand," I said, ignoring the disappearance part and settling for a partial truth, the one thing I could talk to her about right now, "and it's looking very likely my team—my fucking family—is about to be ripped at the seams, once again, and I'll get booted to a group I probably won't be able to tolerate for longer than a day."

I widened my eyes to push the point—even if the impending apocalypse and all the doom and gloom weren't at the forefront of my mind, I had good reason to be off.

"No, that's not it." She pursed her lips, her eyes narrowing so that only flashes of bright blue were visible. " And it's not just a bad different either that I'm talking about. Besides, I've seen you when your world falls apart. I know what it looks like. And don't get me wrong—there's plenty of that behind those pretty green eyes too. But you've also been kind of glowing since I've been back here—like there's some new purpose, a new pep in your step. I don't know, just—" she leaned forward, making me feel like I was suddenly as translucent as wax paper, "something."

I rolled my eyes, ignoring the flush I could feel creeping up my neck. She wasn't usually one for deep and probing conversations. But she was always great at cutting through the bullshit and seeing to the heart of things—I'd give her that. The girl never looked away from the things that would send most people packing.

"Okay," she inhaled dramatically, "I'll pretend this isn't about that new girl I constantly find you undressing with your eyes. Though she is cute. Not what I'd typically consider your type, but something about her—*fits*. If that makes sense?" her eyes darted to mine briefly, before she shook the thought off. "Of course it makes sense to you. You're in love with her."

My cheeks burned, and suddenly staring at her all-seeing eyes was impossible.

Staring Lucifer down had been less intimidating.

That word.

Love.

My stomach flipped, warmth spreading through me like my skin was coated in melted butter.

"And as for Atlas," she shrugged, "yeah, that fucking sucks. I'll give you that. But maybe when things quiet down, Tarren and the rest of them will come around and let your band of merry cronies get back together. Who knows?" She shrugged, "if you're okay with adding Her Almighty Reza to that pairing, that is."

I shot her some side eye.

We both knew that the odds of Tarren relenting were almost zero—especially now that he thought Wade was gone and Atlas was his only chance of leaving a decent stamp to his name. Not that he'd ever really put much weight behind Wade to begin with, but something about having him as a pseudo-back up probably added some buffer.

"Even if that happened," I shook my head, laughing at the thought of it, "I'd end up killing Reza within two days."

Dani clapped, rubbing her hands together, a giant grin tugging at her lips. "That would solve both problems!" Her expression darkened suddenly, the light in her eyes diminishing slightly. "Your aunt spoke to me last night. You know she's pushing for you to bond. Like immediately." She grabbed my hand, squeezing softly. "I just want you to be prepared—it's not going to be avoidable. You're powerful, of age, and the higher ups are getting scared. I'd be shocked if you're not going through your own ritual within the next week. They're having a member of council stay here for the next month—trying to jam in as many ceremonies as they can like some sort of Hail Mary for us up against...whatever the fuck we're up against right now."

The mere thought of bonding to someone—now that I finally allowed myself to acknowledge the connection I had to Max—felt like drinking acid. "Like fuck I'll let that happen. Tarren's always hated me. Hopefully he'll use that hatred to push me further down the line for the *great privilege* of bonding."

"It's not so bad, you know. Eli's like a brother to you. It will bring you closer." She tilted her head, a knowing smile on her face. Dani had a bond mate once—as far as I was aware, nothing romantic or sexual ever came of the relationship, but they got along well. Until he died. Just two years after the love of her life and best friend met the same fate. It was one of the reasons we got on so well—she understood loss, understood how it could turn a person inside out and make them into something new, sometimes something harder, something darker. "And what if you joined me?"

I sat straighter, not sure I'd heard her fully. "You'd join a team?"

Dani was kind of a loner, a nomad. It was incredibly rare for a protector to operate without a team. And she didn't go on many heavy missions because of it—mostly intel and monitoring lesser-patrolled areas of the country.

After every member of her team had been wiped out, she'd tried to join another. When that turned sour—quickly—she vowed never to be part of a team again. If The Guild wanted to use her talents, they'd do it on her terms.

I admired the hell out of her for that.

"I'd join a team with the right people," she nodded, like she'd given this some thought already. "And I trust myself to have your back more than I trust some random meatheads you and Eli will inevitably get stuck with." She smiled, less with her mouth and more with her eyes, as she kicked my feet under the table. "Just do me a favor and think about it. We could get up to some pretty fun trouble, the three of us." She ducked her head towards me, low and exaggerated as she whispered, "maybe add that pretty new recruit who seems to like trouble as much as you do?"

My chest warmed at the thought—at keeping part of my family together, at the familiar comfort and warmth of her sincerity, her friendship. But the potential future disintegrated at the thought of losing Atlas, of leaving him behind. Losing him was like a blade to the gut. And there was the fact that I wanted to keep Dani as far fucking away from hell and the exorbitant dangers we were inevitably up against.

I had no choice but to charge into those dangers—that's where Max would be. Where Eli, Atlas, and Wade would be—once we figured out how to keep Reza and their parents out of our hair.

But Dani had options—tidier paths in her future. I didn't want to get in the way of that.

"I'll keep that in mind," I said.

It was enough to satisfy her probing stare. For now.

MAX WASN'T HOME when I went to check up on her, so I came back to the cabin. I was trying to give her a bit of space—to let her mourn the loss of her friend with the rest of Ten.

But another part of me wanted to be there for her, to help walk her through the grief she was feeling. Protectors were unfortunately pretty damn used to losing our own, and losing them way too young.

She didn't grow up with that culture, not really. This kind of loss was new to her.

For now, I'd hang back for a few hours, let her unpack things with Ro and Izzy, before I tried to check on her again.

Eli was out, probably either visiting Darius and Wade or getting wasted off his ass by the pond.

I glanced at the living room wall, where two unfixed holes sat next to the TV.

Definitely Eli's handiwork.

Probably how he took out his frustration waiting for a month for Max and I to find our way back here.

So much had happened, and this cabin didn't feel quite as homey as it used to. This was probably one of my only chances to soak in some of the few Reza-free moments I would get.

It was still absolutely absurd to me that Atlas wasn't fighting this bonding ritual more than he was. To be tied to her? For life? When it was absurdly obvious to everyone that he was more attached to Max than he'd ever been to anyone before?

It made his bond to Sarah look like it was held together with dental floss.

A loud hammering sound at the front door disrupted my few moments of silence.

I was glad Eli wasn't around to witness my jumpiness—he never lost an opportunity to cackle away at it.

The hammering grew more furious, so I rushed to the door, my heart pounding in perfect rhythm.

Was it Max? Had something happened to one of the guys? Did Atlas decide that he ultimately couldn't go through with it?

When I swung open the door, I was met with a pair of familiar blue eyes, set in a round face that usually carried a warm smile.

Today, that smile was nowhere in sight.

"Aunt Jay?" I opened the door wider, taking in her frazzled appearance, her tear-streaked cheeks. "What's going on?"

She'd been so busy since I'd gotten back that we'd had time for little more than a simple hello.

With a quick glance behind her, like she was checking to see if she was being followed, she stepped into the cabin and shut the door quietly behind her. "They have Sarah."

My lungs collapsed. "What?"

"Sarah," she whispered, her chin dimpling as she tried to hold in the tears threatening to start up again. "Are you alone?"

I nodded, ushering her towards the kitchen.

"Sarah's alive." She ran a shaky hand through her wild dark curls before turning to me. "I know it's going to sound unbelievable, like I'm losing my—"

My stomach clenched. "It's not." I grabbed two glasses from the cabinet. "We found her, when we—when we were on that mission for Seamus."

Betrayal flashed across her face. "And you didn't think that I deserved to know? My daughter was alive and you let me continue on for weeks thinking that she was dead?"

I sucked in a sharp breath. "She didn't want us to tell you. Things are...complicated with Sarah now."

"Yes, she's a werewolf. I am aware." Her lips were in a tight, flat line.

I couldn't bring myself to look in her eyes. Instead, I turned on the faucet to fill the glasses with water, but Aunt Jay's hand turned it off before the liquid hit the glass.

"This situation warrants something a bit stronger than water, Declan, don't you think?" She scanned the kitchen. "Eli lives here, so I know you keep the hard stuff somewhere."

"She is a werewolf, yes." With a tight smile, I reached for the liquor cabinet and pulled down the scotch I knew she liked. "But she's also not dangerous or cruel because of it. And we were worried about what would happen if anyone at The Guild —including you—found out."

"Exactly why you should have told me," she stammered, bringing her fingers to her lips as they started to tremble. "I could have kept her safe, could have gotten her away from here. Now, she's been captured. They won't let her out, even though I'm—" she shook her head, "They'll kill her. They just threw her into one of those cells l-like she's a mons—" Her voice wavered. "Sarah's good. You know that, everyone knows that. She's always had a temper, sure, and she can be a bit impulsive and reckless, but she's a good girl. She doesn't deserve—"

Her words disappeared into a sob.

Seeing her fight so hard to keep it together made it all the more difficult for me to. All I could focus on was the sudden urge to vomit. Sarah was down there. She hadn't decided to split without a word, like we'd hoped. And now she was absolutely fucked.

"We'll get her out," I promised, feeling the vow deep in my bones. "I swear it."

Jay took a deep swig from the bottle, bypassing the glasses altogether. Her eyes met mine, glazed with unshed tears as she nodded. "We will. They were shocked when they brought her in. Will probably run tests, question her—they'll keep her for awhile, they keep many of them for weeks, months on occasion. Years if they think they're powerful enough. It always seemed inhumane before, but it works for us now. We have time to orchestrate a plan. And then, when we've succeeded, when we've broken my baby out of there—" she took a deep breath, "then we're going to expose every last dirty secret I've kept for The Guild all these years. There is no loyalty here, no safety. I'm done turning my head and pretending like this organization is purely benevolent. It's far from it."

"We—" I paused as I processed what she said, "what?"

Her jaw was tight. She poured me a healthy helping of the light amber-colored liquid. It wasn't my drink of choice, but I took it gratefully. "It's time you and I had a talk about your parents."

I wasn't sure what I was expecting her to say, but the mention of my parents dropped like a heavy weight, low in my stomach.

Aunt Jay almost never spoke of them—I wasn't sure if it was to protect me, or because talking about them brought her too much pain.

I followed, unable to utter a word, as she turned towards the living room and settled on the edge of the couch.

"Sit," she nodded to the spot next to her. "There's a lot that I've kept from you girls. I thought it was the easiest way to keep you safe—to keep you ignorant. When you came to me you were so—" she shook her head, took a small sip of her drink, "you were filled with so much anger. So much pain. I knew that if you learned the truth, it would only be a matter of time before you took things into your own hands and wound up dead." Her eyes met mine. "Can I trust that is no longer the case? Can I trust that you'll hear what I have to say without doing something that will get you killed?"

I narrowed my eyes, drained my glass, and considered her. After a long moment, I nodded. There was no other choice.

"Good. This is going to be difficult to hear." She set the

bottle down, then turned to me. "What do you know about your parent's death? About your uncle's, after them?"

My hand shook as I clutched the cool glass. We never spoke of this, not once. I licked my lips, my entire mouth dry as toast. "There was a breach," I said, staring down at my glass, like the scene would suddenly materialize in the liquid there. "When they were down in the labs. A vampire got out," my eyes darted to hers, "and killed them both."

The words spilled out of me like someone else was saying them—cold, detached, and, for the first time, a little unsure.

Aunt Jay bit her bottom lip, glancing around our reasonably tidy living room—save for a few Xbox controllers tangled in the corner that hadn't been used in months—like she was expecting someone to jump out at us any moment.

Finally, she took a deep breath, set the bottle of alcohol down on the table in front of her, her posture rigid. "It was a cover up."

My body stilled. It felt like I was watching this conversation from somewhere above us, part of it but not totally in it.

"Your parents spent a few years working with a vampire who was brought in under odd circumstances."

"Odd circumstances?" I echoed, though I didn't recognize my voice or remember moving my lips.

She nodded. "She was pregnant. The Guild has captured several pregnant demons before, but they rarely survive to term and, if they do, the child never does. Their bodies are put through too much stress, too much trauma to handle the diffi-culties associated with supernatural pregnancies."

"This vampire survived?" I guessed.

"Yes, she gave birth to a little girl. Your parents grew very attached to the pair of them—they remained under Guild surveillance for years." She paused, fidgeted with the sleeve of her dark blazer. "I have no proof of what happened to them. But towards the end, they started questioning some of their superiors—started resisting and downright ignoring requests to put the child through more studies. The Guild has never looked fondly upon those who resist their teachings and orders —particularly when those who resist start to do so loudly."

"You think The Guild had them killed?" It was a strange feeling, like I could physically feel the memories and truths I thought I knew shifting and reshaping into something unfamiliar—but something that aligned quite well with the things I'd learned about The Guild in the past few months. "They killed them and blamed it on the vampires?"

Jay's mouth was pressed into a firm line, her skin clammy and ashen, like it was taking all she had to voice these suspicions out loud. What kind of stranglehold did the labs have on their researchers—that simply voicing these thoughts in a private cabin could cause such anxiety?

"The night of their death, I think they were planning to take you away—to disappear from The Guild and all its hypocrisies forever. They could no longer go through with their work, not when their worldviews had shifted so dramatically."

"We were supposed to go on holiday," I whispered, remembering the excitement of the night before—packing our things, planning our route. Was it a start to a new life, not a vacation all along?

"That's what they called it. What they told their superiors. But I don't think they planned to come back. That night, they let the mother and child out of their cages—intending to free them before leaving behind their work and legacies forever." She sighed, the breath moving through her with a tremble. "They were found with their necks slit, drained of blood. The party line was that they were killed by the two vampires who escaped—vampires who were presumably immediately slaughtered before they could be questioned or anyone could look too closely. The mother and child were very weak—close to death from starvation and years of tests, chemicals constantly pumped into their system to keep them weak." Jay's eyes met mine. "Your mother and father were strong. It would not have been difficult for them to fight back if they truly were attacked. And no vampire I've ever encountered has drained its prey by wasting so much blood through that kind of incision."

A hollowness overcame me. I expected to feel sadness or anger, but all I felt was empty. For years, I'd used their deaths to fuel my hatred for demons—probably the very thing The Guild intended by framing their deaths that way. I'd given everything to this organization, to trying to be the sort of protector that would make my parents proud. To think that, all along, I'd been doing the very opposite—I didn't know what to feel. "Why didn't you ever tell me this before? You just let me go on believing their lies, sinking myself deeper and deeper into an unquenchable, all-consuming anger for years."

Her expression hardened. The black rings around her irises containing the wildness within them. "Your uncle—when you stayed with him right after, after they—" her voice faltered slightly, "he became consumed with your mother's research. The obsession with getting to the bottom of her work, under-standing the minute details of her death, became almost wild in its urgency. The closer he got to the truth, the more he started to voice his doubts to his peers, the more he found similar patterns in other cases in the labs, all around the world, the more danger he put you in. And the more danger he put himself in. He met the same fate as they did. I couldn't do that to you—to Sarah—I didn't have the luxury of avenging my brother or following my suspicions. My only goal—my only purpose—became keeping you girls safe. And that's what I've done. Until—"

Her voice broke, too clogged with emotion to go on.

"Until now," I finished for her. My chest squeezed knowing that she'd carried all of this alone, for all this time—that our teen years were spent with her living with an acute anxiety that we'd lose her too. Or that she'd lose us.

And now, she was very much at risk of that very fear coming true. We needed to get Sarah out. I refused to lose another person I cared about to the private, vengeful society that masqueraded itself as pure.

"The Guild is smart," she whispered, her eyes flashing with anger where there had been sadness. "We are all told to stay in our lanes—no one person or group is given more information than they need. We only get a necessary, single piece of the puzzle to work on, never understanding how things fit together in a bigger picture. It keeps everything buried in a shroud, secrets on every level. It's how they are able to maintain power —they sew distrust, they sew fear of the unknown and empty promises about safety and duty. Even those of us who do question our assignments, our history—we do so in silence because it's almost impossible to identify those who might share the same doubts. Secrets create fear. And fear is the most powerful thing in the world."

"We'll get her out of there," I said. "I swear it."

Aunt Jay nodded as she took another long pull of the bottle. I'd never seen her have more than one drink in a night before. "You're damn right we will. Do you know what I do in the labs?"

I shook my head, realizing that I knew very little about what went on in the lower levels of the Main Hall. Whenever I'd asked as a teenager, she'd always blown it off, calling her job boring, insisting that field work was far more exciting.

"I don't work with the...captured subjects very often," she said, her focus on the empty wall of the living room, expression blank. "Instead, most of my research is focused on protectors who come back with injuries, and those who come back with worse than injuries. It's why I know about Sarah—that's my sect. I've done a lot of real good—identified genetic markers that have saved lives, worked to save as many of our people as I could. I've—I've done my best, in some ways. But while my tasks are quite singular, isolated, I've seen enough to know that protectors who have genes that we suspect can be triggered by werewolf venom often disappear when they return with bites. And if and when they do reappear, it is often as a lifeless corpse, ready for my study in the morgue. I've seen enough protectors in death to identify deaths that are caused by demons and deaths that are more ambiguous. While I've tried to bury my head in the sand when it comes to things I didn't want to know more about—I know enough now to know that I know almost nothing at all. About our people, about The Guild. But I do know what will become of Sarah if she's left there." She inhaled sharply, her eyes welling with tears. "I've tried so hard to stay in my lane, to not question things, to ignore what was right in front of me. But now I wonder if, in doing that, I failed you girls. If I ill-prepared you for the realities of this life. If maybe your parents had the right idea—if I should have taken you both, the moment you showed up on our doorstep, and hidden you away, lived as humans." She turned to me, gripped my hands in hers. "You can trust no one in our world, Declan. Demon, protector—it doesn't matter. The magic we were born from does not deal with good and evil—it deals only in power. Please, whatever you do, remember that."

I searched for a response, for any words at all.

But a loud, piercing alarm wailed—the sound so deep and all-encompassing that the entire cabin shook with the vibrations of it.

I'd heard this alarm before—but only after days of announcements ahead of time, preparation and planning for a drill.

But there were no warnings.

This was no drill.

This was the real thing.

Headquarters was under attack.

23

MAX

The alarm was enough to make my head ring, the sound somehow both tinny and deep. I was on my way to Six's cabin when it started piercing through the campus, reverberating and bouncing off the trees until it created garbled echoes all around me. My body was already a contortion of nerves from what I'd found—I needed to tell them as soon as possible.

Declan nearly ran into me as I walked the familiar path, her emerald eyes wild and filled with fear that quelled a bit when they met mine. "Max. Thank God. We need to get to the others, immediately. This is bad. This is very very bad."

"What's going on?" I'd never heard anything this loud before. It sounded like some poorly-timed drill or explosively loud tornado warning.

Stray people ran through the trees around us, none of them with faces I recognized.

She grabbed my hand in hers and started running back in the direction I'd come from, towards the center of campus. "Campus has been breached. I think. I've never actually heard of this happening before. I only know this alarm from the drills." Our feet pounded in unison as we wove through brambles of roots and unkempt vines growing off the path. "Atlas and Eli will probably be this way. I hope."

Our progress was halted as something bowled into my side, pulling the breath from my lungs and fissuring the link between our hands.

My arm scraped against a jagged rock, the cut on its way to healing as soon as it appeared.

When I looked up, I found myself face-to-face with a large werewolf, yellow eyes glinting, white and brown fur coated in what looked a hell of a lot like blood. It wasn't Atlas and I was fairly certain it wasn't Sarah either.

The wolf bared its teeth and pounced.

Muscle memory had me reaching for my blade as it sank its teeth into my shoulder, but my blade wasn't there. I hadn't bothered to grab it after teleporting back to the cabin—I'd been too simultaneously exhausted from the commute and amped up from the discovery to do much more than charge out of the cabin towards Six.

I kicked with all of my strength into the wolf's abdomen, hearing a satisfying crunch.

It wasn't enough to pull the creature off me though.

Instead, I felt its teeth dig deeper into my skin, scraping up against and shaving the bone.

Excruciating pain pulled through my arm as I tried to free myself.

Just as I started to conjure my fire, with nothing but a quick prayer that no one other than Declan would be around to see it, the wolf fell limp against me—warm and solid.

When I breathed in, I was enveloped in a wave of metallic musk.

With my uninjured hand, I unhinged the locked jaw and freed myself, crawling out from under the deceptively heavy corpse.

Declan was on the ground, covered in fresh blood—most of which looked to belong to the slightly smaller wolf at her feet. Her blade was buried deep into its chest.

"What the hell are you doing?" Darius stood in front of me, the wolf's heart dangling awkwardly in his palm, like a macabre Christmas ornament. "We need to get out of here. Now."

"Darius? Wade?" I stood up, ignoring the slight waiver in my knees. I was exhausted. All the teleporting had taken quite a bit out of me and I hadn't had time to recover properly. "What the hell are you doing here? Someone's going to see you. Get back to the hotel."

It felt like all the neat little corners of my world were collapsing in a way that didn't make any sense, in a way that felt dangerous.

"Not a chance. We heard attacks in town." Wade stood over Declan and pulled her to her feet, running his eyes methodically over her, scanning for serious wounds. When his shoulders relaxed, just slightly, I assumed he found none. "Dozens of demons in the streets—protectors and humans were dropping like flies. Then, more and more appeared. All of them heading towards Headquarters. I've never seen so many demons together in my life, not even in hell—let alone this close to protector territory."

"They seem to have very little regard for subtlety," Darius added, lip curled in disgust. "Lazy really. Just leaving behind human witnesses. Going to make keeping our world quiet nearly impossible if this keeps up."

"Staying inside while you were all here wasn't an option," Wade said as his fingers examined my mess of a shoulder.

"It'll heal," I assured him, though I had a feeling it would take a bit longer than usual.

"Is that a fork? And a steak knife?" Declan asked, staring at the small serrated blade and utensil dangling awkwardly in Darius's hand—the one without the heart.

"A really shitty one at that." He shrugged and looked down at the strange assortment of objects in his hands. His lips lifted with amusement as he licked some of the blood dripping down his arm. "I was eating a steak when we heard the commotion. I grabbed what weapons I could. There wasn't much time to consider style." He scanned the horizon, posture stiff as he took a step closer to me. "We need to get you out of here now. Knowing our luck, they're probably here for you."

Could I really be the center of all this death and destruction? The thought made my head swim and my stomach clench.

I swallowed back bile and squared my shoulders. "I'm not leaving everyone here to fight off this attack alone. My family is here."

A low, frustrated sigh pulled through his teeth.

"Told you," Wade muttered, eyes darting between me and Declan. "Where's my brother?"

A dark red gash appeared on Darius's forearm, deep and painful-looking.

Eli.

"Fuck," Declan whispered as she pulled her blade from the dead wolf's trunk. "We need to find him and Atlas now."

"Ah," Darius studied his arm, like it was nothing more than a mild inconvenience, "right."

"My brother, Cy, and Izzy too," I added.

Darius looked like he was going to argue with me, but before he had a chance, I took off at a blistering pace instead, fast enough to get us to the main clearing swiftly, but not too fast that Declan couldn't keep up with us.

We passed small groups of protectors—younger students running for cover, the older ones protecting them and hunting for scattered pockets of intruders who hadn't yet made it to the center of campus. There were a few times when I saw someone I recognized, and I wanted to stop and help, to make sure that they were okay, but I knew that if we paused to check on everyone, we would never make it to them. Who knew what kind of clusterfuck waited for us at the heart of everything?

"Wait," Declan said, the word reaching me on the wind as we ran.

When I spun around, I saw her diverge from the path, where a girl was running.

The lavender hair billowing behind her told me it was her friend, Dani.

"Let's go." I pulled Darius after Declan, ignoring his reluctant sigh, where Wade was already following.

Dani paused when Declan called out to her.

I could see her heartbeat hammering in her neck from here, her eyes wired with adrenaline and fear.

"Thank God," Dani murmured, her body caked in dried blood. "I was coming to get you, to make sure you were okay. I knew you were alo—" Her eyes widened when they landed on Wade. She took a step forward, brows furrowed. "Wade? You're alive? How?"

Before he could answer, her gaze latched onto Darius, a flash of recognition flaring across her face.

Fuck.

When I turned to him, I saw that recognition mirrored. He gave an awkward wave, and I found myself immeasurably happy that he dropped the wolf's heart somewhere during our trek.

"You know each other?" Wade asked, echoing the question likely written across my features.

"What the hell are you getting yourself into, Declan?" Dani asked, ignoring Wade now entirely. Her voice was low, shaky as she turned her focus to Declan, her fingers stiffening around the hilt of her blade—a silent warning for Darius to stay still.

A warning that Darius, of course, immediately ignored.

In one swift motion, he pulled back his arm, and let the fork in his grip go flying before any of us realized what was happening or had a chance to stop him.

Dani's eyes widened, but the utensil flew past her face, sinking with a satisfying squelch into the figure who'd emerged from a thick tree trunk behind her.

The demon fell back from the impact and, not wasting a moment on shock and confusion, Dani spun with her blade and settled it into the demon's chest, watching until it took its final breath, her brows scrunched together as she stared at the fork.

She shook her head, refocusing her attention on Darius, her chest lifting with each heavy inhale. For a moment, I thought she might attack him. Instead, she considered him for what felt like forever, but was realistically probably no more than a second or two, before dipping her chin in a single, firm nod.

"Don't worry. He won't hurt you." Wade glanced briefly at Darius. "Probably."

"There's no time for me to explain right now. Have you seen Eli?" Declan asked, seeing Dani's small nod for what it was—a reluctant thank you, but a thank you all the same. Enough to give us a temporary pass for the fact that we were working with a vampire and what must have seemed like a resurrected protector. "Or Atlas?"

Dani nodded again, seemingly unable to find words as she pulled her dagger from the corpse at her feet. She pointed the bloody blade in the direction we were heading. With a deep breath, she found her voice. "Last I saw, Eli was outside the Main Hall. It's a shitshow. They're everywhere."

"Come with us. You shouldn't be out here alone," Declan said as she urged us forward.

"I have to check up on a group of students who were scheduled to be out here, but I'll come find you afterwards. Go. Be safe," she paused, licking her lips, frowning—likely at the coppery taste of blood, "and don't make me regret this."

I wasn't sure if she was talking to Darius or Declan, but with a final glance back at us all—one that lingered for an extra moment on Darius—she took off into the woods.

When Darius went to retrieve his fork, Wade elbowed him in the stomach. He unsheathed his backup blade, stared at it, considering, then handed it silently to Darius—his head shaking slightly like he couldn't believe what he was doing.

Darius nodded, and without another word, we took off. I realized after a moment that he wasn't even using the path to guide him. Instead, he was following the thick, intensifying scent of blood.

When we came into the main clearing, where most of the buildings could be accessed, it looked like a war zone—a blur of clashing bodies and limbs almost impossible to distinguish or follow.

"Holy fuck," Declan whispered, as we all skidded to a halt, lost in a temporary daze at the sight around us.

The light dusting of snow was colored with blood, gore, and mud, as more bodies than I could count struggled to fight against the attack.

It was the largest group of people I'd seen occupy this space before, and with all of the new protectors on campus, it was difficult to identify who was on which side.

My stomach turned as I watched a boy—a year or two older than me, who I'd seen in training a few times—get his abdomen punctured by thick claws, and then, with a blink, ripped out completely. He collapsed to the ground, a pile of stiff limbs, eyes wide open as he drew his final breath.

The werewolf responsible, turned towards me and charged, but Darius met him halfway and snapped the creature's neck before he could reach any of us.

The still-blaring alarm cut through the backdrop of grunts, screams, metal crashing on metal—the noise making it nearly impossible to focus.

My body shook with adrenaline and fear as I scanned the mess for my people. I couldn't breathe when my gaze darted to the ground, covered with corpses, terrified that I'd see one of them there looking back at me with lifeless eyes.

Several protectors had the tranquilizer guns we used on field missions, but it was proving impossible to aim in this madness, the risk of hitting one of their own too high in a cluster this large.

One of them shot at a werewolf, but pierced an older protector I didn't know instead, the man falling to his knees as the creature intended for the knockout ripped off his head.

When I turned the other way, I felt my lungs start to work again.

Ro and Cyrus.

Izzy and Eli were nearby too, in a cluster of protectors—everyone locked in their own intense battle.

As I ran towards them I could smell nothing but the metallic, earthy scent of blood and entrails.

When I reached Izzy, she was carrying herself with a limp, a deep gash carved into her cheek as she threw a demon off her back.

Her coordination was awkward and stilted, her breaths heavy and labored as I reached her. In a swift motion, I wrapped my hands around the wolf's neck, snapping it with a satisfying crack.

Izzy fell to the ground, eyes wide with confusion as I knelt down by her, arm extended to lift her back up.

Her body was heavy and stiff, but not lifeless.

It was like she was suddenly paralyzed.

"Tainted ones," Darius said, eyes darting to me between

blows as he and Declan double-teamed what I assumed was a vampire, but I couldn't be sure, "she's been poisoned."

Tainted ones—in our realm?

A brief scan revealed several protectors on the ground—I'd assumed they were dead or unconscious, but maybe they, too, were paralyzed by a tainted one's blade.

I reached for Izzy's dagger, pulling it from her fingers as they twitched, and guarded her, swiping at another werewolf as it charged towards us.

The memory of being attacked by a tainted one rolled through me as I tried to focus on the present—the helplessness, the strangeness of being locked inside a body I couldn't move.

The implications were severe if they were working with other demons now.

Protectors were already wildly unarmed when it came to the hell realm and creatures that lived there. Add in chemical warfare and what chance did they stand?

A grinning, bright-eyed vampire ran towards me, fangs out, lined with red from his last meal. I felt, more than I saw, Ro edge nearer to me, his expression fierce when I caught him in my peripheral vision.

At the same time, a bit further away, I saw a werewolf pin Cyrus to the ground. It was the first time in memory that I'd seen him unsteady before—losing.

My heart climbed into my throat, as I tried to make an impossible decision—did I help my best friend, my brother, the man who raised me, my team?

Too thin.

I was stretched too thin.

There was no way for me to fight them all with my bare hands.

As the vampire clashed with me, I saw an arrow out of the corner of my eye flash past, landing with a heavy thud in the werewolf on top of Cy, imbedding in the animal's furry shoulder blade.

I clenched my jaw. It would do little more than annoy it, a pest of a sting, nothing more.

But then the wolf stilled.

In confusion, I traced the arrow's trajectory to the shooter.

Tarren.

He was already armed and shooting another arrow, Cy a forgotten save.

His arrows must've been laced with the same compound as the tranquilizer darts.

He pulled a second bow from where it rested on his back and tossed it to his left, not even looking as Atlas caught it.

Atlas's eyes met mine briefly, brown streaked through with yellow, though I doubted anyone would notice in this hellscape.

I kicked the vampire away, half of my focus on him as his teeth scraped against me, half on Cy, waiting for him to stir, to get the upper hand.

It had all happened in less than a blink—a microsecond—but it felt like the world was moving in slow motion as I tried to keep track of everyone.

Finally, Cy shifted. As the heavy body rolled away from him and he crawled out from under it, he seemed frail and vulnerable—a combination I'd never once associated with him.

Atlas pulled back his arm, lined up the shot, and released—the vampire fell against me, a flash of confusion in its eyes blurring the arrogance from a moment ago.

As Ro reached me, three more vampires approached us. Izzy was still stiff and immobile at my feet, her bright eyes widening, like she was trying to signal to me—probably telling me to leave her and go help the others.

I couldn't. Not when she was defenseless, not here.

Wade and Declan were locked in a battle with three—now four—other demons to my right.

Another approached Cy from behind—the brutal dance playing out on my left.

Eli ran towards a slim, dark-eyed girl in front of him, but she evaporated into a strange shadowy smoke before rematerializing next to Izzy.

"Fucking fuck," Darius grunted, his limbs tangled in a clash with two vampires. His focus darted briefly to me——an unbridled terror etched into his face that unsettled me to my core. "Is that a fucking drude?"

I had no clue what the hell a drude was but, in a flash of heaviness, I realized that we were going to lose.

Badly.

Swiftly.

There were too many demons—an endless drove that far outmatched the power protectors had.

I had no choice.

There was no point hiding my powers if doing so only got us killed.

The fire brushed along my skin, the familiar tingle bringing with it a rush of energy. The world suddenly seemed impossibly bright, like my pupils were blown wide.

Pulling every ounce of power I had left, I let it go, releasing the fire in rushes of blowtorch-like waves.

I took down the Drude.

Then the vampires surrounding Ro, being as careful as possible to avoid kissing him with the fire.

Then the demons near Darius.

The one battling Cy.

The fire spread, exploding from my fingers, oozing from my pours—far more powerful and intoxicating than I'd ever felt it before.

Power hummed down my spine, veining out to the rest of

my body—the pathway so intense and deliberate I could sense as it moved through every inch of me.

The earth scorched at my feet, encasing Izzy and Ro in a protective circle.

The battlefield blurred and bled until all I saw were the dark outlines of targets harming the people around me. The people I loved.

No more.

I moved towards them, barely noticing when protectors stopped in their tracks—some pausing in shock, others running from me, rather than the demons they originally fought.

Charred meat and ash washed away the scent of blood. I breathed it in, felt my lips tug into a wide grin at the taste of smoke in the air.

Shades of orange, blue, purple, eclipsed the sight of anguish, leaving beautiful, familiar swirls in their wake.

The dark outlines of lingering demons stopped approaching—many now running in the direction they'd come from instead.

I heard my name traveling along the wind from multiple directions, but the voices felt far off and flat, almost dreamlike.

The power was intoxicating, I wanted to live inside of it forever, bask in it until I disappeared into the massive fire entirely.

A hand, firm and steady, gripped my wrist, the flames licking against the smooth skin, but causing no harm. I spun back to react, but found myself staring into a familiar pair of mismatched eyes, full lips straightened into a tense line.

"Stop, little protector," the voice attached to the lips said— and somehow, over the steady, thrilling hum of the fire, the voice got through, clear and resounding. "Call it back, come back. We need to leave."

It sounded like home.

Slow, murky-like, my vision cleared.

The flames softened, pulled tight, and extinguished.

My bones felt like jelly, my skin taught and uncomfortable, like it already missed the gentle lick of fire.

The trees around burned softly, embers trailing through the forest like fireflies. The neat path at my feet was scorched black and wet from the melted snow.

I felt dozens—maybe hundreds—of eyes on me.

The demons seemed to have mostly scattered during my burning woman show, only a few lingering behind in shackles at the feet of protectors.

I took a few steps away from Darius as the world swam back into focus, as I took in what I'd done.

"You."

The word was sharp, hitting me in the chest like an arrow.

I stiffened, the hair at the back of my neck raising as a new, imposing danger crept over my skin.

When I looked up, I saw Tarren's hard focus on me, his body coiled and ready to pounce.

"Father," Atlas's voice was a low, warning growl, so wolf-like that it seemed almost ridiculous that Tarren didn't recognize the demon burrowed deep inside of his son.

But Tarren took a step, and then another, ignoring him as he came closer, eyes never wavering from where they lingered on my hands, like he was waiting for me to make a bonfire out of him.

Protectors flocked to his side—familiar faces and not.

My body tightened, my muscles clenching—silently alerting me to attack, to protect myself and my family—aware of a danger that I couldn't yet fully wrap my mind around.

I forced the impulse down, buried it deep. I couldn't hurt Tarren. I hated the man, yes, but he was Wade and Atlas's father.

I needed to move. Now. Needed to leave.

But my body was frozen, exhaustion suddenly so deep that my bones vibrated with it, my mind still hazy and fighting back against the allure of the flames.

My heart pounded in my ears as whispers fluttered around me, butterflies in the wind.

I felt everyone watching us—my friends, my colleagues, people I'd never even properly noticed before—all of them waiting for a signal, waiting for instruction. But it felt like I was on the inside of a snow globe, disconnected and separate from them all.

Cy stood up next to me, one hand raised toward Tarren, silently urging him to calm down, the other wrapping tenderly around mine. The rough, familiar calluses on his palm sent a bolt of strength—of love—through me that made it a little easier to focus. I clutched his fingers like a lost child, warmed by the protection and support of a father.

I had no idea how the fuck we were all going to get out of this, how we were going to detangle this mess at all, but having him next to me—firm and unwavering, all vulnerability from before evaporated into his quiet strength—felt like the closest thing to a start.

"You're the one I've heard whispers of. They came for you." Tarren's lip lifted into a disgusted snarl, his voice hollow and wavering with shock. "You'll kill us all." His fingers subtly gripped the bow at his side and my brain prickled and screamed, urging me to do something as Cy pulled me closer into his side. But I couldn't move.

The haunted look on Tarren's face turned to a deep unfixable anger—the entire interaction nothing more than a fraction of a moment.

I heard commotion around me.

"No," Cy yelled, the word ethereal and strong as it reverberated around us, an ominous prophecy.

And then, everything shattered.

A loud growl and several screams collided into a strange chorus.

It happened in a flash of chaos and breathlessness, so fast I couldn't even track all the moving parts.

Cy spun me into a tight hug, and moved us over a few feet, his body warm and heavy against mine.

Yelling and clashing echoed through my ears, but Cy clung to me, shielding me from it all, while my brain tried its hardest to process, to catch up.

And then his implaccable sturdiness turned into a strange heaviness.

The world slowed down as his chest fell against me, the weight dragging us both down until my knees buckled under the pressure and he fell to the side—dark eyes wide and watery and vacant.

A thick cord of metal stuck into his back.

All I could do was stare at it as I felt others begin to surround us.

I leaned over him, protecting him from their attention and fear as he'd protected me.

It took me a moment to process that the stick was the shaft of an arrow—and that the head of the arrow had gone straight into his chest, straight through his heart.

24

WADE

One moment Atlas was standing a few feet away from Max as a man, the next he was between her and my father, dressed in the skin of a wolf, teeth bared and body vibrating with a low growl.

Max clutched Cyrus, and I saw the moment she realized that he was gone.

Something seemed to shatter in her posture as she shook and screamed, hovering over him—the sound that emanated from her, low and devastating.

Pure, unbridled anguish.

That sound would haunt me for as long as I lived.

Darius bent possessively at her side and laid a hand on her shoulder, but that seemed to only make it worse as she dug her fingers into Cy's shoulders and shook him, begging him to wake up.

Eli tried to gently pull her back from the body, aware as I was that the tides were turning—that we needed to get out of here immediately—but she shoved him away and clung harder to her father.

She let out a deep, gasping scream, like the sadness inside was too full, like it was forcing its way out.

And then, when the noise disappeared, so did she.

Gone.

Teleported from sight—only instead of taking just herself, she'd taken Cyrus too.

I'd seen the look of horror in my father's eyes when he realized what he'd done—that he'd killed Cyrus, and that he'd done it in front of everyone.

That look of horror deepened as he stared at Atlas, his skin an ashy gray like he'd seen a ghost, eyes wild with disgust as they traced the unfamiliar features of his son.

And then those eyes landed on me, noticing me for the first time in all of the chaos.

"No," he mouthed, as he shook his head from side to side, like the simple action would be enough to reform his family into the image he wanted, the one we'd reflected only one minute ago—one son dead, one on the path to follow in his footsteps.

I wasn't sure what I thought I would see in his face when I stood in front of him again, what I even wanted to see.

While most fathers would probably feel a wave of disbelief, of joy at the emergence of a once-dead son, the impossible melting away of grief, Tarren seemed to only grow angrier—the lingering regret over Cyrus's death making way for something darker, something more brutal.

Darius's back tensed out of the corner of my eye and I knew he was going after my father, that he'd rip his heart clean from his chest.

"Go," Declan whispered as she gripped his arm. "Go. Find her now. You and Wade are faster—we'll take care of this. Get out of here. She needs you. Make sure she's safe. Now."

I tore my focus away from Tarren and turned to the vampire as I processed her words—the taunting smirk typically plastered on his face was nowhere in sight. He looked as haunted and gutted as I felt.

He nodded once and took off at a blistering pace—one no one would take for that of a protector.

I followed, almost as fast, without a glance behind to see what my father or the others I grew up with would think of me now—resurrected from the dead as the very thing I spent a lifetime training to hunt.

We tore through the trees, ignoring the scattered bodies left from the ambush, moving almost as one as we forged our own path, divergent from the one carved through campus.

I didn't need to ask where we were going or how the fanghole knew which turns to take.

He felt the same pull that I did—could sense Max the same way that I could.

It was like her agony was a beacon, pulsing through both of us, pulling us to her.

After a few moments, I realized where we were heading. Not as far as I would have liked her to be from the gathering of stunned protectors, but far enough that she'd be safe for a few minutes while we regrouped.

We slowed as we came through a small clearing that opened up into Eli's pond.

Cyrus was draped awkwardly over her lap, like an overgrown child. Her head was bent slightly so I couldn't see her face, one hand cradling his head, the other pressed against his chest.

Quickly, we closed the distance to her, but she didn't seem to realize or care that we were there.

"Her eyes," Darius said, voice soft like he was afraid of piercing the strange peace of the place.

Her eyes were black as night, her hair blowing softly, like she was in some isolated breeze that I didn't feel.

Slowly her body started to tremble and shake, her skin growing clammy and draining of color.

"She's trying to heal him," I said. I turned to Darius. "Can she do that?"

He shook his head once, a flash of something dark and terrifying in his expression before he gripped Max's shoulders and gently shook. "No, healers can't bring back the dead. She'll only drain herself trying."

"Max?" I pressed my palms to her cheek, they were soaked in her tears. "Come back to us, it'll be okay."

Darius bent close, whispered something into her ear that I couldn't hear, rubbed soft circles on her back as she continued sobbing. "Please," he said, louder this time, "you're only going to hurt yourself. You have to let him go. Don't let his sacrifice be in vain."

This seemed to send a shockwave through her body as she stiffened, a harsh, painful wail ripping from her lips as she shook us both off of her.

"It hurts," she whimpered, rocking back and forth. "Make it stop, make it stop, make it stop."

She pressed the heel of her palm into her chest, like even though the arrow landed in Cyrus's heart, hers was the one that would never feel anything but pain again.

My fingers shook at my side and I had to take slow, deep breaths to keep from vomiting. I didn't know how to help her, how to take her pain away, how to make any of this okay.

She'd just lost one of the only two people she'd had her entire life. Gone, in a flash.

It seemed cruel, how quickly your entire life could crumble, how quickly loss carved out a new reality that you'd have to find a way to survive in for the rest of your life.

Instead of pulling her from Cyrus, breaking their connection—however futile it was—I pulled her to me in a hug, lending the strength of ours.

She shook against me but didn't resist my touch this time. Instead, she just whispered "no, no, no, please come back, please," over and over again—the quiet, desperate appeals breaking me in half each time.

I heard a soft rustle as Darius ran his hands through her hair, down her shoulder, like he, too, sensed that nearness was the only thing we could offer her right now.

A loud vibration briefly shattered the moment.

It came from Cyrus.

Slowly, I grabbed his phone, while Max laid her head on his chest, her expression the picture of agony.

I stood up and walked away a few steps, to give her some peace and to make sure no one had reached us.

I recognized the number.

"Eli?" I asked, realizing that the chaos we'd left behind had briefly slipped my mind. "Where are you? What hap—"

"Did you find her?"

"Yes, she's at the pond."

The line was silent for a moment, but I could feel him take a deep breath.

"How is she?" His voice was heavy as he let out a sigh. "Nevermind, don't answer that. I know she's not okay. How could she be?" I heard some rustling through the phone. "Fuck. This is so fucking fucked."

"What's going on?"

"We ran—me and Dec. We had to. Barely made it out as it was. We'll come to you. We tried to call Max's phone, the burner we left at the hotel for you guys, but couldn't get through. So I figured we'd try—that we'd—"

"Call Cyrus," I finished, my chest tight from the realization that he'd never answer his phone again. I focused on Eli, on what he was telling me, and then my stomach sank. There was a name missing from that list. "Eli. Where's Atlas? He's with you, right?"

Silence.

"Eli?"

"I'm sorry. I'm so fucking sorry." I heard regret in the gravel of his voice. "He kept them distracted when you took off. They barely even spared me and Dec a glance in the shock of it all." His voice cracked as he fought to take a breath. "But we couldn't do anything, not by ourselves, not once they darted him."

My head felt impossibly light—his words meshing into strange sounds that I couldn't shape into meaning. I leaned against a tree. Our own father? Darted him? "Eli, what the fuck are you saying?"

"I'm saying he passed out, Wade." He inhaled sharply, cursing under his breath. "They have him."

THANK YOU FOR READING! If you loved hanging out with Max and her team of moody protectors, find out what kind of mischief she gets into next. Grab Book Seven in The Protector Guild Series now: Dark Before Dawn.

THANK YOU

Thank you so much for reading. I hope you enjoyed your time spent with Max and the chaotic characters at The Guild.

If you'd like to learn more about books and new releases, please find me at grayholborn.com.